Hard Laughter

a novel by
Anne Lamott

NORTH POINT PRESS
FARRAR, STRAUS AND GIROUX
NEW YORK

North Point Press
A division of Farrar, Straus and Giroux
18 West 18th Street, New York 10011

Copyright © 1979, 1980 by Anne Lamott
All rights reserved
Distributed in Canada by Douglas & McIntyre Ltd.
Printed in the United States of America
First edition, 1979

Library of Congress Control Number: 86062832
ISBN-13: 978-0-86547-280-8
ISBN-10: 0-86547-280-7

www.fsgbooks.com

24   26   28   30   31   29   27   25   23

This book is dedicated to my father, Ken

and to Steve, John, and Nikki Lamott;
to the family and to the cronies.

i thank You God for most this amazing
day:for the leaping greenly spirits of trees
and a blue true dream of sky;and for everything
which is natural which is infinite which is yes

(i who have died am alive again today,
and this is the sun's birthday;this is the birth
day of life and of love and wings:and of the gay
great happening illimitably earth)

how should tasting touching hearing seeing
breathing any—lifted from the no
of all nothing—human merely being
doubt unimaginable You?

(now the ears of my ears awake and
now the eyes of my eyes are opened)

—e. e. cummings

Problem stated at its most succinct—is life too short to
be taking shit or is life too short to mind it?

—Violet Weingarten,
Intimations of Mortality

Hard Laughter

The Family

M y family lived for fifteen years in a castle built more than a century ago by an eccentric man who wanted his Rhine-born wife to feel at home when he brought her to live in California. It was a monstrous rock construction two hundred feet above San Francisco Bay, surrounded by cypress trees, two stories of rock with a trapdoor underneath the kitchen table and two caves in the back of the house, one of which was said to have led to the beach during bootlegging days. The walls were a foot and a half thick, fashioned of railroad ties and rock and plaster, and the doors were only five feet nine inches tall, many inches taller than the builder or his wife. At my parents' frequent dinner parties, almost every man in our circle of friends cracked his forehead on the top of the doorway at least once; I vividly remember a man hitting his head twice, and then removing his prosthetic arm, which he was unable to put back on.

My mother was born in Liverpool a few years after my father, the son of Presbyterian missionaries, was born in Tokyo. They met and married back east thirty years ago, moved to the San Francisco Bay area, had three children and a lot of friends, and my mother loved the three of us more than she loved herself, a beautiful and dangerous predicament. Their sons were dark-haired and handsome, whereas I did not look quite human until I grew hair at two years old, and even then more closely resembled an albino rhesus monkey with an Afro. I was sort of comically cute, and was teased about my hair by older kids until my early teens.

Everyone in the family adored Randy from the minute he was born, seventeen years ago, even Ben, who is twenty-five and hated our parents and me until five years ago when he got off serious drugs. My mother and I finally get along, and my father and Ben finally get along, and Randy still gets along excellently with all of us, although I am the person he talks to most intimately, since I am the person he considers most deranged and weirdest in the family, except for himself. All of us are better friends with one another since the recent diagnosis of my father's brain tumor, which is one of the possibilities of crisis. Another is the constant juxtaposition of forgotten memories and a heightened ability to concentrate on the present. Another is insomnia so intense that by three A.M. you can *hear* the blood vessels in your eyes popping.

The castle was filled with books and records, classical, jazz, and folk. Our family has always had an enormous amount of musical enthusiasm and almost no talent whatsoever. My father, Wallace, had every book William Carlos Williams ever wrote and spent his days writing books and articles in his study. My mother was more active in liberal politics than my father, named me after her twin sister, and sent us to school twenty years ago with gourmet sandwiches on whole-grain breads, sandwiches that we traded whenever possible for a slice of bologna on Wonder Bread. She graduated from law school when I was seventeen, a year before she and my father got divorced, and set up a small law firm in Honolulu. One of the reasons we get along now is that we don't see each other very often, maybe once a year.

My father and Randy began sharing a house in Clement four years ago, and six months ago they both moved in with Dad's girl friend. Sarah's house is a mile away from the cabin my grandparents bought thirty years ago and in which I have been living for a year. All of our relatives live on the other side of the mountain, an hour away, and except for our closest family friends, most of the people I am close to live in Clement. Most of my friends are motley, antisocial, deranged, semialcoholic, and black-humored, each one stranger than the last. One of Wallace's two best friends, our uncle Colin, lives five miles away, on the other side of the lagoon from Clement—the dictionary defines "lagoon" as "any small pondlike body of water, esp. one communicating with a larger body of water," a definition I like quite a bit. Both towns are on the Pacific Ocean, and Colin's letters, which arrive almost every day, sometimes take five days to get here.

My father's mother, who is eighty-five and lives on the other side of the mountain, called Wallace one morning two weeks before the first symptoms of his tumor began and told him she'd dreamt that he was having surgery. Wallace told her that there was nothing to it, because at that point there wasn't. Pretty soon the first symptoms began—aphasia, slurring, a physical inability to write or type the words that were in his mind—and we entered the surreal and immediate world of sickness.

I first noticed that something was wrong with my precise and professorial father when he called one afternoon and asked if I would bring a vegetable to go with dinner. I said sure, and asked what he'd like.

He said, "Well, we already have a vegetable here, but not enough for everybody. Perhaps you could buy some more."

"O.K.," I said. "What is it?"

He paused for a minute. "I can't seem to think of the word, and I'm staring right at it."

"What does it look like?"

"Well, it's a big green thing that turns red before it's ready to cook."

"Hmmm," I said. "Tomato?"

"No."

"A pepper? A chili?"

"Nooo . . . damnation. It's uh . . . uh . . ."

"A leek? Broccoli? Cauliflower?"

"No, no, no."

"You're sure it's a big green thing that turns red when it's ready to cook?"

"Yep."

"Is it red yet?"

"Nope . . ."

"Then it's not ready to cook," I said quickly. "I'll pick up some zucchini."

"*That's* what it is," said Wallace. "A zucchini."

"What was the part about it turning red?" I asked.

"Oh, I don't know," he said, and we both laughed.

Wallace's doctor said it was either a small stroke or a brain tumor, a pronouncement that put our family in the curious position of hoping, praying, that our father had had a stroke.

"Poor Wallace," said Randy. "I sure hope Dad had a stroke. . . ." And then, looking askance, Randy tapped his tilted head with the butt of his hand.

The doctor ordered a brain scan, and a tumor was found in the "word section" of Wallace's brain. Just the other day we were three young children who took baths together. Just the other day my parents were young and healthy, and Wallace didn't have a brain tumor, and now, at the age of fifty-five, with three semi-grown-up children, he does. It's as simple and mysterious as that.

The phone rang at nine o'clock in my cabin on the morning after Wallace told us about the tumor. A young friend had stayed over and left at eight, and my first thought was that she had forgotten something. I was making the painful transition between being ambulatory and being coherent, and the phone, which was under a pile of clothes, rang seven times before I answered it.

"Hullo," I said in my flat, dull precoffee voice.

"Hello, Jennifer," said a cheerful male voice that I was unable to place for a moment. I do not know all that many cheerful people. "This is your dear old father. Did you just wake up?"

"How could you tell?" I asked. "What's up?"

"I called to see if you want to walk to Limpet later on—say, three?"

"Oh. Yeah, sure, that sounds good. Is Randy going to come?"

"If he and that idiot dog are finished with the Dreaded Hawaiian Boar game, they'll probably both come."

"The what game?"

"You've never seen them at it? It's a sight. Muldoon is the rampaging Hawaian boar, and Randy is the brave young hunter saving the villagers from certain death. Randy stalks Muldoon around the yard, on his belly, crawling stealthily through the grass towards Muldoon. He hides behind trees and throws bits of ice plant at that silly black Lab and shouts things like 'Die, violent shoat!' Muldoon whimpers, licks the young hunter, tries to hide, and so on."

"Sounds like Randy. Sounds like Muldoon." We both laughed. Muldoon's canine intelligence quotient is about five percentile. "I think Muldoon's father was a brontosaurus. And we all know about Randy's father."

"Oh, the way she speaks about her father," Wallace said in his pained voice. "But I'll tell you, I'm still putting in four hours at my typewriter every day, and they're four stupid hours."

"Oh, well, after they take out the tumor you'll be back to normal."

"Do I sound a little drunken? I do to myself," he said.

"Yeah, a little bit."

"Hmmm. I suppose that's a small inconvenience."

"Why don't you take it easy today, lie on your ass in the window seat and read a book. . . ."

"It's a nice suggestion, but I've got work to do before I go into the hospital—I've got an article to finish, bills to pay, letters to answer, and so forth. I'm getting about an hour's work done in four hours these days, which is frustrating, of course, but I do want to tie up some loose ends. I'll knock off early, relax for a while, and then we'll walk on the beach. Oh, also, Ben called at seven this morning to say he's coming for dinner. Do you want to come?"

"Yeah. I have to go now. My water's ready. I'll see you at three."

"Good. See you later."

"O.K. S'later."

Neurosurgery was scheduled for three weeks hence. I watched the days of my life pass by through the windows of my birth-control-pill packet. Sunday, pop; Monday, pop; Tuesday, pop. The Tuesday pill was gone this morning: it must be Wednesday. The *San Francisco Chronicle* underneath the aging alley cat on the doorstep of my cabin concurred. The cat glowered when I pushed him off the paper. The *Chronicle* reported the death of a local cop who went after a two-bit thief and got shot through the heart; the increase in environmentally caused cancer in the Bay Area; the rape of a seventy-three-year-old blind woman; the story of a woman from Oakland who had her jaw wired shut to lose weight; and a fashion forecast on the possible return of spike heels. It further reported that a brain surgeon in Los Angeles lost his license recently when he was found to have injected his own urine into two of his patients. There were no discernible side effects. It reassured me beyond words to hear of this sort of stability among surgeons.

As families go, ours is remarkable: functional and appreciative. After all these years we still punish one another for past transgressions, past guilts, but there is no longer malevolence, just habit. Mostly.

It is a twenty-minute walk under a grove of elm trees along the cliffs of the Pacific Ocean to the house where Wallace and his girl friend, Sarah, and Randy live, along with countless cats, dogs, chickens, geese, ducks, and a full-grown miniature rabbit that Sarah got half price when its first owner returned it to the pet store because his boa constrictor wouldn't eat it. Wallace and Sarah live together, with Randy, in her fine wooden house with six skylights and a huge yard, and they eat fresh eggs from the hens almost every morning.

Wallace and Randy were on the porch waiting for me at three, and looked like brothers from a distance. Both are tall, fair, thin, with blue eyes and brown wavy hair, and both were wearing worn blue jeans and Shetland crew-neck sweaters. They waved and walked toward me, with Muldoon bumping into their legs. Randy walks with a style somewhere between Wallace's long, lanky stride and Muldoon's gawky and unsynchronized movements. Randy and Muldoon are in the same anatomical quandary, their limbs suddenly much too long for their available coordination. Randy has never been that athletic, and the six inches he has grown in the last two years haven't helped. He is afraid he will end up looking like Diane Arbus's Jewish giant.

Wallace's face is angular and calm, very New England, and he has a sort of kind inaccessibility about him. Randy's face is also angular, but his is shy, earnest, and nervous. I often look at the people in my family—all of them silent or jocular, always private, never confessional—and I think I have no idea who they are, what it is like for each of them In There. But when I look into their eyes or at the idiosyncrasies of their mouths and voices, an evanescent moment of recognition passes.

We walked whistling down the road into town. We whistled "The Keeper of the Eddystone Light," "Buffalo Girl Won'tcha Come Out Tonight," "Jesu, Joy of Man's Desiring" (badly). Wallace started off most songs. We entered the downtown area on "Colonel Bogey's March," all three of us loud and enthusiastic.

Downtown consists of two intersecting streets dotted with horse manure, beer bottles, food wrappers, and cigarette butts. There is a post office, a Laundromat, a liquor store, a grocery store, an organic greasy-spoon restaurant, a bookstore, a gas station, and a bar. There were five cars downtown, all of them in front of the bar. The only person on the street was Miriam Brown, a gaunt and dissipated woman of thirty. She is the mother of three children, all of them under four years old, and our town's most infamous alcoholic (securing the title when she conceived her last child on the pool table at the bar on a full moon night; she herself has said that the baby, whom she pushed this morning in a carriage, emerged from her womb connected by an umbilical cord of green baize). Miriam was headed into the bar, and from a distance of twenty feet we could all see the red-blue plaid on her nose. We said hello to one another. She left the baby outside the bar, in the carriage, and stepped inside. Wallace grimaced and shook his head.

"I hope she's just getting a beer to go," he said.

"Very, very few people look really good without teeth, and Miriam is not one of them." Randy whirled around and faced the bar. "Oh, nooo," he whispered loudly, "I'll bet she heard."

"No she didn't," said Wallace, rolling his eyes, and turned down the road toward Limpet Beach, whistling the introduction to "Ruby, My Dear," by Thelonius Monk.

Limpet Beach has been the family's favorite for as long as anyone can remember. We have come here, collectively and individually, thousands and thousands of times. The surf is notably thunderous here, except during low and minus tides when the tidepools on the reef lay exposed. There are always gulls on and above the reef, there are frequently pelicans, every so often there are harbor seals, and once, when I was eight, there was a drowned Japanese fisherman on the reef, and Wallace *saw* him dead. We talked about it for a year. Along the stretch of gravelly sand are caves, huge trees fallen and standing, shells, agates, and keyhole limpets. (Keyhole limpets are inch-long graduated cones with a hole through the apex, zebra-striped and abundant. For years they were the basis of presents to our parents— keyhole limpet earrings, brooches, and tie clasps, all very pasty and cumbersome. Keyhole limpets themselves are pretty.) We all know the best places to find bits of fossilized whalebone, the best places to find crabs, the best places to pee out of sight of one's siblings, the best places to watch the glorious white pelicans in wintertime.

Wallace brought us here countless times when we were young, with Randy in a baby pack on his back. He held Ben and me by the hand when we walked out onto the slippery reef to inspect the tidepools. We always pleaded with him to let go of our hands, so that we could inspect the life in the pools more closely, and he would say, "Every time I let go of your hands, at least one of you falls in, and then you complain all the way home because you're cold and wet and sandy."

"But that was last time," we would say. "We're older now."

"All right," he would say, and let go.

Ben and I would bend down to put our fingers in the sea anemones or to watch a sea snail crawl from behind magenta algae into a new shell, and one or both of us would slide into the ankle-deep water, and then complain all the way home.

"Has it occurred to you that you might be trying to get attention by getting a brain tumor?" Randy asked Wallace as we headed down the beach.

"If I wanted attention, I'd wear a pointy bra around town," said Wallace.

"It was just a theory; you don't have to get sore," said Randy. "Why do you think you got it?"

"No one really knows. It's somehow connected to stress, and that's about all I know. My mother thinks it's because I think too much."

"Hah," Randy laughed. "You think we could run through the surgery details some more?" Wallace nodded. The first time he ran through the surgery details with us, last night, Randy leapt to his feet, stormed into his bedroom, slammed the door, and emerged five minutes later as if nothing had happened. "O.K.," Randy continued. "So, first the surgeon shaves your head, and then he cuts a door in your skull with a buzz saw, right?"

"Sort of right. My surgeon is a woman, to begin with, and it's not exactly a buzz saw—it's a fine-toothed Black and Decker."

"It is?" I asked, wide-eyed. "Yo!" I shuddered visibly. A current went through the pit of my stomach. I could not imagine facing the prospect of a Black and Decker cutting up my skull.

"It's a *woman*?!" Randy shouted. "You're going to let a woman—oh my god. Jesus Christ. No wonder you need surgery."

"Shove it," I said.

"She's one of the best in the Bay Area."

"O.K., O.K. So then *she* cuts a trapdoor in your head, and then she lifts it with a surgical toilet plunger-type thing . . ."

"Well, sort of. . . ." said Wallace.

"Oh my god," said Randy, struggling with the graphic details. "She probably lifts it like you lift the top off a pumpkin. I wonder if it makes the same noise." He pursed his lips and made a long, slurpy, sucking noise.

"I can do without that, buddy," said Wallace good-naturedly.

"And then she cuts the tumor off, and does an autopsy on—"

I jabbed Randy in the ribs. He hit himself on the fore-head and said, "Oh, no, Dad, I mean 'biopsy.' "

"I know you did," said Wallace. "Forget it."

"God, what a dork I am," he said. "Some great fox pass, huh?"

"Some great what?" I asked.

Randy repeated it, this time with a strong French accent. "Foxxx Pahhhsss."

" 'Faux pas,' " said our father, amused and kind. " 'Foe pah.' "

Wallace and I sat on a fallen oak trunk at the far end of the beach an hour later, while Randy and Muldoon disappeared in an overgrown gorge between the cliffs. In silence, we watched a fishing boat half a mile out on the ocean, and made holes in the sand with our boots.

"How was Randy this morning?" I asked.

"Oh, a bit down, sad about the mouth—hasn't brought up my surgery until just now. Of course, it's easier for him to talk when you're around. And, generally speaking, he's easy to get along with, considering whatever hormonal per-colations are at work now. He has off days, and days when he's sullen and touchy one moment, full of sunshine and small jokes the next. He'll do anything to make me laugh if he thinks I'm in a brood."

"God, he's funny sometimes; he can crack me up, espe-cially when we're alone. We were talking about snuggies the other day and—"

"Snuggies?" Wallace asked.

"You know, when you grab somebody's underwear from above their bottom and pull them up the crack about a foot or so. . . ."

"Oh, shit, yes," he said, scowling. "You and Ben ruined dozens of Randy's underwear. God only knows what you did to Randy."

"Hey, don't worry. I've had massive guilt on the subject." Ben and I used to drape Randy over a doorknob by his underwear; he would kick and scream until we unhooked him or until our parents arrived. Although we got spanked when we were caught, we gave Randy snuggies off and on for a few years, but did not otherwise hurt or torture him very much. We occasionally force-fed him foods like Chinese mustard or anchovy paste, and removed his baby teeth in a series of creative ways, but Ben tortured me a hundred times more than we tortured Randy. "So, anyway," I continued, "Randy and I were talking about snuggies—we were laughing hysterically—and I said it was amazing that none of us, your kids, became Gary Gilmore types, that the three of us trust each other despite our childhoods, and he said, 'Yeah, but you'll notice I never turn my back on either of you.' "

Wallace laughed, nodding his head. "I wonder what he's up to. He's been gone a—"

"Hey, look," Randy called, emerging from the gorge with a stiff heron over his shoulder. "A heron! God, I really scored. Man, look at this; it's in perfect condition, except for one of its eyes is mashed in." He held it sideways by its legs so Wallace and I could see it better when he got close. It was a magnificent bird, and Wallace and I crowded around him eagerly to study and touch the blue-green and grayish wings, soft, vivid, and muted, and the hawk-red trim.

"Jesus, it's just beautiful," Wallace said.

"From the knees up, anyway," I said. The skin covering its legs was rubbery and looked prehistoric; it had four ugly toes on each foot with toenails like ice picks. Its stiffness was disconcerting, its color ethereal. "Its feet look like Howard Hughes's did in his last years." I said.

"You're just jealous because you didn't find it. I wonder if it's a male or a female." He laid it down on the sand and spread its legs apart. "Nothing here," he said, peering at the heron's crotch. "Guess it's a girl."

"Randy," Wallace said with resignation, "herons don't

have penises that you can see. You can't tell a male from a female by looking between their legs. The penis emerges from inside when the heron is going to mate."

"Oh. Well, I'm going to take it home with me. . . ."

"*Ohhh* no you're not," said Wallace. 'It's beginning to stink. What on earth would you do with it?"

"Lots of things I might do with it."

"Like what? Name two."

"Heron cacciatore, chipped heron on toast. There's two."

Wallace and I laughed, but Wallace shook his head.

"Pleeease," Randy wheedled. "I have *got* to have this bird. C'mon, it's no skin off your nose. . . ."

"But it *stinks*."

"I'll lend it to you whenever you want. No questions asked. Day or night. You could take it to the bar on a leash, leave it at the door and say, 'Stay!' We could have *fun* with it."

"C'mon, Dad, let him have the bird. He's low on dead herons."

"Oh, for Christ's sake. All right. I hope you don't catch some strange heron fever from it."

"O.K. Look, thanks a lot. I'm going to make it up to you. You won't regret this, Wally baby." He slung the heron down his back like a sack of flour, and we set off down the beach toward home.

"You *cannot* bring that beast into the house, though."

"No problem." Randy beamed all the way home, and Wallace, with a sad smile, kept shaking his head.

My older brother, Ben, was sitting on the porch of Sarah and Wallace's house when we returned from Limpet, and stood to greet us. "What the hell is that?" he asked.

"It's my new pet," said Randy, holding the heron above his head like a barbell. "I have to keep it in the shed till he's housebroken." Ben punched Randy on the shoulder, which is how the males in my family express affection for one another. Randy walked around the corner of the house toward the shed, and Wallace and Ben stood with their shoulders just touching, both shaking their heads, until the three of us stepped inside.

"Can I get you a drink?" Wallace asked.

"Sure, I'll have a scotch," Ben said. "You too, Jen?" I nodded. "Two scotches, neat." Ben sat near me on the couch and looked intently into my eyes, concerned yet stalwart. His eyes are dark brown like our mother's and they were sad and watery. "How you doing? Man, I'm really jumpy. Are you?"

"Not right now. We just took a long walk. I'm not sleeping well."

"Me either. How's Wallace doing?"

"He's doing just wonderfully well," said Wallace, walking into the living room with two drinks. He handed one to me and one to Ben, smiling. "His spirits are good, his coloring excellent. As his doctor so adroitly put it, he is an extremely healthy fifty-five-year-old man, except for the brain tumor, of course."

I laughed, and held my drink up to him before I took a sip. "Thanks," I said.

"Not at all."

Randy sauntered in the front door with Muldoon, wiped his hands on his Levi's, and went into the kitchen.

"How's Randy doing?" Ben asked me.

"Don't talk about me," Randy shouted from the kitchen. Ben rolled his eyes.

"He's doing great, honestly," I whispered.

"Hey, Randy," Wallace called. "Would you please bring me my drink, on the counter, when you come home. I mean, when you come in."

"You're speaking excellently today, for the most part," said Ben.

"I've been put on steroids, to reduce the swelling around the tumor, so there's not as much pressure on my poor little brain. Glad you noticed." Wallace looked much less sad and nervous than Ben, but then Ben looked like a grieving coffee-taster. I almost can't believe that this sensitive, emotional man is my brother, the same person who used to throw snakes into my room when the lights were out.

Randy walked into the room with Wallace's drink and a beer for himself. He gave the drink to Dad, squinted at me for no reason, and sprawled sideways on the venerable leather armchair.

"Did you make a little nest for your heron so he or she will feel at home?" I asked Randy, who nodded sarcastically. "You should put an alarm clock with it for its first night."

"Duhhhh," he said. "Wudda you think about Sarah, Dad? You think I oughta tell her about my bird *today*?"

"I'd tell her," said Wallace. "Get it over with."

"I brought dinner," said Ben, who was beginning to feel the scotch; his drink was almost gone and the muscles in his face had relaxed. I was drinking more slowly than Ben, and had felt happier just *seeing* the whiskey, which may be one of the ten warning signs of alcoholism, this and my conviction that I wouldn't want to live in a world without alcohol.

Wallace smiled and took a long sip. "Did you? That was kind. What did you bring?"

"Chicken gumbo, French bread, salad."

"Nice work," said Randy.

"Thanks," said Wallace. "It sounds delicious."

"I love chicken gumbo. I like soups these days better than anything else," I said. "They're like breast-feeding again."

"Do you have to talk about it?" Randy asked.

Wallace stood and walked to the kitchen, and returned in a second, empty-handed and concerned. "Did I mention what I wanted from the kitchen?" he asked, looking at each of us.

"I think you said a big green thing, turns red when it's ready to cook," I said. "It'll come back to you."

Wallace sat down, laughing, shaking his head.

"I'm going to name him Mort, for 'rigor mortis,' " Randy announced.

"Speaking of which, any news on the tumor? ... Oh, nooo," said Ben. "I didn't mean it that way at all. Oh, shit." He put his head down into his hands with a rickety laugh.

"Don't worry," said Randy, "it runs in the family."

"And in answer to your question," said Wallace, "no. There won't be much more information until surgery, and the biopsy." He looked at Randy out of the corner of his eye. "Although they think from the brain scans that it's a surface tumor, without tentacles into the brain. But again, we just have to wait until after the surgery."

The room was silent until Ben finally said, "Hmmm." He reached out and slowly stroked each knuckle of my hand, with the high-strung and kind jurisdiction he has shown toward us since the diagnosis: Ben will be the majordomo through this episode in our lives. "Anybody need another drink?" he asked, and the three of us shook our heads. He walked to the stereo cabinet, took an album from its cover, and put it on the turntable. The first song was "Do Nothing Till You Hear from Me," by Duke Ellington, and he whistled the melody under his breath as he walked back to the couch. "Do you mind if I ask you some more questions about it, Dad?"

"Not at all, Benno. I'll tell you everything I can, if you guys all promise not to get morbid on me."

"Good," said Ben. "You don't have to protect us, you know."

"I know. What are your questions?"

Ben tugged nervously at his mustache and then lit up another Camel. "Two things. One, if it's malignant, can it be cured?"

"Possibly, but probably not. They can slow the process down for years, though. . . ."

"So if it's malignant, does that automatically mean you'll,

uh"—Randy seemed to search for the delicate word—"cack off?"

Everybody laughed. "Yes, I guess so," said Wallace. "Well put."

"Oh, well," said Randy, "easy come, easy go."

"Win a few, lose a few," I added, smiling at Wallace.

"That's the truth," said Wallace. "Think of how many of my friends have already bought the farm. Ben, you had another question?"

"Yeah. Is there any chance of brain damange during the surgery? Could the surgeon sever a nerve or something?"

"It's a *woman* surgeon," Randy said with disgust. "I used to know a joke about a *blind* neurosurgeon, but—"

"Shove it, you little creep," I told him. He stuck out his tongue.

"Yes, of course, that's a possibility," Wallace said, ignoring Randy and me. "It's really the only thing I'm afraid of. Odds are good that it's benign, which is what we hope for, but if it's malignant, then I'm just going to die, which is not an uncommon thing for people to do. And if the surgeon severs the wrong nerve, then I'd be a vegetable, which wouldn't be any great shakes but at least I wouldn't be aware of it—although it would be impossibly hard for you guys and Sarah. But if the surgeon cuts wrong and I lose some of my faculties, and am aware of my incompleteness, I'd be terribly frustrated, I know."

"Would you want us to kill you if you were a veg?" asked Randy. "Or if you were *part* vegetable?" His voice was hesitant and curious and horrified and eager, all at once.

Wallace cocked his head, stroked his mustache, closed one eye, and thought. "Yes, I guess so. How would you do it?"

"Strangulation," Randy answered gleefully.

"Forget it," said Wallace.

"Heroin," I said.

"Hmmm," said Wallace. "An overdose wouldn't be a bad way to go. In fact, terminal patients in extreme pain are given heroin in a shot called the 'Brompton cocktail'—heroin and alcohol and morphine mixed together."

"Yum *yum*," I said.

"Don't they get addicted?" Randy asked.

"So what if they get addicted," I said. "They're dying anyway."

"Would you want us to kill you if you were in terrible pain?" Randy asked.

"I suppose I would want someone to put me to sleep, as it were. I'm not sure, though, that it should be one of my children. Let me think about it."

"Anybody want another drink?" Ben asked, standing with his empty glass. "Jen? Wallace? Randy?" Wallace and I gave him our glasses. "Randy? Another beer?"

"Nah," said Randy, disheartened. "Make it a Bromptom. Make it a *double* Bromptom." He scowled, glared into space, and then looked down, clenching his teeth. "I never thought about it before, about how much pain people could be in. Jesus fucking *Christ*. I couldn't *stand* it if you were in pain. I would definitely kill you if you were in big pain, no kidding."

"You'd be surprised what humans get through," said Wallace. "Tragedy, pain, fear, dying, loss—and you three will get through whatever happens."

"But you might not," said Randy sullenly.

"See, now you're getting morbid on me. I want to tell you a couple of things. First of all, there are all sorts of possibilities concerning the tumor: it may be benign, it may be malignant but operable, I may die on the operating table. And I'm pretty sure that the hardest part for you guys is going to be the waiting; I suspect there's going to be a lot of waiting. But no matter what happens, you have each other, you have me and your mother, you have our closest friends and relatives, you have your senses of humor, and I think the three of you have clear ideas of what is of value in this life. The family—blood relatives and adopted relatives—will provide continuity all your lives, and although I think you're all pretty nuts, I also think you're tough and honest. So I'm not too worried about you guys. And as for me, I promise you that I'm not afraid of death, and I'm not even that afraid of dying. But right now I'm alive and living and I want to make one thing crystal clear about euthanasia." He paused and looked at us with mock sternness.

"What's that?" Ben asked from the doorway.

"Do not," he said, squinting at each of us in turn, "I repeat, do *not* do anything about it until you hear from me."

"You got it, Bunky," said my younger brother.

I got up and rubbed Wallace's neck while Ben made the drinks. Wallace dropped his head to his chest and purred. I pushed my thumbs into the muscles above his shoulder blades.

"That feels great," he said. "You're a fine child."

"I know. I'll do practically anything to please," I replied, in jest and in truth. "And I'll tell you, it's one of the biggest problems in my life."

"Well, don't stop now," said Wallace.

Ben came into the living room with two drinks, one for Wallace and one for me, and tripped slightly over Muldoon, who sat at Wallace's feet. "Here, Dad; here, Jen. How come Muldoon is acting so mopey?" Muldoon looked at Wallace adoringly.

"He's worried about his dad," said Randy.

"I am *not* that dog's father," Wallace said indignantly. Muldoon licked Wallace's ankle and howled very softly, like a humpback whale. Ben returned to the kitchen and then to the living room with his own drink in one hand, a Dos Equis in the other for Randy, and a note in his mouth, which he removed after giving Randy the beer.

"But you *are* that kid's father," Ben said, giving Randy

the eye affectionately, and the note to me. "Did you see this note, Jen? It was on the refrigerator.'

The note was in Randy's erratic half-printed, half-cursive script. The first line was in red, and said, "Dad—please get me a sixpack. XX. Randy." The second line was in blue, probably written after the note had been Scotch-taped to the freezer door. It read, "These are not kisses, you old coot, they mean *dos equis*, two exxes."

Wallace and Ben and I laughed, and Randy scowled.

"So!" said Wallace in a huffy and indignant voice. "So! No kisses for your old man?"

Randy grinned and began making loud sloppy kisses toward the chair in front of the fireplace in which Wallace sat. My younger brother stood, his face scrunched up sheepishly, and walked over to the stereo cabinet to turn over the album, his nose in the air, ignoring us all, then stopped for a moment at the chair where Wallace sat smiling calmly and fondly, and punched his father lightly on the shoulder.

The Town
Where I Live

The cabin beneath the eucalyptuses was encased in fog when I awoke this morning, butt to butt with my ten-year-old friend Megan, who was making waking-up noises. It was nine o'clock and the cabin was still dark enough so that the piles, clumps, and general squalor receded in the gray mildewy air. There were clothes on the table, on the floor, on the top of the refrigerator. There was food on top of the piles of clothes, sometimes on a plate or in a cup but not always—for instance, there was a large bolus of partly chewed pineapple core on a purple wool bathrobe. There were books and magazines and newspapers hovering about like unkempt relatives at a reunion. There was a T-shirt beside the bed with which I had wiped up most of a half gallon of red wine, a big ball of blond kinky hair culled from my hairbrush, which I am now down to using once a week, and there was a decrepit, senile, incontinent alley cat pacing across the room, glaring at nothing in particular. Not to mention the pungent smell of his cat box. Megan had propped herself up on her elbows, scanned the room groggily, and said, "You must be a saint to live in a place like this."

She turned on the radio and picked up the cat. The cat has only one tooth, on the bottom, to the left: at sixteen years old he eats his food like a toothless old man gumming saltines. I would have his teeth fixed somehow but he will probably not last long. Megan's seventy-eight-year-old great-aunt was recently told by her dentist that her dentures were acceptable, but that for twenty-three hundred dollars he would fit her with teeth that would last her a lifetime. Megan held the cat in the rocking chair, beside the Franklin stove, rocking slowly and drowsily: both of us would start talking in about ten minutes. The cat smiled. A long strand of embroidery thread hung from his tooth.

"Farrrrrrr out," said someone on the radio doing an impersonation of John Denver, whose great moment, insofar as either Megan or I was concerned, was an interview in *Rolling Stone* in which he stated, "I think it is so far out that birds fly in the sky and fish swim in the sea."

"That guy's a feeb," Megan muttered. In the anteroom the cat peed on the outside of his box.

The disc jockey played a song called "My Feet Stink, My Head Aches and I Don't Love Jesus."

"*My* feet stink," Megan told me. "I've had this same pair of socks on for three days, and they weren't even clean to begin with."

"So don't tell *me* about it."

"Well, I can't very well go around all day with my feet stinking, can I?"

"You did it yesterday. You can wear a pair of mine."

"None of yours match," said Megan, holding one of her socks at a healthy distance. It looked like it had crumpled cardboard in it.

"But mine don't stink. So you can spray Lysol on yours, or you can borrow mine. And frankly, I think you're going to have to burn your pair." Megan waggled her sock at the cat, who rolled his eyes and looked appalled.

"O.K. I want to stay here and read until you do your housecleaning job. Then we could go to the beach or something. I can't believe *you* make money housecleaning."

I can't believe it either. I used to be an editor with a national magazine, and now I spend my days cleaning schmootz off the inside of refrigerators, and wiping up pubic hairs from the bottoms of bathtubs. There are few jobs available in the small town where I live, and I will not commute over the hill. My time is too important to me. My time is so important to me that I choose to spend it sucking up dust bunnies with upright Hoovers.

When I was dressed and about to leave, Megan looked up with feigned annoyance from one of the bookshelves. "If you didn't have so many books, I could probably find something to read."

"Good luck, toots. See you later."

"See you later," she said. In this town where I live, we rarely say "Good-bye." We say "See you later," or simply "S'later."

Megan likes me more than almost anyone else in the world likes me. She has a seemingly blind eye to my top ten personality defects, and laughs at almost everything I say. She likes me so much that I do not panic too much when in her company I feel an unheralded pimple emerging on my chin, threatening to alter my profile. We have a relationship so special, so easy, so lacking in the complications of most friendships—we have so much fun together—that sometimes at the beach dodging waves I look at her and think, Phew.

My next-door neighbors live three hundred feet away and raise worms in big wooden boxes in their front yard. The father and both children look much like the weird children one ran into occasionally in grammar school—very, very tiny and vaguely Martian. I hide from this family most of the time. They invite me to their yard parties, and I never show up. They drop by the cabin to discuss better ways to raise worms, and I hide in the bathroom while they knock. The ten-year-old daughter, who is outgoing and sort of striking in a tiny weird Martian sort of way, once told me I should brush my hair more. The little boy, who is five years old and looks like Oscar Levant, once put my alley cat in one of the worm boxes. My cat was not amused. The mother is a stunning blond heiress who makes a tremendous effort to be liked, and succeeds in offending and alienating almost everyone with whom she comes in contact, except for her husband, who has as much spark and humor as a cattle tick. On my lucky days—of which this is one—none of them see me sneak past their house to the main road. There are many of these strange humanoids in the town where I live.

On the dirt road that runs above the ocean cliffs, I ran into Frank Morgan, a tawny octogenarian who lives alone nearby. He entertains his friends—and everyone in town is his friend—with a wide variety of birdcalls that all sound alike. Today he was walking with a vicious-looking businessman of about forty who was wearing a green-orange diamond-print leisure suit. I decided that this man was Frank's son, and that he had come to town to see if Frank was still coherent enough to live by himself. Well, I thought, I'll show him that Frank has all sorts of reasonable friends with whom he can carry on meaningful conversations.

"Hello, Frank," I said. "How you doing?"

Frank beamed at me, spread his arms, fluttered his eyes, and flapped his wings, emitting a loud, quavering birdcall.

On the main road of the mesa, a 1964 Chevelle Malibu station wagon pulled over. "Wanna ride?" called the driver.

"O.K.," I said, and got in. The driver was one of our town's innumerable Burn Outs. Most are in their twenties and look like either Charlie Manson or Janis Joplin. This Burn Out was wearing horn-rimmed glasses with no lenses (which he pushed up on his nose before he put the car in gear) and seagull feathers in his hair. He almost immediately drove us into a ditch.

"Thanks for the ride," I said, and walked the rest of the way. One treats the Burn Outs with a distant respect, as some of them are dangerous.

My younger brother and I do not enjoy most of the Burn Outs. They are generally a nuisance, although on occasion they deliver performances of unabashed and cinematically enjoyable lunacy. When I feel benevolently toward the town, especially during our saturnalias, I am reminded of the gentle insanity of the inmates in *King of Hearts*; the rest of the time, the characters of *Marat/Sade* spring to mind. The Burn Outs are usually refugees from Napa State, the Langley Porter Neurological Institute, and Bellevue. The rest of us, and sometimes there is a fine line, are—in the words of my dream consultant—refugees from anonymity. The rest of us have better acts, better packaging. The Burn Outs do not have such good acts, and they do not fool anyone. They continually leap in front of us with empty or imaginary cameras, clicking away. They attack dogs at the Community Center dances. They stab one another with pool cues at the bar. Sometimes they get taken away, but they usually come back.

My younger brother, who is seventeen, and, like the rest of us, ravenously insecure, feels he must be kind and attentive to the Burn Outs or risk having his dog attacked with a pool cue. He was once picked up by the Burn Out in the 1964 Chevelle Malibu, and rode halfway over the mountain in silence, until the Burn Out shouted, "I have a can of beans at home with fifty-seven colors!"

"Fifty-seven," my brother said. "That's a lot of colors for one can of soup."

"You're damned right," said the Burn Out huffily, just before he eased the station wagon into a ditch.

Another time, my brother was picked up by a woman with a crew cut and a large eye drawn in the middle of her forehead with felt pens. She didn't say a word for a few minutes, and then the woman whispered, somewhat hostilely, "Last night my cat threw up a hairball."

"Oh," my brother whispered back. "What is your cat's name?"

There is a Burn Out in this town who gets paid a thousand dollars a month to stay out of his parents' hometown, the last of the remittance men. His name is Moonboy, because he howls at the moon nightly, regardless of its visibility; whether it's waxing or waning he howls at or to it. Moonboy today walked toward me, on the road that leads from the town, with composure and solemnity, until he was attacked from the sky by his demons. He looked to the sky with terror and anger, flailed at the air around his head, and tore the attackers like leeches from his shoulders and back. When he had thrown them all to the ground, he continued his walk, head held high, and nodded stoically to me as we passed.

In this town there is also a group of people who are so hip, so high, so cheerful, so compassionate and concerned and loving and full of high consciousness, that hardly anyone (beside their own) can stand them. They travel in packs of goodwill and vapid conversation. Megan's father calls them the Cosmica Ramas. Megan and I avoid them as much as possible, as they are always trying to touch us. Last week we were sitting in front of the Laundromat eating M&Ms when one of the largest female Cosmica Ramas approached us. Being a tall and large-boned woman, she boasts a composite weight and IQ of about one-ninety; her chosen name is Moss. She sat between Megan and me and began discussing the restorative properties of daily miso soup. Megan excused herself and went inside the Laundromat, giggling uncontrollably by the time she reached the doorway.

"So," I said politely, "what kind of miso do you use, the red or the brown?"

"Oh, sometimes I *mix* them!" she said happily. "I think it is *great fun*."

We are a bitterly political town, perhaps because so many people here are bored. We form factions on every conceivable issue, and frequently they are backbiting factions, such as the people who divided into camps on the issue of painting or not painting a white line down the middle of the main road downtown. Mostly we are afraid of losing the town to developers who would turn us from a mostly agrarian and artistic community of two thousand into another Carmel, but we have become confused and paranoid about the proper means to the proper end. We are mostly counterculture bleeding-heart-liberal types of every age, farmers, writers, teachers, carpenters, musicians, therapists, gardeners, laborers, poets, professionals, fishermen, seekers, Burn Outs, and children, with some geniuses, egomaniacs, lunatics, trust-fund radicals, Republicans and martyrs thrown in for flavor, and the flavor is often bitter. We have a few ex-convicts, a disproportionately high number of Ivy League graduates (my father is one; most are much younger), one Roman Polanski type who at thirty-four sleeps exclusively with girls under sixteen, one Rastafarian, half a dozen male homosexuals and no visible lesbians, hundreds of counterculture clotheshorses, many heirs and heiresses, a dozen addicts, our share of wife- and child-beaters, and no one ever starves to death. There are several dozen adults and innumerable children whom I like and/or admire, and many people I cannot stand, and Clement is the closest thing I have to a home, as ingrown and incestuous and irritating as it sometimes is.

My uncle Colin once said that in this town of almost unspeakable physical beauty, our boredom and conceit has bred the worst sort of self-righteous paranoia, and that our tensions along these lines are so rampant that our horses—and there are hundreds of horses, with which we see the world of the ridges and the waters, stunning natural luxuries that diminish much of our angst—are going to develop long, pointy teeth and attack us.

I clean house three times a week. On Mondays I clean the house of an elderly and feisty environmentalist. On Wednesdays I clean the three-story house of a Prabhavan-anda disciple who makes his living speculating on land in this town. On Thursdays I clean the house of a trust-fund radical, whose major revolutionary act of the last two dec-ades has been to hang the Symbionese Liberation Army's group picture on his bedroom wall. His family owns a chain of drugstores. Every week he tries to cheat me out of a few dollars, but so far he hasn't succeeded.

I hate cleaning house, especially on Thursdays. I hate it even more than I hate brain tumors and cancer and pimples. But I make four dollars an hour twelve hours a week, which gives me enough income to write the rest of the time, and I am buying writing time—it is as simple as that. I would not hate cleaning houses so much, I think, if the houses were not so clean to begin with. Two of the houses, the environ-mentalist's and the land speculator's, are impeccable to be-gin with, and the trust-fund radical's appears to have been sterilized, except for a particularly loathsome toilet. So I spend four hours a week in each house taking swipes at imaginary cobwebs, diligently vacuuming immaculate car-pets, wiping, sweeping, scrubbing, deodorizing, and polish-ing already-clean houses. It is equivalent to corporate paper shuffling. It bores me and frustrates me and angers me. The occasional dust globs, the sporadic refrigerator messes, those random pubic hairs on bathtub floors—these I eradi-cate triumphantly, like a paper shuffler in the moment of glory when he or she discovers a typo in an otherwise im-maculate report on Systematized Reciprocal Contingencies.

The trust-fund radical, who wears extremely tight pants and shouldn't, left me the key to his house and the written admonition that last week I neglected to clean the finger-prints off his toaster. I cleaned his bachelor's house, which cost $120,000 to build, in four hours. When I finished, I left him a note to the effect that he owed me sixteen dollars that I would collect when he got back. At the last minute, I cleaned his toaster with spit and a shirt he left in the bathroom.

He arrived as I closed the door behind me.

"Hello," I said.

"What do I owe you?" he asked.

"Same as usual. Sixteen dollars."

Reaching into his left pants pocket, he brought out a ten and a five.

"Could we make it fifteen?" he asked. "You've cleaned me out."

"Sure," I said. "I'll debit your account."

His pants were so tight that his other hand got stuck in his pocket when he withdrew it to shake my hand. We shook hands and he flinched and grabbed his hand as if I had crushed it. He chuckled heartily and said, "Say, that reminds me, I heard a news story on the radio this morning that I thought would crack you up—I love your sense of humor. . . ." I put my hands in my jeans and looked expectant. "See, this old lady had a poodle, and the poodle got sopping wet in the rain one day, so the lady pops it into a microwave oven for about a minute . . ." He couldn't continue for a few moments, as he tried unsuccessfully to contain his laughter. ". . . and she opens the door and the dog has burnt to a crisp. *Ha ha ha ha ha.* It's *charred!"*

I faked a short laugh—a fake laugh is one of the most obvious and disgusting sounds in the world; it feels awful to fake a laugh—and said, "Jeez!"

"Ha ha ha," he finished up. "I knew you'd like it."

There are any number of people—my friends—who could have told this story with the proper sense of black humor, of isn't-life-the-shits irony, and I would have laughed a bit sadly and then improvised something to the effect that dogs who fit into microwave ovens are usually yappy and hateful anyway, and we would have laughed to make everything all right. But the way the trust-fund radical told the story made me feel sorry for him, and I left liking him more than I had before, which still wasn't much but was tinged with compassion, and compassion, I think, is the hard and estimable one.

I used to clean house for an arrogant but charming Gestalt therapist, until she moved out of town. Very few of us ever move out of town; the real world is very likely even more cruel and scary than it is in our town. The therapist moved because she was offered more money over the hill, and because she got tired of dealing with the parents of our teenagers, who as a whole are confident and undisciplined and sexually active. A father called her once when I was cleaning her house and said that his sixteen-year-old daughter had stolen three cars in two weeks. "I think she needs therapy," said the distraught father.

"I think she needs a car," said the therapist.

I walked to the cabin after leaving the radical's house. I passed the lagoon, two sections of the Pacific beach, innumerable birds, dogs, horses and riders, amid the spectacular and overgrown foliage. Everywhere you look here you see a million trees, a million birds.

Megan was hanging upside down from one of the old cypresses in the grove that grow behind the cabin. There is something, for me, indescribably lovely about the long, thin brown legs of a child: I was glad to find Megan hanging from my tree. I thought she might be gone when I returned.

"Hey, Megan," I said.

"Hey," she said. "I've got two new tricks." She was glad I was back. Her first trick involved a slow, limber backward flip from the branch. She landed on her feet and beamed. I smiled and nodded.

"And now for my next number," she said.

She climbed up the widespread trunk to her branch, and

stood up, holding a thin upper branch for balance. She moved one leg forward and farted, a quiet, ten-year-old-child fart, and blushed.

"What was *that*?" I asked, grinning.

"That," she said with prim composure, "was my next number."

Megan and I left the cabin for the beach, holding hands and kicking rocks, exchanging details of the day. "What did you end up reading?" I asked.

"I just read a bunch of magazine articles. Mostly I hung out in the trees because the cat kept getting on my nerves." Her voice is soft and precise, medium high. "Everywhere I went, he'd follow me and stare. I read one pretty interesting article, though. Do you want to hear about it?"

"Of course I want to hear about it."

"Well, there's a drug called 'Pergonal' or something that makes women pregnant with four or five babies."

"A fertility drug?" I asked. "Does that ring a bell?"

"Yeah, a fertility drug. And you will never believe what it's made of." She looked at me. "Urine!"

"I don't believe it," I said, although I did.

"It's true. And you know who pees most of the urine?"

"Who?"

"You are *never* going to believe this." She looked at me sideways to see if she had my full attention. *"Italian nuns!"*

The cattle in the meadows alongside the road were so fat by this time of year that they were lying down, black and white spotted hulks amid the sparse grass and thick brush. Only two of the beasts were standing. A bull lumbered over to a confused-looking female and heavily lifted his front legs onto her back. The animal being humped—the hump-pee—rolled her eyes indifferently. They looked like two Dalmatian Volkswagens making love. The wrentits sang from the coyote bush. Megan wanted to stop and watch, so we sat on a cypress log alongside the field.

There are many three-legged dogs in the town where I live. A golden retriever with one front leg ran across the field in a well-choreographed limp toward his owner, a small boy named Zapata who lives in a tepee with his mother at the north end of the pasture, and whom my father's lover and roommate has in her third-grade class. Zapata was carrying his lumpy, angry Siamese cat named Gandhi toward the tepee, several hundred yards away from where Megan and I sat. He didn't see us.

Many of the children and animals in this town are named after East Indian heavies, herbs, recipes using soybeans, and imprisoned revolutionaries. There are children named Ram, Blueberry, Jesus, Tania, and Tahini, and many of the children in this town are a joy. There are dogs named Renaissance, Rosenberg, and Coriander. Zapata himself owns, besides Gandhi, a black and slightly retarded cat named Batman, a greenish collie named Liberace, a horse named Eldridge, and a rooster named Junior who twitches continually.

"Have you ever seen *The Glass Menagerie*?" Megan asked.

"Yeah," I said, watching the three-legged dog. "Why?"

Megan was silent for a moment. "Zapata's got a *spaz* menagerie," she said. "And I don't think it's fair that his mother is so nutsy."

"Either do I."

"Usually if you point out that something isn't fair, an adult says"—her voice became nasal and patronizing—"'Now, no one ever said it would be fair.' It drives me crazy."

"Me too," I said.

"See, I can't even tell what's fair and what's not."

"That's one of the things that isn't fair," I said.

"'Now,'" she repeated in her adult voice, "'no one ever said it would be fair.'" We both laughed. "So what do you think?"

Megan was trying to pull a foxtail out of one of her back

teeth: she puts foxtails in her mouth so that she can spit them at nonmoving objects—my back, for instance—but often they become lodged between her teeth. It is one of her recurring dilemmas.

"I don't know," I said. "One thing that I think is that there are a lot of good shows around here. You never even have to look for them. It's like a puppet show in this town."

"Here comes one now," said Megan as Zapata's mother, Aurora, stepped out of the tepee wearing six empty Tampax tubes on her fingers, in the way that children wear pitted olives on their fingers at holiday dinners. Aurora is a Burn Out. For Halloween last year she went to the Community Center dance dressed as a capillary, in a skintight red tube dress with lipstick above her eyelids and ketchup on her hands and neck. She has a strange sense of humor: nothing amuses her more than an especially poignant memorial service. She goes to the Laundromat for entertainment, where she tears the pleated paper cups that the management provides for detergent into animal shapes—a bat, a money, a snake. Once, I slammed my fingers in a washing-machine door, and Aurora laughed off and on through the entire wash cycle. Once, she called the fire department at three A.M. to report a terrifying flying object that had hovered outside the tepee all evening. When the fire chief arrived, she was crying and pointing at the luminous white orb in the mist, which upon careful scrutiny by the chief was determined to be the moon.

Megan was watching Aurora deliberately and sadly. "Some of the shows are sort of sad, aren't they?"

"Yeah," I said, "they are."

"That's what you like most about the town, isn't it? The shows, right?"

"I like you better than the shows. I like the waters and the lands around here better than the shows. I like some people better than the shows. But you're right, I do like them."

"So do I," she said. "But some of them are sad."

When Zapata reached Aurora in front of the tepee, she tousled his hair gently with the Tampax tubes still on her fingers, glared at the three-legged dog, and ushered Zapata inside, disappearing after him. The dog sat down outside and scratched the area where his front right leg would have been if he had one.

Romance

S everal months ago Megan and I were sitting on the hillside above the small commercial section of town,
watching the antics of the mostly long-haired townspeople
as they went about their Saturday-morning errands. Megan
and I at least recognized everyone below, and in many cases
even knew their automotive, romantic, financial, and professional situations. Only two thousand people live in
Clement, a town thought by outsiders to be an ambulatory
psychotic ward. Megan pointed her ice-cream cone at a man
walking alone past the grocery store, past the bar, past the
Laundromat, nodding hello with reserved charm to friends
along the way.

"There's Eric," she taunted. She was a bit jealous of him,
because at that point he was spending the night with me
several times a week, frequently on nights when Megan
wanted to stay over. "There's your *boy* friend. . . ."

"That's your worst voice," I said, "your sneer voice."

"I think my worst voice is when I'm mad," she said. She
looked over at me contritely.

"I don't mind your mad voice at all. I'm not crazy about
your *peeved* voice, and I'm not crazy about the sneer voice."

"So too bad for you," she said, shaking her cone at me.
We both laughed. "All I was going to say was that his dog
looks more and more like a saddle shoe."

"You don't like him all that much, do you?" I asked.

"I like him sometimes, when he's not being conceited, but I just sort of don't like something about him."

"Is it just sort of that you wish he didn't spend the night as much?"

"Well, yes," she said. "It's sort of that exactly." She grinned. One of the many things I like about Megan is that she owns up to her feelings, even the socially unacceptable ones like jealousy.

"Anything else?"

"I wouldn't like it if you liked him more than you like me."

"Well, I don't. I just like sleeping with him."

"I know why," she said slyly. She made a circle of her left thumb and forefinger, and put her right forefinger through it. "Right?"

"Partly right. Partly I just like sleeping next to him."

"Does he like you the same amount that you like him?"

"More or less. He's more afraid of me than I am of him."

"What's he afraid of?" She handed me her ice-cream cone.

"He's afraid of people knowing"—I changed my voice to *basso profundo*—"*his secrets*."

"Like what? What secrets?"

I handed her the cone. "He's afraid that I'll notice that he's going bald."

"What do you mean, *going* bald? He only has about thirty hairs on the top of his head."

"I know," I replied, "but he thinks that if he combs those thirty hairs carefully, no one will notice."

"You're kidding," she said. "You never say anything?"

"Not really. . . ."

"Emperor's new clothes," said Megan.

"I've alluded to it exactly twice. It hasn't gone over well."

"Like a fart in church," she said.

The first time, as I told Megan, I was doodling happily one day and ended up drawing a picture of Eric. I generously drew in extra hair, but there was no question that it was the head of a balding man. He looked over my shoulder and scowled.

"Gee, that's really excellent," he said sarcastically.

"Get me an eraser, would you?" I asked him. "I just realized what's wrong with it. I put in too much hair."

He glared, and went outside huffily.

The second time, I told Eric this story:

During my sophomore year in college I was a hatcheck girl at a Tall Cedars of Lebanon grand ball. Vaughn Monroe and his orchestra played, and drove the women wild. Alcohol was prohibited by the lodge, so everyone brought bottles with woolen poodle covers and got quite drunk, except for the grand poo-bah's wife, who wore a white satin dress with a tall cedar embroidered on it from her neck to her crotch. A very drunk man came up to the hatcheck table midway through the dancing and started to ask for his coat. He stopped suddenly when he caught sight of my hair, my thick, frizzy blond Afro, and tried to focus on it, weaving without moving his feet as he did so. After several moments, he said, "Who scared *you*?"

Eric laughed, and said, "Five years later and your hair still hasn't cleared up."

"Eat your heart out," I said.

"Are you going to sleep with him tonight?" Megan asked as Eric walked down the street toward us.

"I might," I said, and shrugged with exaggerated nonchalance. "I want you to come for tea this afternoon anyway, with my grandmother. Are you going to come?"

"I might," she said, doing a brilliant parody of my nonchalant look, and then laughed. "Good! Yes, I can," she said.

Eric caught sight of us on the hillside above him, out of earshot, and waved to us. We waved back. "Don't do anything to embarrass me," I whispered.

"Like what?" she asked, standing up with her forefinger-into-the-circle gesture for Eric's benefit.

I started laughing and looked away. Megan was in hysterics, and sat back down. Eric looked up at me questioningly. "Please," I whispered, "don't do any bald shtick. . . ."

"Like what?" she said, standing up theatrically and then looking to see if I appreciated that she wasn't going to go through with it.

Eric, on the street, first raised his thumb, then turned it upside down, and then shrugged inquisitively.

I looked back at him, raised my thumb, shrugged; he nodded, waved, and walked away.

"Does that mean you're going to sleep with him?" she asked.

"Yeah," I said.

"That certainly was romantic," she said.

Eric and I met on the tennis court almost a year ago. It was an uneven game of pickup doubles; Eric played backhand to the forehand of the town's dentist, and I played backhand to the forehand of one of Clement's holistic doctors, whose name is Fenton Smail but who works under the name of Dr. Rainbow. Dr. Rainbow is a vicious and thieving partner who cheats when he is losing and gloats out loud when he is winning; I think it is because he is just over five feet tall.

I had never been formally introduced to Eric, although we knew each other by sight and I knew several stories about him. Eric had a competent and unassuming tennis demeanor, and paisley boxer underpants that hung two inches past his khaki shorts.

Dr. Rainbow's strategy was to let it flow, let it happen, and to go for the throat. Eric passed him continually at net, and said, "Well, Rainbow, if you can't beat 'em, cheat 'em, eh?" when Rainbow called in-balls out. Midway through the second set, I began to think that Eric showed great promise.

(I went to see Dr. Rainbow as a patient on three occasions, *before* I had played tennis with him: I would not have entrusted my urinary infection to him otherwise. On all three occasions, despite my having made appointments, I had to wait. His girl friend and receptionist, who travels under the name Olivia To*Nite, referred to him as "Doctor," as in, "You'll have to wait; Doctor is doing his yoga," or "You'll have to wait awhile; Doctor is on another plane.")

When we finished two sets of doubles, each side winning one, Eric and I sat down on the court bench and watched Dr. Rainbow cheat the dentist through a set of singles. We both made frequent and droll comments on the game, and laughed appreciatively.

"Well," he said when he stood to leave, "I'd like to play again with you sometime."

"Good, so would I," I said. He looked at me levelly, and I thought I detected a vibrational beep. I looked at him levelly, returning the beep.

"So where are you going now?" he asked.

"Up to my cabin, for a beer."

I felt sure enough of the beeps to ask him if he would like to come along, and he said, "Sure."

I drove us up the hill, making small talk and surreptitiously looking at myself in the rearview mirror to make sure there were no bits of flug in my nose or eyes, which there weren't. I looked surreptitiously at him also, and noticed not only that there were no bits of crud on his face, but that he was very close to being handsome, in the same sort of way as my father (coincidentally), part Kennedy, part Arlo Guthrie, part Smokey the Bear. He was casually rearranging the sparse hairs on the top of his head for optimum coverage. One of the stories I had heard about him over the years was that he began going bald in his late twenties. I had heard that his ex-wife had had three nervous breakdowns, and that any number of women in town had been driven to obsessive distraction because of him. I had heard that he rarely had long-term girl friends, and that on his thirtieth birthday, two years ago, he roasted a pig on a spit in his back yard and left quite early and quite drunk with two Bunny-type knockouts. I had heard that he was an impossible man to know intimately, and that his romantic delivery was cool and irresistible. I hoped that he had not heard about the time I helped push over the pool table in the bar, or about the time I was arrested with my dream consultant for peeing on the ground at the Catholic cemetery.

He stepped inside the cabin and looked around admiringly. "Nice place," he said. While I got two beers out of the refrigerator, he looked at the clothes in the middle of the floor and the newspapers and books strewn about, and at the aging alley cat who lay on a pile of dirty dishes in the sink, and at the spaghetti-sauce tracks that ran down the stove like a trail of snail spit.

"Uh," I said, "the girl obviously hasn't come yet today. You know, my slavey."

"Don't worry," he said. "I'm not one of the world's most compulsive housecleaners either."

"Well put," I told him, and gave him a beer.

He opened it and walked around the cabin, kicking things lightly—the edge of the refrigerator, the Franklin stove, the table leg. He studied the two batiks that Megan made for me, one of which says WE LIKE UNCLE ROSCOE and the other I USED TO BE A MOVIE STAR BUT NOW I AM A STAR IN THE SKY.

"Have a seat," I said. He kicked the rocking chair and sat down in it. The first time he rocked backward, his body jerked forward as if he didn't believe that the chair wouldn't crash over backward.

"So," he said, pretending to be unruffled by his lack of aplomb, "do you, uh"—scratching his beard, clearing his throat—"live here alone?"

I cleared my throat, scratched my armpit, and said, "Uh,

yes, I do live here, uh, alone."

He laughed. "Do you want to smoke a joint?"

"I think we'd better, under the circumstances," I said.

He took a joint from the pocket of his khakis, lit it, and inhaled deeply. His hands were large and beautiful and well worn, his eyes large and gray, his teeth huge and wet. When he handed me the joint, and looked at me with his level, aloof look, it became obvious to me that we were going to end up in bed. I inhaled, eager with anticipation and relief—knowing that chemical help was on the way—and began to cough and choke.

"This your first joint?" he asked.

I took another toke and passed it back to him. We sat around talking and joking through two more beers and one more joint. We talked about tennis, penguins, nuclear power, and mutual friends. In Clement, all of us gossip shamelessly about our friends and neighbors.

"Well," he said when we finished our third beer, "do you think we would both fit into your bed?" It was five-forty-five. His smile was just shy enough through the bravado and almost-smug charm to satisfy my suspicion that there was a real person In There.

I got up and closed the door. "Only one way to find out," I said jauntily, palpitating with nervousness and lust. We got in bed and made friendly, athletic love while the old cat watched, and pretty soon we were sleeping together as often as not.

Megan's father drove by the hillside and signaled for her to come down.

"See you at three, Jen," she said, wiping the ice cream off her mouth with the back of her hand, and then wiping the back of her hand on the back of her pants. "Thanks for the ice cream."

"You're welcome. See you later."

Megan looked at me and smiled. She put the back of her

hand to her forehead, and looked at me with dramatic tenderness.

"Good night, sweet princess," she said. She had just started reading Shakespeare. She raced down the hill to her father's car.

Megan arrived at the cabin at quarter to three, dressed in a short Mexican skirt, an embroidered white blouse, red knee socks, and her tennis shoes. She is tall for ten, and thin. She made a mock-stylish entrance, her hand behind her head, her nose in the air, her eyes closed haughtily.

"Hello, my dearest darling," she said, shaking my hand. *"Enchanteé,* I'm sure; *je suis, je vais."*

"You look great," I said. I was wearing blue jeans and a T-shirt.

"Yes," she said, "I think I'm looking particularly sheveled right now. Do you think your grandmother will remember me?"

"Of course she'll remember you," I replied. Megan looked pleased. "Last time she saw you you spilt your milk on her purse."

"Oh, that's right," she said. "I thought she'd remember me for my grace and brilliance. Well, don't remind her about the milk. I thought she might not remember me because she's so old. No offense."

"What do you mean, 'no offense'?" I asked.

"I didn't mean to say that your grandmother was *old,* or something."

"She's eighty-two, for God's sake," I said, laughing. "Why are you being so polite?"

"My father said to act polite in front of your grandmother."

"Well, she's not here yet. You can act normal for a few minutes."

A car pulled up in front of the cabin twenty minutes later, and soon there was a light knocking on the front door's porthole.

"Yo!" Megan said to me. "What light through yonder window breaks?"

" 'Lo,' ' I said. "Not 'yo.'"

"Oh," she said.

My maternal grandmother has shrunk from five foot eight to somewhere around five foot two in the last ten years, and she now weighs about ninety-five pounds. She used to worry inordinately about her slightly large calves, but now they have disappeared altogether except for the shinbone. Her once-flaming-red hair is now sparse, and very white. Her eyes are the same color as mine—hazel, on the greenish side—and thick-lidded. She is quite abstracted now, although nowhere near senile.

"Hello, dear," she said to me when we kissed. Megan stood shyly off to the side with her hands behind her back. "And who is this pretty little girl?" she asked, smiling to Megan.

"I'm Megan," said Megan. "I spilt milk on your purse last time, remember?"

"Oh, yes," said my grandmother. "How nice to see you again," she said kindly.

While I made tea, Megan told her the plots of two movies. She and my grandmother make a funny pair. No one else reads the same books they do, and no one else will listen to Megan's movie renditions—which frequently last longer than the movies—with any enthusiasm whatsoever. Megan and my grandmother compared their favorite sections of a book they had both finished recently, *The Pushcart Wars*. Megan's vocabulary is extensive, with only periodic misusages. She told my grandmother that she thought oldish people should be legible for more state money. She also told her that she and her mother inhibit a house in Portland. My grandmother did not correct her, and Megan did not correct my grandmother when she referred to *Dandelion Wine*, by, as she said, Ray Bromberry.

After my grandmother's friend came and picked her up for the ride home, Megan kicked off her sneakers and said, "So what time is *he* coming over?"

"Soon."

"Crumb," she said, looking down.

"You can stay over tomorrow night."

"O.K.," she said, and did not at all give me a hard time.

The first time I ever hugged Eric while vertical, about a month after we started hanging out together, it was like hugging a totem pole. He was reserved and undemonstrative to the point of defensiveness. But the early days of our alleged romance were always exciting, as the sexual tension and obvious affection made for delicious companionship.

Eric continued to show great promise for a long time; it seemed that he was always on the verge of opening up a bit, although after a particularly close night together he always retreated psychically for several days. He divulged little about himself, except for past adventures, and almost nothing about his family. He told me that his mother was a saint who adored him, and that his father was a silent man who preferred Eric's younger sister, with whom Eric did not get along. Both of his parents had died many years ago. On the night he died at the age of fifty-six of a heart attack, Eric's father had eaten an experimental dinner prepared by his wife, the saint, and upon finishing had said, without looking up, "Don't make that again."

So, outside of the fact that Eric was an emotional tightwad, we had an easy and comfortable time of it for many months without making any sort of commitment to each other. We played tennis, hiked to Bass Lake, made each other laugh, made love. Our times in bed were vehement and tender, sometimes alternately, sometimes concurrently. I began reading his horoscope (Gemini) as well as my own (Aries) in *The San Francisco Chronicle*. We sat and listened to the stereo stoned—classical music before 1850, rock music before 1974, any jazz—and read separately together. I read more-esoteric books than he. He read only three kinds of books: Horatio Hornblower adventures, books about American Indians, and books of an Eastern spiritual nature. He brought me two books on Valentine's Day: one called *Those Eternal Questions*, by the great Eastern scholar Quentin Bostick; and *Great Indian Chiefs*, by Mildred Boyer Schultz. When my alley cat peed on *Great Indian Chiefs*, Eric suggested having him put to sleep.

We were immoderately fond of each other's bodies. I loved his long, muscular trunk and legs and his soft, fuzzy baldness. He loved women with ample bottoms, and said, with real esteem, "Fat ass, warm heart."

On the night before our first Easter together I came down with the flu. I had a headache, the shakes, a fever, and the megashits. Eric rubbed my back for an hour, and made me toast and chaparral tea, which tastes vaguely like burning hair and is rumored to have great healing properties. I fell asleep as we were watching the semifinals of the NCAA basketball championships, and when I woke up at midnight, he was gone.

I waited up for an hour, cried a little bit, and threw up once. My vomit tasted like chaparral tea and I decided that he had tried to poison me. I knew that he was off sleeping with someone else, and decided that as soon as possible I would have to sleep with another man: no one owns anyone else, and all that.

In all of my sexual relationships something curious happens, after four or five months, when I have to wait for a lover to arrive. If it is a friend or someone in my family whom I am waiting for, and he is quite late, I am convinced that he has been killed in a horrible, fiery car accident. (In college I waited for a close friend to return from upstate New York, and she was several hours late and it turned out that she had been killed in a fiery car accident. Positive

identification was made by checking her dental records.)
But when lovers have been late, I have assumed not that
they are dead but that they are in the back seat of a car
screwing a close friend of mine. And on Easter eve, I was
right, or at least close: it was not a close friend of mine he
was with but a close friend of his.

Eric came back at eight Easter morning with two marzi-
pan bunnies that his friend had given him. We lay on the
bed in silence. He was sheepish and concerned and obviously pleased with himself, and I was snotty and tired and
my glands were swollen and my eyes were crusty and my
feelings were hurt. He liked it—during our romance—when
my feelings were hurt, just as long as I didn't want to talk
about it. There was nothing to say.

At noon we turned on the NCAA finals and watched them
in a mood of distant decorum. It was some great Easter.

My father left a note in the cabin a week after Easter.

"Billie used to sing a song called 'Fine and Mellow,' " he
wrote. "The last verse goes, 'Love is like a faucet/It turns
off and on/Sometimes when you think it's on, baby/It has
turned off and gone.' It's a lovely song, maybe her best, but
it ain't true. It's hardly ever that clear, that black and white.
So you get confused and your pride gets hurt, but that's the
risk, that's the game. And sometimes it's worth it."

I dreamt that I had written "ha ha" on Eric's bottom with
toothpaste as he lay sleeping. My dream consultant said
that I was the toothpaste, and that I was his bottom. Furthermore, she said, the world is filled with weak, shitty little men, and not to take it too personally.

My dream consultant said that there is all the difference
in the world between sleeping alone and sleeping with
someone that you get along with fairly well. Eric and I got
along fairly well through the spring, although we did not

trust or confide in each other, and did not know where we stood with each other, and kept our emotional brakes on most of the time, except while making love. But when I wasn't punishing him for being a coward, and when he wasn't punishing me for what he considered to be nosiness, we were pretty good friends. He could really make me laugh, almost as hard as my dream consultant can. Eric couldn't stand my dream consultant, who is strong and direct. He thought she was a lesbian.

Eric's best friend was an anxious, evasive neurologist who tasted wine with a group called the Medical Friends of Wine. This neurologist, Gordon, bought a case of 1952 Pierre Ponnelle Echezeaux on the day his only daughter was born. He was going to give it to her when she married. It turned out that his daughter was a lesbian. Eric thought this was one of the saddest stories in his repertoire, although he loved to tell it.

Eric and Gordon met once a week for beer benders, during which they cruised around in Gordon's Mercedes and talked jovially about many things. Literally—things. Gordon told him six weeks after the fact that he had separated from his wife. Eric did not understand why I thought it strange that Gordon had kept it a secret for so long.

"He didn't keep it a secret," he said defensively. "He just didn't get around to telling me."

"So what do you guys talk about all the time, then?"

"Oh," he said evasively, "things. You know, projects, adventures. That sort of stuff."

"Who do you talk to about your feelings?" I asked.

"Me," he said. "I talk to myself about my feelings, and I don't talk out loud."

"It's starting to make me feel lonely, never to know what any of your feelings are. And it's boring. And I think you're afraid of letting anybody know who's In There," I said. We had been sleeping together for about seven months.

"So take it or leave it," he said. "It's the way I am."

"It's the way most males are," I said. "And I know it's the way you are. Whenever we start to get closer, you get panicky, and go away or just push me out. You're going to wake up someday and be ninety-two and you will never have let anybody in."

"And you're going to wake up someday and be ninety-two and your skin will still be breaking out. So in the meantime, I'd appreciate it if you would get off my case. Either it's worth it or it isn't."

"It *is* worth it to me, sometimes. I just wish you'd stop taking the Fifth so often when I ask you questions. If I ask, 'How are you feeling tonight?' you say, 'What do you mean by *that*?' "

"Look, Jennifer, I'm tired of you taking the car all the time, but I don't make a big deal about it."

"But it's *my* car!" I said.

"I know," he said, "and it's my privacy."

Exactly two months ago I got a Xeroxed rejection slip for a short story called "Bury My Heart at Wounded Pride," which was not a very good story. I moped for most of the morning, and cried a bit, and when I showed the letter to Eric, he touched my face tenderly. Then he lay down on top of me on the bed and hugged me until I stopped crying.

"I *hate* being rejected," I snuffled.

"But you can only reject yourself," he said.

"Uh-uh," I said. "Magazines can reject you, too."

"But being rejected by a magazine is like being rejected by a man wandering around the Mojave Desert wearing a wetsuit and reciting the poetry of Edgar A. Guest. No big deal." And we both laughed for a long, long time.

Later in the day, I told him that he seemed to be rejecting me also.

"Oh, for God's sake," he said. "I'm not rejecting you. I have a special place for you in my heart. . . ."

"Oh, for God's sake," I said. "Then how come you jam

on your brakes whenever we get closer? How come you're impersonating yourself all the time with me, never taking any risks? . . ."

"Oh, for Chrissakes," he said. "Don't you tell *me* about risks, Jen. I take a huge amount of risks, but they're not the risks you want me to take."

Three years ago Eric careened off the mountain in a Fiat going around a curve at forty-five miles an hour. He escaped with only nine broken bones, all of them major.

"All the risks I'm interested in make you nervous—"

"They do *not* make me nervous," he thundered, lighting up a Camel and then placing it in the ashtray with a Camel he had lit half a minute before. "I'm just not interested in them. *You* make me nervous."

"Well, you make me bored, and frustrated."

"We're certainly the golden couple, then, aren't we?"

"I don't think this relationship is going to take, to gel," I said. "Even if we're just biding our time together until someone better comes along for one of us."

"Why don't you just relax about it?" he said. "It's a lot better than a poke in the eye with a sharp stick."

Megan came over early the next morning when Eric and I were still in bed. Eric made her leave the cabin while he got dressed. He made pancakes for all of us, and told Megan how penguins make love. He told her that penguins can't tell the difference between males and females, so that when a male penguin is horny, he just walks up to any available penguin and knocks it over on its side. Then he gives it a stab, and if nothing fits, he just leaves the penguin lying there on the ice and tries again with another random penguin. Eric told Megan that the horny male penguin knocks over other penguins like dominoes. All three of us laughed.

"Is that true, about the penguins?" Megan asked after Eric left.

"I don't know," I told her.

"He sure is funny," she said. "Sometimes he sure is weird, too."

"What are you thinking of specifically?" I asked. "Making you leave while he got dressed?"

"Partly that. Last time I was here, he went into the bathroom and ran the water the whole time, even though you could *hear* him taking a dump anyway."

"I know, it is weird. It's one of his little secrets. . . ."

"It's supposed to be a secret that he takes poops?" she asked.

"His parents were weird about that sort of thing. His mother the saint always called the toilet 'the twilight.' "

"How old is Eric again?"

"Thirty-two," I said.

"I don't think I'm ever going to understand the adult world," said Megan. "Except that it sure sounds stupid."

"Here are some guidelines on how to be an adult," said the consulting editor at a magazine where I worked several years ago. "I wrote them in honor of your twenty-first birthday, which if I'm not mistaken is today." The man handed me a sheet of paper. The list began, "Adults always speak in a calm quiet voice. When angry an adult says, 'I think I must tell you that I am angry.'" The list ended, "Adults are very careful about the drains, and often have trouble walking on beaches: sometimes they cannot synchronize their legs properly to adjust for the sand."

"I think I must tell you my feelings are hurt," I told Eric a few days later.

"I think I must tell you that I'm thinking of leaving Clement for a while," he said, mimicking my seriousness. "I really am. I want some room to move, for a while. I'll be back."

"You're going to go away?" I asked. "Where to?"

"Wyoming, probably. I don't know anyone there, and I sort of want to be anonymous for a while. If you understand."

"Of *course* I understand," I said, irritated. "You're getting sick of my hurt feelings, and you're probably getting sick of my demands, and you're probably getting sick of having to avoid my questions."

"Wrong," he said, "on all three counts. Ask your brilliant dream consultant," he said sarcastically. "I want to figure out what I want. I think you should figure out what you want, too, 'cause I think you want Megan and your dad and your dream consultant rolled into one, and I don't think you're going to get it."

"So too bad for me, huh?"

"I guess so," he said. "Too bad for you."

My dream consultant said that as long as I wasn't going to get any real intimacy from Eric, I might as well settle for functional comfort from him, psychic and sexual. I told her that Eric was going away at the end of the month. She thought about this for a minute, and then said, "You're better off."

Two weeks later, a week before Eric was to leave for Wyoming, my father told us about the brain tumor. Wallace told us very calmly, and I responded with stoicism and optimism, until I got home to my cabin. Then I proceeded to cry very hard for a long time, and then began to get drunk. It seemed the only thing to do under the circumstances. Eric called at eight, after I had stopped crying.

"Hello, Jen, how you doing?" he asked.

I started crying again.

"Look," he said. "I was going to come over, but I'm really not in the mood to get a hard time from you. . . ."

I hung up the phone. He called right back.

"Listen," he said, "I'm getting a little bit tired of—"

I hung up the phone again, and then called Megan.

"Hullo," she said. "Why does your voice sound so funny?"

"I'm real sad. Can you come over and spend the night?"

"I think so. Are you crying?"

"Yeah."

"Hold on a minute. I have to ask my dad if he'll take me to your cabin." When she came back, she said, "He said he will if it's important. He says to say he's not pleased to do it, but that he will if it's important, since you're crying and all. So I'll be over in about ten minutes."

"O.K.," I said. "Thank you. Thank your dad."

I was lying on the bed when Megan arrived. She walked gingerly to the bed and said, "Hullo. You sure look sad, Jen. Good thing I got here, huh?"

"It sure is," I said. My eyes were wet and red, but I was no longer crying.

"What happened?" she asked.

"I just found out something awful," I said. "My father has a brain tumor."

"*Oh no!*" she said, and her eyes filled up with tears. "Wallace has a brain tumor? I can't believe it. He's so nice; he's so funny." She was silent for a minute, and then said, "Goddamnit crumb nation!"

"That's what I think," I told her.

"Well," she said seriously, "I had a dog with a brain tumor once, so I know what it's like, sort of." I thought she was trying to make me feel better.

"And your dog recovered?"

"Nope, it died, about two months later." Silence. "I don't think that was the right thing to say."

"It doesn't matter. Anyhow, Dad's having brain surgery in a few weeks. Eric's leaving in a week. . . ."

"What did he say when you told him about the tumor?"

"I didn't tell him. I don't think I'm going to; he'll feel like he has to stick around. Actually, I just hung up on him."

"Who are you going to sleep with, when you get sad and he's gone away?"

"I don't know. I don't really like any other men in town that much right now, not enough to sleep with when I'm sad."

"So are you going to break up with Eric?" There was just a *trace* of hopeful expectation in her voice.

"No. He's just going away. We're not even close enough to officially break up, if you know what I mean."

"God," she said. "Poor Wallace."

"I know," I said.

"It's too bad you don't have a boy friend who likes you as much as I do," she said.

"It sure is."

"Well," she said, "it's so lousy; it's sort of like a joke."

"I know," I said. "You're exactly right."

"Maybe I should make some sandwiches," she said, looking at me expectantly. "Would a fried-egg sandwich make you feel better?"

"It might," I said. "In fact, it might be just the thing to take the edge off." Together Megan and I have eaten many fried-egg sandwiches. I am a vegetarian, and vegetarians really have so few first-class vehicles for ketchup.

Eric left for Wyoming a couple of days later, earlier than expected. We made sad, resigned, and slightly nervous love before he left, and I didn't tell him about the brain tumor.

A week later I got a color postcard from Wyoming, with six frames, each depicting a rodeo horse and rider, and *Wonderful Wyoming* in yellow across the middle. The postcard read:

Hello Jennifer.

As you can see it's opera season here, and I've been every night. I am glad to be out of Clement, and I'm thinking many good thoughts of you. I no longer think that you were trying to get me to sign on the dotted line, and I feel good all the time to like you so much and to have you for a friend, even from—or because of—the distance. I think I'm going to stay here longer than intended. Life goes on etcetera.

Love and gooses from Eric.

Beneath his name he had drawn a blackbird with a cartoon balloon coming out of its beak, which was puckered. The balloon contained musical notes, in reference, I knew, to a poem by Wallace Stevens, one stanza of which goes, "I do not know which to prefer,/The beauty of inflections/Or the beauty of innuendoes,/The blackbird whistling,/Or just after," and I do not know which to prefer either.

I thought for a while that I had learned these things from the affair: that the handsome hidden men do not deliver for me; that next time—for certain—I would not let myself be hurt by a man too dumb and frightened to love me and to be loved by me; that perhaps it would be more satisfying, and less painful, to have a long-term and exclusive affair with my Water-Pik.

And these are the thoughts I was left with: that romance is stupid and sometimes worth it; that fellowship is risky and always worth it; that I am ridiculous, and that I am not.

Gatherings

I t has been a most strange and difficult era in our town, these last few months. We have been bombarded and caught off guard by the number of deaths, accidents, suicides, and automotive catastrophes. For months we coasted along with the usual smattering of head colds, separations, broken septic tanks, and inexplicable physical anomalies, and then—bam!—one thing after another, never raining, always pouring.

In the month before the diagnosis of my father's brain tumor, a young equestrian died of brain damage after he was thrown by his horse; a two-year-old boy died on the beach; two venerable homeowners died of heart attacks; the owner of the bar nearly died of a stroke on the tennis court; three car engines blew up, leaving one of the drivers with awful burns; a close friend was informed that she had uterine cancer, which would require megasurgery; and three of our Burn Outs were transported back to Napa State Hospital in cop cars and straitjackets. The most widely touted theory was that Mercury was retrograde, and that when this phase passed, our town would once again become salubrious.

On the day that Mercury ceased to be retrograde, the local organic-pizza maker sat in his bountiful garden gobbling down phenobarbital with vodka chasers underneath an old oak in the sun. My younger brother and I arrived by accident at his farm moments after his body was discovered by his ten-year-old son, who was in the old oak tree screaming when we got there. The pizza maker looked very calm, very rosy, much healthier than he ever had alive. Many in the town had suspected that he would kill himself eventually: he had no real friends, too much money, a suddenly receding hairline, and drank a pint of vodka a day. But no one knew what to do to assuage his loneliness, so no one did anything. Someone called the coroner, who dispatched the death car, which looks like an ambulance on the outside but has no life-support equipment in it; it has only a stretcher and a plastic death bag that looks like a Hefty Zip-Lock garbage bag. The death squad had trouble zipping him in, as he was six foot seven and his arms were by then sticking straight out.

My father, Megan, and I went to the memorial service for the pizza maker, which was held in the valley behind his farm at sunset the day after his suicide. The sky was the color of a pigeon's neck, and the moon rose slowly over the ridge. There was a fire by the creek that fed his crops and animals, and there were a couple hundred mourners in a circle around the fire. Someone stood and read a Navaho poem of bodily liberation. Someone led the mourners in a husky, quavering version of "Kumbaya" while many cried. A Burn Out, dressed for the event in a black graduation gown and a raccoon-skin hat, wailed loudly on the periphery. The son stood to talk, and sobbed instead. Megan put her hand in mine; I leaned against my father, and the moon evaporated in the mist over the ridge.

A minister from the Divine Light Church of Universality read from *The Prophet*. Megan rolled her eyes and whispered, *"Schlock."* My father read from Pascal. In his L. L. Bean khaki pants and camel-colored chamois shirt, easily the most conservatively dressed in the gathering, he read, " 'Nothing is so unbearable to a man as to be completely at rest, without passions, without business, without diversions, without study. He then feels his nothingness, his forlornness, his dependence, his weakness, his emptiness.' "

The Burn Out in the raccoon cap howled and spread his black gown like a shroud. The son wept great, racking sobs in his sister's arms, so hard that he peed on himself. When Megan saw the spreading wetness on his pants, she went and stood in front of him. When he escaped in his disgrace and climbed back into the branches of the oak, she waited with his sister at the bottom. He began to scream again. Megan came back to stand with me, staring at the ground. Our town's holistic doctor, Dr. Rainbow, led the chanting of the *om*, after a short speech on the emotionally strengthening properties of garlic. Only his girl friend, Olivia To*Nite, stood within five feet of him. Finally the howling Burn Out took the hand of the woman who makes yogurt, who took the hand of the weaver, who took the hand of the tree doctor, who took the hand of the dixieland band's oboe player, who took the hand of the alcoholic Muktananda disciple, and in a swaying *Totentanz* they led the other mourners up the trail from the valley to the farm, where we sadly dispersed.

We, as a town, were noticeably more sympathetic to and delicate with one another for a good ten days after the service. People invited their lonely acquaintances to dinner. People touched one another on the street as they passed. Old copies of *The New Age* were put back in circulation. A crisis hotline was proposed and enthusiastically discussed for the entire ten days, and then we returned to our habitual and gregarious indifference.

A week before his brain surgery, my father was given a month's notice from his landlord. Two days later his car was hit-and-run in front of his girl friend's house, to the tune of seven hundred and fifty dollars. Later that day his chicken coop caught on fire and four chickens were burned beyond recognition. The next morning he got a notice about his overdue IRS bill, which was for three thousand dollars. It all became vaguely amusing.

We as a family have buried many of our friends. My father alone has had three of his four best friends die. All three were writers, like my father, and all three were alcoholics, whatever that means. One, Warren, took off all his clothes and jumped off the cliffs above the ocean in front of my cabin. He left a note referring its readers to the chapter in *Moby-Dick* in which Pip, the boy, falls overboard and drowns. One friend named Noel ate a bottle of Talwin and chased it down with a plastic tumbler of Wild Turkey. Noel left my father's name and phone number taped to the bottle. My father contacted Noel's father, and together they sifted through the belongings. His father saw the Gauloises that Noel smoked as he waited to disappear, and he pocketed them, saying, "No use letting these go to waste." One friend blew his brains out in his mother's kitchen last Christmas, an hour before the other relatives arrived. His mother was touched that he had chosen her kitchen wall as the screen for what my father described as a "pizza-sauce Rorschach." She did not seem to get the point, at all.

My father and his three children went to services for all three. The mourners were largely alcoholic writers, and the services intellectual, sardonic wakes. My family got very drunk on all three occasions; there didn't seem to be anything else to do.

Every year in Clement there is a night of poetry in which twenty or so poets read, and every year Wallace and I go to hear four of them, two men and two women, four dissipated people with massive imaginations and souls and problems, all four of whom are politically silent.

This year's poetry reading was held two days before Wallace went into the hospital, and we arrived in time to hear a wizened and commended poet wearing a black vinyl visor with nautical flags on it recite a poem by Edna St.

Vincent Millay. ("I'll tell ya," he told the audience when he finished, "fifty years ago she really turned our heads.") The last poem he recited was called "Days," and Wallace got a very faraway look in his eyes as the old man recited: "'Daughters of Time, the hypocritic Days/Muffled and dumb like barefoot dervishes/And marching single in an endless file . . .'" The crowd cheered when he was done, and the old man asked, "Anybody know who wrote that?"

There was a silence of ten seconds, until a young man waving a bottle of Jack Daniels, very drunk and the writer of remarkable plays, shouted, "Emmmmerson."

"Right!" said the old man happily. The young man staggered to the microphone, put his arm around the old man, and smiled lovingly.

I have a distant crush on the man who read next, and the only poem he read went like this:

> I like smells of jello
> And tastes of jello
>
> My heart is pure
> My feet are clean
>
> And all the worms inside the world
> Are turning cheese to cream.

Everyone in the audience clapped loudly and called for an encore, but the poet stationed himself at an exit with a bottle of beer and stared at his feet. There were many friends of mine at the poetry reading that night, all of them casual, and most of us, including Wallace and me, were at least semidrunk; the good feelings at these town gatherings are contagious, and every so often I forgot that Wallace was soon to have a brain tumor removed.

The woman who ended the show was in her fifties, beautiful and shy, dressed in a Guatemalan skirt and alpaca sweater. She shakily read a convoluted and ultimately glorious poem about wanting to live in a land where the Great One cares, and Wallace bought her a drink at the bar later. As a town, our best gatherings are our celebrations, our performances, our memorial services, and the evenings in the bar together afterward.

On the night before my father entered the hospital, he ran through the will with us. My older brother was to be executor of the so-called estate, which consisted largely of books. My father said that it all—the will, the executor of the estate—is just a formality, and not to take it too seriously.

"Can I have the car and the dog if you croak?" asked my little brother.

"You can take it more seriously than *that*," my father said.

"Dibs on the silverware," I said.

"Dibs on the binoculars," said my older brother.

"I'll trade you the dog for the binoculars," said my younger brother.

My father pretended to ignore us, cheerfully. He found our gallows humor to be a good sign of something, perhaps the survival instinct.

"I'll give you the silverware, the stereo, and two dollars for the car," I offered my younger brother, who replied, "Throw in the binoculars and then we'll talk." And so we went on, until it was time to go, at which point we became silent and stricken. No one looked at anyone else. My older brother drummed his fingers on the dining table. My younger brother drummed his fingers on the top of the Labrador's pointy head where he suspects the soft spot grew together incorrectly. I drummed the fingers of my right hand against the fingers of my left hand, and then switched.

"Well," said my father, "I guess I'll see you tomorrow."

"Well, here we go, I guess," said Randy slowly.

"Well," said my father, "here we go."

My brothers stood in the doorway of my cabin in the morning. Today our father was to enter the hospital; tomorrow they would operate.

"Are you ready?"

"No," I said. "Are you?"

"No," said my older brother. "Let's go."

The three of us were nervous and exhausted, as no one slept much last night. Tonight was probably the night that we should lie awake anxiety-attacking ourselves, and we might anyhow, but last night was our anxiety rehearsal, and it went flawlessly for all. No one slept before three o'clock. My younger brother tried to count sheep, but they were all sheared—as my father soon will be—and it upset him.

I called my father before he and his girl friend left for the hospital in San Mateo. We were going to meet them there.

I said, "Well!"

He said, "Well!"

I said, "Well, well, well, well, well, well."

There was really nothing else to say.

"Well," said Ben as we began the two-hour drive.

"Well," said my younger brother, "this is going to be interesting."

"I suppose," said my older brother, "that we just have to be old and tough about this."

"Except that we're young and wimpy," said Randy.

"Feels to me like the Twilight Zone," I said as we drove around the curvy mountain road alongside the Pacific. It was foggy, and an easterly blew over the water. Goethe once said something to the effect that the spirit of humans is of the waters, the fate of humans of the wind. Which is true, I suppose, but not reassuring.

The hospital is located just off the Bayshore Freeway, named the "Bloody Bayshore" because of its fantastic death rate. From the outside the hospital looked like a factory, which is not entirely inappropriate. The people gathered in the lobby were generally gray and tired, except for the receptionists, who were annoyingly chipper.

My father's room was on the twelfth floor, which is the floor for surgery and maternity patients. To the left of the elevator is the baby department. There was a baby-display window at the entrance to the maternity ward, where for today's viewing pleasure a set of two-day-old twins wailed in harmony. The twins' names, according to their name tags, were "Livingston A" and "Livingston B." They were pin-headed and purple, and bore an unfortunate resemblance to Irish wolfhounds. My brothers and I turned to the right and located my father, who was sitting in his room on his bed in Brooks Brothers pinstriped pajamas and a black kimono. He was dental-flossing his teeth. His girl friend, Sarah, was filling out hospital forms. My father said, "Well well well well well well" when we came in.

Randy immediately picked up the urinal. He asked if every patient got a vase and if it depressed patients who got these complimentary yellow plastic vases when no one brought them flowers. My older brother rolled his eyes and took my father's hand. I sat on the bed and tapped my father's foot. A nurse came into the room and said, "You are breaking two hospital rules. Two visitors at a time, and no sitting on the bed."

"We're one family unit," said Ben.

"I'm sorry," said the nurse. "Two visitors."

We smiled politely at her and said, "O.K." When she left, my younger brother shook the urinal at her. From the window we could see the immense parking lot; beyond the parking lot was the freeway off-ramp (a huge billboard reads, A PRETTY FACE ISN'T SAFE IN THE CITY: FIGHT BACK WITH SELF-DEFENSE. "Self-Defense," it turns out, is a new type of moisturizer); beyond the off-ramp and the billboard was a hulking K-Mart shopping center, and beyond that an industrial dump. It was a lovely view.

The nurse came back in. She didn't look pleased. She looked at the urinal in my brother's hand. "I do not want to have to repeat myself," she said.

"Then don't," said Ben.

"The rules are, two visitors at a time, and no one on the bed."

My younger brother looked at my father and said, "O.K., Pops, move along, off the bed, come on, hup hup."

"*He* can sit on the bed," she said. "You can't."

"Well *that's* something," Randy said. "I mean, for three hundred fifty dollars a day I think it's fitting that he gets to be on his bed. And by the way," he continued, although my older brother was giving him the eye, "these pillowcases were stolen from the Stanford hospital. 'Stanford' is stamped on them. To whom shall I report this?"

The nurse looked at my father, who was trying not to laugh. He swallowed, gritted his teeth, and said, "My children will be leaving in a few moments. I'd appreciate it if we could be together for just a little while."

The nurse left.

"She's going down to tell the kitchen to slip Ajax into your fruit juice. I'm afraid she feels she has to punish you now," said Randy.

There were three beds and one television in the room. There were Huckleberry Hound cartoons on the TV, which was being watched by the patient in the second bed. My younger brother peeked around the curtain dividing the beds and told us in hushed tones that there was a Trekkie in the next bed.

The wife of the man watching *Huckleberry Hound* peeked her head around the corner and said, "Yoo-hoo."

"Hello," we answered.

"Shut up your globby mouth," her husband said. "Don't bug them people."

She was wearing purple ski pants and an Olympia Beer T-shirt. She was fortyish and quite fat. Really fat people should not wear ski pants, or T-shirts, and especially not the combination, as it tends to make them look like vertical couches. She said, "So this is your first day, and this is our last day. We been here a week." Her voice was friendly.

"Tell them our whole goddamn life story while you're at it," said her husband.

I went around the curtain to investigate. He was squat and reptilian and wearing *Star Trek* pajamas: there was a picture of Mr. Spock on his breast pocket.

"Bring a flask," said the woman. "That's my advice. Bring a flask."

"O.K.," said Ben numbly.

"I like Livingston B best, don't you?" she asked.

The door of the room across the hall was wide open. The patient had tubes going into his nose, into his mouth, and into both arms. His mouth was gaping and he was making a racking, guttural sound. He looked like he weighed about seventy-six pounds. It was not encouraging, and I started to cry. "Ohhh, shit," I said.

"Two for eight and a quarter will get you a fart," said the wife of the Trekkie, brightly.

"What?" I asked.

"Two for eight and a quarter will get you a fart," she repeated. "I always says that when someone says 'shit.' I think it's amusing."

"It certainly is," said my younger brother, not unpleasantly.

When we told my father that we were leaving, the woman peeked around the corner and said, "Okey-doke. Bye-bye."

We said 'bye to her. She disappeared for a minute, and then put her head through the curtain again.

"A flask," she said conspiratorially. "That's the secret. Bring a flask."

She winked at us. My younger brother winked back. I kissed my father on the lips, and then his girl friend. My older brother kissed Sarah, and then put his arm around my father, and for just a second put his head against my father's. Randy extended his left arm, and then didn't really know what to do with it, and ended up spastically thumping my father's chest. " 'Bye, Dad," he said, and didn't look at him.

When my brothers dropped me off at the cabin, two hours later, they both kissed me a dozen times, on my cheeks, forehead, eyes, and mouth.

My father turned fifty-five in April. For the occasion, the three of us ran a picture of him in the town newspaper; in it he is holding a chalice of champagne in one hand, with the aging alley cat draped bonelessly over the other arm. Below the picture we wrote:

> Our father is fifty-five today. It is the oldest he has ever been. Not content with the usual lot of American men, this man has struggled to attain his current status, which includes divorce, unemployment, and false teeth. He imparted many words of wisdom to his charming and devoted offspring, nine of which were "Sharper than a serpent's tooth is an ungrateful child." His children do not think he is getting older, just grayer and more wrinkly.
>
> —His darling children

We knew that he was deeply touched, although he did not exactly say so, because he read it aloud to the old friends who gathered at the cabin for his birthday celebration, and he laughed like a madman.

After the boys dropped me off at my cabin, I sat around for a while trying to be certain that we had really spent the afternoon at a hospital where Wallace was going to have brain surgery tomorrow. Then I sat around for a while trying to think sane thoughts about life and living and death and dying: dying seems to me to be the real bug in the system. When I thought about Wallace and his tumor, my stomach began percolating and my whole body flushed.

The old cat, Samuel P. Taylor, who is going to die soon, paced around the cabin between naps. When I was seven and a half, a neighborhood dog bit a gaping hole in the cat's neck and almost killed him, and I cried hard. Not long afterward, my grandfather died and I invited my friends over to the house for ice cream. It was the first and almost only time I ever saw my father cry, and I tried to cheer up my grandmother and him by telling them every joke I knew. It seemed the logical, appropriate thing to do, but my friends and I were sent outside.

Watching Westerns as a child, I thought that outlaws who were shot on television were, in real life, criminals who chose to die on television rather than be gassed. (My father had taught English at San Quentin, and I knew about the gas chamber.) I thought animals who were killed on TV really died. I was nine years old when President Kennedy was killed, and I was more shocked that the teachers were crying than that Kennedy had died, until I was in bed that night. I knew by ten years old that life would be happier if only I were quite stupid and devoutly religious, but unfortunately I wasn't. Late at night, with the lights out, alone, is the best and the worst time to think about death and dying.

My dream consultant and I talk about death frequently, usually when someone we know has died or got sick, but we mostly make jokes, or concede calmly that, really, it is to be expected, that everybody does it eventually. Kathleen thinks she will go kicking and screaming. I think that if I'm conscious, I'll be mostly annoyed.

I reread *The Lives of a Cell* the night before surgery and felt less confused for a while. I read and thought and smoked dope all night. I thought about the proposition that to share the big experiences of life and death, joys and griefs, with other people makes those experiences more authentic. I thought that this was true, and I was also glad to be alone that night. I came across the word "apodictic," looked it up, found that it meant, in terms of propositions, "logically certain," and remembered where I had heard the word for the first time: Megan and I had been playing dictionary one night after dinner with some of our favorite adults, and one of the words to define was "apodictic." Megan defined it as "Walt Disney's dying words."

Bodily death seems to be the only logical certainty about life, and I much prefer Megan's definition. I read for six hours and smoked four joints the night before the surgery, and fell asleep soon after I turned off the lights, with a calm, worldly sense of impending doom.

I was still alone in my cabin on the morning of Wallace's surgery, with Randy signing up for college courses over the hill, Megan at her grandmother's, my dream consultant at work, and Ben at the hospital with Wallace and Sarah. I drank too much coffee and then cried a lot and thought once again that nothing that was going on made any sense, and for moments here and there I was not at all sure what was going on. I thought that Wallace might really be at home, with no brain tumor, and that I was just losing my mind. Ben called me from the hospital just moments before I was going to call Wallace's house to see if Wallace was there.

"They just shaved his head," Ben said. "It looks like this is it." Our quasi-godfather, Michael, was there with Ben and Sarah waiting for the surgery to be over. I wanted to be with them, but Wallace thought it would be too hard for me or Randy to be at the hospital, just waiting (or else he thought we would fall to pieces and get in the way). Randy and I were a bit angry that we had been banished for the day, but because we were also somewhat relieved, we grumbled only a bit and took it like troopers.

"I'll call you when surgery is over," Ben said. "Hang on; I love you; take a Valium or something; I have; Sarah has."

I would have taken a Valium if I had had any, but I didn't, and I decided to write instead and perhaps have a minor breakdown from which I would recover by the time surgery was over. My minor breakdowns manifest as numbness, and numbness that morning was as welcome a thought as sleep, and sleep, as it turned out, was going to be impossible for eighteen more hours. I decided to spend the morning writing outside. The major obstacle to this endeavor was that there were no pens or pencils in the cabin. Finally, under the bed, I found a foot-long fluorescent pink pencil that said, "ENZELAC LEADS THE WAY with Flexible Simplicity for Baby, Doctor and Mother." I had to chew a point on the pencil. Some writer, I thought, and gave up.

I decided to pet the cat instead, but he was in one of his moods in which the touch of human flesh seems to repulse him. He escaped from my clutches and spent the morning on the roof of the cabin, glowering like a vulture. When I went outside to coax him down, the little boy who lives next door was leaving for school. "Good-bye, everybody!" he yelled cheerfully. This is exactly what Hart Crane is *supposed* to have said before he neatly laid his jacket on the railing of the ship that he jumped off: "Good-bye, everybody!"

I sat on the step of the cabin, beneath the eucalyptuses, beneath the sun, beneath the cat, and threw pebbles into the ice plant for close to two hours. Ben called, finally.

His voice was shaky. Surgery had just ended. The good news was that my father had come to immediately after being wheeled into the postoperative room. A nurse was standing over him, and said, "Hello there." "Oh," said my father, looking up into her face, "hello there." This was a good sign, as it meant there was no brain damage, that all of his faculties remained intact. The bad news was that the surgeon thought the tumor might be malignant. It was the size of a shooter marble, and plum purple. "Oh," I said, and started crying.

"The biopsy could take a long time," Ben said. "Like a few weeks." Then he started crying.

"So we have to wait some more. I thought it was going to be all over today, one way or another. Shit."

"Two for eight," said my older brother. "I'm going to see him soon. I'll call you back. And then I'm going to pick up the kid and come over to your cabin. I want us to be together. O.K.?"

"O.K."

He called back in an hour, and his voice was much lighter.

"Listen," he said, "Dad looks wonderful. He's very clear, very coherent. He tried writing a bit, and it was only a little bit spazzy. He made little jokes."

"He really looks wonderful?" I asked.

"Well, 'wonderful' is not exactly the right word. His *eyes* really do look wonderful. But the left side of his face and neck are pretty swollen, and there are incredible purple and green bruises all the way to his chest."

"Wonderful," I said.

"And his head is all bandaged up in a gauze turban. He looks like an Ivy League swami. If you could see him, I think you'd feel better."

"Can I see him today? I could be there in two hours."

"No. Not until tomorrow. You have to wait."

Waiting waiting waiting waiting. I had to wait until tomorrow to see him. We have to wait weeks on the biopsy. I didn't think I could wait any longer, but there was nothing else to do. My brothers would come wait with me tonight, to drink Wild Turkey and to hold my hands, and to have their hands held.

Our family has a friend whose mother died of Hodgkin's disease two years ago in the spring. She waited for months to die. She was only sixty years old. When she was down to seventy pounds and was about to die, our friend brought her to his house above the ocean in the town where we live. The house was also sixty years old, and very beautiful, and very remote. Our friend put a stereo, many plants and flowers and thick fur rugs on the floor around her brass bed. Many friends gathered every day, and lay on the rugs below her bed, and played music for her of every variety. Candles were lit, and our friend gave his mother—who looked like an apple doll—large and continuous doses of LSD, which has been proven to alleviate pain. For the two weeks before she died, she was the center of the household, the center of the gathering. Friends lay on the bed with her. The day before she died, she asked my older brother if he had seen any unoccupied ice floes around. My older brother said that he thought he might have. She died without pain or fear, filled with the beauty of the universe. Her last LSD vision was of white light and poppies. "No angels," she said, but not sadly.

I think these were the most exquisite gatherings of which I have ever heard.

My Brothers

On the day after our father's brain surgery the three of us stood outside the hospital waiting while Ben got a grip on himself. He was on edge to the point where he looked like an insane fugitive trying to act calm: his hands were jammed into his khaki pants and his round brown eyes blinked like neon. The voice with which he addressed Randy and me was half an octave higher than normal, and he was clearing his throat between every sentence. He was giving us a lecture on composure.

"See," he said, "Wallace looks *very* good for having just come through brain surgery, but he doesn't look at all good in terms of how we're used to him looking. So I just want you—"

"We'll be all right," said Randy. He was pushing a penny around on the cement with the toe of his sneaker, up against a leaf, around a gum wrapper, between two bottle caps.

"Well, let's just stand here and relax before we go up," said Ben. "It's really quite a shock to see him."

"Let's stand here while you relax," I said. "Randy and I will be all right. The more you tell us to relax, the more I think I'm going to have a breakdown."

We have had several of these nervous, bickery moments since the diagnosis. Ben was having the hardest time of the three of us, I think. He is the child who, although the oldest, has been closest to Wallace for the shortest amount of time—about five years. Randy and I often let him deliver his big-brother speeches because we like him so much and because these speeches make *him* feel so much better. He had delivered lectures on our need for extra vitamins during this most sad and stressful time of our lives, on how we must express our anger when we felt angry about It All and cry when we felt like crying, and how at all costs Randy and I must avoid the *mea culpa* trap. (He himself thinks he caused the tumor via his tempestuous teenage years, and therefore he told us with great authority that neither Randy nor I was responsible for it.) Randy and I interrupt his speeches about half the time, not because his information lacks validity but because of the tone of voice, the big-brother, oldest-child voice. Sometimes it is endearing, and sometimes it is irritating.

"Pennies ought to be outlawed," Randy said, pushing the penny onto a piece of chewing gum. "You can't even give them to kids anymore. Old men used to give me pennies all the time, and it was a very big deal: 'Oh boy he gave me a *penny*.' Now I give them to little kids and they just chuck them into a bush."

"Son," I said in a crotchety, old-age voice, wagging my finger at him, "five pennies used to buy me a hot dog."

"Have you ever noticed that people call boys and men 'Son,' but they don't call girls 'Daughter'? Like, 'Hi, Mom; Hi, Dad.' 'Oh, hello, Son.' No one ever says 'Hello, Daughter.'"

"It doesn't seem to me," said Ben tensely, "that you guys are taking this situation very seriously. I mean, here we are at the hospital about to see Dad. . . ."

"But right now we're just waiting for you to calm down," said Randy. "So don't give us a hard time. . . ."

"Listen, I just want for you two to understand that—"

"Let's just go up now," I said.

"Are you sure you're ready?" asked Ben.

"Anytime you are," said Randy.

Ben took one last suck on his cigarette and stubbed it out. He cleared his throat and tucked in his shirt. "All right," he said, "let's go up," as if he himself had just that moment made the decision.

Livingston A and Livingston B were looking less like Irish wolfhounds than they had two days earlier. We stopped to look in at them, partly because they were such peculiar looking infants and partly because we were stalling for time. Randy was enormously fond of these babies, having known them almost since birth.

"Hello, babies," he said, standing directly in front of the window before their bassinets. The babies were awake, and, for once, not howling. "Gucci gucci gucci," Randy said, scratching the window. "Hello, babies."

"Let's go," said Ben.

"I want to watch the babies," said Randy.

"All right," said Ben.

"Dad was their age once," said Randy. "That's what's interesting to me about these babies. Someday *they* might be fifty-five and have brain tumors. Isn't that weird to think about, that they're only three days old and the next thing they know, they'll be forty-three and maybe have prostate troubles? Just like that," and he snapped his fingers.

"You were twice their size when you were born," said Ben. "A little fatty."

"No I wasn't," said Randy.

"Yes you were," I said. "You looked like Winston Churchill."

"Hmmmphh," said Randy. "I was that *age* once, though."

"Yeah," said Ben. "None of us is getting any younger."

"Especially Dad," I said. "He's getting less young more quickly."

Ben ushered us down to Dad's ward. Randy gangled behind us, all six-three, hundred forty-five pounds of him, saying hello to everyone he passed. Ben nodded with friendly sternness to everyone, the nurses, orderlies, patients, families. The only person I made eye contact with was an elderly woman with green bruises covering her wasted legs. A microwave oven in the middle of the corridor went *ding* every fifteen seconds, to signal that another meal had been heated, and each time, the woman with the bruises looked around, to both sides. The food coming out of the microwave and the adjoining refrigerator—unearthly vegetables that looked like green oatmeal, frozen beefsteaks, gelatin cubes, and "fruit-juice *drinks*"—should not be consumed by healthy people, let alone post-op patients. Randy, the junk-food faddist, looked longingly at the hospital's chicken-fried steak.

Wallace was asleep on the blankets in a single-occupancy room, in his Brooks Brothers pajamas and his Japanese kimono. Sarah was embroidering a heart on another pajama shirt. She stood up and put her finger to her lips (she teaches elementary school) and smiled to each of us. We looked at Wallace in unison, and began swallowing loudly. His face was swollen several inches all over, and deep-purple birthmark-type bruises extended from beneath the gauze turban to (at least) the top of his pajama shirt. His neck was as thick as a stovepipe, and his left eye was black and swollen. It was horrible, and mesmerizing, like coming off LSD under fluorescent lights in the Twilight Zone.

"Jesus Christ," said Randy, who looked furious and sad.

Sarah directed us out into the corridor, next to the microwave oven.

"He's doing just beautifully," she said. Ben put his arms around her paternally and protectively, the same boy who twenty-four years ago appeared naked at one of my parents' dinner parties with concentric circles drawn around his penis with finger paints.

"He looked better yesterday, Ben, when you saw him. But the doctors already told us that would happen, that today the bruises would be awful. They'll start disappearing in a week or so, and in a few days he'll be able to talk normally again. He slurs because of the pressure on his brain. The surgeon is amazed at what great shape he's in, really. He came through the surgery with flying colors. . . ."

"I wonder what he'd look like if he hadn't come through beautifully," said Ben.

"It was an absolutely successful operation," said Sarah. She is large and blond and pretty, and looked tired, but calm, and sad. "The only thing we don't know about is the biopsy. The surgeon said she *thought* it looked malignant, but the pathologists are the ones who will know for sure."

"How long until they tell us?" I asked.

"I don't know. The surgeon didn't know. It could be tomorrow, it could be weeks."

"He'll be all right," said Randy, almost defensively.

"How are you holding up?" Ben asked Sarah.

"Oh," she said, shrugging her shoulders, "fine. I guess. How about you three?"

"Oh, fine," we all said quickly, nodding our heads.

My voice sounded, to me at least, as if I had been sucking down helium, and my brothers' shoulders were much too close to their ears. I started laughing.

"Fine," I said, "fine," twitching, winking, blinking, letting my tongue fall out of my mouth.

"Well, your father really is fine," she said. "He's real stoned also. Why don't you guys go in and wait for him to wake up, I'm going to get something to eat, a hamburger or something." She wanted for us to be able to be alone with him.

Randy looked envious when he heard the word "hamburger," but said, "Yeah, let's go in."

For half an hour we sat in chairs around the bed pretending to read but watching Wallace for signs of waking up. Randy read *The San Francisco Chronicle Sporting Green* all the way through, twice. Ben pretended to read *The New York Times Magazine*, and got up every ten minutes to pace around. He gave me a neck rub while I pretended to read the *Chronicle* front page. Bert Lance was being forced tó resign. Richard Pryor had lambasted the Los Angeles Gay Rights Celebration. A twenty-five-year-old man—the same age as Ben—claimed that he had murdered a family of seven because he had been intentionally poisoned by his mother over the years, his mother having left dishwashing detergent on his plates, cups, and utensils.

"This doesn't seem very real to me," said Ben.

"M'either," said Randy.

"I think we're in shock," said Ben, "because he looks so battered."

"I think we're in shock because the biopsy hasn't come through yet. He might have brain cancer. And we have to keep on waiting. A whole other round of waiting," I said.

"It's both," said Randy.

"Sure is a lousy way to live," I said. "Waiting."

"It sure is," said Ben, "but it's the only game in town. Right now, anyway, until the biopsy comes through. Then we'll be able to relax."

"So we have to wait for the time when we can stop waiting," I said.

"Makes as much sense as anything," said Randy.

It did not seem possible to me that the tall man walking around the hospital room in khaki pants and an Arrow shirt was once the teenage boy whose long, greasy hair fell into his meals during the several years of serious drug involvement, or the cherubic little boy who once gave crew cuts to all of my dolls. He seems such a reasonable person, now. And it did not seem possible that the gangly, gawky boy reading the *Sporting Green* was once the little boy who read before he was three, and who once, at one of the dinner parties, poured a glass of milk over my mother's glorious *crêpes fourrées et flambées* to save us all from incineration. It did not seem possible that Ben, rubbing my neck, used to beat me up so frequently, often on days when he also beat up roughnecks in the playground who teased me. And what especially did not feel real—what seemed most like something that was happening in the inexorable present *that simply could not be happening*—was that the swollen, bruised man with his head wrapped in gauze, whose thick wavy brown hair was collected in a Baggie by the sink, was a transformation of the man who *four days before* had walked briskly with his children to the lagoon, hale and weathered and well favored, one last bird-watching for the road.

Randy stood up and knocked a vase off the bed table with one of his five-and-a-half-foot arms and caught the vase before it hit the floor but not before it hit the table, loudly, and had spilled all of its water. Randy swore and gritted his teeth, embarrassed and mad at himself, and began wiping up water with Kleenex. Wallace opened his eyes.

His blue eyes were sleepy and clear, and he blinked heavily several times.

"Hullo, kids," he said groggily.

"Hello, Dad," we said moving in close to him gingerly, smiling brave, nervous smiles.

"I didn't mean to wake you," Randy said, holding a wad of wet Kleenex.

I kissed him on the lips, and my brothers kissed him on the forehead. I took one of his hands, and Ben took the other, which had a glucose IV running into it.

"Hair the dreb?" asked Wallace, and then, shaking his head, "How's the drive?"

"Oh, fine," said Randy. "No traffic at all." We had been stuck in a traffic jam on the Bayshore Freeway for twenty minutes and had agonized the whole time.

"Hair are . . . how are you?" asked Ben.

"Ooookay," he said, nodding his head. "All things considered," he enunciated carefully. "I kent talk gerry bell . . . weld," and shook his head again. He looked at us with great affection.

"The drebs are good ... the drugs are fud ... the drugs are good," he said.

"Looks that way," I said. Wallace smiled.

"Save some for us," said Randy.

"Sounds like the surgery went great," said Ben with enthusiasm.

Wallace nodded. "I cud wrote this morning, a bit."

"Great," I said.

"Go get me juice," Wallace said to Ben, pointing to the closed door. When Ben opened it, the microwave in the corridor went *ding*.

"Great bruises, Dad," said Randy respectfully.

"Tell us who did this to you," I said to Wallace, putting up my fists. Randy was sitting at the foot of the bed, rubbing Wallace's ankle.

"Your legs are as beautiful as ever," said Randy, pushing Wallace's pajama leg up to expose more of the long, skinny white leg. "Our dear sweet Birdlegs," he said affectionately. Birdlegs is a name from the past, when as children we used to slap his legs when he went past us in a bathrobe. Egrets and herons have always been Wallace's favorite birds, and it is no coincidence.

Ben brought a can of apple juice with a straw in it to Wallace, and closed the door behind him. "That microwave *ding* is sure therapeutic," he said.

Wallace took a sip, put the can on the bed table, and knocked it over. It fell onto the floor.

"Shuck fit," he said, shaking his head.

Randy began wiping it up with more Kleenex, and Ben went to get another can. He was back in half a minute. Wallace gripped the can tightly, took a stiff sip, and handed it back to Ben.

"I hear the doctors are astounded at how healthy and clear you are today," Ben said.

Wallace nodded. "I feel gud," he said. Ben was shaking his head, and then nodding it, with wonder and sad triumph.

"I heb a hadache," said Wallace.

"So do I," I said.

"Keep thinking these white healing rods . . . thoughts," he said.

"We are," said Ben. "We've been bombarding you with them, with white-light healing thoughts. So are all your friends, and all of our friends."

"Good," said Wallace. "Thank you."

"I thought maybe the surgeon would notice a faint whirring noise in the operating room," I said.

"Me, too," said Randy. "Did she mention it? The sound?"

"She thought it was mashanical malution . . . machine malfunction," said Wallace. He looked around at us drowsily and fell back to sleep.

We sat and looked at him for a few minutes. The difference between a sick person and a well person is phenomenal. This difference in—the lessening of—the lights in the eyes and the skin and the voice of a well person seems to me to be perceptible evidence of something.

One of the reasons that Ben and Randy are my two best male friends, besides my knowledge that their thoughts can be as sick as mine, and their actions just as underhanded and pathetic as mine, besides the fact that they seem to love me unconditionally and make no bones about wanting to see me, besides the enormous pleasure and trust I experience with them—besides these excellent reasons for loving them so much is the fact that I do not have many male friends in the town where I live who are older than fourteen. I used to have three actively close male friends in Clement, all at least ten years older than I, and now I don't. I miss terribly having male peers with whom to play, drink, and talk, and see no new possibilities on the horizon; in town I feel like I am looking in the refrigerator with a hearty appetite, and nothing on the shelves calls to me. If Randy or Ben were to die too young, which is the only way

I'd ever lose them, I would have to become an addict to keep on living.

"I'll tell you what I think about the business of how good Wallace looks," Randy whispered. "More emperor's new clothes. Lots of it going around." I nodded. Randy looked like a boy trying to see something a mile away. Ben held Wallace's hand, stared at a series of pale-blue herons on the kimono, and looked stricken. Wallace looked like a man who might die of looking so horrible and so old so suddenly.

I jabbed Randy in the butt with my foot, out of nervousness and habit. He smiled menacingly at me, so I jabbed him again. "Daaaaddd," he whispered, "she's bugging me."

"Shhh," Ben whispered, looking up crossly.

I held my hands outward with a look of innocence and, as soon as Ben looked back at Wallace, jabbed Randy again. Randy and I laughed under our breath, scrunching up our shoulders and laughing silently into our chests.

"Daaaaddd," Randy whined in a whisper, "she's still bugging me. Make her stop." Wallace, of course, said nothing.

"I feel much better than before we saw him," said Ben, standing up after he had removed Wallace's hand from his own and realigned it on the bed.

"So do I," said Randy. "Are we going?"

"Do you want to?"

"Yeah. I have low blood sugar," said Randy.

We stood to leave. I felt better, too. It had occurred to me when Wallace first opened his eyes that it was such grotesque and arbitrary luck for him to be one of the relatively few people who get brain tumors. So why shouldn't Wallace be one of the brain-tumor patients who fully recover?

Ben drove the car on the way home. I had driven us down to the hospital, had filled the car with gas before leaving town, and had pulled into a gas station an hour later and asked the attendant to fill it up. For some reason my brothers did not say a word, possibly because they didn't want me to be embarrassed, and when the bewildered attendant said, "A dollar fifty?" it turned out that I'd forgotten my wallet. Ben paid. When I pulled up in front of the hospital, Ben asked me for the keys in his gentlest big-brother voice, and said that maybe I could get some sleep on the way home.

"I think Dad'll be okay," said Ben, starting the car.

"Me, too," said Randy, who was riding shotgun. "I'm hungry."

"We'll stop in the city," said Ben.

"I hate the hospital," I said. "I hate it when one of us is in the hospital."

"Just think of them as repair shops," said Ben. "Just forget all the melodrama; just think of them as human Midas Muffler shops or something."

"Midas Mufflers," said Randy, shaking his head. "This is a family of crazy people."

From the back seat Ben's and Randy's heads looked almost exactly alike, with medium-length, dark brown, slightly wavy hair. Ben told me when I was eight that Mom and Dad had run out of benevolent hair genes after he was born, and that the only genes left when I was born were blond-Afro genes, and that it took the seven years until Randy was born for the wavy genes to be replenished.

"Did you hear about the experiments the Rand Corporation did on hair?" I asked.

"What experiments?" Ben asked. "What made you think of hair experiments?"

"I was looking at your hair, and thinking what sounds it would make."

"Crazy people, crazy people," said Randy.

"See, judging from the laboratory results, both of your hair would make a soft rustling sound."

"What laboratory results?" asked Ben.

"These scientists got some canine volunteers, poodles and boxers, I think, or Airedales and Dobermans, and rigged up wires to the frontal lobes of their brains. Then they monitored the sound produced by the nerve endings between the scalp and the membrane that surrounds the brain. The brains of the straight-haired dogs made a soft humming noise, and the curly-haired-dog brains made a sort of *scritch scritch scritch* noise, suggesting that the kinky hair was growing *into* the brain, causing possible cranial irritation."

"That explains a lot of things," said Ben, looking at me in the rearview mirror.

"Sproing!" said Randy, turning around to look at me. "Your hair would go *scritch scritch sproing*! *Scritch scritch sproing*."

"Dad's head would make the sound of a baby's breath," I said.

Ben turned onto Lombard Street soon after we'd come off the Bayshore. "Your choice," he said as we drove along the garbage-food boulevard of San Francisco. "You want Doggie Diner or Jack-in-the-Box. . . ."

"Dad calls it Jumping Jack's," I said.

"Or Clown Alley," he continued, "Or Kentucky Fried . . ."

"Mom calls it Captain Sanders," said Randy.

". . . Or do you guys want to wait until we get to Mill Valley and go to the delicatessen?"

"Deli," said Randy.

"Me, too," I said.

"Good," said Ben. "I'll treat you both."

"Good," said Randy, " 'cause neither of us has any money."

"I got plenty," said Ben. He often has to pick up the tab for Randy and me, as he often takes over in family crises. I think he does it partly to make up for the years of torture he inflicted on Randy and me when we were young children, and partly because he is a good man who happens to be the eldest in our family. This function is not without its compensations; for instance, our grandmother's holiday checks to Ben are for twelve-fifty, to Randy and me for ten dollars. And it is not without its special problems, as Ben and I knew even before one of my friends, and one of Ben's friends, both first sons, killed themselves.

My friend Wendell was a brilliant and shy nisei with a stutter who went to UC Berkeley after a straight-A high-school career. When he got his first-semester grades, three A's and a C-plus, he went to his dormitory room and blew his brains out.

Ben's best high-school friend died of internal injuries at the age of twenty-five, suffered when he fell off a cliff in the Salmon River Mountains. He was an excellent and experienced hiker. He had told Ben a week before he died that he had just found out that he had leukemia, and that he couldn't imagine telling his parents. He was embarrassed about it—leukemia, for Christ's sake—guilty that once again he was going to cause his parents shocking grief. His mother had fallen apart when Tim got his seventeen-year-old girl friend pregnant, and again when he dropped out of college during his first year to go to India, and again when he and Ben got busted for possession of speed. His father had only recently begun speaking to him again.

Tim told Ben that he thought he'd blown it again, like all the times before when he had angered and frustrated and hurt and embarassed his parents. He said he didn't know what he was going to do, or even what his choices were, but he didn't think he'd be telling his parents because they'd either fall apart again or be relieved, and he couldn't stand either.

We drove across the Golden Gate Bridge; the fog over Alcatraz glowed white and silver. Tammy Wynette was singing a choking song about Mama and the angels, and for a moment I had no idea why I was on the bridge with my brothers or where we were going, and just after that moment, Randy said, "None of this feels right to me."

"None of Dad having a brain tumor, you mean?" asked Ben.

"Yeah." He turned around and looked at me. "I keep feeling that it's all a dream, but I'm not sure which of us is having the dream, if it's my dream, or if I'm making an appearance in one of your dreams, or Ben's dreams. But your dreams are all so sick and weird, and Ben hardly ever has dreams. So it must be my dream, but I feel like it's all happening on Mars, or that I'm really from Venus and somehow got on the earth by mistake, and I'm totally unable to understand any of it. Do you know what I mean?"

"Yeah," I said. "It's exactly what I was thinking. I feel like it's my brain in the wrong body, or some lunatic brain in my Jennifer body. It doesn't feel at all comfortable. It feels like kids must feel if they're born left-handed and their parents and teachers forced them to be right-handed, and so everything is slightly off center."

"Me, too," said Ben. "It's much less nerve-racking to be with you two, though, because I'm not self-conscious with you guys. With everyone else, I keep thinking I'm acting totally strangely, you know, looking like a loony classic paranoid-schizophrenic eye-and-body jerkiness . . ."

"You *are*," I said.

"So you and Randy don't seem real paragons of stability," he said. "So I'm comfortable with you both. With everyone else, I keep worrying that people will think I'm losing it and becoming dangerous."

"Why do you care if people you're not comfortable with anyhow think you're nutsy?" I asked.

"Because I blew it for so long, and now my life is pretty well together, and I like it that people think I'm fairly reasonable. I mean, I think people take me seriously now, and it's really the first time in my life—"

"But your friends know you're under incredible stress,

and they're not going to ditch you if you're nervous or crying or whatever. And as far as I'm concerned, everyone else
can suck wind."

"Well, I don't feel that way."

"Maybe it's because you're the oldest," said Randy.

"Maybe. But the only people I trust to not ditch me are
you guys and Mom and Dad."

"It's a good thing everyone in our family is so deranged,"
said Randy.

"Except for me, of course," I said.

"You *especially*," said Randy. "The rest of us at least *pretend*
to be functional, but you don't fool *anybody*. You don't even
try to fool most people; you just say whatever you feel like
saying all the time. . . ."

"So what?" I said.

"So, Ben and I can imitate mentally healthy people. And
we have reputations to protect, because we're the men in
the family. But you can go ahead and be a raving maniac
because of your hair." He turned around and squinted at
me. "*Scritch scritch*," he said, with ineffable love in his eyes.
"*Sproing sproing*."

We stopped at Sonapa Farms in Mill Valley and bought
black bread, Brie, chicken salad, Greek olives, three pirosh-
ki, a half pint of herring and sour cream, marinated mushrooms, and a six-pack of Ballantine's India Ale, to go.

When we left the delicatessen, Randy carrying the food
and I the six-pack, Ben paternally putting the paper change
into his wallet, Randy beamed with anticipation.

"The three of us are going to have some delicious
breath," he said. "Good thing we're related."

Somewhere along the line a good meal with my family took
its place among the other estimable things: good music,
good hard laughter, good sex, good industry, and good
books. It wasn't always this easy. For years a meal with my

family was hostile and competitive and to be finished with as quickly as possible, but that was so long ago.

We took the food to Ben's apartment in San Rafael and ate with our fingers, sitting on the living-room carpet. Randy promptly knocked over a beer, and cleaned it up with Kleenex.

"I'm getting to be good at this," he said, throwing the wet wad into the fireplace.

"I bet that when we're in our eighties we'll still be sitting around eating with our fingers and having weird conversations during dinner, and Randy and I will still be spilling things," I said, spilling chicken salad on my leg.

"Probably," said Ben.

"Hopefully," said Randy.

Ben lowered a piece of herring into his mouth. "I like that we're stuck with each other."

"You're so sentimental," I said.

"Attached by blood and years," said Ben.

"'Stuck with,'" said Randy. "I like it, too. I couldn't stand it if I didn't have you guys. I couldn't stand it if either of you died before I do. My brain would explode."

"Me, too," I said. "I couldn't keep playing if either of you died. I'd just pack my bags and wait for the angels to come and get me."

"It makes me sad that it took so long for it to be this easy," said Ben. "I don't think I'm ever going to stop feeling badly about the way I treated you both." He had finished his second beer. "I was really an awful brother for a while. I don't think I can ever make it up to you."

"Why don't you just write us each a large check," I said. "Then we'll call it even."

"I just wonder why it took so long for us three to get along," said Ben.

"It's because you're both so goddamn difficult," I said.

"Oh, yeah," said Randy sarcastically, "and you're an *angel*...."

Skunks

E very Tuesday night at eight-thirty my dream consultant and I meet for drinks at the bar in town. That is,
we arrange to meet at eight-thirty, but regardless of what
time I arrive, she ambles in ten or fifteen minutes later. Being as she is a Capricorn—a notoriously late species—she is
simply not comfortable in public unless she's late; I am not
sure whether she likes to make entrances, or is even more
self-conscious alone in public than I, or is testing the affec-
tions and devotion of the people she keeps waiting, but, at
any rate, I have finally stopped haranguing her for her late-
ness and she in turn has stopped giving me a hard time
about my smoking.

When I arrived on foot at the bar on Tuesday last week at
seven minutes past nine, her MG was not one of the seven
cars parked in downtown Clement. It was unlikely that she
had walked, owing to the fondness and pride that she feels
toward the car, which she procured in her divorce settle-
ment years ago, after eight years of marriage to a prominent
surgeon who taught her to induce vomiting after dinner in
order to keep her body slim. And besides, she is not one of
the world's prodigious walkers, restricting her foot travel to
the nearest car.

Four of Clement's Burn Outs stood outside the doorway,
stage left, discussing epileptic fits—specifically, whether
one should cut out the epileptic's tongue so that he or she

won't choke on it. When I approached the doorway, Juno the Burn Out, dressed fit to kill in a toreador jacket and lime-green leather pants, gestured for me to walk through the door, with a grandiose flick of his wrist, like a maitre d'.

It was a slow night in the bar, no jukebox music, no dancing, no shouting, no obvious overdoses. The bartender applied her lipstick leisurely by the cash register, and the four veteran drinkers slouched over the bar nursed their drinks sullenly and, for the most part, silently.

Frank Belford, a towering, well-known writer and drunk, stared hostilely at his reflection in the mirror and grizzled something incoherent to himself. Everything about him is grizzled—his voice, his beard, his clothes. His wife, Dolly, four seats away, watched him watch himself with drunken disdain, rolled her already-out-of-focus eyes, and turned her attention to the large white plastic purse in her lap. She withdrew a dollar bill, shook it at the bartender, and rearranged her squat, ponderous body on the stool, grinding her bottom around on the seat while crossing and uncrossing her legs, which were sheathed in orange stretch pants. When she had arranged herself into exactly the same position as before, she took a tube of lipstick from her purse and applied it to her gummy, caved-in mouth. The bartender brought Dolly a vodka-tonic. The difference between brightly colored young lips and brightly colored old alcoholic lips is remarkable.

She and Frank almost never speak to each other in public except to borrow money. It may be one of the secrets of their forty-year-old marriage.

"Hello," I said when I passed her chair. She jutted out her bulldog chin as a greeting.

Two male hippies were playing pool in the wing. No one else was in the bar. I ordered a Heineken and took it to a table in the corner where the lighting is most pleasant, bright enough to illuminate and soft enough to tolerate. I sat patiently waiting for Kathleen.

I am not as a rule a rational or calm waiter, especially when I am alone and not absolutely positive that the person I'm waiting for is really ever going to show up. I punish the friend or bus driver or clerk if and when he or she does. I would almost rather go to a dentist or a large department store than have to wait in a line for any length of time— say, over ten minutes.

Waiting alone in the bar has led to some of my worst bouts with self-consciousness, and impatience with the drunks, Burn Outs, and losers who on a bad night seem to make up the town. So that night I was surprised to find myself waiting so tolerantly, wishing that the four drunks and two hippies made for more arresting theater, but generally content with my beer, Camels, and the knowledge that Kathleen would show up eventually, and would be able to make me laugh, and that I would forgive her and make her laugh, and we'd be close again. I felt mildly pleased with my pragmatic benevolence.

Half an hour later I ordered another beer, drumming my fingers rapidly against the bar while waiting. When I put my empty bottle on the counter, it was with much greater force than intended—*bam*! Frank Belford jerked his head off his chest and looked at me, as I assumed everyone in the bar did, so I looked at him as if *he* were the person slamming bottles around.

"Come here, cool lady," he said to me. "I want to tell you something."

"Tell me from there."

He looked at me, hurt, turned his head away back onto his chest, and then looked up at me sideways.

"Jennifer," he said, his gaze level and bleary, "I am not an oil can." He clenched his jaw, let it sink in. "I'm a guy."

I had no idea what he meant. The bartender handed me a Heineken and some change.

"Oh, uh-huh. You're probably right. I'll talk to you later," I said to him untruthfully, as in the last ten days I had made a special point to stay outside of conversational distance from him.

Midway through the second beer I glanced up to find Frank staring at me. He didn't look away, so I turned my eyes away coldly. When I looked up a few minutes later, he was still staring. I gave him my mean look—a ridiculous squinty scowl. It did not make any sense to me that Frank Belford, who is the most aggressive bore I know, was sixty-eight and in good health while my father had just had a brain tumor removed. Why not the hostile bores?

When I was nine years old, a hostile bore and his wife dropped in for lunch when only Wallace and I were home. After lunch his wife—who was *not* a hostile bore—put on a record and asked me to dance. I was painfully shy with strangers, but somehow got up the courage to dance with her. We danced to the Weavers' singing "Tzena, Tzena, Tzena." She was cheerful, a *bissel zaftig*, a fine and easy person for me to dance with.

The hostile bore turned to my father and said, laughing with a certain derision, "She sure is *skinny*." I cringed with embarrassment.

"Yes," said Wallace, "like a gazelle."

The bar door swung open and without looking up I knew it was Kathleen. I stared at the beer label with sudden concentration, smugly making plans for her impending punishment, perhaps a little initial grouchiness or apathy. Only it wasn't Kathleen but a casual and mildly bothersome friend named Lynda who was flanked by her two Newfoundlands, who lumbered dumbly beside her. Lynda is large and beautiful and voluptuous, and was dressed entirely in red, from the clingy red silk dress to the red fingernails to the red Capezios to the red rose between her large, red-lipsticked lips. The dogs drooled waterfalls down their chests. When several people called greetings, she waved and bade them hello as if she were in a motorcade. She gave the rose to Dolly Belford, who put it into her purse, and walked to my table. Kathleen's punishment was going to increase in direct proportion to how difficult it was going to be to reject Lynda.

"May I join you?" she asked, oozing charm.

"Well, Kathleen is meeting me here any minute," I said.

She took a red bandana out of her purse and wiped the dogs' mouths. Their chests glistened with rivulets of spit.

"Fine," she said starchily, "fine . . . fine, no problem," and walked to the next table where she sat with her back to me, the dogs at her feet.

After waiting an hour, I called Kathleen from the pay phone and rehearsed my snitty but controlled opening line. "Un, didn't you for*get* something?" But no one answered. I let the phone ring a dozen times, and began worrying that everybody in the bar was watching and wondering if I was calling someone, anyone, to keep me company while I drank, and that I couldn't get hold of anybody. I mouthed some words into the phone, listened for a moment, mouthed some more words, listened, mouthed "Goodbye," and hung up. Then I worried that Lynda had heard the sound of the phone ringing while I was talking and would think I was losing it.

I got another beer and went back to my table. I looked up and Frank Belford was *still* staring at me, so I gave him my meanest look. I was torn between being furious with and sick of Kathleen and worrying that she had been killed or mangled in a freak car accident and that I was going to feel bad for thinking lousy, accusatory things about her. I realized that when I finished the third beer, I wasn't going to care as much.

Frank Belford got up unsteadily from his bar stool and began walking toward me with a menacing friendliness. I looked in the opposite direction and determined to leave as soon as I got rid of him. When he got within a few feet of my table, he suddenly lurched, and his knees bent under him, sending him sprawling forward onto one of Lynda's dogs. He broke his fall with his hands and, pushing himself upright, said to no one in particular, "Trick knee." He got to his feet and looked at his hands, which were covered with black dog hairs and saliva.

"Goddamnit!" he said to Lynda, who reached into her purse and handed him the red bandana. He loftily wiped his hands, and then froze, revulsion on his face and the damp, hairy bandana in his hand. He stormed away drunkenly into the bathroom.

I got up to leave, carrying my beer, and smiled to Lynda, who smiled back. I walked out the door and pulled it closed behind me, much too loudly.

I walked up the hillside toward my cabin in a brood, rehearsing my confrontation with Kathleen wherein I told her that I was *really* angry this time, and *really* sick of waiting, and no longer sure that all of our laughing and confiding was worth all of the frustrations. I stopped at the overlook when I reached the top of the hill and looked out at the ocean, which was scintillant under the moon. A pattern of white ripples branched out on the surface of the water for miles. At first the ripples looked like a covering of the finest Irish lace and then, upon careful bad-mood scrutiny, like stretch marks. One sees many such distortions on this overlook; once, I saw what I thought to be pelicans flying way out over the Pacific, and it turned out to be monarch butterflies flying not very far away, above the eucalyptus grove.

I slammed the door of the cabin after I stepped inside. There was one dim corner lamp on and the usual pile of dirty laundry in the middle of the floor. I turned the radio on loudly, started a fire in the Franklin stove, poured a large glass of cheap red wine, smoked an already rolled joint, and waited to feel better. I didn't. Visions of Kathleen flitted through my mind. Drunk and tired and seething, I called

Kathleen's house, but she didn't answer. I rolled and smoked another joint, poured and drank another glass of wine, and began to feel better; my heartbeat slowed down from its anxiety-attacking whir to a rate at which I could discern spaces between the beats.

I stood and walked to the kitchen sink sluggishly, and looked around for my toothbrush, which finally turned up in the silverware drawer, with the forks. I brushed my teeth in half a minute and climbed into bed. The cat was asleep on the pillow next to mine. The radio played a Mozart concerto with a sad, slow oboe line, and I got up to turn it louder. Yehudi Menuhin wrote, "I still look to music to heal and bind; I still think the musician can be a trusted object offering his fellow-man solace but also a reminder of human excellence." I turned the radio off by accident, got back into bed, and sat puzzled for a moment until I realized my mistake, at which point the cat stirred, arose, and stepped onto *my* pillow with his dirty, cruddy cat feet.

Suddenly I was wide awake and furious and frustrated and desolate, and I grabbed the cat, yelled, "Goddamnit you stupid fucking douche bag," and hurled him against the wall. He hit with the awful dead thud that only a sixteen-year-old bag of cat bones can make, and dropped onto the bed, dazed. The phone rang. I looked at the cat, who had lifted his head to see what hit him, and I began crying in low whining sobs. I picked up the cat forlornly and put my head down onto his and walked with him to the phone.

"Hullo," I said, sniffling back tears and snot.

"Hello, Jen," said Kathleen. "I bet you're mad at me, aren't you?" I hung up the phone.

I stood holding the cat, sobbing and shaking and much too stoned, staring out the window into the shadows of the eucalyptus trees under the waxing moon. The phone rang again. I picked up the receiver and hung it back up. My heartbeat once again had no spaces between the pounding. I lit a Camel and tried to pour another glass of wine but first knocked over the glass, and then the bottle. I stood staring out the window into the light evening, and pretty soon there were no eucalyptus branches or shadows, but instead a team of doctors and nurses with clipboards who were looking in the window at me, taking notes.

"Hmmm," says one doctor. "Subject seems to be slipping. Attacking the cat, attempting to break various glass vessels."

"Impaired motor coordination," replies his colleague, a woman with a tight bun on her head. "Possible aphasia, some evidence of brain damage—toothbrush in with silver-ware. Subject may be reacting retardedly to trauma of father's illness."

"Drinks like a fish," says a nurse.

I turned off the lamp so that the doctors couldn't see me as clearly, and climbed into bed. I rehearsed another speech to Kathleen in which I patiently explained that I no longer wished to be subjected to her power games, that all I had revered in our friendship was no longer enough to balance the crap. I dredged up past transgressions, past indications of neurotic personality defects—stinginess, fastidiousness, questionable loyalty and priorities. I anticipated future confrontations and injustices.

I felt calmer as the warehouse of ammunition accrued, until I felt a twinge of pain in the lower part of my calf, cramplike but unmistakably more serious, possibly fatal, and I held my breath unconsciously. The pain moved slightly upward and I suspected that it was thrombosis from birth-control-pill use. The blood clot crept resolutely toward my heart, where it was probably going to cause a cardiac infarction by morning. I felt panicked and resigned. I had sad thoughts about someone finding my little dead body in the morning, and sadder thoughts about someone finding me in a week. God only knows what the old cat would think of or do on my body.

I turned on the light next to my bed and got out to sit in the rocking chair before the Franklin stove. Wrapped in a quilt that my grandmother made sixty years ago, I felt the clot inching past my knee. For a few moments I debated giving my face a Mint Julep Face-Glo Facial, but decided against it for two reasons, one being the doctors, and one being that I still assumed that Kathleen would arrive eventually and that my stoic fury would lose something in the rendering if my tired, drunk face was covered with green slime. I climbed back into bed, turned off the light, and lay heavily on my back, as lost and low as I can ever remember. At some point I started to drowse. At some later point Kathleen was standing above my bed in darkness.

She sat next to me on the bed. I was not exactly pretending to be asleep; nor was I acknowledging that I was awake. It was absolutely silent in the cabin. Her gin fumes surrounded me.

"Jen?" she asked. Silence. The thrombosis abated somewhat, only to be replaced by a hot bubble wedged up in my ribcage. "Hello?" she said. "I know you're not asleep." Silence. "How long did you wait in the bar?"

The bubble moved to the left, indicating that either the blood clot had reached my heart without causing pain in my trunk or that I was having a heart attack. I didn't want Kathleen to be in the cabin, because I was beyond talking and I wanted to have my heart attack in private and I wanted to die without having forgiven her.

"Jen, I know you're not sleeping. I can tell by your breathing. Or the lack of it thereof." I had been holding my breath. "I'm going to tell you the truth and then if you want to be a shithead about it, go ahead...." Her voice was whiny and frustrated. "I was with Peter Anders." Silence. "I tried to call you but you'd left the cabin already, and I wanted to get laid, and I *needed* to get laid and I didn't feel like sitting around the bar intellectualizing with you. So I got drunk and screwed Peter. So big deal."

"Hunh," I said dully.

"Listen, I know you think you're having the hardest time

of anybody because your dad is sick, and that you're suffering more than anybody and blah blah blah. But all day today I thought I was having a breakdown; honest to God, my voices were going full steam all day, like a three-ring circus, and I was on the highway for the four hours down and back to see your father, and I couldn't make any decisions, I couldn't remember if I wanted low-lead gas or regular, and I couldn't remember who I was supposed to be impersonating and how I was supposed to walk and talk and . . ."

Suddenly she was hitting the mattress next to my head, shouting, "*Goddamm it you coward phony, talk! I hate it when you pull this crap on me and hang up the phone and make your crappy moralistic judgments, you hunk of shit. Talk to me!*"

Silence.

"I don't think either one of us is all that well," I said finally in a tired, flat voice. This is me at my worst. "For instance, I think I should tell you that I'm having a heart attack. . . ."

"I *hate* that cool voice of yours," she said, her own voice higher than is normal for her, and wavering, and mad. "I tried to call you but I couldn't. . . ."

"Didn't," I said. "You *didn't* call. You *could* have."

"I *couldn't* call; I tried once. . . ." she said defensively.

"Didn't," I said.

"All right. Didn't. But it doesn't make a difference if I cop to it, right? You're still going to resent me." Her voice became sarcastic. "So how long till you're going to be friendly again—a week, a month?"

"I don't know how long. Maybe forever, maybe not until the snow melts, I don't know. I'm *totally* sick of the same old shit. I'm tired of you testing my love, and I'm tired of punishing you and I'm tired of testing your love and being let down and being punished by you. We're supposed to be close friends and we do all these stupid cruel rejection games. I sort of want to quit."

"You want to quit me?" she asked. She was crying.

"Right now I do. I think," I answered, but truthfully, I didn't care at that point one way or the other. I didn't care right then about anything.

I could see eucalyptus branches where the doctors once stood. My eyes had adjusted to the dark. Kathleen's eyes were so huge and black and filled with water that it almost scared me to look into them.

"Will you talk to me about it in the morning?" Her voice was washed out, defeated.

"Yes," I said. Silence.

"Can I spend the night?" Silence.

"Yes."

She undressed and climbed into bed beside me. I was lying on my side, facing away from her. She lay with her back and bottom against mine.

"You're as much of a pain in the ass as I am," she said, not meanly.

"I know I am," I answered. "So why do I need two major pains in my ass in my life?"

No reply. I was about to doze off.

"Did I tell you I saw Wallace today?" she asked.

"Yeah. So did I."

"Your brothers were there when I was there."

"How was it?"

"The usual," said Kathleen. "Everybody being very cavalier and nervous except for Wallace, who'd just gotten a big shot of Demerol. Wallace was sitting on the bed in his kimono with his head bandaged, and his big handsome purple and green face all drugged out, and every time he slurred something, your little brother would say something like, 'Well, we can't very well take you to parties for a while, can we?' Your brothers both call him Wallacedananda, because of the bandages. That kind of thing."

I made a grinning sort of noise, an almost-laugh, an almost-grunt.

"I didn't think it was all that funny," she said. "It depresses me to watch your family being so stoic and tough about it all, none of you copping to how bad and scared you feel. . . ."

"Oh, fuck off," I said, but I didn't move my body away from her. "Give us a break. I'm going to sleep now."

"O.K.," she said. "Did I tell you I was sorry about the bar?"

"No." My heart attack had gone into complete remission. "Thank you."

"Good night," she said. The luminous alarm clock said one-fifty.

"Oh, shit," she said loudly, five hours later, bolting upright beside me in bed. I turned over groggily to look at her. Her round, black eyes were red and scroonched up in reaction to the morning light. "I have to leave for work at eight."

She hung her head down on her chest and shivered. The deep pockmarks beneath her jutting cheekbones look like pebble imprints. She has huge bones, and little fat, but Kathleen will not let her boy friends see her naked body in the morning light, because of the stretch marks and the five surplus pounds. It is a fine, ample body with no belly fat and much character—the dimples at the base of her back, the muscles in her arms. When she got out of bed that morning, she dressed so quickly that even had I been functioning and coherent, I might have missed her nakedness.

"Jen," she said, lacing up her boots, "I have to run; I have to get things together before I leave. I want to spend some time with you when I get off; I want to talk to you some more because I don't want you to write me off. O.K.? Do you understand?

"What?" I asked. My eyes were out of focus and I wasn't sure what we were talking about. "What?"

"Forget it," she said. "Go back to sleep."

I did.

I dreamt of gazelles grazing in the grass outside my cabin. They were very beautiful and I was surprised that they

were in my back yard, because I thought they lived only in
Africa. They looked up at me occasionally. I went to the
phone to call someone to tell him or her my yard was full of
gazelles—I don't remember whom I was calling—and then I
hung up and went to the window to watch them, and they
were gone, and there was loose, runny shit on my arms, and
I started crying and panicking because someone was coming
over right away and was going to see shit on my arms instead of gazelles in my front yard.

I woke up tired and unhappy, at nine-thirty. I pulled a
blanket around me and went to the phone, and called Kathleen at her office. She has a part-time job as a research assistant for a pharmaceutical company. While the receptionist
transferred my call, I rehearsed a short speech about how
this phone call did not mean that I wasn't still mad, but
when Kathleen picked up the phone, I said, "Hello, this is
your friend the asshole."

"Hello, Asshole," she said cheerfully. "What's up?"

"Do you have a minute?" I asked.

"I have exactly three minutes, and you can have them."

"Well, I just want to tell you my dream quickly, even
though our friendship is on the rocks, and all that."

"Oh, O.K. Go ahead."

I gave her the details.

"Is that it?" she asked.

"That's not enough? Gazelles and shit on my arms?"

"I think it's an obvious dream. . . ."

"You always think my dreams are obvious," I complained, beginning to wish I hadn't called her.

"So would you tell me your dreams if I had no idea what
they meant?" She changed her voice to an analytic, professional basso profundo. "Uh, let's see, you dreamt of a po-
liceman chasing you with a snake. Hmmmm. Well, you got
me. . . ."

"No. I guess I wouldn't."

"O.K. Obviously we can't work on this right now; your

time's almost up. But I think it's the same theme as your skunk dream, trying to hide away your black scary disgusting side, and being afraid you're going to be exposed. That when people find out how weird and awful and pathetic you *really* are, or at least how awful you think you are deep down, they're going to be repulsed, and they're going to reject you, and so on. You can work on the dream yourself. Talk out loud about the dream in the first person, present tense. Be yourself first, then be the gazelle, then be the shit on your arms, and so on. Everything in the dream is you, or some aspect of you. O.K.? I gotta go; I really do. I'll see you at about five."

"O.K.," I said. "Thanks. See you at five." Maybe.

Kathleen is essentially a Gestalt dream consultant and, like all Gestalt therapists, an occasional dope. But often her dream games work, and I see the message of my weird and vivid dreams. The work we did on my skunk dream several weeks ago made a strong impression on me, although it did not make my life any easier.

"Tell me the dream," she said after I'd casually mentioned it. "First person, present tense."

I said (as always, with an eye roll and an "Oh, for Christ's sake"), "I'm in my room, and somehow there are two skunks in my room, and I'm trying to get them out of sight because someone is coming for a visit and I don't want the skunks to stink up my room or my guest. So I try to stuff them into a cellophane bag, but every time I'm about to zip the Zip-Lock closing, one of the skunks pokes its head out of the bag. Like when a cat pops its head out *just* when you've almost got the cat carrier's lid closed. I have the bag locked for a second, and then one of the skunks pokes through the top, and I'm panicking."

"So what do you think of when you think of skunks?"

"Cute, furry, et cetera. And they spray these stinking fumes when they're threatened," I said.

"When they're afraid of being hurt or captured, right?"

"Right."

"And you realize that the skunks are some aspect of yourself."

"Like what?"

"You tell *me*. It's your dream. I only dream of angels and flowers and bunnies." Her dreams are usually sicker than mine.

"I think I see," I said. "Something to do with my black side, my primal side or something. The part of me that people don't know at all, the part that I have to protect, the part that I think is repulsive and stinks."

"Keep going. Be the skunks now. Tell me about your skunky side."

"Nah, I see the dream now," I said. "Thanks—I mean it; I do understand it now. Let's just drop it."

"See?" she said in a slightly patronizing voice. "You're putting the skunks back in the cellophane bag with the Zip-Lock. . . ."

"You're so profound," I said with nervous disdain, and would not talk anymore about the dream. And she didn't push.

About two days later, when I was no longer peeved with Kathleen for her Gestalt condescension, and no longer so worried about her increasing knowledge of my psychic rats and worms, I apologized for my sarcasm, and I expressed appreciation for the dream work, and I told her truthfully that she was the best friend I've had, and that she knows more about me than anyone else. But I still wouldn't tell her about my skunks.

Lumpoid Masses

W hen I awoke on the morning before my father was to
leave the hospital, the sun was materializing through
the fog almost as fast as an image on Polaroid film, and the
old alley cat in a circle of sun on the floor was not at all
looking his best. He was, in fact, lying somewhat stiffly on
his side with his tongue hanging out of his mouth and eyes
wide open. I got out of bed, walked naked to where my cat
lay, and nudged him with my foot, but he was dead and
didn't respond.

I put him in a white polyethylene garbage bag, fastened it
with a rubber band, replaced the rubber band with a piece
of twine, carried his starched body outside into the sunshine, and dug a hole in the earth for his body to disinte-
grate into. It did not occur to me until later that the white
polyethylene bag was not—as were the twine and the cat—
biodegradable.

I stopped crying after my second cup of coffee, and considered my current situation. Wallace was in excellent postoperative shape and there was still no word on the biopsy.
My younger brother (the co-owner of our former cat) was
leaving Clement for college in the East. The cat had kicked.
My father's car, in which I had been commuting to the hospital, had developed an ominous noise that on the freeway
sounded like an engine catching on fire or a rear axel working loose. Things could be worse, I decided, until the mirror

disclosed two pimples on my chin and two on my forehead, at which point I kicked the wall and poured another cup of coffee.

I called Wallace at the hospital, misdialing only once.

"Hello," he said. "The freedom train is coming."

"Hi, Dad," I said, "you sound wonderful."

"I feel much better today," he said. "No headache, and I'm not slurring must. Much." His voice was softer than before the operation, but more animated than it had been since. "You sound like you've got a cold."

"My cat died."

"Oh. I'm sorry. I know how fond you were of that incontinent beast."

"Up yours," I said.

"Uh, let me start over," he said. "I know that wasn't the right thing to say under the circumstances." He paused, and then said with great emotion, "No cat is an island unto itself, a peninsula blah blah blah." I laughed dryly. "Hey, no kidding, too bad, honey. You know, I was actually *sort* of fond of the deceased. Where is he now?"

"Outside. I buried him in front of the cabin. Anyway. I'm coming down this afternoon. Need anything?"

"Let me think. Yes, would you bring Sarah a sandwich from a delicatessen? Roast beef, maybe, on rye? She's had Howard Johnson's fried clams four times this week."

"Yeah, sure. Anything else? Books?"

"I've got plenty of books. Why don't you pick up my mail, and bring me the *New York Review* and the *New Yorker*s. That would be great. Are you bringing Randy with you?"

"He's filling out college-roommate forms today."

"Roommate forms? 'Do you do anything particularly disgusting or bizarre which a future roommate should know about?' That sort of thing?"

"Something like that. I think I'll be down at two or so, with Megan. Okay?"

"Good, anytime. I'll see you when I get here. Or when you get there, I mean."

"Hello, Megan," I said over the phone. "Do you still want to visit Dad with me?"

"Of course," she said resolutely.

"Oh, wait," she burst in. "I have to see my great-aunt for a while today, because I'm going back to Portland next week. Do you want to see her with me, on the way to the hospital?"

"Sure," I said. With an adult friend I might have vocally grimaced just enough so that the friend would know that it was just an ever so slight inconvenience.

"O.K., good, thanks. You'll like each other, because you're both sort of senile. And we don't have to stay long, but I have to warn you about something: she drools a lot, because she's so old—she's eighty-five. She's sort of like your cat that way. . . ."

"My cat died. This morning," I said.

"He *did*? Oh noooo . . ."

"Well, we all gotta go sometime. Don't cry, kid; he's buried and everything. We Must Be Brave."

She was smiling. I knew she was smiling by the sound of her exhalation. "You know what bugs me most about Wallace getting a brain tumor? That it's *Wallace*, who's the nicest person in the world, and he's so young, and it's all so stupid."

"Bugs me too," I said. "It makes me crazy. Only a mean jackass should get a lumpoid mass. Wallace should get free tickets to the theater instead of a tumor."

"Pick me up as soon as you can," she said. "We gotta talk."

There was every possibility that the lumpoid mass that the neurosurgeon removed from my father's brain was malignant, and there was every possibility that it wasn't. There is every possibility that many of the people I know will develop lumpoid masses, if they have not already. None of the lumpoid masses in my life—the brain tumor, the various tumors that friends are growing, the pimples, and the hostile bores with whom I have contact—are acceptable. The problem is, as unacceptable as they may be, there they are.

Lumpoid masses are, on the whole, a terrible embarrassment. When a lumpoid mass appears, something important has gone seriously wrong, and there is sometimes the shame and the guilt and the defensiveness of a major mistake.

Wallace dealt with his tumor with such grace and humor that had I not asked him directly I would not have known that along with the fear and concern was the embarrassment. I have had a more outwardly traumatic time dealing with pimples than he has had with the possibility of brain cancer. Brain cancer, at least, doesn't show.

When Megan told me, a couple of years ago, that she thought pimples looked nice on me, I made an appointment with a dermatologist, who turned out to be young, handsome, and funny, and who had a pimple on his lip. I asked him if he had any cures for me. He prescribed a tube of anti-acne gel that can probably be used effectively in removing furniture polish or as a drain unclogger. What it did was to leave the pimples intact and irritated, and to cause the skin around them to turn red and peel. I threw the tube away when I began to look like an adolescent burn victim, and from then on tried to think of my skin as a protective covering whose sole purpose was to keep blood from getting on my clothes. But to no avail, for I am still deeply embarrassed by my pimples, which is largely why, I think, they continue to develop.

"Romany is the language of the Gypsies," said Megan when she climbed into the passenger seat. She was wearing a green sweatshirt with an airbrushed stallion on it, and her long hair was in braids.

"Oh," I said. "Where'd you find that out?"

"In a book I'm reading about Gypsies. I thought maybe you would want to know what language they speak."

"Well, you were absolutely right," I said. "And I just found out that gorillas are being taught to communicate in sign language with scientists."

"Are you reading a gorilla book?"

"Nope, just a magazine."

"What can they say? Do they talk like babies or something?"

"Oh no," I said, turning down the road toward the mountain and the freeway. "They're totally brilliant. . . ."

"Like what?" she asked.

"Like one of them chewed up a bunch of pencils when the researcher left its room one day, and when the researcher came back, and saw the pencils, she asked the gorilla, 'What happened?' And the gorilla replied, via sign language, 'Naughty teeth.' "

"You call that brilliant?" asked Megan.

"O.K., I'll give you another example. The researcher kept asking the gorilla what it was, over and over, and the gorilla kept thinking and then finally said, 'Fine gorilla animal.' "

"Well, I think that's *interesting*, Jennifer, but I don't think it's *brilliant*."

"What would you say if the tables were turned and a gorilla was asking you what you were?"

" 'Fine human animal,' " she said. "What would you say?"

"Maybe 'fine human animal,' maybe 'fine speckled human animal.' "

"Are breasts lumpoid masses?"

"God, no, they couldn't be less alike. Breasts are one of the finest things about being human; you simply *can*not go wrong with breasts. Unless you get a lumpoid mass in them."

"You mean a tumor, right? Is that what lumpoid masses are?"

"Partly. Pimples are lumpoid masses, too. . . ."

"God! Jennifer! I wish you'd shut up about your pimples. . . ."

"Why, because it's embarrassing?"

"It's not embarrassing to me," she said. "Just boring."

We drove along the lagoon until she said, "We're almost
there. In two more turns you take a right."

"O.K.," I said. "Does Honey know I'm coming, too?"

"No, I forgot to tell her. But even if I'd told her, she
won't remember by the time we get there. And she definitely won't get your name right. And I forgot to tell you one
thing: she has an ulcer on her whole leg, from the knee
down. It's totally gross. But it'll probably be bandaged."

"O.K., let me see if I got this right. She's senile, she
doesn't hear well, she doesn't have any skin from the knee
down, and she drools. . . ."

"And she's real nice. Try not to say anything about her
leg, if you know what I mean. . . ."

"You think I'm going to say 'Jesus Christ, that's repulsive, Honey; I mean, Megan warned me but I had no idea it
was so *sickening*'?"

"No," Megan said huffily. "Just don't mention it."

"If your aunt doesn't mention my pimples, I won't mention her ulcerous leg."

"Jennifer, you have four lousy pimples."

"I knew you'd noticed."

"And I *know* that Honey won't say anything about them,"
said Megan with assurance, and then she began to crack up
when she shouted, *"Because she can hardly see!"*

Honey's home stood in dilapidated splendor on the last
long stretch of beach before one starts up the mountain,
with lush and colorful overgrowth, and a white plastic bird
bath, in the front yard. On the gate was a sign of crooked,
spastic lettering that said BEWARE!! VIOLENT DOG!

"There's no dog at all," said Megan, walking up to the front door. She knocked—pounded—very loudly, and then opened it. "Hello!"

"Hello?" said a scratchy, feeble voice from another room.

"It's Megan," said Megan, stepping inside and pulling me behind her. "It's me, Megan," she said loudly, looking around.

The living room was large and empty. There was a table with chairs around it, an easy chair in front of a wall heater, the kind of cheap collapsible table generally used to hold TV dinners, and a couch that was covered with tissue-paper boxes. There was an ashtray in the shape of a beagle on the TV-dinner table and a half dozen postcards of beagle puppies taped to the wall. The entire living room wall on the west side was a window, and the back yard was sand and waves and beach vegetation.

"Hello, Megan," said Honey. "I'll be right there." We heard the sound of wheels and shoes on linoleum, and Honey entered the living room in a wheelchair, moving her feet in rapid tiny steps in front of her for locomotion; she held her arms stiffly in her lap.

"I thought it was Chet," she said. Her face was the size of a large fist, and her puffy sparse hair was almost as blue as her sharp viscous eyes. "But it's Megan," she said, "and a friend." She was wearing men's cotton pajamas, at least a size too big, with one pant leg rolled up to her knee. The leg was bandaged.

Megan went over to her wheelchair and kissed Honey on the lips. "Honey, this is my friend Jennifer," she said.

"Hello, Evelyn," she said, smiling at me.

"Jennifer," said Megan.

"Hello, dear," she said, and then, to Megan, "I've been looking for my hand."

"Oh. Well, let us help you," she said, without the slightest bit of patronization. "I'll go look in the kitchen. Honey, you just sit there; Jennifer, you go look on the couch."

"Right," I said, as Megan went into the kitchen. I smiled at Honey, and walked to the couch. There was a Kleenex box with needles, bobby pins, and paper clips, a Kleenex box with postcards, a Kleenex box with gauze, adhesive tape, coupons, and a hairbrush, but there were no hands.

"Found it," said Megan, coming back into the room, holding a two-foot steel rod with an orange fluorescent hand on it. Megan was squeezing a lever at one end, and at the other the thumb bent across the two flat fingers as in a grasp. She handed it to Honey, who shakily grasped it with her real hand and laid it across her lap like a rifle.

"Now, where were we?" asked Honey. "Have we had a snack yet?"

"Nope," said Megan. "But Jennifer and I can't stay too long, because we're going to the hospital to visit her father. He just had brain surgery."

"Oh, that's nice," said Honey. "Guess what time it is?"

"Twelve-thirty," said Megan.

"Twelve-forty," I said.

"Wrong; you're both wrong," Honey said with great satisfaction. "It's twelve-thirty-three."

There was a digital clock on the table, and Megan had full view of it.

"I'm going back to Portland in a few weeks," said Megan. "School starts pretty soon."

"That's nice," said Honey. "Are you going back to school?" she asked me.

"No, I don't go to school anymore. I dropped out of college six years ago." Six years ago!

"So did I," said Honey, "sixty-six years ago. Seems like three weeks ago. Couldn't stand it, no drinking, no smoking, no boys, no fun."

"I don't mind school at all," said Megan, "because when it's over, I get to ride my horse every day."

"I used to have a horse," said Honey. "But my husband made me get rid of it when we got married. Herman Hung said that no wife of his was going to go around smelling like horse hairs. Course, Herman smelled like scrambled eggs most of the time, something to do with faulty sweat glands."

"You shouldn't have gotten rid of your horse just because your husband said so," said Megan.

"Nope, I shouldn't have, but I did. Don't know why I did now, but I did do it, did get rid of my palomino. . . ." And her eyes fill with tears.

"Damocles?" asked Megan.

"What?" said Honey.

"Damocles?" asked Megan again.

"Damocles?" asked Honey, slumping forward with her chin raised and great concentration on her tiny, aged face.

"Damocles," said Megan. "That was your horse's name, wasn't it? Damocles?"

"Oh yes, my horse, Damocles. Damocles, my horse. What about him?"

"Never mind," said Megan.

"The red whatsername is cooking my dinner tonight," said Honey. "She's a better cook than the blond whatsername. She can make meat loaf, and something Greek called 'mazookie,' and biscuits. The blond whatsername is a health loony, always tries to get me to eat seaweed. Always tries to get me to quit having drinks before dinner, but I tell her I've been drinking for almost seventy years now, and smokin', too, and no health loony is going to get me to stop. She says it's going to shorten my life," and Honey cackles appreciatively at the irony. "Says that whenever I have a craving for nicotine I should just suck on a piece of seaweed instead. I told her that when I have a craving for nicotine, I just suck on a lit cigarette."

Honey's wheelchair was facing the wall window. "This is my favorite painting in the world," she said to us. "Sometimes it's blue waters and sky, and sometimes it's green waters and blue sky, and sometimes it's gray-green-blue water, right before a storm. It's like watching television, only you never have to change the channel. Oh my God!" she said suddenly, with shrill excitement. "Guess what time it is?"

"One o'clock," I said.

Megan, directly facing the clock, said, "Five minutes after," and looked at me with annoyance.

"One o'clock exactly," said Honey, glancing over at me with a slightly nasty look in her eyes and mouth. "One point for you."

"May I use the bathroom, please?" I asked.

"No. You can't use the bathroom; just try to hold it," said Honey.

I couldn't think of anything to say. People had told me I couldn't smoke in their house, and that I couldn't wear shoes into their house, and even that I couldn't sit on specific pieces of furniture because they were too valuable, but no one had told me I couldn't use the bathroom, and I was confused until I saw that Honey had her hand over her mouth and was snickering.

"Heh heh, one point for me," said Honey gleefully, and she and Megan laughed. "Sure you can use the bathroom; just don't flush it if you only make water."

"O.K.," I said, somewhat sheepishly.

"Gotcha, didn't I?" she asked, much pleased with herself.

"Yep, you got me," I said, standing up.

"Go get me the girl," she said to Megan. "We'll play her for Evelyn when she's finished doing her business."

The bathroom was equipped with a special toilet, two feet higher than most, with arm rests. Lined up next to the sink were a toothbrush, tooth powder, talcum powder, baby oil, a round box of Parisien powder with OOH LA LA! on it, and a black phallic tube of Brut Extra-Strong Roll-On Deodorant. There was a note under the talcum that said, "Marie—I washed and powdered Honey this morning. Just oil her. Susan." Oil her, like a car?

In the living room Megan was brushing out Honey's fine, puffy hair, and Honey was slumped over with her head held up and eyes closed, with a look of sensual satisfaction like that of a cat being scratched under the chin. I sat down and looked at the waves and the sand and the rushes in Honey's back yard until Megan stood up and put the brush back into one of the Kleenex boxes on the couch.

"Wind up the girl now," Honey told Megan.

Megan picked up the porcelain Swiss girl on a round pedestal, wound a key that was stuck in her back like a knife, and set her down on the TV-dinner table. The girl revolved slowly on her pedestal and "Happy Birthday to You" played tinnily. Honey beamed.

"Isn't that a lovely little song?" she asked. "Megan gave her to me last year."

"I was going to get you a music-box doll that played *Eine Kleine Nachtmusik*, but it cost a dollar more," said Megan. "I couldn't even pronounce it right, because I was only nine. I thought it was 'Einnie Kleinnie Nachto music.'"

"I would have never forgiven you," said Honey. "This tune is so happy."

There was a loud pounding on the door. "I'll get it," said Megan. "Happy Birthday to You" was beginning to wind down.

She opened the door, said, "Oh, hi, Chet," and stepped aside to let him in. A tall, blondish man of about fifty stepped inside holding a bouquet of wildflowers; he had a look about the eyes of snobbish chivalry. "Megan, my dear, how nice you look today," he said, patting her on the head. "And hello there, Honey, dear," he said, picking her gnarled hand off her lap and kissing the back of it. "I've brought you some flowers." He replaced her hand, and patted her on the head. I stepped back. I didn't want him to pat me on the head.

"Oh, they're lovely, thank you, Chet, dear. Megan, go get me a vase," she said. Chet stood twirling the ruby ring on one of his long, thin, and very elegant fingers, waiting to be introduced.

"This is Megan's friend Evelyn, Chet. And this is my best friend, Chet," she said to me. We nodded to each other.

"Hello, Evelyn," said Chet, bowing slightly from the waist. *"Enchanté."*

"Hi, Chet," I said. He wore an incongruous assemblage of Eddie Bauer slacks, a Donny Osmond blouse, black penny Loafers, and yellow socks.

"Have a seat, dear," said Honey.

"Oh, no, I really must be going; my bougainvillea are simply crying for water. But I'll be here for a drink before dinner, same as always. I just dropped by to bring you the flowers." Honey reached for the pack of Marlboros on the TV table, shakily removed one, and equally shakily brought it to her lips. Before she could reach for the matches, Chet whipped a Cricket lighter from his pants pocket and held it to the end of her cigarette.

"Thank you, dear," she said. Megan returned with a small vase and put the flowers in it.

"Pretty flowers," she said to Chet.

"Aren't they lovely?" he asked. "Makes me think of something from Katherine Anne Porter." The allusion was completely lost on me. When I think of Porter and plants, I think of hemorrhaging trees. "Or Rod McKuen," he said. "Not that I truly consider McKuen to be a *great* poet, but he has written some lovely odes to flowers. I'm sure," he said to Megan with erudition, "that next year you'll be familiar with some of McKuen's major works, the cat poems and the odes to wildflowers."

"I've already read a lot of McKuen," Megan said with an absolutely straight face. Megan and I have sat around reading McKuen poetry to each other, howling with laughter.

"And do you go to school, Evelyn?" he asked me.

"She's a dropout," said Honey.

"Oh, I'm *sorry*," he said.

"Guess what time it is, Chet," said Honey.

"Time for me to go, I'm sure, but I'll be back tonight, Honey, same as always. About five-ish, I hope. . . ."

"Guess who's on TV tonight, at eight," she said. "It's someone you like a lot."

"Fred Astaire?"

"No, he's dead," said Honey.

"No, he isn't," said Megan.

"Yes, he is," Honey said sadly. Her eyes filled up with tears. "H-h-h-he h-h-he died last year." She stopped for a moment. "No, that was Jack Benny," she said, squinting, and was calm for just a minute until her eyes refilled as she thought about Jack Benny's death.

"Please don't cry, Honey," said Chet, patting her hand with great tenderness. "There are still so many people alive whom we love just as well."

"Yes, you're right," said Honey bravely. "Is Florence Henderson still alive?"

"Yes, she certainly is," said Chet reassuringly. "Now tell me who's on the telly tonight, because I simply have to get back to my garden. Someone I like a great deal, you said. . . ."

"Liberace," said Honey. "He has his own special."

"Oh, he's marvelous, isn't he?" Chet said, nodding his head at Honey. "Such a pianist! He's really quite a guy." Megan looked at me out of the corner of her eye.

"*I'll* say so," said Honey. "He's my favorite, him and Myron on the Lawrence Welk show. Of course, Myron plays the accordion, not the piano, so I guess Liberace is my favorite piano player. Now, I'll tell you," she said, looking at the three of us with indignation, "a *lot* of people think he's a show-off for dressing that way. They think it's a *gimmick* that he wears those clothes." She squinted her eyes determinedly and said, "But *I* think he just wants to look nice."

———

"We better go now, Honey," Megan said ten minutes after Chet had bade us all a fond adieu. "I guess I won't see you until Christmas vacation."

"Is it almost Christmastime?" asked Honey. "Because I don't even remember anything about turkeys, and now you tell me—"

"It's not for four months," said Megan, "but that's when I'll be back to California. But I'll write you."

"You always write me; I know that. And Chet always reads me your letters. So you have a good time in school, and you have a lot of fun with your horse, you hear me?"

"Uh-huh."

"You write me about your horse, and you tell your mama that old Aunt Honey is just fine, and I'll see you at Christmastime, if I'm still alive."

"You'll still be alive," said Megan.

"No way to tell, though," said Honey. "So give me a kiss now, and I'll let you be off to the movies."

"The hospital," said Megan, walking to Honey's wheelchair. "We're going to the hospital." She bent down and kissed Honey on the lips and smiled her kindest smile. "Well, 'bye, Honey," she said, tenderly.

"Bye-bye, Megan. Push me over to the window, would you?" Megan pushed the wheelchair to the window where the green-gray waves partially covered the bone-colored sand. "Perfect," she said.

" 'Bye, Honey," I said.

"Good-bye, Evelyn. You drive carefully."

"I will," I said. Megan and I walked to the door. Honey had her back to us, was watching the Pacific Ocean through the window; her fluorescent orange hand lay on the linoleum near the door.

We got back into the car and drove the rest of way around the lagoon, watching the egrets and sandpipers and mud hens eat, swim, take off, and land. As we began the climb up the mountain, Megan turned her head toward the ocean, toward the tiny islands on the horizon, toward the sky, where billowing gray nimbus clouds covered the sun. The first cloud in the succession looked like a Macy's Thanksgiving Day–parade balloon with a Truman Capote head and the body of a duck. The second looked like a skull with depthless eye sockets attached to the body of a horse. A *V* of geese flew over the ocean; several minutes later a solo goose followed in its path. Poor bastard, I thought; I wonder if he'll catch up, and what happens to geese who don't.

"Do you think the other geese ditched that guy?" asked Megan.

"I was just wondering that also," I said. "Maybe so; maybe he has garbage breath, or herpes, or maybe the other geese thought he was just generally a pain in the ass."

"Maybe he talked too much, or interrupted. Or else maybe he was daydreaming." She thought for a minute. "So who would you say was the worst lumpoid mass you know?"

"Well, the classic lumpoid mass of this era is Nixon."

"*Was* Nixon," said Megan.

"And he still is, in fact; he's *still* pulling off some of the great moments in lumpoid massism. You know what he's done? Ever since he, uh, retired, hundreds of thousands of people have written to him in San Clemente with sympathy and support letters, in spite of all the crimes against nature, in spite of the millions of deaths he's been responsible for. They write and say, 'Gee Mr. Nixon, I sure think the media has given you a hard time,' and so on. And he saved all the letters, and has sent each sympathizer a letter offering him a special deal on his new book, the special deal being that he's trying to rook them out of two hundred dollars for a leather-bound autographed copy of the memoirs."

"Did you think Chet was a lumpoid mass?"

"No, no, not at all. I think he's so lovely with Honey, such a good friend to her."

"He comes over to see her every day, you know."

"I know."

"And Honey isn't always the easiest person to get along with."

"I gathered."

"A few times this summer I was hanging out with her, and she fell asleep in the wheelchair, so I just got cookies and read magazines until she woke up, and she got real mad at me for not waking her up to make sure she was only napping. Not dead. So one time when she fell asleep I woke her up after half an hour and she was totally crotchety that I'd woken her up from her nap. And every time I leave to go back to Portland, she says that she might never see me again because she's so old and is going to die soon, she thinks. And if I say something like 'That's what you said last year,' she says, 'Last year I was only eighty-four.' And you know what: Honey's brother died when he was a little kid; he got stompled on by a horse. . . . Jeez, he wasn't even my age yet. I mean, even your cat got to live longer than Honey's brother. My dad calls this kind of thing a 'head scratcher.' You know what I like about Honey most of all? That she's still so lively, you know; she still makes jokes and does tricks on you and drinks rum."

"I'm not sure if there's a connection," I said, "but a few days ago when my cat was moping around and showing all the signs of being sixteen years old, he suddenly, for the last time, became the Flying Red Horse, entered the cabin with his wild Flying Red Horse look, tore as fast as he could across the cabin, hit the wall by the bed, turned around, and tore back outside. When he was six weeks old, I let him outside and a dog got him and tore away a lot of his throat, and he ended up living all these years, and even ended up with one last round of the Flying Red Horse in him."

"I wonder what decides how long you live."

"I think it boils down to luck of the draw."

"Do little kids get cancer?"

"Yeah, sometimes."

"Just because of bad luck of the draw?"

"Mostly, I think."

"Are the kids in pain when they have it?"

"Oh, they have miraculous painkillers these days."

"Did Wallace take them?"

"Yeah, after surgery. But he wasn't in so much pain."

"Does he have cancer?"

"Not that we know of."

"But he has lumpoid masses?"

"He had one, and the surgeon cut it out."

"And how will you know if he'll be O.K.?"

"We'll just have to play it by ear, just like everybody else."

"Are you very afraid?"

"Yep."

"Like you're afraid of snakes?"

"Sort of. Except that I was always terrified of snakes, from when I was little and Ben dropped a snake down my sunsuit, and for all these years they were the blackest, scariest thing I could think or dream of. But then when I lived at the hot springs I kept running into rattlers, almost stepping on them—honest to God, I was inches away a few times—and they never bit me. So pretty soon I was out looking for them. I would have adrenaline pumping when I saw them, but I was more fascinated than scared. Then I started having good snake dreams as opposed to bad snake dreams: a good snake dream is when you watch one glide by somewhere, when you know it's totally mysterioso and capable of ending your life but you're just watching because it's so captivating; a bad snake dream is when you're in a sunny glade with the people you love most and all of a sudden black mambas are falling out of the sky. But I don't have that much experience with Dad's brain tumor yet; it's brand-new material, and some of the possibilities are so grisly it scares me shitless. . . . But, Megan, I want to talk about something else. I mean, what sort of delirious crackpot tells some sane kid like yourself about all these obsessions with snakes and cancer?"

"You better keep talkin' or you're gonna stop one," she said, making a pistol of her hand and pulling it on me.

I zipped my mouth shut.

"Unzip it," she snarled, squinting, waving the gun wildly.

I shook my head and said through the tiniest possible opening in my lips, "Nothing you can say can get me to talk . . ." but then burst out laughing. "Let's go into petty crime," I said. "You're a perfect gangster; we'll disguise you as a killer midget."

"*Jennnn . . . I want to talk about this stuff some more.* You just think you're boring or weird or talking too much but you're not and I'm really interested so just shut up and keep talking!" There had been some real frustration in her voice, and when we finished laughing, I told her I'd shut up and keep talking if she shut up and asked me her questions.

"O.K.," she said, "and keep your eyes on the road. So, you don't know why somebody gets cancer at some particular age?" I shook my head. "How can doctors not know how to cure it?"

"It's a mystery, why it starts, when it starts, who it gets. We don't know yet. Doctors can cure all sorts of cancers now, lots of them."

"Oh Jeez, you mean there's more than one?"

"Hundreds."

"O.K., O.K., I don't want to talk about it anymore. But don't you think it's stupid when a five-year-old has to get it? I just think it's the shittiest, nastiest thing."

The stupidest, nastiest, shittiest death I ever heard of happened to my dream consultant's brother, who was twenty-one and in the novitiate. One weekend he went to visit his parents, and their TV set was on the blink, so he unplugged it, took it apart, and got electrocuted. There's a great deal of voltage stored inside picture tubes, even picture tubes of unplugged television sets. But I did not mention this to Megan; it was *much* too obscene.

"Can I ask you something about when your college friend got creamed in the car accident?" she said, stroking her chin with her left hand and wrapping a braid around her ear with her right. "When it happened, were you mostly furious, or mostly sad?"

"I don't know," I said. "Very sad, very furious. And very nervous. She was my age exactly."

"How about with your dad?"

"Both. All three. But he's still alive, and he may get completely better, so it's different."

"Maybe he'll live to be eighty-five, like Honey," said Megan.

"Maybe."

"But I really don't think he will, if you don't mind my saying so."

"I don't mind your saying so," I said. "I don't think he will either."

Megan looked at me with a sad and affectionate smile, still stroking her chin. "Oh well," she said.

"You haven't cleaned any houses for a long time, have you?" she asked as we neared the top of the mountain.

"Nope. Not since the brain surgery was scheduled."

"Because you wanted to spend your time with your dad?" she asked.

"Partly. And partly because I got nervous again. I thought, Wallace has a brain tumor; Wallace might not get to live forever. And then I thought that maybe *I* wasn't going to get to live forever. I decided it was totally possible that I might die next week, and I didn't want to have cleaned a toilet the afternoon before I died."

"Do you think this all is as interesting as I do?"

"Oh yeah. And I'll tell you something really interesting from the *Chronicle* this morning. This guy about my age got pierced by a metal rod which went through his stomach and out his back—it was about as thick as an orange-juice can—and he's going to *live.* . . ."

"Godddd!"

"Yeah, and the story goes on to say that his kids have been inviting all their friends over to look through their daddy's stomach. . . ."

"Noooo. . . ."

"O.K. I made the last part up. I admit it. But the other part's true. The guy was working on the ground floor of a building, and from the top floor, out of the blue, the rod fell and went through him. And he gets to keep living. There's a perfect example of the sword of Damocles."

"What happened to Damocles again?"

"He was bragging about how good his life was, and this king friend of his made him sit at a banquet table with a sword suspended by a single hair over his head—the point being that at any second, his life and happiness could have ended."

"Drive carefully," she said.

At just those moments when I would start to be depressed about Wallace's condition, Megan would say something, funny or serious, and the pictures of Wallace would disappear. Traveling up the curvy road with Megan was the best possible therapy. We almost never resort to discussing the farts in the windstorm—niggling complaints, economics, politics, or any but the most bizarrely unattractive fashions—and it is always worth it to pay attention to what Megan says, unless she is telling me the plot of a movie. Even then I like to listen to her voice.

Megan said she thought it was sad when one daughter was beautiful and one daughter was homely, and I said that this was true, but added that some of the world's worst people have the world's greatest teeth. We talked about the parts of our mouth we didn't like to touch with our tongue—the ridges above your front teeth, the little punching bag.

I said that I thought the secret of life was obvious: be here now, love as if your whole life depended on it, find your life's work, and try to get hold of a giant panda. If you had a giant panda in your back yard, anything could go wrong—someone could die, or stop loving you, or you could get sick—and if you could look outside and see this adorable, ridiculous, boffo panda, you'd start to laugh; you'd be so filled with thankfulness and amusement that everything would be O.K. again.

"We gotta get one for Wallace," said Megan, "so when he comes home from the hospital, he can look outside from the window seat and see this giant panda beaming at him."

"And Muldoon would have someone to play with," I said, and the picture of Muldoon and the panda wrestling on the lawn at the house where Wallace and Sarah and Randy live made Megan laugh so contagiously that we were unable to stop until I started coughing.

"If you quit smoking, Jen, you could laugh longer," said Megan.

"Or else I could just stop laughing," I said, and lit up a Camel. "And then I'd be a big lumpoid mass. But I think I'm going to stop using 'lumpoid mass.' I might as well just say 'tumor' or 'pimple' for that sort of lumpoid mass, and I think it shows a certain lack of compassion to call lumpy boring despicable people 'lumpoid masses.' "

"We'll probably forget about it in a couple of days anyway."

"Yeah. I hope so. I sure like the sound of it, but it makes it too easy for me to judge people too quickly. For instance, if I saw Chet in that stupid yellow blouse at the store and he was telling someone about the odes to flowers and that his bougainvillea were simply crying for water, I'd write him off as a lumpoid mass. And I wouldn't know how kind he is to Honey, and how much time he gives her, and I'd be wrong in my assessment."

"But we could at least talk about it, about lumpoid masses, just so we'd laugh about them, even though we aren't quite sure what we mean. It's *still* so much more interesting than the stuff I talk to most adults about, like where I want to go to college or where I bought my shoes or something."

"O.K. I'll tell you everything I know about them. You and my giant panda are the exact opposites of a lumpoid mass. And I still maintain that Nixon is the classic lumpoid mass."

"But Pat's pretty nice, I think."

"Oh yeah. But my uncle Colin says that secretly she's been dead for years. The White House had a Pat robot, like Artie Dootie except it looked exactly like her."

"R-two-D-two, stupid. You should've seen the movie."

"You better stop telling me what I should and shouldn't be doing, shouldn't be smoking, should see *Star Wars.* . . ."

"Oh, that's nothing; I could go on for hours."

"I bet you could," I said, smiling.

"Frinstance, you should start spending a little more time with your hair."

"I spend all day with my hair; in fact I never leave it alone for a minute."

"You know what I mean."

"If you promise not to mention one more thing I should do, even if you're right, I won't make you get out at the top of the mountain. Deal?"

I glanced at her and she nodded.

"So go on then, about lumpoids," she said, mock-glaring.

"You really want to hear? I'm not being boring?"

She closed her eyes, snored loudly, woke up abruptly. "I'm sure."

"O.K. I was going to say something about how everyone hates lumpoid masses because they're ugly and life-threatening or they blow your façade because you have to confront these scary, vile things, and you can't understand why you have to be involved with them at all. You don't get to say, 'Oh, no thanks, no lumpoid masses for me today!' You develop them, and at first and maybe forever it seems like there's no good reason for them. They're like my fears about poisonous snakes: I could *never* imagine any good reason for the earth to include snakes; I thought they were a big mistake on somebody's part. And then I confronted them and read about them and saw that they weren't out to get me and my perspective changed enough to see them as being O.K.; as being necessary, et cetera. Beautiful, even, although I don't really believe it for a minute, and God only knows I may lose my mind permanently the next time I see a rattler. Anyhow, there may be some weird reason for tumors. It may be that surviving the brain tumor will change Dad's life forever for the better. I've read that it can. And we'll look back in ten years and we'll know that confronting this scary, shitty thing made our lives better. Scary things are not always as they seem. I hope."

"I see what you mean, I think," Megan said, chewing on a braid, and staring off into the distance. "You mean like that, up there, on the mountainside, below those vultures—see?" I eased the car around a curve and then saw what she meant directly in front of me. Amid the greens of the mountain foliage—deep pine greens, muted gray greens, dark spinach greens, bluish greens, yellowish greens, olive greens—was an expanse of glistening red beauty, of stunningly beautiful poison oak.

Rallying

O n the morning Wallace was to come home, a woman of my father's age brought over some tapes for him to listen to while he was recovering: Schubert's "Trout" Quintet, some Mozart piano sonatas, the Modern Jazz Quartet at Monterey. She is one of my favorite people in Clement, not an especially close friend, just a fine one.

On the same morning, Richard Braithewaite stopped Randy at the post office and told him he'd heard that Wallace was mortally ill. Randy said this wasn't true. The man asked if Wallace had suffered brain damage. Randy said no. Richard asked if our mother was still alive. Randy said yes, she was, and so was Wallace, and that he foresaw no changes in their status. Richard asked if Wallace had cancer. Randy said not that he knew of. Richard told Randy that the only reason he asked was that his own uncle had had a tumor removed and died three months later. Randy told Richard that he was a nosy, stupid asshole and left the post office.

Randy called me from the pay phone downtown and related the conversation. He told me that he thought Wallace would have wanted him to act more politely. I said that Wallace would probably have said the same thing had the tables been turned. Randy said he wished he'd said, "Well, too bad for your uncle," and I said, "Too late now." I told him he'd done fine, and that Wallace would be proud of him. Randy said he felt bad. I told him to meet me at his house, and that we could wait for Dad to come home. I also told him that as long as he and I were going to continue caring about what acquaintances in Clement think of us, we should be more selective—I do not want nosy, stupid assholes like Richard Braithewaite to have any effect on our lives.

It does not necessarily make it easier to write off a person—Richard, for instance—simply because he announces as fact that he was born under a pyramid on the planet Betelgeuse of a special race of beings who would one day save the planet Earth. It doesn't make it easier that Richard has spent the ten years since he received a doctorate in physics from Harvard as a trust-fund psychedelic adventurer, a combination of pastimes that has resulted in an unstable and tactless paranoiac. That Randy and I once overheard Richard ask the man at the produce stand why the broccoli wasn't happening should make it easier, but it doesn't. It must be the doctorate from Harvard.

Randy and I met at his house just after noon. Wallace had told us that he and Sarah would be home around one. Over the phone he sounded like our preoperation father, cheerful and strong, not at all like someone who ten days earlier had had a fairly large plum-purple brain tumor removed.

We sat outside with a beer for a while, throwing sticks to Muldoon and pebbles into the ice plant. We were more cheerful than we had been in weeks. We went inside and opened another beer each, began straightening up the living room, and listened to the stereo, loud. Randy rearranged the stack of periodicals on the coffee table into three two-foot piles, and showed me a women's fashion magazine with an article on how to plump up your lips, which for some reason made us both hysterical. We played our favorite reggae album of the hour, and Randy told me that the guitarist was recovering from surgery for the removal of a tumor on his foot, and that when interviewed from his hospital bed, he had said, "My foot no hurt no more mahn." When there was nothing left to straighten up, we sat down with our beers and began tearing napkins into little bits, which we left on the floor by our chairs.

"You think he'll be all right?" Randy asked.

"Yeah," I said. "I do. Turn the record over, will you?"

I still order him around a bit, a habit from earlier years, which I am not proud of but which I still do. Usually he performs little services that will benefit us both, like turning over records, or bringing the salt to the table.

"You turn over the record," he said. I think he is recovering from having had me for an older sister and Ben for an older brother all these years. Still, it meant that *I* had to get up and turn the record over. "I'll get the next one," he said. I got up and turned the record over.

"I think he's going to recover, too," I said. "I'm not sure whether it's because I can't picture it otherwise, or whether it's because he has done so well since surgery."

"I guess we have to wait and see," said Randy, "and you know how goddamn sick I am of waiting and seeing."

"You and me both," I said.

"Things are never going to be the same again for us."

"A lot of things will still be the same, but we'll just have more knowledge about how weird and lousy and sad things can get."

"No kidding. I keep thinking, What on earth is going on here? Brain tumors are supposed to happen to other families. I keep thinking someone is going to call the whole thing off, you know, announce that it was all sort of a joke. . . ."

"It *is* all sort of a joke."

"It doesn't exactly feel like a joke to me," said Randy. "It feels a lot more like taking a dump on LSD."

Two beers later, at quarter to one, there was still no Wallace. We kept getting out of our chairs to look for their car;

the last time I remember feeling this way was while waiting for my mother to come home from the hospital after Randy was born. I thought I had lost this hopeful-waiting feeling, after too many disappointments when the awaited party actually showed up, or didn't.

"Colin wasn't expected to recover after the fifth heart attack," I said. "The doctors told him to pack his bags, get his papers in order, not that he has any 'papers' to speak of, and now he's in excellent shape. He even died in the ambulance for a few minutes, and they brought him back to life, and he completely recovered."

"He died?" asked Randy. "Colin died? No one told me that."

The youngest child in families is often denied important information, because no matter how old the person gets, he or she is still thought of by parents and siblings and relatives and family friends as being "so young." I think that no one wants to see the last baby grow up; it makes the rapid passing of time so tangible.

"Yeah, he died for three minutes. I met the ambulance attendant who brought him back to life—pounding his chest—and she said it was a miracle he survived."

"Does he remember being dead?"

"No, not at all. There are a lot of people these days who've been medically dead and then come back to life, and mostly they report absolute tranquillity while they've been dead, white-light visions, being greeted by relatives, and so on. But Colin says that all he remembers is the sensation of being poured back into an old potato sack."

"I think all that life-after-death stuff is stupid; there's no proof. . . ."

"There's no proof for death after death; it's all circumstantial evidence. . . ."

"Oh, come on," he said. "There's scientific proof."

"No, there isn't. There's scientific evidence. Scientists can only perceive certain frequencies, even with computers and machines."

"You just want to believe in all that stuff," said Randy.

"You just want to believe in science. I think that you might as well believe in whatever makes you feel better, since there's no proof, and if you believe in God or the Other Side all your life, you can never be proven wrong."

"That's so stupid," said Randy.

"You're so stupid," I said reflexively, and then started laughing. I stuck out my tongue, squinted my eyes, and said, "Nnnnyyyaaahhh."

Wallace and Sarah arrived home at two, both much thinner than they had been ten days ago. Wallace wore a Navy watch cap, and of course no hair showed beneath it. We stood around the car hugging and patting one another, saying, "Hello! hello!" and "Well! Well well well."

"Why don't you kids bring in the stuff from the back of the car," said Sarah.

"Sure," said Randy. We grabbed the clothes and books and cards and Sarah's embroidery bag, and followed Wallace and Sarah inside. Wallace walked slowly.

When we had set down the hospital gear in the living room, Wallace turned to us and said, "Shall I unveil?" We nodded. He lifted off the cap, and we stared. His head was glabrous and well shaped, with a three-inch trapdoor Frankenstein scar above his left ear. We stared. Wallace smiled.

"Yo," said Randy. "Kojak."

"Pretty neat, huh?" asked Wallace. "That woman did good work. Good surgeon, good seamstress. She came in this morning to remove my bandages, and Sarah and I were expecting a dramatic unwrapping, like in the movies when the surgeon unwinds the bandages and the patient blinks and says, 'Doctor, I can *see*!' So she comes next to the bed, gets a handful of bandage, and lifts it off in a split second." He pantomimed the surgeon's popping his gauze cap off.

"Did you blink and say, 'Doctor, I can *see*'?"

"No," said Sarah, "he didn't say anything; he just gingerly felt his scar, and then ran his hand over his head. He was smiling."

"Was I?" asked Wallace, smiling.

"Yep," said Sarah. They looked at each other with the fondest looks in the world.

"Sarah looked at my scar closely and told the surgeon that she sewed beautifully. The surgeon said, 'Only scalps. Otherwise I baste my fingers to whatever I'm sewing.' "

"I'm glad I didn't know that before surgery," I said.

"What if she deliberately sewed her hand to your skull because she had the hots for you," asked Randy, "and you had to go through life with her hand on your head?"

Wallace laughed and sat down in the window seat, leaned back against the pillows, kicked off his L. L. Bean moccasins, and said, "Jesus Christ, it's good to be home."

He slept in the window seat off and on, an hour awake and an hour asleep, with his watch cap off and his bruises only slightly faded. He looked so good in relation to his early days in the hospital, so much more old and tired than in the family pictures on the wall. When Wallace awoke, he had juice instead of the beer that the rest of us drank; if the scar and the baldness and the purple-green bruises weren't enough evidence that all of this had happened, the incongruity of Wallace drinking juice confirmed it.

While Wallace slept, Randy asked Sarah about her third-graders, whether she had missed them, whether she thought the ones with junkies and drunks and Burn Outs for parents would recover.

"They'll either be tough and special or they'll be Juan Coronas," she said. "Suzuki Bradey's mother shoots junk, and his father is usually bottled up at Napa State, but Suzuki is one of the truly great kids in my class. He collects wounded animals—cats, birds, banana slugs—and takes care of them till they die, which they always do because he's rough with them, inadvertently. He has a sort of animal hospice, gives them eyedroppers of alcohol when they cry. He also brought me one of his mother's bras for Valentine's Day. I think he's in the process of transcending."

The people in my family have always had strange views of who the "sane people" are. For instance, we consider ourselves to be archetypes of sanity in a twisted, demanding sort of way. And Randy's role model for years was a kid named Johnny whom he swears he saw years ago on the old *Bozo the Clown* television show. Johnny was chosen to play the bean-bag toss, missed the cutouts with all three bean bags, and said, "Dammit!" Bozo shook his finger at Johnny and said, "Now, Johnny, that's a Bozo no-no," and Johnny said, "Cram it, clown."

At four o'clock Randy announced that he was going over the hill with a friend to do an errand.

"What sort of errand?" I asked.

"Uh, an errand," said Randy, who is terrible at lying. "To do. You know, like an, uh . . ."

"Like an *errand*," I said, suddenly realizing that it was a secret errand. "An errand to do, right?"

"Yeah," said Randy. "I'll be home in a few hours."

"Good to see you, Randy," said Wallace.

"Good to see *you*, Dad; it sure is good to see you back; we sure missed you," he said, walking backward toward the front door. "It sure is good," he said, backing out the door, "to see you," and disappeared.

"God," said Kathleen when she walked into the house an hour later, "it sure is good to see him home." Wallace was asleep in the window seat, Sarah was embroidering next to him, and I was at the refrigerator getting another beer for myself.

"You want a beer?" I asked.

"You need to ask?" I handed her a Ballantine India Ale, which is for special occasions, Ballantine Ale being the usual house beer.

"Thanks," she said. "I've just made an enemy, Adelle Firth, via those open-mouth-insert-foot routines that your family specializes in."

"What'd you do?" asked Sarah.

"I just told Adelle how cute her baby was and how glad I was that she hadn't given her a stupid hippie name like Peace or Energy. . . ."

"Oh, no," said Sarah.

"I said, 'Carmen is such a pretty name,' and Adelle looked at me as if I'd just tried to *lick* her baby, or something, and she said in this high, tight voice, 'The child's name is Karma.' I said, 'Ah, Karma, well, uh, Karma, well . . .' "

"I wouldn't sweat it," I said. "Adelle is a total write-off, in my book; she's a woman-hater, I think. She once told me I'd never catch a man if I didn't stop wearing tennis shirts; she said tennis shirts were unattractive and unalluring, and that I should wear orange scoop-neck blouses. She said, 'You've got everything in the world going for you. *Forget* the bad hair; *forget* the bad skin. . . .' "

"I would have told her to shove it," said Kathleen.

"No, you wouldn't have," I said. "I didn't, anyway. I just wrote her off."

"Yeah, well, you're saner than I am."

"No, I'm not," I said.

"Yeah, you are. Your parents are still alive, for one thing, and you weren't raised a Catholic, for another, and your skin is clearing up. . . ."

"And yours is totally cleared up. . . ."

"Yeah, and I'm thirty-five. It cleared up last year."

"I wish you both would stop talking about your pimples in public," said Sarah, who has annoyingly clear, perfect skin. "It makes me uncomfortable."

"It's good for us, though," I said. "It's like talking about the brain tumor; it makes it less horrible."

"Why don't you start wearing a fake beard if your skin bothers you so much?" asked Sarah.

"My cheekbones and eyes would start breaking out," I said.

Kathleen laughed, and Sarah stood up. "I'm going to take a bath, while Wallace is still asleep," she said. "Make yourselves at home, but keep your mitts off Wallace's juice."

"Wallace is drinking *juice*? God, this must be serious."

"I think it's pretty serious," I said, "as tumors go."

Sarah left the living room.

"Any word on the biopsy?" Kathleen said.

"No. It turns out that there might not ever be a definitive word on the biopsy. Oncology, pathology aren't absolute sciences. They're talking about a couple weeks of radiation, just to be on the safe side."

"Ughhhh," said Kathleen. "Shit."

"Ughhhh shit," I said. "Wallace is coping, though. He told us that everything since the tumor diagnosis has felt like theater of the absurd, and that seeing 'it all' as theater of the absurd makes it a good deal easier."

"He looks wonderful, doesn't he? I mean, in spite of the bruises? And the baldness? And the scar? I wish my father had been as sane as Wallace. O,, man, I almost forgot to tell you my latest perverted dream, speaking of parents, and theater of the absurd."

"Good. What happened?"

"I'm in a hospital bed with a view of the house I grew up in, and my arms and legs are burning, and it turns out that they've all been amputated. So I'm lying there without arms or legs, screaming for my parents, but no one comes, and somehow I manage to start masturbating. No arms or legs and I'm abusing myself like a disturbed adolescent."

I broke out laughing. "That's the healthiest dream I've heard in weeks," I said.

"Your idea of health is very, *very* twisted."

"No," I said. "Look, your parents killed themselves when you were my age—most people would never recover from that sort of guilt—and in your dream you're screaming for them and they don't show up, and without both of them, without arms or legs, you're masturbating, you're *nourishing* yourself, you're giving yourself an orgasm."

"Maybe I am recovering; hell, it's about time. I sort of thought that when my skin cleared up it would mean I had made some sort of cellular decision to stop punishing myself. Of course, my face is always going to look ravaged."

"It doesn't look ravaged at all."

"You're just saying that because your face looks ravaged, too."

"No, I'm not. I *prefer* faces like ours, faces that look like they've gone through the mill and survived."

"I suppose you meant that as a compliment?"

"Practically all of the women I love most in the world have faces like ours, have faces that look like the women played hard. I take hotshot women with scars much more seriously than beauties."

"Yeah, but if you'd had excellent skin, you'd look at women like us and think we must be incredibly neurotic and self-hating."

"How do you know?"

"Because *I* would think it. And I'd be right," she said, smiling at me. "Jesus, look at the skin on Wallace's head; it's as smooth as a baby's bottom." We looked over at Wallace, who stirred, blinked, and looked back at us. "Hello, Wallace," Kathleen said. "Welcome home, you old shnook."

"Hello, Kath," he said. "Come here." She walked to the window seat and they hugged and kissed. Kathleen rubbed her hand over Wallace's shiny head. He closed his eyes and smiled.

"I hope you kept Jen out of trouble while I was gone," he said.

"God knows I tried."

"She's a great influence on me, Dad. In spite of her drinking problem. She told me that we had to drink for three now, since you're on the wagon."

"I certainly appreciate you girls covering me like this."

"Girls?" asked Kathleen.

"Forgive me. I meant dolly-rolls."

"I'll let it go, in light of the surgery. Anyway, your alleged daughter has decided that she and I aren't alcoholics yet; she thinks we're vivacious social drinkers."

Wallace reached for Kathleen's beer bottle, held it up, and asked, "Jennifer, is this bottle half full or half empty?"

"It's probably almost gone," I said.

"Oh listen, Kath, I hope you didn't think you were boring me the other day at the hospital, when I fell asleep."

"I thought you were on drugs, stoned beyond madrigal potential."

"I was," said Wallace. "Very, very good drugs. Demerol, which I got as often as I wanted, is absolutely wonderful stuff. Everything becomes warm and soft and pleasant, and you drift into sleep on it, very high, On Beyond Zebra."

"Did they give you some to take home?" she asked.

"Not after they saw you two, and Ben and Randy. They gave me Dilantin to prevent brain seizures, and some steroids to reduce the swelling, but nothing euphoric."

"Is he holding out on us?" Kathleen asked me.

"Probably," I said. "You can't trust anyone in my family when it comes to chemicals."

"Speaking of which," Wallace said to us, looking back and forth at us sternly, "I hope you guys realize what a lousy psychological time it would be for LSD."

"You think we're stupid idiots?" I said. "We haven't done any acid for a year now, and I don't think we'll do it again for ages."

"Never again for me," said Kath. "Never again. The last time we took it—did we tell you about this?" Wallace shook his head. "We drove . . ."

". . . your car . . ." I said, and Wallace grimaced.

". . . up to the ridge at four in the morning, hallucinating like mad; we'd been tripping for about ten hours at that point. We're driving along the lagoon—Jen's driving five miles an hour—and it was totally beautiful. If you think the lagoon is exquisite normally, you should see it with three hundred mikes of LSD surging through your veins and brain. And we were both wildly happy and looking at the trees and the water and the sky—before the first morning lights had broken—and Jen was laughing and pointing at all the cobras and pythons that were outside. . . ."

"In Northern California?" Wallace asked.

"Yeah, but I wasn't *scared* of them," I said. "I knew they were really just tree branches, pretty much."

"She kept saying, 'Look at all those fucking cobras,' as if she was saying 'Look how low the tide is.' And then we got pulled over by a cop, and I said, 'Please, Jen, please don't start joking around with him; let me do the talking,' and she said, 'Trust me,' but she had that wild-eyed look she gets—"

"I know that look well," Wallace said. "She had it when she was three."

"And I kept saying, 'Really, Jen, don't start joking; we'll end up in jail,' but she just beamed and rolled down the window of the car. And the cop comes over and says, 'Good morning, girls, may I see your license?' So Jen hands him her license, and he looked at it for a real long time, and then at her, and then back at the license, and Jennifer said, finally, 'If you're trying to think of who it reminds you of, it might be Angela Davis.' So the cop hands it back to her and says, 'Do you have any idea what speed you were going?' And Jen says, 'Well, I think it was about five miles an hour,' and the cop says, 'That's right. Now doesn't that strike you as a bit slow, since this is a highway of sorts?' And Jen says, 'Not under the circumstances.' She says, 'Since we're on LSD, and we're hallucinating wildly, and I can't really feel my hands or feet, and it's my dad's car.' "

"Oh, no," said Wallace, putting his head into his hands.

"So the cop starts laughing, and says, 'Sure, lady,' I swear to God, and Jen says she likes being out at this time because no one else is on the road, and the lagoon is most beautiful just before the sun rises, and the cop nods his head and says, 'All right, but be very careful about cars coming up behind you' blah blah blah, and Jen says, 'You bet, Officer; I guess there are a lot of *drunks* out at this time,' and the cop nods solemnly, and lets us go."

Wallace was laughing. "And you got off scot-free?"

"Yep," I said, "and lived to tell. Then we got up to the ridge, somehow, and when I was turning around at the top, I thought we were stuck in a five-foot snowdrift."

"In Northern California? In the summer?" Wallace asked.

"Yeah," said Kathleen. "And I believed her."

God, she has a wonderful laugh, from the belly, with her head thrown back.

"Great story," Wallace said. "But please, please don't play around with that stuff, that acid."

"Hey look, bub, you take your drugs and I'll take mine," I said.

"But my drugs are necessary for recovery, to keep me out of pain, to keep me happy so I can recover."

"So are mine," I said.

"Promise me," he said.

"I promise."

He smiled at both of us; his eyes looked tired, very clear and white but tired, as if he had *just* got up. "Hey, I think I'm about to conk out on you."

"I think I bore him stiff," Kathleen said to me. "Every time he's around me, he drops off."

"Never," said Wallace. "You never bore me. It's just that I'm so tired . . ."

"I was just kidding," said Kathleen.

"Sarah's in the bathtub," I said. "We're going to go downtown and get ice cream. You want me to bring you some? Blackberry?"

"I'd love some."

"O.K. Well, actually, to be perfectly *frank*, I need some money for the ice cream."

"How much?"

"A couple bucks."

"There's money in my jacket, on the chair," he said, pointing. I went and got two dollars from it, and stuffed the money into my jeans. "Are you flat broke again?"

"No," I said, smiling.

"How much money do you have these days?"

"Oh," I said, "about two dollars."

Kathleen and I sat with our ice-cream cones on the hillside above Clement, in the sun.

"Sure is good to have him home," she said.

"Sure is," I said.

"So how come you're so quiet all of a sudden?"

"I don't know. It's so weird to me that Dad went into the hospital looking healthy and perfect, and then he comes out and he's bruised and swollen and exhausted with a huge bloody scar cut into his head, and we all sit around commenting on how beautiful he looks now, but to me he looks awful."

"But it's all relative; he does look excellent compared to how he looked a week ago, and that goddamn tumor is gone."

"I know. Maybe it's different if someone you love gets hurt *first* and then they get put in the hospital and patched up and they look better than when they went in, but with Dad, first he looked fine and now he looks hurt."

"But the tumor had to be cut out."

"I *know*. I'm glad it was successful; I'm glad he's home. I'm not in a bad mood; I'm not even sad. I just think the whole situation sucks wind and it's sad for me to look at him."

Neither of us said anything else for a while. We watched the parade below. When I am in a fairly good mood—which I was—the townspeople below seem benignly eccentric, and I am moved to feelings of warmth, interest, friendliness, toward the strange and sometimes talented and often kind people of Clement. When I am in a bad mood, most of the

people strike me as ridiculous and terribly paranoid, pho-
nies, cowards, and losers.

There was a woman below, named Ellen, standing on the
curb in front of the gas station with her baby in a stroller,
looking down the road from time to time as if she were
waiting for a bus, but no buses come into Clement. Her
smile, as always, was empty and happy, and from up on the
hillside we could see the huge spaces between her teeth;
many of the Burn Outs have more gaps than teeth. Kathleen beside me had classically, almost aggressively perfect
teeth, huge and white and straight, with no cavities to boot.
It is one of the few things I don't like about her.

"Ellen's lost it completely. I wonder what it was. Too
much alcohol in her test tube, maybe."

"Too much acid," I said. "There but for fortune."

"I like to think we won't take it again," she said, "especially because we have that horrible impulse to drive to the
ridge, but I wouldn't put it past us. And I don't regret a second of it, even the part at the cabin where I thought my
parents were still alive and I almost freaked out. Even that
was worth it, but I don't ever want to have the experience
again. I wasn't at all sure that we'd recover from that one."

The view from the ridge on LSD is the most beautiful in
the world, especially in the late night and early morning.
The lagoon and the Pacific and the trees below us on the
ridge fill with lights of every color and change as the sun
very slowly comes up and the stars fade out; it is truly a
Disneyland E-ticket ride. It was worth every minute: those
times with Kathleen on the ridge were the most insanely
happy of my life, and my most spiritually convincing, but I
suppose it was worth it only because we recovered completely, made it back home safely, and no longer have acid
flashbacks. Or maybe not; maybe if you *don't* recover,
you're too burnt to realize it and you walk around with a
much lower dread and guilt level, maybe even peace of
your burnt-out mind. But then, too, maybe it isn't as
interesting.

One of my favorite women in town passed below us on the street in an African wedding dress of red linen. She looked up at us and waved. We waved our ice-cream cones at her.

She is about forty-five, brown and weathered and squinty and beautiful, the antithesis of modern beauty, square of face and body. She is one of the many, many serious drinkers in town, and a terrific drinking companion: she has lived on every continent at least once, and tried a little of everything and a lot of the things that kept delivering. For ten years, a long time ago, she was even a suburban housewife with spike heels and fish forks. For the last fifteen years she has traveled, physically and psychedelically, and until recently has carried a deadly African mushroom in her Moroccan pouch, wrapped in tinfoil alongside her psychedelics. She carried the mushroom just in case she ever got into a predicament from which she did not think she would—or would want to—recuperate. One day last year she accidentally left the Moroccan pouch at a friend's house after they had shared some mescaline. When she returned for it an hour later, the children of the house were playing with the pouch. She threw the mushroom down the friend's garbage disposal, and later told me that the only situation from which she would not be able to rally would be the death of a child resulting from her own stupidity.

"Too much heavy potential," she said of the mushroom.

When I returned to Wallace's house with a pint of blackberry ice cream, Randy was back from his errand. When I walked into the house, Wallace and Randy and Sarah were standing in the living room in hysterical laughter, one of the great sounds to walk into, so good to hear that I started laughing even before I saw the heron on the table.

The three-foot heron that Randy had found in the gorge at Limpet Beach a month ago was standing on the table, mounted on a piece of driftwood.

"Jesus God," I said. "It's beautiful, Randy; it's just a knockout. No kidding, it's phenomenal." Randy beamed. Wallace, between laughs, was shaking his head, as usual.

"Randy had it stuffed for me, illegally, of course. It's against federal law to have a heron stuffed. It's magnificent, isn't it?" The wings were folded, soft, subtle blue-green and gray with rust trim. "For the bird-watcher who has everything," said Wallace. He put his arm around Randy's shoulder. They didn't look at ease together, but they looked affectionate.

"I had an underground taxidermist do it," Randy explained. "I'm an outlaw now."

"Where'd you get the money?" I asked, and then regretted it.

"Oh, I just got it," he said. "And it's none of your business."

"Did you get it legally?" asked Wallace.

"Of course I got it legally. You think I'm selling smack to Sarah's third-graders or something? I sold some things. . . ."

"What things?" Wallace asked suspiciously.

"Oh, uh, your car, and—"

"No, seriously," said Wallace.

"Goddd," said Randy. "Nobody trusts me. I had most of the money in the bank from last summer."

Wallace tousled Randy's hair. "Well, shit," he said kindly, "it's such a lovely present, really it is, I can't think of anything to say. Thanks."

"You're welcome." Randy looked down at his enormous feet for a minute, rearranged his slightly lopsided mouth into an embarrassed smile, and then looked up with *his* wild-eyed look. "Look at that goddamn bird!" he roared, and all four of us laughed harder than I can remember any of us laughing in a long, long time. The heron looked out at the proceedings with his or her yellow marble eyes, unruffled, and I saw signs of recovery all around me.

Paranoia

There was no mail in our post-office box on the morning after Wallace returned home. I stood staring disconsolately into the empty box for a moment and then called through the box to the postmistress, "Angela! Someone has been stealing my mail again! There is nothing in the box!"

"I haven't put out all the first-class mail yet," said a female voice. "Come back in half an hour."

I went outside and sat on the bench to enjoy another glorious Clement summer day—the fog had burned away by noon and the wind today was not quite as bitter as yesterday—and to watch the parade of Clement friends and acquaintances. The town was buzzing with gossip of a heroin bust, Julia Randall's recent diagnosis of lung cancer, the destruction of the bar's jukebox by a young man who hated the disco-music selections, and the recent abdominal surgery of Melanie Reese's cow (who had swallowed a piece of wire from a bale of hay and had had a magnet sown into her belly to attract any future wires). I sat on the bench like a ship's rat, absorbing the details; gossip thrives in Clement, defines Clement, poisons Clement, and fascinates us all when we wonder how much of our own aberrant, sordid lives is on public file. The wind drove me back inside the post-office lobby, where the loudest male voice was insisting that They had tried to besmirch his name and reputation with the business about the utilities bribe, and that in fact, shortly after he was released from Napa State, They had knocked him unconscious and injected cancer cells into his arms, which now ache all the time. He glared at me when I walked past him to my mailbox. Help me, help me, I thought, the paranoids are after me.

There was a letter from my uncle Colin, who has known me since I was born and has been one of my best friends for at least five years. He knows me as well as my dream consultant, or my family, has frequently brilliant and amusing insights into human nature, has several preposterous theories whose validity he insists upon (to wit: that beer bubbles can sneak into your bloodstream and kill you), and has written to me every day since my father's surgery.

"Darling Neurotic," the letter began,

"Of *course* I don't think it is wrong for you to be the way you are: unmeticulous, disorderly, absent-minded. These are characteristics that often are wonderful and interesting and loving, and to reject them is to reject artistic ability and joy in living. All the tight-assed perfectionists in the world aren't worth one Pablo Casals or one Einstein or one Margaret Mead. I find your stylistic differences to be endearing as long as they do not inconvenience me, or cause my feelings to be hurt. You and I have now gone for almost two months without a major Personality Conflict, which for two such difficult, demanding people is no small feat; and as always we will be able to discuss Things when and if they go sour, and will be closer for having broached the issues.

(I thought we had long ago agreed that I was the soul of patience, understanding and general excellent humor, and that such interpersonal difficulties as may occur between us were due entirely to your inabilities in the area of rational behavior and maturity and goddamn fucking good MANNERS, you little shit. And yes, I love you very much: perhaps I am developing even higher levels of sublime consciousness, wherein I don't even notice your indiscretions, and people will collect and save my toe parings and put them in a shrine.)

Come see me soon. I know you are in the midst of great inner angst and confusion and mistrust because of the royal cosmic screwing your father has gotten. I hope and know that you are relieving much of the pressure with humor, love and physical exertion. We will all love your dad especially well these days and he will be all right, and you will be all right also, tempered by the experience and back in the psychic saddle. Tennis and friendly sex are excellent therapies, as is awareness. Remember two things which we have discussed before: one, that obsession breeds paranoia, and two, that the world of sometimes unbelievably gross and silly and cruel and pitiable "adults" which you now observe with proper distaste is always there, waiting for the unwary young to join it in a few years.

Can you come for lunch Friday? Around noon? I will even let you give me a haircut, if you promise not to sell the clippings to other women.

I read the letter over, smiling, and walked jauntily outside, where I inadvertently nudged the utility briber in passing. He jumped. I apologized. Poor bastard, I thought smugly as I began the walk up the hillside to my cabin. It must be hell to be so paranoid.

The phone was ringing at the cabin when I walked into the familiar and comfortable clutter; two weeks ago in a fit of reform and remorse I had put all the clothes in the closet, stacked the books and magazines neatly against the wall, shaken out the rug, shaken the crumbs out of the toaster, washed the dishes and the sink and the stove and the refrigerator, and zealously vowed to be organized and tidy for the rest of my life. One week and four days ago the magazines and books and clothes had found their way back to their favorite haunts—the bed, tables, refrigerator, desk, and floor. The toothbrush was back in the silverware drawer, dirty cups and glasses sat on the papers on my desk, and my Things Not to Lose file was nowhere to be found. (Even so, I am much neater now than I was five years ago, when I moved from San Francisco to the cabin with a large carton of dirty dishes among my belongings.)

The phone stopped ringing a moment before I picked it up. I opened a beer and looked at the grandmother clock above the bookcase, which read five-thirteen, which is what it has read for the last fifteen years; it remains for purely aesthetic reasons, a fact that does not deter me from looking up at it occasionally and thinking, Hmmm, five-thirteen; must be time for a beer. I called the Time Lady, who said that the time was five-eleven and twenty seconds. I listened to her recitations until she said that the time was five-thirteen, and then hung up, glancing at the clock and nodding to myself.

The phone rang again. I rolled my eyes and picked it up.

"Hello?" I said.

"Hello! Tony Beerbohn. How you doing?"

"Fine." I am not an animated phone conversationalist.

"I'm calling to invite you to a pot-luck tonight, my house, sevenish. I think it's going to be a lot of fun. Will you be able to come?"

"Gee," I said, "I don't think so, not tonight. I've already got plans." My plans involved lying on my bed, reading.

"Damn! I thought it would be an excellent time for us to get to know each other. Well, I'll try to give you advance warning next time."

"O.K. Thanks anyway. I hope it's fun."

"Really. See you later. Good to talk to you again."

"Yeah. O.K. See you." I hung up and congratulated myself on having turned down yet another party invitation. It is sometimes a difficult decision to make in spite of the fact that many Clement parties, of the cocktail or pot-luck persuasion, that I have gone to in the last four years have been dull and irritating and nerve-racking, difficult because there are just enough really excellent parties to keep one playing the party game. In this case the lure of party food and entertainment was easily outweighed by the fact that I cannot stand Tony Beerbohn, who is a dolt and a hypocrite (my dream consultant refers to him as a walking bundle of neuroses and hostility with good teeth) and who retains a booming New England accent despite having lived twenty-five of his forty years in California: his accent increases with every drink until he sounds like Bobby Kennedy for a while, and then he forgets to do his accent altogether.

The less I have to do with community endeavors the less paranoid my life is, especially since the diagnosis of the brain tumor. Parties have become breeding grounds of paranoia for me unless they are given by family or good friends. There are three possibilities that usually manifest at the parties I attend: one is that I will not know the people well, and perhaps the party food will consist of a nasturtium salad and a Scotch-broom sauté, and I will be so shy and intimidated and condescending that, in Virginia Woolf's words, I will sit in a corner looking like a deaf-mute waiting for a funeral to begin; another possibility is that I will find myself having a good time drinking, and smoking marijuana, find myself talking a good deal, and then find myself saying incredibly vapid, nervous things that then hang in the air above my head sounding not only empty and inappropriate but also as if Minnie or Mickey Mouse were speaking; and the third possibility is that people I do not know well will ask tactless questions about my father's illness ("Is it true your father is dying of lung cancer?").

All three possibilities became reality at the last party I attended and I still managed to have a good time until the music stopped and the hostess read an hour-long poem that went like this: My man / our breath / our love / the ocean breathes into the fullness of our moon-love / of my man / of myself / on a plane of light and child-breath / in the womb of the earth / my man / in my womb / breathing / he / I / ONE. It was at this point that I made my decision to do myself and the community a favor by not attending Clement soirees, unless conditions were very promising, and a pot-luck at Tony Beerbohn's did not qualify.

Well, I thought, opening a beer, that was easy. Another paranoia-free evening coming up. My father is recovering from brain surgery, and I am recovering from my undiagnosed hebephrenia. I am wont to make self-congratulatory discernments whenever I act significantly less stupid than I might have in the past, and I often end up wolfing down my words.

I spent the next two hours calmly and productively, with a live broadcast of Joan Armatrading on KSAN, a roaring fire, another beer, and the sense that all was all right with the world. I washed the dishes, made vegetable soup, and sorted through the papers on my desk, finding in the process a long-lost description of recent laboratory experiments involving rats and various acne theories. (Half the adolescent rats were kept clean, well fed, and were free of facial blemishes, whereas the other half were kept dirty, fed on junk food and coffee, hassled all day long by the scientists, and consequently developed little rat-sized pimples on their chins and foreheads. I think I was stoned when I wrote it, and am not at all sure why I was pleased to find it.) At eight, when the sun was only a few inches above the horizon, I rolled a joint, dressed warmly, and headed down the road to the Point, which is the best seat in town for the sunset and only a few hundred feet away from my cabin. There were no people or machines on the road, and I thought that if the continuing work on my own pathologies progressed as admirably as it had been, I would soon find myself the sanest, healthiest, freest person in town, if not the world. Smugness, while alone and amid almost indescribable natural beauty, is one of the finest emotions in my repertoire.

The Point is a salience of earth and vegetation overlooking the reef and the Pacific Ocean, and is one of the sanctuaries in Clement—along with the ridge and the lagoon—to which I come daily. It takes an enormous amount of distraction to slow down the voices in my mind to the point where I lose the sense of having a body solely for the purpose of transporting my head around. I lay in the grass on the visibly penultimate ledge, ten feet away from what was either the cliff or a ledge, beneath which there was another, and I smoked most of the joint as I scrutinized the sun, an inch above the water, and the sky above the sun, roses above the reds, purple above the rose, and then successively darker areas of blue. I propped myself up on elbows to watch the pelicans on the reef, and relaxed enough so that one elbow promptly buckled under me and I collapsed onto my back. I rolled my eyes, looked over my shoulder at the three houses fifty feet away, to see if anyone was watching—no one was—and I laughed at my self-consciousness, having vaguely suspected that at least one person was watching me with binoculars, chuckling. I turned back to the seascape, took a few deep breaths, and relaxed again. Marijuana does absolute wonders for sunsets, sex, and music, but has the unfortunate side effect of occasionally heightening feelings of anxiety. I closed my eyes and listened to the very lovely sound of no wind, to song sparrows singing from the coyote bush, to seagulls above and on the calm, steel-gray-blue ocean, and to footsteps that were undeniably headed in my direction. Rats, I thought, I want the whole Point to myself. The interloper's footsteps got very close and then veered off to the right, where there is another subpoint ten feet away. I very, *very* surreptitiously glanced over, moving my eyes without moving my head, and for a microsecond made eye contact with the Hulk, who was looking at *me* clandestinely and holding a long-handled trowel.

The Hulk lives somewhere in the vicinity of the cabin,

keeps an extremely low profile, is roughly the size of Orson Welles but taller, and sports a crew cut. I have seen him perhaps ten times in four years, and have never seen him in anything but gunmetal-gray sweat clothes—the old-fashioned kind that athletes wore before the advent of Sweat-suit Chic—with Loafers and yellow socks. I have never spoken with him, but Megan claims that once she said hello to him and he made a dinosaur noise at her. It was getting darker, I was slightly stoned, and ten feet away stood a three-hundred-fifty-pound man with a *trowel* and a crew cut. Oh, dear, I thought when my adrenaline attack had subsided, I'm going to be murdered.

I looked over again out of the corner of my eye. The man was staring at the ocean and I started to breathe again. I was amused for a moment by my paranoia, until the Hulk looked over again. I looked away and started humming softly. Relax, I told myself; breathe. The most popular media murderer of the hour, Son of Sam, came into my mind, and I decided that there was all the difference in the world between his victims and myself, the difference being that I was not a person who was *supposed* to be murdered, whereas they obviously were, because they were dead.

I have never known a person who was murdered except in Vietnam, although I do know one murderer, the mother of a high-school friend who beat her second husband to death with a champagne bottle. This is ridiculous, I thought. Relax; you're not going to be murdered; just ignore him—I immediately glanced over just as he was glancing away from me. Please, God, I thought, get me out of this one; I'll stop smoking; I'll start dental-flossing and jogging; I've got a softball game tomorrow, for Christ's sake. . . . Oh, this is stupid, Jennifer; he's your *neighbor*—

At this point my neighbor made a loud, racking, primal noise. I jumped, sitting down, and looked over. He was kneading his nose with a handkerchief, and when he finished, he began walking slowly toward me.

He was staring at the ground as he walked, and although he did not look psychotic and was not exposing himself to me, the twilight created surreal lighting in which a humongous male with a trowel was quite close, and the soundtrack of the shower scene in *Psycho* began to play in my mind. In the twenty seconds it took him to walk the ten feet, I thought briefly of the really sordid secrets and belongings people would find in my cabin after my death, I thought about how badly my relatives and friends would feel when they learned of my mutilation, I thought about possible karmic explanations, and I thought about escape.

The only escape possibility at this point was over the cliff and I didn't know if it was a straight drop or a gradation of eroded slopes. If it was a straight drop, it would mean a disgusting and messy death, and it could also be that the Hulk *knew* it was a straight drop and that this in fact was his *modus operandi*, to intimidate young women into jumping off the cliff (after which he would stand above the cliffs looking down at their bodies, rubbing his hands together and possibly getting an erection). I thought about how posthumously *embarrassing* it would all be, especially if I ran over the cliff and fell three hundred feet onto the reef, and how the neighbors (who were watching me through their binoculars) would tell the police and the press that they'd seen the whole thing: "It was the damndest thing; Jennifer was sitting there on a ledge watching the sunset, and Jim Baxter—you know, the heavyset guy who runs the Guide Dogs for the Blind school in the city—walks past her and she jumps up and looks wildly around and then runs over the side of the cliff; it all happened in a split second. . . ."

"Hello," he said in a dull baritone as he walked past me and headed back up the dirt road. "Hello," I said much too loudly.

Phew, I thought as his footsteps receded. I almost exploded with a sense of ease and deliverance and felt as if I had been pumped full of helium: relief is an extraordinarily satisfying state of mind, as powerful as its antithesis, as overreactive fear. Perhaps I conjur up these horrifying possibilities so that when they prove to be unfounded, I will experience the succor of a load off my mind, a good, if unnecessary, trade. I walked buoyantly back to my cabin, and laughed somewhat patronizingly at myself: David Bromberg wrote a song that goes, "Run and get the hatchet, there's a fly on the baby's head," and I whistled it, cheerfully, in the moonlight, filled with antiparanoid resolve.

After dinner I sat in the rocking chair, reading, for about an hour. I read six pages in that hour and later that evening had absolutely no idea what book it had been. Eventually I figured out that my interest was not in reading, and I thought of someone I wanted to talk to, went and dialed the number, and had forgotten whom I was calling by the time it started ringing. No one answered. I stood staring at old pictures of my family on the wall; I couldn't take my eyes off what my family used to be: my grandparents as college graduates; my parents when they were my age; my brothers and I as young children; my recently deceased alley cat as a kitten; my father, who now looks so old and bruised and scarred, as a handsome, skinny young man holding Ben, who was an infant.

Looking at old pictures, especially after a family crisis, is as profound an experience both cellularly and intellectually as is staring into one's own eyes for a long time while very stoned. It was sometimes disturbing—to think for instance that, barring death, I would turn out to be a middle-aged person and then an older person; that by the time my skin cleared up, I would have wattles, and those crepey flaps of skin at the top of the arms called "kimono arms"; and that I couldn't help but believe that everybody in my family would eventually die. It makes me sad to see pictures of myself at young ages, and to know that though I had it easy (relative to, say, my friend who was fellating her father and uncle when she was eight), there were great terrors and cruelties and humiliations that parallel anything I have found and experienced in the adult world. Looking at old pictures of my brothers and myself, I find it hard to believe that the three of us survived with our psyches as intact as they are.

I sat down at the typewriter and wrote about earlier days for two hours. I wrote about when I was five years old and Ben told me that he'd overheard my parents planning to stab me to death that night because they were broke and couldn't afford me and besides, I'd broken the car window the day before. I wrote about the years when Ben tortured me with snakes, letting them loose in my room when my lights were out and then calling affectionately, "Oh, Jennnn. Wake up. I just dropped a snake on your floor, but don't worry, because it's only three feet long." I wrote about early hikes with my father, about my mother as a young beautiful woman, about our first house and earliest holidays and about when two other grandparents were alive, about my childhood crimes and adventures and insecurities. A story started to form in my mind, about a race of people who were born aged and got younger and younger until they finally disappeared back into their amniotic fluids, which turned out to be what heaven was.

I abandoned my story, picked up the dictionary, and took it to bed. I looked up the word that had been on my mind all day, "paranoia," and found its roots: "para," a prefix meaning both "alongside of" and "faulty," or "amiss," and "nous," meaning "mind" or "intellect." I saw it as a voice alongside the intellect giving faulty interpretations as the mind went along reverberating with sensory information, a whiny and defensive voice that saw hostility where, perhaps, there wasn't any.

Just before I fell asleep that night, I learned also that "antipasto" means "before the food," whereas I have thought all my life that it meant foods that were the opposite of pastas, i.e., nonstarchy, and I laughed out loud happily for a minute before dropping off soundly.

Several hours later I awoke from a nightmare in which my father, with bloody bandages on his head, was trying to put out a fire on (of all things) my bed while the phone rang and a dozen household machines (which I don't own) whirred. I felt instant relief upon waking, until I had the sensation that someone was in my cabin. I turned the light on, and was alone. It was two-thirty and I was wide awake but the light hurt my eyes and I turned it off. There are only a few things one can do alone in the dark, one of which is to anxiety-attack oneself, another to calm oneself through breathing and relaxation exercises, and yet another is to abuse oneself, which is the best.

I rubbed my belly for a long time, slowly and sensuously, and thought what a really warm, soft stomach I have, and in fact what an excellent body I have, strong and coordinated and responsive. I moved my hand downward and began tracing various routes around my pubic hair while I fantasized about making love with two homosexual men while Merv Griffin watched, but then my finger stopped suddenly alongside a pea-sized lump next to my crotch. A lump! Within seconds I had decided that it was cancer, and that I had possibly six months to live, and that, furthermore, it was cancer of my privates; I had cancer of the *yoni*! Creeping Jesus, I thought, how embarrassing.

I had an adrenaline attack that resembled a moment of sudden fright on LSD, or those moments when time stops in an out-of-control car. The network of nerves called the celiac plexus, located at the top of the abdomen, in front of the aorta, was charged with electricity suddenly and my body went rigid, and—the worst part of fear attacks—my inner voices started whirring, like a Robert Altman soundtrack.

God! I thought, cancer; I've got cancer; I'm going to have to *tell* people I've got cancer. Jesus Christ, how embarrassing; I'm going to die *young*. I know that if your parents have tumors or cancer, you are more apt to develop them yourself, but I'm twenty-three. This is ridiculous. I thought maybe I'd last another thirty years, but no, here I've gone and grown a tumor; everybody is going to think I'm neurotic and self-destructive; I *am* neurotic and self-destructive. People will think I'm such a *jerk* when I tell them. Jesus, *cancer*, the Big C, just like the skinny pathetic Americans posing for *Newsweek* at the Clinica de Laetrile or whatever it's called. Why me? Why not Idi Amin? *What on Earth did I do to deserve this?* I fingered the lump. Definitely malignant. The more I thought about it, the more things I had done to deserve it. It could be the really hateful manipulative things I've done over the years; it could be the indirect means I have used to get people out of my life who didn't want to go—lovers, friends who had come to bore or irritate me, Jehovah's Witnesses. It could be all the lies to save face and money; it could be all the punishments I have inflicted on my brothers and my mother. It could be my moral indiscretions. It could be that I am being punished for being an imposter, a charlatan, a hypocrite, a manipulator, a conceit— my *skunks*, I thought; it has something to do with my skunks.

A faint and patronizing voice said, "Relax, there is some explanation for this; tomorrow a gynecologist will tell you that it's something routine and banal; you're a *good* girl, Jen; keep calm till tomorrow; you'll see, truth and beauty will win out once again." I touched the lump, pushed it from side to side, rolled it under my fingers. Another adrenaline attack and I was once again condemning myself to death in six months from a tumor, which, the more I thought about it, had some advantages, such as the Brompton cocktail, guaranteed to take the edge off anything. So there was that to look forward to, and there was an enormous amount of attention and affection to look forward to, and there were the added enticements of no more painful relationships, no more having to watch people in my family get sick, no more pimples (death being one of the few known cures), no more

dental drilling and root canal, no more laundry or night-
mares or adrenaline attacks. And no more sex or music or
laughter or chocolate or family or friends or sunsets or
drugs or my writing or getting to be this person that I am
and am becoming. A lousy trade, and the panic set back in.

How can I tell my family? I wondered. They'll fall apart,
I'll fall apart, and my dream consultant will definitely fall
apart. I will be indirectly responsible for all sorts of nervous
breakdowns and psychic collapses but at least I won't have
to watch over the years as the people I love most get sick or
go nuts or die. My dream consultant and my brothers will
have the worst time of it, but maybe they'll be subliminally
relieved, maybe they'll get so much sympathy and love
after I die that it will have been worth it to them. Cancer!
Cancer has become incredibly popular lately. *Everybody*'s
getting cancer; it's as popular a subject at cocktail parties as
nuclear annihilation or human potential or Gary Gilmore.
But I am not one of the people who are supposed to get
cancer; there has been a tragic mistake made; my dream
consultant has told me that I do not have to worry about
breast cancer for a few more years but that I am in the
prime age group for multiple sclerosis—why on earth did
she tell me this? she's my best friend—and I've felt miscel-
laneous and ominous aches and twinges since she told me.

There was absolutely nothing in the house along the lines
of chemical comfort—no alcohol, no dope, no tranquilizers,
no Brompton cocktails—so I breathed rhythmically into my
belly and thought about the possessions I had to get rid of
before I died to spare myself posthumous exposure—the
Clearasil, the dirty books, Frank Sinatra's *Greatest Hits,* and
the festering clothes at the back of the closet. As long as I
don't die before the morning, I thought as I began to fall
asleep, I can dispense with the really *icky* evidences of my
existence. The first prayer I ever knew came into my mind,
and I smiled as I thought about the terror it had inspired in
me as a six-year-old to think, as I prayed "If I should die

before I wake, I pray the Lord my soul to take," that there was even the slightest chance that I would die before I woke. *This* is the sort of stuff adults give to children for reassurance? I thought. No wonder we're all so afraid. And, so saying, I fell asleep soundly and woke up alive in the morning.

I called my father while the coffee water boiled.

"How are you?" I asked.

"Excellent! I feel better every day. And you?"

"Oh, fine," I said. "I'm going to need your car sometime today, to go over the hill."

"O.K. by me; I won't be using it. What are you doing over the hill?"

"Well, I'm doing all *sorts* of things over the hill, like, uh, going to the Civic Center Library, and, uh . . ."

"Uh, you don't have to, uh, tell me, you know," he said, chuckling. "Just don't get caught."

I called my gynecologist after three cups of coffee and four cigarettes. While dialing the number, I decided to be perfectly straightforward—this was, after all, my *life* I was talking about—but when the receptionist answered, I felt guilty and rattled.

"What would you like to see the doctor about?" she asked.

"I'd like to get a pap smear and a VD check," I replied.

"Have you been exposed to gonorrhea or syphilis?"

"Not that I know of." I *have* been exposed to cancer, however, and I'm afraid I've caught it and have only six months to live; no, I couldn't tell her that, and I also didn't want her to think I slept with the sort of people who get venereal diseases (although I actually did get gonorrhea four years ago, from a lawyer).

"Well, if you haven't been exposed, I'll give you an appointment for next week when Doctor isn't so busy. . . ."

"I forgot to mention that I've been itching like crazy, if

you know what I mean. I was sort of embarrassed to mention it. . . ."

"Yes, of course, dear. Come in at noon; I'm sure Doctor will be able to see you then."

I drove over the hill singing loudly along with the radio and taking in the extraordinary beauty of the mountain greens and the sky. One of my favorite Clement poets wrote a book called *All This Every Day*, which I consider to be the finest mantra, and I thought, Gee, all *this* (trees, sun, birds, flowers) every day, for the next six months.

A friend of my father's who was dying of cancer said, "Well, at least I won't have to read about Patty Hearst anymore," an attitude I found somehow reassuring, although I would not mind reading about Patty Hearst for sixty more years, if that were part of the bargain.

My gynecologist is an elderly woman with white hair and kind blue eyes. I am only a little afraid of her, whereas with male gynecologists I have always been paranoid and slightly hysterical. (And sometimes for good reason. Three years ago I went to a male doctor, told him I wanted to start taking the pill and to have my IUD removed after I had been on the pill long enough to be protected. "Fine," he said. I was lying on my back with my legs in the stirrups, feeling vulnerable and exposed. "This is going to hurt," he said, and since it was a routine examination, I asked casually, "*What* is going to hurt?" He held up a pair of gynecological pliers and said, "You'll feel a slight twinge as I am removing the IUD." I bolted upright and said, "Chrrrist! Three seconds ago I told you I wanted it removed after I had been on the pill for a couple of weeks! Weren't you listening?" I gave him my meanest look. "Oh, yes, of course. Now be a good girl and lie back down." I didn't. I got dressed and left, found my current gynecologist, and have given her all my business ever since.)

"Itching, huh?" said my doctor. I was sitting upright on

the table, naked, worrying about whether my socks smelled or not. "Lie back and relax, dear, and I'll have a look."

"I'd like a pap smear and a VD check, also, please."

"All right." She looked around for a few minutes, took pap and venereal-disease smears, examined my breasts, and then shook her head. "There's no evidence of infection, no yeast; in fact, you look very, very healthy. I have no idea why you should be itching. . . ."

"Actually, the itching has gotten quite a bit better in the last couple of hours," I said. "But there was one other thing." She looked at me with kindness and interest. "There's a . . . lump near my crotch," I said in a melodramatic voice, "here," and I indicated the site of my malignant tumor. She felt it lightly with her fingers.

"A lymph node," she said, smiling. "A very slightly infected lymph node. You have them all over your body. This one could be irritated for any number of reasons, and I'm sure it will clear up by itself within a month or so."

"Ah," I said nonchalantly, flooded with relief, "that's pretty much what I thought. I really wasn't worried, just thought I'd mention it, better safe than sorry hah hah hah." Now that I didn't have to worry about losing my life, it was once again important that I not lose face; I didn't want her to think I was a *hypochondriac*, for Christ's sake.

"Call me in a month if it hasn't gone away, and in the meantime, drop these slides off at the lab across the street and we'll give you a call if anything shows up."

"Well, thank you," I said, beginning to get dressed. "Thank you very much." She nodded, smiled affectionately, and walked to the door.

"Good-bye," she said.

"Good-bye. Thank you," I said.

"You're welcome, dear."

"O.K., well, 'bye," I babbled. "Thanks again."

The stunning, delicious sense of relief filled my body. I fairly ran across the street to the lab, smiling to pedestrians, whistling, laughing about the last twelve hours in my life, and so thrilled by my health and vitality and impending sanity—so thrilled that I got to keep being alive for more than six months—that the lab clerk's nasal officiousness did nothing to dampen my spirits. I gave him the slides, my name, doctor, and phone number while mentally listing the blessings of my life.

He wrote down the information and then, looking up mechanically, said, "That will be fourteen dollars."

"Fourteen dollars!" I said with incredulous hostility. "Highway robbery!"

One Day with
Wallace

O
n the first day of September, a year to the day since I saw Wallace naked for the first time in twenty years, I awoke at the crack of nine from a dream in which I chased a tiny and mysterious old man, of whom I was absolutely terrified, through dark alleys: I was chasing him because I had to see his face, but chasing him was as frightening as being chased. When I caught up, he whirled around to face me, a three-foot man with open sores on every inch of his face who held his hands like a cat, with claws exposed, eyes and mouth leering.

I was sitting upright when I awoke, screaming at the top of my lungs, and I looked to see if I was alone in bed, which I was. For the last month I have not been all that much fun to sleep with: sound asleep, I shout or talk loudly until whoever I am sleeping with—Megan, Kathleen, or a lover—wakes me. I was gapingly alone that morning, rattled by the dream, rattled by a sudden and unshakable hunch that something important that had to do with the brain tumor was in the works, and rattled by how often these days I was feeling fear, anger, and sadness.

I called Wallace but he didn't answer. Sunshine streamed through the cabin windows, and I heated up yesterday's coffee in a saucepan with an enormous amount of milk. I poured myself a mugful and took it outside to the front step of the cabin. A light, waffled fog hovered over the ocean, and I sat waiting for Wallace to appear, because I knew, for no reason, that he would.

I stared at the ocean, the sky, and the vegetation at my feet and around me, partly chanting Joanne's line, "All this every day," and partly thinking about the man's face in my dream, until my father pulled up in his Mazda, ten minutes later.

"Surprise," he said without much enthusiasm, and got out of his car. He had made a remarkable recovery in the three weeks since surgery: the bruises were gone, his hair was starting to grow back, and his neck was only twice its original size.

"I thought you'd never get here," I said.

"Were you expecting me?"

"Yeah, sort of. Do you want a cup of coffee?"

"Sure." He looked like a rosy Buddhist monk with a headache, and sat down on the step. "The biopsy results are in," he said as I stood up. "My doctor called and wants to see me this morning."

"Ohhh," I said, freezing up inside. "So the *biopsy* results are in. God! Maybe it's good news. . . ."

"They tell you the good news over the phone. They say, 'I wanted you to know as soon as possible.' My doctor said he wanted to talk to me, in his office. I'm sure it's the biopsy."

"Can I go with you?" I asked calmly. My pulse was whirring.

"Yeah," he said. "Sure. I haven't been able to reach Sarah—she's off with the faculty. I'd love your company, as a matter of fact." I went to the kitchen for the coffee, and Wallace followed me inside. The phone rang, and I handed Wallace a mug.

"Hello?" I asked.

"Guess what?" Megan asked.

"What?"

"I'm leaving today, instead of next week."

"Oh, no," I said. "I thought maybe you'd enlisted, or developed a goiter. . . . ."

"Nope, but I'm leaving. Some friends of my mom are driving to Portland tonight and they have room for me, and we won't have to pay for a plane ticket. And I'm leaving in a couple of hours."

"Well, that's terrible news," I said. "And I'm leaving for over the hill in a few minutes." Wallace raised a finger. "Hang on," I told Megan, and looked questioningly at Wallace.

"You don't have to go," he said.

"Who's that?" Megan asked.

"Dad. I don't know what he's babbling about." I waved to him and continued talking. "I really think you should reconsider this, Megan. What do you need to go to school for? All you learn in seventh grade is the capital of Bolivia. Stick around awhile; I'll teach you everything I know." Wallace laughed. "I'm going to miss you wildly," I said, which was true, and at the same time I was aware of the relief mixed in with the sadness: when I left college friends and my friends at the magazine, I cried off and on for several days, but was glad that I got to be alone again.

"Well, I want to see my mother—and I live there, you know, and I like that school, but maybe I'll come down for Thanksgiving. And I sort of don't want to see you today, because, well, you know, and I haven't even packed yet."

"O.K., Megan, I guess this is it. Thanks for everything; hello and love to your mother. I sure had fun."

"Well, O.K., me too. Tell your family good-bye; tell Randy I hope he likes school; tell the college graduate goodbye; tell Wallace love and good-bye, and Colin also."

"O.K. Geeee," I said sadly, but it was one of those sadnesses that are clean and temporary, one of those sadnesses that come when you are saying good-bye to somebody you love. I looked over at Wallace, who sat with his coffee and read a *New Yorker* in the rocking chair, serious and sad.

"Well," I said to Megan after a long pause, "good-bye, I guess."

"Well, good-bye, Jen; see you around; I'll miss you."

"Me too. Good-bye." There was a long pause, and neither of us hung up.

"O.K.," she said. "Good-bye."

"O.K. See ya round."

"O.K. You got any last parting words?"

"As a matter of fact, I do. Megan," I said with utmost solemnity, "as you go through life, remember one thing: the opera's not over till the fat lady sings." Megan and Wallace both laughed. "Eavesdropping, you old coot?" I asked Wallace with my hand over the receiver. He nodded.

"Who said that?" she asked.

"I don't know. Did you say that, Wallace?" I asked.

"I didn't say it. You just said it."

"I didn't say it," I told Megan.

"Is this a crank call?" she asked.

"It most certainly is. Good-bye, good-bye, good-bye. I love you; I'm about to hang up; good-bye," I said.

"'Bye," she said softly, and hung up.

"Sure is hard to say good-bye, isn't it?" I asked Wallace. "To the happy few?" I sighed deeply, and smiled at him. He nodded. He has had jowls ever since the surgery, which quiver when he shakes or nods his head. It is a shock to watch a human body and face that you are intimately acquainted with age quickly, "overnight." My mental picture of him was evolved over twenty-three years, and I have not had time to adjust to five years' worth of facial aging in the course of three weeks. It changes every aspect of my time sense: time has simultaneously been devaluated (five years for the price of three weeks, or vice versa), and time, the time that we have now, has become everything.

"Do you want another cup of coffee?" I asked.

"No, I think we'd better get going. Do you mind?"

"No, of course not." He stood, took his coffee cup to the

sink, brushed a few dog hairs off his pullover, and stood holding the door open. He did not even remotely resemble a person who was about to find out whether or not he had brain cancer, although I think I might have, behind my concerned yet stalwart façade. My family specializes in the concerned yet stalwart façade when one of us is in trouble, and each can see through the others' façades but assumes that his or her own is impenetrable. I grabbed a sweater and walked to the door, where I stopped, and looked up at Wallace for a minute. He seemed at first to be staring off a million miles away, but was looking at a large school picture of Randy at ten that hung next to the schoolroom clock (which said five-thirteen, of course). When Wallace looked at me, there was just a trace of foreboding in his face, and he winked slowly. What a lousy joke this all is, I thought, and we left.

We drove in silence out of town. I felt scared, angry, impotent, and a sense of relief—the relief of knowing that the other shoe was going to drop—and assumed, knew somehow, that Wallace felt the same. I think in most ways I know Wallace better than anyone else does, but because Wallace does not brag, complain, drop little details about his achievements, or make loud noises (except when he is telling stories), there are hundreds of things I don't know. His friends have told me more about his accomplishments than he has. Several months ago when Wallace and I were sitting around drinking Irish whiskey, I mentioned for some reason that my brothers, his sons, are two of the most generous people I know. Wallace agreed, and then told me something that he'd never told another person: the head of the English Department at Yale has written in Wallace's academic file that Wallace possessed one of the broadest streaks of generosity that the professor had encountered. Both of my parents are so generous that they almost never have any money to speak of. That Wallace is generous is as much of a secret to the people who know him as is the fact that I have exceedingly curly hair.

I looked at Wallace as we approached the lagoon and knew him not only as a grown-up child can know a parent but also as an adult friend might know another.

We drove around the lagoon, which was still and green-blue and filled with birds, shore birds pecking for food, mud hens and ducks and egrets in the water, pelicans and gulls and more egrets in the air.

"O.K., what's that?" he asked, pointing at a dark-blue bird on the telephone wire. He has tried to teach us everything he knows about bird-watching ever since I can remember, to not much avail, except that he has instilled in me a great enthusiasm for watching birds. I can describe them to him with a detailed eye ("brown hooked beak, brown primaries, yellow wings") but I usually can't name the species.

"A jay," I said. "But not a blue jay"—I imitated his slightly professorial voice—"because we don't have the common blue jay on the Pacific Coast."

He laughed, recognizing his tone and words, and said, "What kind of jay?"

"Hey, man, I'm not into labels, ya know?"

"Any idea? Look at the crest, and the darkness of the blue . . ."

"Stellar's jay," I said.

"All right!" he said cheerfully. "And that one." He pointed to a zebra-necked killdeer above the water.

"You insult my intelligence," I scoffed. "A killdeer."

"Right! And that one." He indicated a small, long-beaked shore bird up ahead of us on the bank of the lagoon. Most shore birds look alike to me, and I like to think of them all as sandpipers.

"A vulture," I shouted triumphantly.

He laughed. "Try again."

"A cormorant?" I asked, stabbing in the dark. "Cedar wax wing?"

"Noooo," he said, pained.

"O.K., I give up."

"It's a sandpiper," he said.

"Beautiful, beautiful day," he said a while later, as he eased the car around the first curve on the mountain road.

"Yeah. Did I tell you about Joanne's book, *All This Every Day*?" He nodded. "I told her what a great mantra it makes, and how often I think of it whenever I'm outside in Clement, or on the mountain, and she said, 'You can think of it in other ways, too, like "All *this*?" ' I held my hands outward and up, like Job. ' "Every day?" ' "

"Or 'All this, *every* day?' "

We climbed up the mountain, headed toward the oncologist's office. I kept looking at Wallace, wondering uneasily about the biopsy—benign or malignant, life or death. If God appeared to me and said, "You'll be at the doctor's soon, there's a fifty-fifty chance that the tumor is malignant, and here's my deal: if you give up one of your arms, it'll be benign; otherwise I can't promise you anything," I would accept it. I wouldn't give it a second thought, which may be infantile and neurotic but which is crystal clear to me. If the deal was a guarantee of fifteen or twenty years of good health for my father, and then his instant death, I would be inclined to accept it, but luckily I wasn't offered any deals.

"Hey, Dad, do you have any feeling one way or another as to whether it will be benign or malignant?"

"Well, baby, I'm a lifelong optimist—cynical but optimistic—so most of me thinks it will be benign. I simply cannot imagine a world without me. And then there's a small part of me that loves life so much that I think it—my future—will be taken away from me. Either way, it's my destiny unfolding. If it's cancer, I'll accept it, and be able to live with it, I hope, until, of course, it kills me."

"You think it's destiny, and not good or bad luck?"

"It's both; it's many things. It's genetics, it's my conditioning, it's the way I've chosen to live my life, which of course involves a fairly high stress level—I'm a male, and a free-lance writer, and so forth—it's the times we live in, and the chemicals in our food and air and water, and then, it may be a freak molecular accident, which is one of nature's specialties. If it weren't for freak accidents, there wouldn't be mammals or birds—there wouldn't even be guppies."

"Did you ever notice how many major aspects of your life—I mean *one's* life—like where you live, or who you decide to live with, or your job, have absolutely nothing to do with plans or calculations? How sometimes you're going to one place, and for no reason whatsoever you go somewhere else and it turns out that you ended up at exactly the right place at exactly the right time? And you had absolutely no intention of being there, that you're there because of whim or good luck, and your life takes a radically new direction?" Wallace nodded. "Do you think it's karma, or do you think that's too flaky?"

"I don't think karma is *too* flaky, life being as strange as it is, but I think it's *pretty* flaky. I'm inclined to think that karma is wishful thinking, and a bit unrealistic, and not nearly as interesting as the possibility of free will...."

"But you said that your tumor was destiny...."

"It's my destiny because it happened to me. I don't think it was determined at conception or birth that I would get a tumor when I was fifty-five, but it has happened—I developed a brain tumor—and therefore it's part of my destiny."

"I still think the drunken-stoned-gods theory holds water."

"It appears that way, doesn't it? When things strike me as being particularly arbitrary, either arbitrarily shitty or fortuitous, I tend to think you're right."

"Today's a big one: what we find out today will affect us for the rest of our lives. Today we have a rendezoid with destiny." Wallace laughed lightly for a second, nodded, and then we were silent and sad for a minute. I looked at his face as he drove, and felt, as Wallace once expressed it, a gentle melancholy.

At the top of the mountain he spoke again. "Did you read the Edmund Wilson essays?"

"Some of them. I didn't like them as much as the Orwell essays you gave me. But I loved that one where he says the most terrifying thing in the world is to look a chicken straight in the eye."

"So did I. After I read it, I went out and looked one of Sarah's chickens in the eye for several seconds. It scared me shitless."

We laughed. I love to travel with my father.

"Hey, you know what? It's exactly a year since we took our first bath together at the hot springs."

"It is? How do you remember?"

"It was September first; I just happen to know. I remember waiting for you to arrive. I hadn't eaten all day, and my stomach had eaten itself up, and was about to start in on my kidneys. Then we had three glasses of wine, and sat around stalling, saying, "Well. Well well wellll."

"That was a lovely day. Oh, perhaps a bit nerve-racking."

"No kidding, man, I was a wreck. I paced until you got there. I kept thinking, Oh no, he's going to be naked and he's going to have *genitals, pudenda*. Holy shit, he's going to have pubic hair; he's going to have the whole works. You know, none of my friends have seen their fathers' genitals, not since they were very very young girls, if ever."

"Die Schamteile!" he said. "The parts of shame."

"I remember that it took us both about half an hour to undress at the hot baths; we'd take off our sweaters and then hang them up and then unhang them and fold them up, and then our shirts, and then our pants. Then I got in the bath first and you were ever so slowly taking off your socks, and I thought, Gee, if I look up three feet, I'll see his *penis*, yoiks! And finally I did. . . ."

"I didn't notice."

"I know. And I looked at them—I mean, the whole general area, if you know what I mean—for a few seconds, and then looked away at something more interesting than my naked father, like my fingernails."

Wallace laughed. "I was a bit nervous too. . . ."

"Nervous?! You got into the bath holding your socks. I was trying so hard to look cool and nonchalant—you know, worldly—that I got a cramp in my foot underwater. The first bath was scary, Dad, no kidding."

"Like looking a chicken right in the eye." He looked at me, fondly and amused. "Wouldn't have missed it for the world."

I have done many things in hot baths, ranging from Esther Williams aquatics, illegal sex acts, and solitary sea-lion impersonations to having my toes pulled out of their sockets by a three-hundred-fifty-pound woman who swore by toe-cracking. But the first of five baths that I took with Wallace last year was the most intriguing and profound, retrospectively the bath I am most glad to have taken.

"I think it makes karmic sense—in terms of the tumor—that we saw each other naked a few times recently, without our uniforms on."

"I think I know what you mean, but tell me more," he said.

"Well, six weeks ago our worlds changed pretty dramatically. There's been so much fear and unhappiness since the tumor showed up, and everybody in the family is grappling with new territory—sickness, hospitals, our more or less grown-up family being brave and terrified, et cetera, and we're all being flooded with memories. And it seems appropriate that we—you and I—were naked together, in hot water. I can't explain it very well."

"I agree—it *was* a powerful and breakthrough sort of

day—but I'm not sure it makes *karmic* sense. And it was about time."

"I was totally self-conscious."

"You didn't seem the least bit so."

"I know. I felt like an enormous bottom with little legs to carry it from one place to another, especially since your buns are about three inches wide, each."

We were both silent again. The oncologist's office was just over ten minutes away, and I had a mild adrenaline attack when the somewhat monumental meaning of today's visit to the doctor sank in. A malignant brain tumor or a benign brain tumor, diametric possibilities as black and white as the land and the sea, and yet, observing our faces and demeanors, listening to our conversations, you might think we were going to the library with overdue books, or looking forward to lunch with a slightly tedious friend.

Wallace folded and unfolded his *Times Literary Supplement* a dozen times in the doctor's office, tapped his foot rhythmically as if he were keeping beat to a slow song, and looked over my shoulder at the advertisements in *McCall's*.

"What do your panties say about you behind your back?" I asked him, reading. I held the magazine so that he could see it better. One set of panties (from underneath a tight dress) said, "Messy, goodness me, doesn't she care about the way she looks?" and the other set of talking panties—the advertised product—said, "Ummmmmmm. Nice," or something like that.

"Jesus Christ," said Wallace, shaking his head and returning to the *TLS*. "Sheer madness."

We both flinched when the nurse called his name. Wallace stood up, gave me the crossed-finger sign, and took a breath. I pinched his bottom very lightly, and he disappeared with the nurse.

It was the longest half hour of my life; it began to feel like at *least* the day after tomorrow. I was positive the news was good and then positive the news was awful, and then good, and then awful. I kept breathing into my stomach. I read five issues of *McCall's*, six minutes each, and mostly the advertisements. I drank five cups of Alhambra water, and peed twice, just for something to do. The door to the examining room opened once and I flung the magazine behind me. Heyyy, who's nervous? I thought. And then finally, and irrevocably, Wallace stepped back into the waiting room with his news, and a look of controlled relief on his face.

"Hi," I said, standing up.

"Hi." He raised his eyebrows once, and shrugged and said, "I might be all right."

"You might be all right?" I said without much emotion.

"The consensus of the doctors who looked at my brain cells is that the cells were precancerous." My stomach froze at the word "cancerous." "Or," he continued, "that they were just beginning to be cancerous, and that the surgeon got them all when she cut me open. Because there were no tentacles into the brain. My doctor feels optimistic, and says there's every chance that there's no more cancer in me and that I'll live forever." He was looking closely at me. "It's a strange predicament to be in," he said, "to find this news—that it was cancerous, or precancerous—to be good news, a big relief. But consider the alternatives. And the lack of tentacles is in my favor. So the doctor is recommending a two-week course of prophylactic radiation, although it's entirely up to me, of course. Just to make sure. I start Monday."

"You start radiation Monday?" I asked.

"Yeah. I'm afraid so. And I'm also encouraged by what the doctor had to say. It seems that the prognosis is good."

"Well. That is good news, then," and we both laughed, with dejection and irony and some relief. "So I guess it really *is* good news, then, relatively speaking."

"You know what I feel like?" asked Wallace as we

walked toward the car. "I feel like having a bittersweet-chocolate ice-cream cone, from Swensen's."

"Me too." Throughout my childhood Wallace drove me to the emergency room on perhaps a dozen occasions—when I fell out of trees, stepped on glass, or painted my body with poison-oak juice—and every time, we stopped for ice cream afterward.

We drove to Swensen's with a Laurinda Almeida cassette playing. I played the bass line on my knees, and Wallace sang the melody.

"*De dee dum dum dummmmm, de dum, de dum dum dum . . .*" he sang.

"What else did he say?" I asked. I was beginning to worry that Wallace was holding out, or had decided to give the family a version of the doctor's report that we could live with, except that I also knew he'd tell us the truth as he heard it. I have thought, since the diagnosis, that if Wallace had a choice, he would want to be completely alone in dealing with the tumor, would want to spare his children and lover all the fear and sadness and anxiety. But of course he was stuck with us, just as we were stuck with him, for better and for worse and for the long periods in limbo as well.

"Not much, really. That I have a good chance, that we caught it early, that I'm in excellent physical shape otherwise, and blah blah blah. My guess is that somehow this fucking tumor is going to kill me, but it could be years. It won't be today, anyhow. . . . Here we are."

We got out of the car with some dejection and walked to the store. Cancer, cancer, cancer, I thought, walking. Brain cancer, precancerous brain tumor, radiation, cancer, *cancer*.

When, walking into Swensen's, it occurred to me that I hadn't considered the possibility of the tumor's being neither benign nor malignant, hadn't considered the possibility that Wallace would have what sounded like a little touch of cancer, I felt a wave of frustration, torn-to-pieces-ness about having to keep playing things by ear because nothing was turning out to be cut and dried. Wallace and I leaned against the counter, shoulders touching, waiting for the girl to take our order. Wallace stared at the list of flavors with great concentration, although he always orders bittersweet chocolate. It occurred to me almost for the first time, viscerally at least, that Wallace might really die, that in fact all the people I knew and loved were going to die at some point. The only reason that they are going to die is because they were born and they breathe. I was even almost convinced that I might die also, but not quite, only enough to have a sudden conviction that Janis Joplin was right about getting it while you can.

"What do you want?" Wallace asked me.

I want you not to have precancerous brain tumors, ever again, that's all. "Bittersweet," I said. In a tweed jacket Wallace looked like a professor of Eastern Studies with low blood sugar. His face was so beautiful and familiar to me. Maybe death exists as a deadline that forces the issues, so that you have to learn what there is to learn—which is how to enjoy this life—before you die. Or maybe it exists as the ultimate population control, or maybe it exists for no meaningful reason whatsoever.

"Let's eat in here, so we can watch," I said. Watching strangers perform is one of the most pleasurable distractions I know of. It almost always makes me feel sane and dignified in comparison, and I am never bored.

"You got croy sents?" asked a lumpy polyester businessman. "Or craw sents, however you say it?"

"No," said the young woman behind the counter. "If you want *croissants*, try the bakery, four shops down."

Wallace and I smiled at each other, and the waitress came over to us, shaking her head with a grin. "What can I get you?"

"Two bittersweet chocolates," Wallace told her, "on sugar cones." The woman returned in a minute with our cones, and Wallace handed her a dollar.

"I'm sorry, sir, we have new prices. Sixty-five cents for a single." I took a bite of the rich, dark, creamy chocolate, and Wallace extracted thirty cents from his chinos and gave it to her with a smile. We headed for a booth, licking our cones.

"Who wants to live in a world where a single scoop costs sixty-five cents?" I asked.

"I do," he said.

There were several packs of teenagers sullenly ordering and eating their cones; two men wearing open blouses and medallions; one woman wearing stretch pants; three women wearing the very latest fashion, which is spray-on-tight straight-leg blue jeans with the cuff rolled up two inches; and a cherubic little boy whose ice cream dropped off the cone after his first bite. He yelled, and his eyes filled up with tears, and he planted his foot firmly on the ice cream: a long, apelike arm reached out, slapped his head, and dragged him out of the store.

"Ahh, childhood," said Wallace.

"Look," I said, indicating the door.

A well-dressed couple who were obviously not enjoying each other's company or existence entered the store.

"I don't even want a cone," the husband hissed.

"Then go sit out in the car," the wife hissed back.

"You need ice cream like you need another mother."

"Will . . . you . . . leave . . . me . . . alone?" she said.

"Go ahead," he said, "buy a cone. Oink, oink."

They were at the counter by this time, and Wallace and I were transfixed.

"Ahh, marital bliss," I said.

"Last week I lost five pounds," the woman said, tightly.

"Well, I think if you look behind you, you'll find it," he said. The woman ordered a double, and squinted meanly at him. He squinted back at her, clenching his jaw, and ordered a milk shake. "Nyahhhhhh," I expected him to say.

"Shall we?" said Wallace, standing up.

"Yeah," I said, "let's go home."

"So now I'm a cancer patient of sorts," he said when he started the car.

"Yeah. How do you feel?"

"A little worried, but not nearly so much as this morning. And I still believe that life is supposed to be good, and my life as a cancer patient can be good, lived one day at a time, and at some point it may be determined that I am no longer a cancer patient, and my life will be better for this scare we're having. We're all on borrowed time anyway, and it's good to be reminded."

We drove along the highway, and spoke in the shorthand that close friends develop, in which one phrase conjures forth a complete memory or portrait or story, and sometimes we did not speak at all.

As we approached the mountain road, Wallace said, "What are you thinking? Kind thoughts of your dear old father?"

"No, I was wondering how long it will be before there are cancer-medicine commercials on television. I'm picturing this woman with two cancer-contaminated glass plates, where the cancer cells are dyed so that we home viewers can see them. And she dunks one glass plate into Brand X, one glass plate into the advertised brand, which is spotless in seconds, while the glass plate in Brand X is ominously smudged. . . ." Wallace laughed, shaking his head. "Oh, and I had a few random thoughts about my dear old dad. What were *you* thinking?"

"I was thinking how good some reggae would sound. Do we have any of the tapes?"

"Oh, yeah, I got your favorite," I said. "Bob Marley." I looked in the glove compartment and found the cassette.

"Bob Marley and the Maytals?" he asked.

"How many times do I have to tell you?" I said with

feigned irritation. "Toots and the Maytals, Bob Marley and the Wailers." I put the cassette in the machine and turned it on.

"And this is Toots?"

"Noooo! This is Bob Marley . . ."

"And the Maytals?" he asked. I laughed, and shook my head.

The first song, "Lively Up Yourself," began.

"Too much ganga, mahn," said Wallace after listening for a moment. "Good beat, good guitar, dumb words. What's that song I like so well?"

"It's next."

We went up the mountain in second, slowly maneuvering the curves, hairpin and otherwise, listening to the beat and the words—most of which we couldn't understand—and watching the hillside for birds. There are more greens on the mountain than there are adjectives that attempt to define various shades, every green under the sun, and for thirty seconds at a time I forgot about the biopsy.

When the introductory guitar line to "No Woman, No Cry" began, Wallace recognized it immediately and began to sing along enthusiastically, only he was singing "No Woman in Christ." (Wallace is an ardent singer, in the same way that I am an ardent bird-watcher. He sings loudly, on key, and with mostly improvised words. When my brothers and I were young, he took us and our friends to countless outdoor concerts—Pete Seeger, Joan Baez, Odetta—and sang along, loudly, on all the songs he "knew." Wallace, for all his dignity and erudition, has several qualities that Randy refers to as "goofy-ducky"—qualities all the more endearing for their contrast to the relaxed precision of his demeanor.)

"No Woman, No Cry" is such a beautiful song that it always makes me cry if I am sad to begin with. My eyes were brimming with tears and I was determined not to cry. My father sang, "Noooo woman in Christ."

" 'No *cry*,' " I said. " 'No *cry*,' not 'in Christ.' "

"O.K., smartass, what's that?" he said, pointing to a blue jay on a wire.

"Common blue jay," I said solemnly.

"Tah!" said Wallace, which is his lapsed Presbyterian version of "Feh!," and he went back to singing. "No woman *no* Christ."

"There!" he said with great satisfaction. "Happy?"

"No," I said, as a few tears worked their way past my eyes and down my cheeks. I stared out my window.

"Neither am I," he said. When I looked over at him, his eyes were watery, too, but did not brim over. "It's just the shits, isn't it? That's almost all that can be said for it, and we'll all get through it together—and alone—one way or another. I'm in much, *much* better shape than I might be, and the fact that it's only two weeks of radiation is a good sign: if it were definitely cancer, or advanced, I'd have five, six weeks of it instead."

"Yeah, I know, I know. But what distorted reality," I said. I wasn't crying anymore.

"It is," he said. "It's the theater of the absurd, and it's life pretty close to the edge." His voice was serious but not sad. "And never a dull moment. *Carpe diem!*" he said jovially. "Seize the day! Here, have a candy!" He handed me a tin of De La Vosgienne black-currant candies and, when I opened the top, helped himself. I took a few and noted that Wallace was one of those people (unlike Randy, Megan, Kathleen, and me) who can have a *tiny* tin of tiny candies around for weeks. Wallace is one of those people who *never* gobble food.

"Thanks." We sucked on our candies and listened to the reggae. We reached the top of the mountain, where suddenly there were miles and miles of glimmering ocean and clouds, whereas before, our view had been of trees and land.

———

Filled with memories, I kept glancing over at Wallace. Several years ago Wallace told me that when men first meet, they size one another up immediately in terms of accomplishments and stature, instead of how much they have loved and have been loved, or how happy they have been in their work, regardless of the successes. There are people who consider Wallace unapproachable because of his successes—eight published books, articles in almost every important magazine in the country—but he has said he is just a man, and that we are all on common ground at three in the morning, grappling with the fears and sorrows of the human condition. The men who have loved him most have not loved his achievements; they have loved his kindness and sanity and humor and sensitivity, and they have told me so. These are the qualities I love him for, too, alongside the innumerable hikes he took with us, the outdoor concerts with picnic lunches, the books and the insights he gave to us, the birthday expeditions to Playland-at-the-Beach and Japantown, and if I live to be a hundred, I will never understand why this man got a brain tumor.

Thirty-two years ago Wallace was my age; in thirty-two years, if I'm still alive, I'll be a fifty-five-year-old woman, but I do not really expect to live that long. Wallace said that this feeling—which he also had at twenty-three—is a phenomenon of youth, that you assume you'll die young because you cannot picture yourself looking and being much older. Wallace told me that it takes a *long* time to assimilate the knowledge you find along the way; these last few years have been his most calm and free and satisfying, I think. He said that in his early twenties he thought that at twenty-eight one became an adult, and that he only recently realized that one never really grows up, or, at least, that one never loses the child inside.

"I *do* feel relieved," he said at the bottom of the mountain. "I still don't know all the answers that I want to, but now I know that my tumor was in some way cancerous, and that I seem to have a good chance."

"Answers to what questions?"

"Well, Why me? of course. And, How does cancer begin to develop, assuming that the virus theory is right, and that we're all exposed to or carrying the cancer virus? How is it that some people get cancer and others don't, even under identical stress conditions? Why do some people's immune systems break down? And why on my brain? Now, I know there's a correlation between my being a writer, a person who uses words, and my getting the tumor on the word section of my brain, but it's not so simple as that I think too much, or didn't use the words I wanted to. It's something more subtle, more delicate than that. And why *now*? And what's next?"

"Oh," I said. "Those questions."

Wallace turned onto the "highway" that leads to town, the highway that runs along the lagoon. "And I do feel relieved, now that I think about it," he said, and I could see by his eyes, and by his mouth, that he did. He slowed down after several curves when we spotted a Highway Patrolman lurking up ahead. "They're on to us, baby," he said in a mild gangster voice. "The jig's up."

"Which jig?" I felt relieved, too, since he felt relieved.

"The police are out rounding up escaped cancer patients these days. You must have read about it in the paper."

"Oh, yeah," I said. "Now it all comes back. The dragnet, right?"

"Right, the dragnet and the cancer concentration camps. It's become against the law to have cancer in California; it's such unpleasant business, you know, all that weight loss, hair loss, rapid aging. It gives the state a bad name."

The Highway Patrolman did not pursue us.

"Phew," I said. "That was a close one."

"Skin of our teeth. See that guy up ahead, in the lagoon, with the wading boots and binoculars, *pretending* to watch the egrets?" I nodded. "Undercover."

"Ah. I might have known. You can tell by his sunglasses. They're the wrap-around sort, instead of the hinged kind.

Undercover people and Arabs are practically the only people who wear them." When we passed the man in the lagoon, I turned around and said, "He's got his binoculars on us. He's probably radioing the CHP man down the road, via the mike in his armpit."

"One thing we escaped cancer patients have going for us is that the cops are afraid of catching cancer—*everybody* knows it's contagious, that you can catch it from a patient's saliva and breath. So when the cop pulls you over, you just start coughing and sneezing like mad, all over him. It scares them to death, and they leave you alone."

We drove along the lagoon, laughing off and on.

"Have another candy!" said my father. "We escaped from the police for yet another day." I opened the tin, offered it to him, and when he took just one—they are the size of peas—I took just one also.

We were home in five more minutes. It was a sunny day, with none of the fog and wild wind of the last few days, and Sarah came out to greet us when we pulled up. Before we had got out of the car, Sarah told us that Muldoon had been jailed by the pound again, that Randy had called the college and told them he wasn't coming this year, and that the toilet had overflowed at a most inopportune moment.

"Hunh," said Wallace, putting his arm around her shoulders and kissing her. "What a day, hunh? You ready for a drink?" he asked her, and she nodded. He looked at me and I nodded also.

"I got your note," she said. "What happened at the doctor's? Any news?"

We began walking to the house, and then Wallace said, "Let's have drinks out here, in the yard. I'll do the honors."

"Well, tell me, what happened?" There was suddenly worry and excitement in her face.

"Let me get Randy first," he said.

"I'll get him," I said. Wallace nodded in appreciation.

"*Randy!*" I yelled. "*Randy!*" He appeared in a few seconds with a determined but nervous look on his face.

"Now, Dad," he began very quickly, "I just *thought* about it for a while and realized I didn't want to go this year. . . ."

"Wait!" said Sarah. "Wallace has news."

Randy stopped short, and his mouth dropped open. "What?"

"Well, the biopsy report came in this morning, so Jen and I went over to see him, and—"

"It's good news!" said Sarah, looking excited and beautiful.

"Well, yes, it is good news, but not what you're expecting," said Wallace.

"Ahhhh," said Sarah slowly, nodding her head.

"The tumor is thought to be either precancerous or early cancerous. And the doctor says everybody is optimistic because they caught it so early."

"Precancerous?" asked Randy dully.

"And I'll get two weeks of radiation just to be sure. . . ."

"Radiation?" said Sarah.

"Radiation" was one of the words we most wanted to avoid hearing.

"Just two weeks," said Wallace. Sarah and Randy were staring at Wallace in a way that was *supposed* to look relieved and encouraged but that looked politely alarmed. "It takes a while for it to sink in as good news, but it really is. Think of the alternatives."

"It does sink in," I said, "after the initial shock of its not being benign wears off. It really does."

Sarah put both arms around Wallace's waist from the side and leaned against him. "Well," she said. "That's good to know."

"I'll go get some drinks," Randy said. "Everybody relax."

The three of us sat staring off into space, and I felt a now-familiar surge of fury and frustration: my stomach cramped, my mind raced, my jaw clenched, my eyes almost filled up, and I said nothing. We almost never acted angry about the tumor around Dad, because we didn't want him to feel worse about it, which he would have. So I would bottle my feelings until I got home to the cabin, where I would turn the radio on loudly, shout, and cry.

I wrote to Colin recently about how much I shouted in the cabin and on the ridge, a technique I had learned at the hot springs; that none of us, except Randy, acted furious; and that I was just generally sick of hearing about anger, because everybody was talking and writing about anger and I always stay out of popular fads, but that the fact remained that I was mad.

"Darling," Colin wrote back the next day,

> Of course you're pissed off about the tumor, all of us are. Every so often we are reminded of how sad and shitty the world can be. Part of the secret, as you know, is to siphon anger's self-destructive qualities into a sense of humor, a sense of comic irony, and when that fails, to cry and scream and shout and shit on the floor of your cage.
>
> You were better at being mad when you were a young child, all three of you kids were, and in fact most of us were. You had a joyful side at three, and you had a shy retiring side where your voice would become very soft and you would seem almost near tears, and I mostly thought you were great, *except* when you screamed in anger. Then all of us adults wanted you to shut up. You were punished, non-physically of course, when you were pissed off and loud: many small children are beaten when they express anger. Many children are denied their meals (read: love) when they are angry, but as you know, the anger festers inside us when we don't get it out of our systems. Your so-called shouting therapy sounds like just what you need. I would not expect to see Wallace express anger at his misfortune, but don't *you* go worrying about this, because your dad is going to do just fine, in his own way.

My anger passed when I looked at Wallace: Sarah was massaging his shoulders, and he was whistling "The Great Spreckled Bird," and he winked at me when our eyes met.

We sat down in the back yard of the house, a back yard filled with grass and wildflowers and planter boxes of herbs, vegetables, and marijuana. There were pens full of geese (two geese fill up a pen), rabbits, ducks, and chickens, and all were squawking but the rabbits. Randy came out with a drink for Sarah and Wallace, and then a moment later with one for me and one for himself.

"Cheers," I said. "*Carpe diem*."

"Cheers!" Wallace said, raising his glass.

"Cheers," said Randy and Sarah without enthusiasm.

"So what's this about calling the college?" asked Wallace.

"Oh, well, see, I just *realized* that I didn't want to go to college this year. I want to stick around, get a job or something, maybe an *apartment*. And we didn't send the college any money yet, so there was really no *reason* to go, if you think about it."

"Well, listen, I don't feel especially strongly about your going to college, if you don't want to."

"You don't?" he asked. It had obviously been much easier than anticipated, and I'm sure he rehearsed all day what he was going to say. "Well, that's great."

"I think it's great you're not leaving," I said. "Megan left this morning. I'm glad you're sticking around."

"Me too," said Randy. "*What a relief!*" he shouted, with controlled joy. "Especially because of this . . . I mean, the biopsy . . . I mean, not that I think you're in trouble now, Dad. I didn't mean that . . ."

"Well, of course I'm in trouble," said Wallace levelly. "But I'm not in nearly as much trouble as I might be."

"That's exactly what I meant," said Randy. "I just meant that, you know, the radiation and the, uh, you know . . ."

"Why don't you stop while you're ahead?" I suggested.

"It's starting to sink in," said Sarah. She and Wallace

were sitting together on the porch step, holding hands. All of us had almost finished our drinks. "One more shot and it will have sunk in as *really* good news—which I know it is. I mean, Jesus Christ, it could have been awful news."

And I know that all of us at that second thought, And it could have been benign, too.

"Will it make you radioactive?" Randy asked. We were sitting in studio chairs in the grass. Randy was throwing pieces of ice plant at a sack of alfalfa cubes twenty feet away.

"No," said Wallace.

"Will all your hair fall out?" he asked. "I mean, what there is of it?"

"Yep." Wallace was looking down at his and Sarah's hands.

"What will it be like?"

"I don't know. I'll have to tell you after Monday."

"You don't know?"

"Not really. I know there's an enormous X-ray machine which will aim a beam between my ears, just for a few minutes every day. And the radiation will burn the cancer cells away...."

"If there are any left," said Sarah.

"How does the X ray know which cells are cancerous?"

"Well, it doesn't *know*, of course. It doesn't scout around and then pounce on the cancerous cells, but the cancerous cells are dividing abnormally fast, and brain cells don't divide at all, and it's much easier to destroy a cell when it's in the process of dividing, so the cancer cells go first. And some healthy cells will be destroyed."

"You won't have much radiation sickness, will you, after only two weeks?" Sarah was staring at her ice cubes.

"I don't think so."

"What *I* want to know," said Randy, "is *how* it got started, the tumor, and why it got started."

"So do I," said Wallace. "No one knows. It's still a mystery."

"Just like real life," said Randy.

"It *is* real life," said Wallace. "No matter how surreal and rotten it seems, it very definitely is real life."

Randy was sitting next to me on the grass, building little piles of pebbles on my tennis shoes, absently. His jaw was clenched, and I thought about how terribly he and I would miss Wallace if Wallace died, and how everybody would have to love us because we were grieving so much, at least until we became an inconvenience if our mourning took too long. God, I'm sick, I thought suddenly, and hoped that Randy, too, escaped into fantasies like mine to avoid the confusion of the present. I thought suddenly of the horrible dwarf with open sores on his face, and decided it was a brave and sane dream, to pursue and confront such terror. My mind was in its three-ring-circus state, and I thought about how many millions of people mourned all over the world every day, and I hoped I would not be joining their ranks. I looked at Wallace's tired and old and handsome face and thought, I do not get it at all. I looked at Sarah and knew that her presence in our lives—in Wallace's life—was saving the day in all sorts of ways, and was jealous of her importance, psychic and physical. I looked at the piles of pebbles Randy was engineering on my feet, and thought about Stonehenge. I thought that there is every chance there *is* something bigger, more cohesive and sublime, than our individual psyches, and every chance there isn't. I thought that even if we had to say good-bye to Wallace at some not-too-distant point, we would still be way ahead of the game, because so few people have as many fine days with their fathers as we have had. I took a long, long sip of Jack Daniels, and then a deep breath.

"I'm feeling happier about the biopsy now," said Sarah. "I'll make us all another drink." She kissed Wallace, and stood.

"Thanks," said Wallace. "I really truly think that I'm going to be all right, and I, for one, will drink to that."

"Oh, you'll drink to anything," said Randy, finishing his

whiskey. "And furthermore, your fly is down, and you balds should be especially careful about that sort of thing."

"Oh, go to hell," said Wallace, smiling as he zipped up his fly. The sun still shone on the four of us, but fog crept back over the ocean from the south.

Kathleen

On a warm, windless morning a month after Wallace's surgery I awoke from a dream so sad that I was still crying ten minutes later. I was in a large glass house on the top of a hillside covered with closely cropped and brilliantly green grass, with the ocean beyond and nothing else in sight. I stood watching the hill and the water, filled with terror and sorrow as I thought about Wallace. From the far right of the hillside a black speck emerged and became larger as it moved up the slope; when the figures got closer, it turned out to be Martin Luther King, Jr., of all people, who walked slowly toward me with such dignity and humility that I was filled with infinite sadness and fear. He walked up to the window where I stood, gazing at me through the glass, and said, "I just don't want you to be afraid when I come back." I nodded, and we looked at each other, and then he walked slowly down the left side of the hillside.

I wrote the dream on the back of an envelope, computed the hours until I would fall asleep again, and with great resignation climbed out of bed. I have got to get a grip, I thought. *I have got to pick myself up by the bootstraps.* Enough of this gloom, enough of this depression. Wallace will be fine, I will finish my short story today, I will not have a breakdown, I will be kind to myself all day, and I can go back to bed in fifteen hours.

I put the water on for coffee, washed my face, tossed my hair, and went outside to get the paper. The sun was shining above the ridge to the east, the sunflowers in my neighbor's garden were flourishing, and the sky above the blue-green Pacific was filled with pelicans and sea gulls. Not bad at all, I thought, a split second before I stepped barefoot on a banana slug, whose green slimy insides oozed into the spaces between my toes. "God!" I shouted. "God! Shit!" I hosed my foot off angrily, and then with sudden and affected maturity realized that on a scale of human trauma, stepping barefoot on a slug was insignificant. I walked back inside with the paper, turned on KSAN, and scanned the front page; there are so many urges in me that I do not value and that I do not or cannot curb, and reading the *Chronicle* every morning is one of them.

Another massacre in Rhodesia, more incoherent and hypocritical drivel from Jerry Brown, the arrival of *Jaws 2*, the theft of Charlie Chaplin's body, an eighteen-month-old baby with oral gonorrhea, an interview with John Aristotle Phillips (who designed an atomic bomb as an undergraduate and was then approached by the Yugoslavian government, which coincidentally had just got all the necessary material for building nuclear power plants from the U.S. government), and a three-inch story about an accident in an East Coast nuclear power plant that was caused by a lit cigarette. Oh well, I thought, too bad, and stood to make coffee.

The phone rang while I was pouring hot water through the filter.

"Yo," said Kathleen.

"Yo. How you doing?"

"I thought I might come over for coffee. How does that sound?"

"Fine. I'm just making it."

"O.K. I'll be there in ten minutes. There's a hysterical story on page four of the *Chronicle*, by the way. It sounds like you wrote it. Check it out."

"O.K. See ya."

"O.K. Well, see ya."

"O.K.," I said.

The story on page four was an interview with the county coroner, who divulged the manner in which he breaks the news to a dead person's family. "I have two methods," he was quoted as saying. "Sometimes I say, 'Is this Joe Smith's residence?' and if the person says yes, I say, 'I'm afraid I have some bad news.' And the person says, 'Yes, yes?' and I say, '*Very* bad news.' And sometimes I say, 'Is this Joe Smith's residence?' and the person says yes and I say, 'Hello, this is the coroner . . .' and they know I don't call them to invite them for dinner, so they're a little bit prepared by the time I tell them. Of course there's really no way to prepare them for their beloved's expiration. . . ." Ha! Expiration! "It's not an easy job," he concluded.

"Hello," said Kathleen when she stepped inside the cabin. "This is the coroner, and your husband croaked this afternoon, cashed in his chips, you know."

"Hello," I said. "I'm afraid your husband will be late for dinner tonight. Very, very late."

"Is the coffee ready?"

I nodded, and she poured a mugful.

"Hello, this is the coroner," I said. "I'm afraid your husband has expired, and cannot be renewed."

"Did you see that spike heels are about to be the rage?"

"Oh yeah. It figures."

"How's your dad doing? I saw him at the vegetable stand a few days ago, thought he looked wonderful. His hair is *really* growing in now. . . ."

"He calls them his little hairlets. He says that when a breeze blows through his little hairlets, his scalp feels cool and pleasant. I *guess* he's doing excellently. His doctor is totally optimistic, thinks the surgery was a success and the radiation will get anything that's left, and says that Wallace is going to live forever. He really does look healthy, and has good coloring and spirits, and he's getting a lot of writing done, which makes an enormous difference."

"I hope he lives for thirty more years," she said.

"I do too. God, cancer. What a terror it is; it's the biggest scare word of the age. Cannnncer. *Cancer, cancer, cancer!*" I shouted, and we both laughed. "It's incredibly popular these days, media-wise. It's the hottest thing since Jackie Onassis. Everybody who's anybody is getting it, or has someone in the family with it, practically; it's kind of a craze in some parts. It's the latest no-nonsense no-gimmick weight-loss method around. . . ."

"God, you're disturbed."

"No kidding. So is everybody. So is everything. There's a clinic in Beverly Hills where you can have anorexia nervosa induced. Hundreds are flocking to it, since protein powder has been outlawed. . . ."

"You're making this up." She was laughing.

"No I'm not. Well, yes I am. But I bet you when they discover a cure for cancer, there'll be clinics for rich people who can be given a little dose of cancer and then cured after they've reached their desired weight, wait and see." I stood up and poured myself another cup of coffee, sat down in the rocking chair, and lit up a cigarette. "Look at this. Look at me sitting here poisoning myself."

"I don't understand why you smoke. . . ."

"Because I think it looks *coollll*," I said, inhaling deeply.

"Do you think everybody thinks they've got—or are going to get—cancer?" Kathleen asked.

"Oh, sure. Except for the people who think they have heart disease. People with really devastating brain damage might not think about it, but I bet almost everybody else thinks that their or their families' aches and pains and growths and fatigue are cancers. Especially late at night, in the dark. And they're usually not."

"But sometimes they are. I haven't told you this before, but I've gone to the doctor a lot of times convinced that some pain was cancer—throat cancer, bone cancer, cancer of the complexion. And when the doctor says I'm in great shape, I just think he or she is incompetent, or that it's just a bit too early for detection."

"I do prone yoga now when I start thinking about cancer. I think thinking about it, being worried about it and hypochondriacal about it, causes it partly, in that it causes great stress which breaks your body down, and you get a cold, or cancer."

"Have you been doing much prone yoga?"

"Oh yeah. Several hours a day, including evening sessions."

Prone yoga is a therapeutic system of relaxation that Kathleen and I developed several years ago. It consists of lying down on the bed and not thinking of much, just relaxing until you have enough strength to cope with another day of the roller-coaster ride. We have yet to introduce prone yoga to the community at large, as Clement is already glutted with therapeutic options, Tai Chi and high colonics (especially coffee enemas) currently being the most popular.

"Jesus Christ!" Kathleen said suddenly, putting her mug down and removing a piece of milk skin from her bottom lip. "It's disgusting stuff," she said, and laid it with much distaste in my ashtray. "It's *demoralizing*. It's like getting a piece of eggshell in your scrambled eggs. . . ."

"Or getting your hair stuck on a fly strip when you're hung over. . . ."

"Or menstruating, or both. It's like sitting on a wet toilet seat—it's the sort of thing that finally pushes you over the edge when you're staving off a nervous breakdown, the big NB. And you somehow deal with mortality and sickness and nuclear power and war and blah blah blah, and you can be just devastated by it all and still hold on until—bam!— you wake up and there's a daddy longlegs walking across your chest, or your pets have diarrhea, and . . ." She yelled and pantomimed raving insanity, pulling at her hair and contorting her features. I laughed.

"You forgot tinfoil on fillings, and getting your pubic hair caught in your zipper. I think when I finally lose my marbles, something will just snap in my brain and I'll become catatonic, never say another word."

"Nah," said Kathleen. "You'll be a screamer."

"I never scream."

"You scream on the ridge. I've seen you, heard you. . . ."

"That's shouting," I said. "That's shouting therapy."

"When my dad went nuts, he broke every single machine in the house except the stereo. And then he mostly wouldn't talk; he'd tell war stories once in a while, and sing."

We were silent for a minute. The radio was on. A string quartet filled the cabin and Kathleen began to sway ever so slightly, smiling with a sad faraway look in her eyes, moving to the rhythm of the bass line. I lit a Camel.

"You've got one lit already," she said, indicating a half-smoked cigarette in the ashtray.

"Oh, yeah." I snubbed it out. "Smoke should have tipped me off."

"And I couldn't help but notice that there's a tennis ball in the refrigerator. I wasn't going to say anything."

"Anyone could make that mistake."

"And there's a can of green chilis outside on the step."

"There is? Oh, I remember, when I came back from shopping I—"

"I was just wondering in general if you'd noticed that you are acting a bit peculiarly. As if you had ten major things on your mind and were sort of stunned or numb at the same time."

"Oh yeah, I definitely noticed it. A few nights ago I woke up from this horrifying dream where something was attacking my left foot, and I threw the covers back and turned the light on and it turned out to be my right foot. I think what's happening is that I was so stiff-upper-lip-ish in my own way during and since the surgery and whatnot, you know, acting like I was pretty much composed about it all, and now that Wallace is pretty much out of trouble I feel like I want the luxury of falling apart a bit. I know it's not the big NB; I *know* I will keep functioning and stay in control, et cetera, but at the same time I *feel* like I'm imploding, as if all the things I've been feeling but not expressing much, like rage and fear and sadness, are turning in on me. You know what I mean?"

"Oh *yeah*. I know exactly what it's like. So *that's* why you shout so much, on the ridge. Think of what a wreck you'd be if you didn't."

"And I feel like running away from town all the time. I want to go back to the hot springs, and I want to go to a *Magic Mountain*–type sanatorium in the Swiss Alps and I want to join a fairly strict religious order."

"Last year when you were at the hot springs and I was having a totally difficult time of it all, I had a fantasy of running away to Paris to become a high-priced call girl. I thought, Why not get paid for it? And then you came back *just* when I thought I was in real trouble psychically, so I never went ahead and had a breakdown. That's how it's worked since we've been friends, more or less. I think it keeps me going to know that I'm never *that* much sicker than you, and you keep your head above water, and still laugh, and so on. And I have to go. Let's go to the bar after dinner. Can you?"

"Sure, I'd love to. I have a dream to tell you about, and the usual sordid goings-on, and I haven't seen you for a few days—it seems like weeks. . . ."

"*Years,*" she said, standing up. "It's my goddamn job, cuts into most of my free time."

"You could retire, like me, and then all your time would be free."

"But then who'd pay for the drinks?"

"You better get going; you're going to be late," I said. "Come pick me up after dinner. No, wait, I'll meet you there; the walk will be good for me. That's exactly what I'd like to do—have drinks with you after dinner, and after I've had a walk. *Please* try to be there on time, at say eight. I'm not at all well enough to be left alone in public."

"Okay, eight o'clock. Eight sharp." She winked slowly.

"Please," I said, laughing.

"Hey," she said very slowly, "*heyyy*, you can bank on me."

"If you come in at quarter of nine, and I'm howling and barking and throwing pool balls against the liquor bottles, call my father. He'll know what to do."

"O.K. See you at eight. I hope your writing goes well. And you can call me at the office if you ever need to. If you ever needed for me to come home, I would, like *that*," she said, and snapped her fingers. "See you. Love to Wallace when you see him."

"I will."

"Hang in there."

"I will. I'm O.K."

She walked outside to her car. Someone had drawn a swastika in the dust on her back window, which she erased with her hand. (Her ex-husband gave her the MG when they got divorced, and he kept the Alfa; things are always going wrong with the MG. If it's not a blow-out on the freeway, it's a swastika on the window. Last year I told her that she should just get rid of the damn thing—it was obviously saturated with bad karma—and that she should in fact give it to me and I would give her a ride whenever she needed one.)

When I was living at the hot springs retreat last year, Kathleen wrote me a letter, a full page of adjectives, which began "Hello dearest, I am afraid I am losing my marbles. I am anxious, willful, young, beautiful, smart, funny, clinging, possessive, scared, scarred, swarthy, talented, stupid, angry, stretchmarked, special, neurotic, insane, surviving, strong, falling apart, sensitive, obsessive, hypochondriacal, kind, cruel, honest, manipulative . . ." and ended "Come home. All is forgiven. I love you and you are the most deranged and mentally healthy person in my galaxy. I would marry you in a second if your skin ever cleared up. Your confused Kathleen."

I did not understand until I met Kathleen how someone so beautiful and wealthy and intelligent, with such great teeth and wit, could be as unsure of her worth as I am of mine, and as arrogant as I am, and as psychotic as I am. And then when we became close enough to start sharing our deeper secrets—about our parents, and ex-lovers, and skin, the true details of our girlhoods; in short, the true flavorings of our lives rather than the revisionist histories that we recite to others—I understood. When it became evident that our souls were similarly textured despite the differences in our packagings, when we let each other in, I entered into the most difficult and essential friendship of my life.

I met her ex-husband a month or so before I met her— they were in the process of splitting up—and slept with him three times. He was handsome, charming, and aggressive; he was also, as I learned after we went to bed, imperious, selfish, and thoroughly, laughably incompetent. I have had better sex with an assortment of fruits and vegetables, *much* better sex. I went to bed with him the second time after a party, because he was so charming and I didn't want to sleep alone and I knew the price, the sex, would be over in eight or nine minutes. And it was.

I met Kathleen at a party shortly thereafter, and fell for her immediately. We talked quite drunkenly for an hour about the monotonous Bad Girl–Good Girl voices in our minds, laughed uproariously, exchanged horror stories about food benders, and arranged to meet for a beer several days later. She left the party at midnight; at one-forty-five her husband and I climbed into my bed; by two he was snoring, appeased, and he was gone in the morning when I woke up with a very bad taste in my mouth.

Kathleen and Kent separated soon after. Kent left town with a blond teenager, and Kathleen and I became closer and closer. We played together several times a week, regularly had drinks together, and talked voraciously about our lives. We showed off quite a bit for each other; made each other laugh hysterically; casually and with some self-consciousness dropped names and achievements; and, usually stoned, played our most dazzling, absorbing music for each other.

One afternoon, during the peach season three years ago, we sat in my cabin eating peaches with cream, smoking dope, and drinking tequila, straight, with lime. We were talking about the men in town with whom we had slept, and I proposed that in twenty years we have a party of all the men, everywhere, whom we had slept with.

"God," said Kathleen, "what an appalling thought. Think of the really revolting one-nighters, and the married men. I had a lover who talked with a Donald Duck voice when he got drunk; he thought it was amusing and childlike or something. He was married to a woman I went to college with. Have you ever done that—slept with the husband of a friend?"

"Oh, yeah," I said, and had an adrenaline attack. "Once."

"Did you get caught? By your friend?"

"Ohhhh," I said, taking a generous sip of tequila, "well, no, I didn't, well, what was interesting about it, well, I, I, no, I didn't get caught." I put down my drink, took a deep breath, and said, "I slept with Kent a couple of times. Before I was friends with you." She was looking at me with friendly astonishment. I wasn't breathing, and tried to look aloof.

"You did?"

"Yep. Twice. Before we were friends."

"Oh, God, that's wonderful!" She looked very pleasantly surprised, and started laughing. "What a relief! I thought I must have been such a moron masochist to ever be attracted to him; I never thought an excellent, feminist woman would have anything to do with him, honest to God; it makes me feel much less stupid to know you fell for his game, too. Honest." She really, truly looked happy. "I *know* he liked you—he was always telling me what a hotshot you were—but I never thought you'd even *talk* to him, he's such a sexist, phony jerk."

"He sure is charming," I said.

"He sure is," she said. "And, of course, he's really an extraordinary lover," she said, and burst out laughing. "I tried to train him in the early days, and then I gave up completely—he's got the Evelyn Wood dynamics down perfectly." She passed me the joint.

"I clocked him at just over seven minutes the first time, and that included undressing and kissing."

Kathleen was laughing hysterically, and as I thought about it, and about what a tremendous relief it was for her to know now, I began laughing also.

"Thank you for telling me," she said. "He never said a word, although he intimated it very slightly a few times when we were fighting—but I was so positive that you wouldn't be able to stand him for ten seconds. It would have been easy for you to lie about it, or not even tell me. . . ."

"And once after," I said. It seemed suddenly important to get it all out. "After that party when you and I first talked, I brought him home with me." I paused. Kathleen wasn't smiling, but was looking at me with now-serious eyes. "I know it was a shitty thing to do; I know it seems antifeminist and two-faced, I mean, I know it *was* these things. But there it is. I wanted a body to sleep next to, and he was easy to get, and quick, and uncomplicated, because there wasn't a chance that I'd get involved." I looked away from her because I did not know what the look in her eyes meant—anger, betrayal, condescension, or simply strong curiosity. She was inspecting me with huge black eyes that I assumed were full of judgment, and the look around her mouth was amused but not pleased. "So," I said. "What do you think?"

"I think we could overblow it into a very big deal, which I don't think it was. And I do feel relieved that you fell for his act."

"He does a good Sterling Hayden," I said.

"A *brilliant* Sterling Hayden, and a good John Wayne."

"Do you think there are moral issues here, as opposed to aesthetic issues?" I asked. "Because I do feel slightly guilty, but mostly I feel stupid. And that this Incident is somewhat pathetic but otherwise meaningless, which is why I told you about it. It's too pathetic to keep as a Secret from you. It's just a little turd in the punch bowl."

"I agree," she said, "mostly. I hate it when women choose men, especially stony men, over women friends, especially when I'm one of the women, on either end." She stood up. "I have to use the john. Let me think about it." She went into the bathroom, and seconds after I had thought about how lucky I was to have found Kathleen, I began to think malicious thoughts about her overbearing moralistic stance—as capsulized in the word "mostly." I am never so ridiculous as I am when criticized, even if it is implied criticism of my ethics or behavior. I do not take it well, not well at all. I begin plans for retaliation, or revenge, or vindication, and almost immediately decide that whoever is casting aspersions on my impeccable character is a hypocrite, a moral plebeian, or a bonehead. It is, I'm afraid, one of my big hypocrisies, this business of condemning people who condemn me *for* condemning me, and it is closely related to the ritual of gossiping maliciously about people who have gossiped maliciously about me *for* gossiping maliciously about me. It is all very sickening and toxin-generating, and it is also one of my patterns, and because it is an automatic response, I am sometimes able to turn it off very quickly after becoming aware of it. Sometimes. By the time Kathleen had sat back down next to me, I was winding up for a heartfelt and mildly indignant lecture on how sick I was of other people's morals and of other people's suggesting or telling me what I *should* do and what I *should* think and how I *should* act. I took a breath and uttered five words—"I think I must mention"—in a voice that could have been described as shrill if it had not been for all the flug in my throat. I coughed and cleared my throat, but it was too late, and Kathleen was laughing.

"What on earth was that?" she said. She was fidgeting, as usual, with her long brown hair, and laughing. " 'I think I must mention,' " she bleated. "Damn, I can't do it quite right, because I don't smoke." I started laughing also and canned the lecture. "And if what you were going to mention had anything to do with your thinking that I'm judging you, just drop it. I'm not at all in the mood for it, and I want you to recognize that if there are any moralistic bad vibrations right now, they're yours."

"Because you're perfect and forgiving?"

"Yes. I'm practically a saint."

"So you don't feel the *slightest* bit scandalized? Or moralistic?" and I smiled roguishly.

"Oh, O.K., a tiny, tiny bit of it all, out of habit; an angstrom unit of betrayal...."

"God, you're uptight!" I leapt to my feet, hands on my hips and rolling my eyes with hostile exasperation.

"Goddamn cheap hussy!" she shouted back at me. *"Homewrecker!"*

"I'll drink to that!" I shouted, and we broke up. When we stopped laughing, I poured us each another shot, we clinked glasses, drank large sips, and settled back down in our chairs.

"Phew," I said. "Truth and beauty wins out again."

"Your shoulders are about three inches lower," she said. "They were almost touching your ears there for a moment, like Nixon's."

We sat around for another hour, comparing notes on our

mothers, our eating habits, our early childhoods, and our feelings of not fitting into the Real World, and not wanting to. I thought, as we spoke, about what a beautiful face she had, with black eyes so *obviously* manifesting soul, scars and laugh lines that showed how hard she has played, those huge white teeth, and I thought about how hard she could make me laugh and vice versa, and about her understanding, and pretty soon I thought, with some horror, that I was falling in love with her.

"Lesbian homo pervert!" I thought to myself. "Narcissist! Fool! Better nip *this* one in the bud." As I watched Kathleen tell a story that made us both laugh, it occurred to me that there were worse actions in the world than falling in love with a brilliant kind maniac who acts like she thinks I'm an extraordinary human. And then it occurred to me that my sexual relationships with men had almost always become frustrated and possessive and creepy at some point, and that, ergo, if I got involved with Kathleen sexually, *our* relationship would end up similarly. Cop-out, I thought; you're afraid. And what if Adelle Firth found out? What would my *mother* say? But think of it—a sexual relationship with a friend who loves me. But what if it were awful and terrifying and revolting and I couldn't ever stand to see her again? And, good heavens, *what if I loved it?* I did not mention any of this that day, although by the time she left, the enlivening tension was unmistakably sexual in nature, and playfully so, and was to go unconsummated for two years.

I seduced Kathleen for the first and only time on the night I returned from the hot springs. I had been gone for four months and we sat drinking tequila at the bar, in celebration. After our fourth drink, right after I asked if she had ever *really* liked my cat, I asked if she would like to spend the night with me.

"Sure," she said. She looked beautiful, and her eyes were dilated. She had spent the night at the cabin a few times before, in slumber-party style.

"And, uh, defile one another?" I asked. I looked at her, tried to look worldly, and held my breath.

"Oh." She looked stricken for a split second and then composed, as usual. "Yes, let's."

"God, you're an easy pickup," I said, laughing nervously. "Well, good, uh, well, good. I mean, it's destiny, it's inevitable."

"Now don't go getting romantic on me," she said.

"And, uh, defile one another?" was the hardest question I have ever asked anybody. I could hardly get it out of my mouth. If she had said no, I would have been devastated and humiliated, and because she said yes, I was filled instead with massive anxiety, slight nausea, and proud excitement.

It was the sweetest, slowest, most awkward lovemaking in town that night. There was candlelight, Mozart, much laughing, much hesitation, and I had locked the door. I worried that I would be incompetent, and I worried that at any minute the door would be kicked in and we'd be caught *flagrante delicto* by God knows whom—the police, my mother, Adelle Firth, the media.

"God, this is scary," I said at one point. She stopped doing whatever it was she was doing and looked up at me. "But not *that* scary," I said.

We would have cut our fingers and pressed blood if we were young girls, and it was this quality, or maybe perspective, that I most appreciated, or at least appreciated as much as the pleasure and closeness and the consequent good sex and the relief of having it over with, once and for all. It was the best one-night stand of my life.

We were, by this time and henceforth, traveling companions in drunkenness, mental derangement, honesty, psychic struggles, psychedelia, adventures, and massive, extraordinary fun. We weathered our depressions together, weathered our disappointing affairs together, forced each other to cop to manipulations, evasions, and emotional blackmail. We were inseparable, except when one of us was trying to write the other off. (I wanted to be sure, as did she, that if the relationship were to end, *I* would be the one to end it. I did not want to be ditched, although on several occasions I decided to ditch her because the friendship was so complex, so intimate, so important, that a certain terror took over.) We weathered our periods of accusation—we accused each other of self-destructiveness, self-pity, megalomania, hypochondria—and we weathered the periods when real or assumed injustices went unspoken and caused tension and hate between us. We treated each other quite badly on occasion, in order to test the strength of our relationship. We acted, and often still act, like vicious, Jekyll and Hyde married people; when we fought, or were disappointed, her voice always went up half an octave, while mine lost all of its wind.

She is a lapsed Catholic; I am a lapsed atheist. She is beautiful and I am not. I read books and she mostly *intends* to read books. We are so insanely close, and so different, that it is a miracle to me that our friendship still thrives: her imagination and humor and truthfulness stun and rejuvenate me, and her particular brand of madness is not unlike my own.

After Kathleen left, I clipped the article on the coroner and began my first therapeutic exercise of the morning. Prone yoga is remarkably simple, as it involves only two steps: one, taking the phone off the hook, and two, lying down on the bed. I lay staring at the old pictures of my family on the wall, and most intently at the picture of myself at three years old, in which I looked remarkably like I do now, complete with an untied shoe and a serious, demented, and mischievous look in and around my eyes; the major differences are that the person in the photograph looks one hundred years younger and without guile or self-consciousness.

Half an hour of prone yoga was followed by ten minutes of coffee and cigarette therapy, outside under the sun, at which point I felt relaxed and energetic enough to sit down at my typewriter. I was working on a short story about an evening at the movies with Megan and Randy. I put a piece of paper into the typewriter, indented five spaces, laughed out loud as I remembered Randy's telling Megan that Kirk Douglas's chin looks like it does because he got shot there while filming a World War Two movie. I typed eight words about Kirk Douglas, stared into space, and stood up suddenly to turn the radio on. I fiddled with the volume, bass, and treble for a couple of minutes, and then sat back down. I typed two sentences, stared into space, and got up to make another cup of coffee, which took about ten minutes. I sat down, looked at the words I had just typed, crossed out four of them, and got up to put more milk in my coffee.

Stick with it, I told myself. Writers write. Sit down and write. Stare at the paper instead of the floor; resist the daydream. I wrote a few paragraphs and thought one of them was good. Without really thinking about it, I walked to the refrigerator with a picture of a burrito on the screen in my mind, and then noticed that I wasn't hungry. It occurred to me to do the dishes as long as I was up; I smiled alone in the cabin. I do dishes only when I want to get out of doing something disagreeable, such as the work I love so much.

I sat down and thought of five people I ought to call, typed a few sentences, sat with my fingers on the keys, stared intently at the last sentence, became filled with *furor scribendi* and poised for action, only to find that I had completely forgotten how to write. Eventually I typed four words, x-ed them out, thought for a minute, typed the same four words—"choice of traveling companions"—started daydreaming about my Clement traveling companions and travels with my family, then snapped myself out of my daydreams. Write! I stared at the paper in the typewriter, fingers on the keys, wrote five words, and watched a fly land on the carriage. When I pushed the carriage back to the left side of the page, the fly went along for the ride. I per-

formed several experiments on the fly, like blowing on him
softly, and when he didn't move, I got up and went to the
bathroom. When I got back, I looked first to see if the fly
was still there (he wasn't) and then to see what I was writing. One paragraph made me laugh, and I began writing
again with enthusiasm, for approximately fifteen minutes. I
got up to make another cup of coffee, decided against it for
gastrointestinal reasons, and chided myself for trying to get
out of working. This went on for about an hour and a
half—this business of leaping up and then forcing myself
back to work, unable to concentrate and castigating myself
for my reveries—until finally the voice of sanity inside of
me said, Calm down. Breath rhythmically into your belly.
Nurture yourself; get off your own case; stop poisoning
yourself with doubts; *give yourself support*, you stupid asshole.

Somehow confidence and concentration set in and I wrote
for three hours in a row. When I finished writing for the
day, I felt calm and pleased and disciplined and smug: I had
once again got away with all the benefits of hard work
without having a boss or an office or a cubicle in an office. It
might be added that I hadn't made any money, but all the
same I hadn't been bored for a minute and was in an excellent mood. Happy work is as gratifying as sex or hard
laughter or love or good drugs.

I opened a beer and sat on the doorstep, looking at the
harsh white ocean, and debated whether to go to softball
practice or not. Softball practice is one of my most reliable
therapies these days; three times a week, with ten women I
like enormously, a coach I like to harass from left field, two
hours of physical exertion, fun and beer, all especially satisfying if I have worked well that day and therefore *deserve* a
good time. I was considering skipping it because Kathleen
wouldn't be there, and it is much, much more fun when she
is. I decided that I wanted the exercise and the contact, and

got ready to walk to the field, walking being another excellent and convenient therapy. I would not need so much therapy to survive and prosper if I were extremely stupid, or devoutly religious, or if Wallace weren't sick, or if I stopped reading the front page, but as it is, I do need it. Walking, softball, dinner, and then alcohol therapy with Kathleen, the last possibly the best of them all to look forward to, and as I tied the laces of my sneakers, I envisioned being at the bar with Kathleen, talking to her about anything, everything, and drinking, and showing off, and talking to friends, and maybe bringing home a Date afterward. Yes! I thought, this all sounds very, very good.

The phone rang. My first thought was that it was bad news—that someone in my family had been hurt or killed, or that suddenly Wallace's condition had taken a bad turn. My second thought was that my agent in New York was calling to say she finally sold a short story of mine, for hundreds of thousands of dollars. It was none of those things. It was Kathleen, calling from the office.

"Hi, Jen, how you doing?" There was a hazy edge in her voice. She's going to cancel, I thought. Here we go again.

"Hi, Kath. I was just leaving for softball. What's up?"

"I've decided to spend the night in the city tonight. I sort of have a date with this guy at the office, who I've been watching, if you know what I mean." She laughed. I didn't. "So we're going to a movie. Do you mind very much if we don't go downtown tonight? Could we do it tomorrow instead?"

"Sure," I said reflexively. "Fine." My voice was very tight, although I meant to sound nonchalant. "Fine."

"Fine, fine," she mimicked, and laughed. I didn't. "You're disappointed, aren't you?"

"No," I said petulantly, "I don't care." I sounded like a hostile seven-year-old. Kathleen exhaled loudly.

"I didn't think it was any big deal, going to the bar. . . ."

"It isn't."

"Obviously it is," she said. "Your voice has gone all haywire and unhappy."

"I wanted to see you tonight. I felt like playing, and going to the bar and having drinks and goofing off and flirting. . . ."

"You can still go to the bar. . . ."

"I never, ever go to the bar alone. You already know that."

"Tomorrow, then? Because what *I* want to do is go to the movie with Tom, and hang out with him. And now I feel like coming back to town and going to the bar with you, so you won't be mad or feel bad or whatever, but if I *do*, I'm going to resent it. Because I'd be doing it out of guilt. And every time one of us does something with the other that we don't really want to do, there's resentment. Every time." As she spoke, I was, of course, making feeble mental moves toward writing her off, even as I knew that I was trying to infringe on her freedom; I wanted to go to the bar with her, or just be with her, and she didn't want to go to the bar tonight with me. My evening was *ruined*, and I hate to be stood up by women for men. "Tomorrow?" she asked. "So could we do it tomorrow?"

"I don't know what my plans are. . . ."

"Oh, come off it," she said.

"This has happened so many times!" I yelled.

Kathleen was silent. I hated the words that were coming out of my mouth, and I hated the vibrations that I was emitting over the phone, and I hated Kathleen because I love her so much and she didn't want to be with me. I almost threw in some terrible, guilt-mongering blackmail lines—threats of breakdown, suicide, self-pitying indifference—because I wanted to see her so badly. I almost mentioned Wallace's cancer so that she would come back to town. Instead I went silent, one of the reactions I hate most in other people.

"I'll call you tomorrow," she said. "I want to stay in the

city, and you want me to come back to Clement, and I'm
sorry you're mad about it but I'm going to stay. I know this
has happened a few times and I know it even happened recently, and we both know it's going to happen again, and
that you'll probably punish me and then I'll probably punish you for punishing me, and we'll weather it. Take it or
leave it. I'm having a hard time, too."

This "take it or leave it" business is one of the few secrets
of friendship I know, a validity I accept—even preach—intellectually but that still causes cellular distress when my
desires are thwarted, especially when I feel on the verge.

"I know I'm being a shit," I said hollowly. "I know you're
'right,' or whatever, but I want to see you. So I'm mad."

"So what do you want me to do? If you are really having
a breakdown, or falling apart, I'll come home. But I don't
think you are."

"I want you to . . . I don't know . . . I would have wanted
you to tell him that we had a date, and you'd see *him* tomorrow night. *I* would have."

"And *I* didn't. You're not me, and I'm not sure *you* would
have anyway. Do you *need* for me to come back?"

"No."

"O.K. I'll call you tomorrow."

God, I'm a bad loser, I thought when I hung up. Such a
baby when I don't get my way, an unbalanced, dejected
baby.

I lay down on the bed and immediately started crying,
racking sobs interspersed with whimpering interspersed
with furious shouting. I have had it, I thought; I don't want
to play anymore. I want to take my ball and go home, only I
do not know where my home is. I was born in a Martian
hospital, I thought, and, due to a tragic mix-up in Registra-
tion, ended up on Earth, where I am thoroughly ill-
equipped to deal with life in the Earthling adult world. I
want to go to a sanatorium in the Swiss Alps, have the big
NB, and spend the rest of my life taking Thorazine and

having affairs with kind older women and shy crazy men, or maybe with kind older shy crazy hermaphrodites. I want to stop being brave, stop being in control, stop having affairs, stop thinking that I will ever understand the purpose and intricacies of human life. I want to stop having a father who might have cancer. I even want my father to die sometimes, just to get it over with. I want to die before anyone in my family, or Kathleen, or Megan dies. I don't ever want to die, and I don't want to play anymore. I don't know what I want. It was not until I finally finished crying, much later, that I knew what I wanted: a drink.

I got up and poured myself a generous glass of wine, and essentially inhaled it. I called Wallace and Sarah, but they weren't home. I called my older brother, hoping he was drunk and would tell me that he loves Randy and me more than life itself, as he often does now when he's drunk, but he wasn't home either. I called my seventy-year-old friend Sylvia, who wasn't home either, and then there was no one left to call. I called my own number, wondering if I was home, and the line was busy. (Two years ago Kathleen and I drove down to the lagoon at dawn on LSD and passed a car exactly like my father's, which I was driving. "Was that *us*?" Kathleen asked, and I wasn't sure that it wasn't.)

I found the envelope on which I had written my Martin Luther King dream. It seemed no longer profound and illuminating but rather contrived and melodramatic. I reread the story I had written that day, and thought it convoluted, didactic, sophomoric; I imagined someone reading it aloud to someone else, and roaring with laughter at its pretensions and stupidity, as Kathleen and I laugh when we read Marabel Morgan, or as Megan and I laugh when we read McKuen. I will be ridiculed, I thought, and exposed as an imposter.

I poured another glass of wine and called Wallace again but he still wasn't home and I thought he had probably been killed in a car accident. I called my older brother again, but he had apparently also been killed in a car accident. I called my seventy-year-old friend again, but she had evidently just had a heart attack or a stroke. I called myself again and the line was still busy.

I found by the phone a letter from Kathleen that she had written to me soon after we met, from a spiritual retreat in New Mexico. Upon finding that the people at the retreat were no saner or calmer or less hypocritical and, if possible, even duller than people in the so-called real world, she had made a feeble attempt to drown herself in a hotbath, and had been rescued by a young man who told her that everything was everything.

The letter said:

Coming home soon. I hope this letter doesn't Bum Your Trip. I am beginning to feel like a Joan Didion heroine with acne scars. I no longer feel that I am on to anything. My parents are dead and I have no home. All I want for the rest of my life is to get away with as much fun and freedom and adventures and love as possible: I think I would like to be a moral outlaw when I grow up, and to stop getting in my own way. I am sorry for such a sad numb letter, but I feel sad and numb, like an old bottle of Kool-Aid with wrinkles. Modern life sucks wind, is one thing I know, and that men still hate women and women still hate men and that many women still hate many other women, and that the machines and weapons and technology of our age make a mockery of anything but what I have already mentioned—love, fun, adventures, freedom. Sex and avocados are nice also, as is music. Read Berryman's *Dream Songs*—they are very beautiful and hopeful, and a balance to this letter. Somewhere I think there is something to learn or know about balance and humor, balance and humor, but I can't put my finger on it. Here is a taste of Berryman, who as you know killed himself:

I feel a final chill. This is coldsweat
that will not leave me now. Maybe it's time

To throw in my own hand.
But there are secrets, secrets, I may yet—
Hidden in history and theology, hidden in rhyme—
Come on to understand.

My parents are dead and I have no home. Poor, *poor* Kathleen.

I was semidrunk when I found Kathleen's letter. I was drunker than a skunk an hour later when she appeared at the cabin door. She walked into the cabin, took one look at me, and poured herself a tumbler full of wine.

"How many glasses have you had?" she asked, smiling.

"Two." It is difficult to slur one-syllable sentences, but not impossible. "Two twelve-ouncers." I was so happy to see her, because she *understands*, that I sat down in the rocking chair and cried. "So heppy to see you," I said.

"So heppy, so heppy," she said, smiling and shaking her head.

"Wrecked beyond madrigal potential," I offered, and stopped crying. "On beyond zebra." I stood up, and almost lost my balance.

"I'll get it," she said. "What do you want?"

"I'll get it," I said. "Not sure what I want." I careened around the cabin for a couple of minutes, desperately and drunkenly trying to remember what I had got up for. I found the letter she had written from the spiritual retreat, and I found the envelope on which I had written my Martin Luther King dream, and I found by the phone a William Steig cartoon of a man being carried away by two ostriches; the man is shouting, "This is *ridiculous*." I gave them all to Kathleen, and lay down on my bed. "Prone yoga," I said as she began to read. She nodded.

"I'm glad I came home," she said, looking up from the rocking chair. When I came to at midnight, she was still in the rocker, still drinking wine, and staring out the window at the full moon above the white-blue ocean. When I woke again at dawn, she was in bed beside me; and when I awoke for the last time, just before eight, she was gone. Sixteen more hours, I thought when I looked at the clock, only sixteen more hours. I put the water on for coffee, washed my face, tossed my hair, and went outside to get the paper.

Getting Older, or
Life's Little Joke

On the evening before the beginning of radiation Kathleen pulled up in front of my cabin in her MG with a Bach cantata playing loudly on her radio.

"It is going to be one hell of a sunset," she said, holding up a joint. "I have three Becks, a Pauli Girl, this excellent joint, which I pinched off you last time I was here, and I'm looking for a date."

"Look no further," I said, and climbed into the passenger seat. I opened two Becks as she backed up, and gave her one. I lit a Camel and rolled down the window, with the beer and cigarette in my left hand. Kathleen lit the joint, smoked it for a moment and handed it to me. I put the Camel in my mouth but did not inhale, took the joint in my left hand, put the bottle between my knees, removed the Camel from my mouth with my right hand, and then put the joint in my right hand (I smoke right-handed) and the cigarette in my left.

"Jesus," said Kathleen, looking at me from the corner of her eye, "your hands sure get overworked sometimes."

I inhaled, and nodded. I stubbed the cigarette out in the ashtray, and stinking dead cigarette smoke filled the car for a few seconds.

"*Schmutzig, schmutzig,*" she said gravely. She drove to the dead end downtown where the beach begins, and turned off the engine. Another Technicolor sunset was in progress above the channel and the ocean, and we listened to the radio until the cantata ended and some organ grinder music with harps began. We sat in silence staring at the water and the sky and at the vague figures on the beach, some of whom became bigger and eventually recognizable. A girl with a surfboard walked toward us, and when she was close enough, we could see the glittering letters of her T-shirt, which said SEVENTH GRADERS DO IT BETTER. Not far behind was her younger brother, also with a surfboard, followed by a dog so raw with mange that not even St. Francis of Assisi would have touched it. The story in town goes that when Mickey was born, Stephanie sang "Happy Birthday to You" as he emerged from their mother's womb in the bedroom.

Stephanie walked past our car, nose in the air, while Mickey stopped at the seawall to which we were parallel. He leaned his surfboard against the wall, and leaned over the side to look into the channel, with his feet up off the ground.

"My dad and I were fishing here once when I was about five," I told Kathleen, "and I walked behind a man who was casting and his hook went into my butt and got stuck. I was horribly embarrassed. Dad got the fish hook out of my butt, and the guy who did it gave me a Hershey bar. With almonds."

"How can you remember that it had almonds and not be able to remember what month it is most of the time?"

"Isn't that obvious? It's on my memory tapes; it's part of my memory slide show. I've remembered it so many times for so many years, it's almost more real to me than Dad's surgery."

"What's that kid doing?" Kathleen asked. Mickey had got down from the seawall, picked up a bunch of rocks, and leaned back over the side. Kathleen rolled down her window and we heard him shout "Bonzai!"

"You big fucker!" he shouted, dropping a rock the size of

a tennis ball down into the channel. "Gotcha!" I got out of the car and called, in a friendly voice, "Hey, watcha doing?"

"Big fucker turtles," he said, looking at us with excitement, dropping another rock off the side.

"Hey, knock it off," I said. "Leave them alone." Mickey glared at me for a long minute, slid off the wall, picked up his surfboard, gave me the finger with his free hand, and said, "Cram it, lady." He laughed and walked down the road and I got back in the car, thinking of *The Lord of the Flies* and the little boy who told Bozo, "Cram it, clown."

"Sweet boy, isn't he?" Kathleen asked.

"He called me 'lady,' did you notice?" I asked. "Kids on the street have started calling me 'lady,' like, 'Hey, lady, gotta match?' and it gets me every time. I have to look around to see who they mean." A dozen pelicans flew in a line over the channel toward the ocean, and the sun was flattened into an orange-red strip on the horizon.

"I saw an episode of *Maude* last week," said Kathleen after a minute, "in which Maude—Beatrice Arthur—had turned fifty, and she says to her best friend, 'I'm old, Vivian, I'm ollllddd, ollllddd.' She holds her hands out in front of her and says, 'These aren't my hands, Viv, these are my *mother's* hands.' " Kathleen looked at me and we laughed weakly.

"I was Stephanie's age once," I said, "not all that long ago. In fact it was about six weeks ago, and in another three months, barring accident, I'll be fifty. I wonder if I'll have some kids. I wonder if I'll have the sort of kids who break turtles' backs with rocks. Some of the truly great adults I know have some of the most atrocious children . . . and vice versa, actually."

"I think that if you had a kid, you'd misplace it. That's why I don't worry about you getting pregnant."

We were halfway done with our second beer and the red strip of sun had all but disappeared. Reds, roses, and purples became the navy blue of night over the ocean and over our heads.

"How can this all be so beautiful, so fucking perfect, so obviously inspired by the gods—I mean, how could the same gods create all this perfection and then let Wallace get a brain tumor? How can everything look so beautiful and function so exquisitely if a god or gods weren't involved, and if there *is* a god involved, how could the world's nicest man get a tumor? I mean—"

"You're just about the only person I know who still believes," said Kathleen. "I don't have any answers for you, except I think your theory of the drunken stoned gods is as good as any. Sometimes they've had two beers on an empty stomach and they're all light and happy and inspire good things, and sometimes they're hung over and divinely diarrhetic and inspire lousy shitty things like Hitler and cancer. I'm quoting you."

I stared out my window, away from Kathleen, and chewed on my thumbnail. "Radiation starts tomorrow," I said.

"Yeah, I know."

"I picture the gods saying, 'Okay, let's see, we've scared the living bejesus out of Wallace and his family; we made him look ten years older in the course of a few weeks; we got a surgeon to cut through his skull with a saw—what shall we do next? Hey! We'll have him get radiation, but we won't let him know for sure whether he really needs it, and he'll lose all of his hair again and look another ten years older. Hah hah hah, that's a good one. Any of You Guys got any more Angel Dust?' "

"I'll come over tomorrow night," she said, "I want to hear all about it, and you'll probably want some company. And I'll want some, too." She started up the car, and asked, "Do you know who said that we are not children or gods?"

"No, who?"

"I don't know either; it's been on my mind for the last few minutes. Ask Wallace tomorrow; he'll know. Not that I believe for a second that you'll remember."

When Kathleen dropped me off at the cabin that night, I

sat on the front step and threw pebbles into the ice plant, knocking God knows how many insects unconscious and not giving even the mildest damn.

Wallace and I stopped at the post office on our way over the hill for radiation ten weekdays in a row. We followed the same ritual every day: I drove; we picked up the mail, which Wallace read aloud; we played tapes on the cassette player, and sometimes sang along. Sometimes we talked, and sometimes we sat thinking silently. I read magazines in the waiting room while Wallace was irradiated, and then we stopped for a snack before I drove us both back home. Every day we pointed out the undercover cops who were carrying out the cancer-patient dragnet, and every day I thought about how many times Wallace had driven his children to the doctor when we were young, and the ironies and beauties of the cycle.

Nothing was more depressing than to leave for the clinic on an empty mail box, or a mail box that contained a Gray Panther pamphlet for Wallace and a Christmas catalogue for me. Somewhere along the line following the brain surgery I had stopped seeing most of my adult friends in Clement, who were inclined to offer great affection and encouragement and to then launch into intolerable complaints on every conceivable subject, up to and including the delicatessen's nefarious coffee, the wet towels their teenagers left on the floor, and finances. (Several days before radiation began, a woman I barely knew named Cathy Buns launched into a documentary on her recently diagnosed ptilosis, which is an ophthalmological disorder that causes one's eyelashes to fall out, and I had to put my hands in my pockets to keep from choking her to death.) I played with Kathleen, and the people in my family, and a few twelve-year-old boys, and only a few adult friends, and the mail became increasingly more important for extracurricular human contact.

There was a letter from Colin to Wallace on the first day of radiation. When we went to the post office these days I always hoped there was a letter for Wallace more than I hoped for one for myself, a reversal of the sacrificing parent-child relationship, I think. Wallace probably hoped there was a letter for me.

" 'Dear Wallace,' " my father read as I drove us to the doctor.

"If all goes well you are reading this on your first day of radiation, and knowing that you will be trapped in a car with Daughter for three hours a day, I am passing along two items of automotive interest.

"Yesterday, when I walked to the store, I found a letter on the ground from Old Mrs. Wolfe who lives up the street, to Jack Benton, who has just returned to town. The letter concerned the driver's-license exam, which Old Mrs. Wolfe will be taking again soon. O. Mrs. W. is eighty-four, has cataracts in both eyes and advanced arthritis, and Jack is seventy-six, with glaucoma. Both drive regularly over the mountain, and O. Mrs. W. wanted to compare notes on the routes that the driving inspectors use when they test. It is my clear impression that O. Mrs. W. *memorizes* the turns, stop signs, and parking tests. Caveat!

"And the really big news around here is that Ruth [his landlady who lives downstairs] bought a new (used) car, a Plymouth Barracuda in which she will henceforth transport me to my monthly cardiologist appointments. It is a rather vicious-looking machine as befits its name, and Ruth is busily not being delighted with the change from her rather primitive VW, and I pretend to give the Barracuda only passing glance and offhand comment, as it is always difficult for us old left-wingers to accept luxury and added comfort. The other part is that I think we are both a bit frightened of the damn thing.

"Now you tell Daughter to drive slowly; love to you both."

"Good letter," said Wallace, folding it up and putting it back in the envelope. Colin and Wallace and my "uncle" Michael were just a bit older than Ben is now when they met, all newly married, all just getting started. And now Colin has had five heart attacks and Wallace one brain tumor. Both, as Colin has said, have been in the Dark Room now. Both know that life is short, destiny inexorable, and that life is precious only because they are not going to live forever.

I have a photograph taken in 1950 of Colin and Wallace and Michael on the latter's sailboat, and they look like my older brother and his friends. Colin says that before his first heart attack he had never been able to live in the here and now, had never understood that the moment is the only reality. I know now that the past (which holds maudlin or bitter and certainly revisionist memories) and the future (which holds hope and anticipation and, by extension, anxiety—stage fright) can be experienced only in the present, but the problem, as I see it, is that the present, the here and now, is the shits.

Colin's answer is that in Chinese, the character "Crisis" means two things: danger and opportunity. Wallace agrees, but he and I spend hours and hours reminiscing. The past is so safe.

"Remember the time Colin painted our kitchen floor?" Wallace asked as we drove around the lagoon. "You must have been four. It was the kind of paint that takes twenty-four hours to dry, and your mother and I had to leave the house, for a cocktail party, I think. So we left all the food and liquids you and Ben would need in the living room while we were gone and we made you both promise you wouldn't go in the kitchen. But while we were gone, it turned out that you simply *had* to go through the kitchen, so you very carefully laid newspapers down on the floor and walked across the newspapers, which dried into the paint. . . ."

"Oh, no," I said, laughing. "Did you beat us?"

"Of course not. We were laughing so hard about your sincerity that we wept, but Colin was furious the next day. It was impossible to get a lot of the newspaper off, and you know how meticulous he is. He still brings it up."

I remember being spanked only a few times in my childhood. I also remember the parents of several very young friends beating, literally beating, their small daughters in my presence in the suburbs where I grew up, for crimes along the lines of a "needs improvement in classroom conduct" on first-grade report cards, and then shouting, when my friends wept, *Now shut up or I'll really give you something to cry about!*

I vividly remember my fourth year, and almost nothing of earlier years. It was the year when I saw God for the first time, on the album of *My Fair Lady*, in the form of George Bernard Shaw as a white-haired and mischievous grandfather in the clouds dangling the marionette strings of Julie Andrews and Rex Harrison. It was the year I saw the first death that moved me, in a Walt Disney movie in which a mother leopard was shot in midair by hunters. Her cubs and I wept wildly as I suddenly understood something about death: that the cubs no longer had a mother. It was the year when I began altering my consciousness, via hyperventilation and spinning rapidly in circles, from someone's arms or from a rope swing. It was the year before I started school, and the older boys were already teasing me about my hair. Wallace was in his early thirties, and already a successful writer: my memories of Wallace as a young man in his thirties and forties are almost more real to me (and maybe to Wallace) than the man he has become, dangerously close to sixty and no longer in robust health.

We drove up the curves of the mountain road, silently. Wallace was staring out the window, pursing his lips, and I was thinking about first grade. There wasn't a nonwhite in my class (and there wouldn't be until fourth grade, when the Mexican janitor's daughter enrolled). There was a little girl whose mother burned to death in a fire, a chubby six-year-old boy with breasts, two kids with divorced parents—almost unheard of then, and a big stigma—three adopted kids who frequently said in response to taunts, "Our parents *chose* us, but your parents were stuck with you," several stammerers, a boy named Lester Snorts who used to mash his cheese sandwich into his milk and then drink it down and who on several occasions made it come out his nose, a few kids who periodically peed on themselves and their chairs, and then there were the rest of us, the "normal" kids of varying intelligence who indulged in routine acts of derision and cruelty toward the misfits.

One of Wallace's sociological theories is the Shitty-Assed Child Theory of Human Behavior, by which he means that in our subconsciousness we are still shitty-assed children who need to be wiped, and who are always afraid of being discovered with a dump in our pants, shameful for reasons we don't understand, yet we know our parents will not be pleased, at all. When I listen to adults in Clement eloquently restate standard childhood lines like "Oh yeahhhhh?" or "Lookit me, lookit me!" or "If you give me that, I'll be your best friend, I'll give you a penny," it feels like first grade all over again, with just enough Peyton Place thrown in to cause large-scale schizophrenia. In one way I wish that our motives and meanings and feelings did not have to be so carefully disguised so that we will not appear to be misfits or laughable or to have age-old dumps in our pants, and in one way I just don't want to play anymore.

Violet Weingarten, in her journal of chemotherapy, wrote, "Problem—stated at its most succinct—is life too short to be taking shit, or is life too short to mind it?" All my life, when I have perpetrated or experienced some disaster, Wallace has said, "Think of it as an Educational Experience," and the unavoidable shit has always become amusing and ironic. When Wallace got sick, Randy told him to think of it as an Educational Experience, and Wallace glared at him, jokingly. But as for the avoidable shit we take and dole out—the pettiness, the games, the pretenses—it all diminishes greatly when I step outside of the so-called real world of Clement society, when I spend most of my time alone.

We arrived at the clinic ninety minutes after leaving Clement, and found a space right in front, a good omen. I turned off the engine, and we sat staring at the front door for a minute.

"So here we are," said Wallace. "This is it." We got out of the car and went inside, as casually as if we were going in to buy shoes. The waiting room was empty, as it would be on seven of the ten days we came. Wallace went to the receptionist's window and introduced himself.

"Why don't you come on back," she said. Wallace turned around, smiled dryly, and semisaluted. I gave the thumbs-up sign, and he went into the back room. I sat down and began leafing feverishly through women's magazines. There was an advertisement in *Women's Day* that showed a model whom I knew when she was a chubby, surly child. Her face was being touched by a hairy hand, and the caption read, "I love you without make-up." The model's makeup looked like Mae West's did at seventy. I stared at her very beautiful face for a long time; she was one of the kids who used to pee on herself.

I sat reading magazines and waiting for Wallace to come into the waiting room. I sort of expected him to reemerge any minute, saying with great relief, "Well, let's go; it turned out to be a big mistake; I don't have *anything* wrong with me; it's some other person that had a possibly malignant brain tumor. Let's go have a drink!" But he didn't.

Finally I got up and asked the receptionist where the ladies' room was, knowing full well that it was behind the door. I simply had to see what was back there, and when she told me it was in the back hallway, I opened the door with blind expectancy.

There were a half dozen elderly men and women sitting on couches outside office doors. The men wore pajamas and bathrobes, and the women wore nightgowns and bathrobes and had the six skinniest legs I have ever seen. They looked exhausted and used to waiting. The lucky ones believed in God, and not one of them looked up at me. I went into the bathroom at the other end of the hallway, washed my face and hands, stared at what suddenly seemed the most youthful face in the world, in the mirror, and went back into the hallway. Nothing had changed, no one had so much as shifted position, and again no one looked at me. I went back to the waiting room and sat down.

The door to the clinic opened, and an orderly stepped inside, pulling behind him, as it turned out, a stretcher on wheels with another orderly at the other end. On the stretcher was a huge, horizontal man of about forty with a shaved Neanderthal head with a trapdoor scar at the top of the forehead. I looked at his face as he passed, and smiled tightly. He stared at me with intense black eyes and a twisted, almost malevolent, almost leering but actually amused mouth. He continued to look at me as he was wheeled into the back room, and I didn't look away. "Hi," I said. He winked. I waved as he disappeared into the back, so that he wouldn't think his presence was making me uncomfortable.

As a child, it goes almost without saying, I was taught to keep my eyes off peculiar-looking people—retarded children and adults, the lame, the very old, the very fat, the deformed, those of different races, and so on. I was taught that it was impolite—cruel even—to look at them, and even worse to ask them questions, like why they had only one arm, or what it was like to be an old man who was shorter than I was at five. I was taught that ignoring these people, compassionately, was what good girls did, and I developed my parents' feelings of discomfort with physically and mentally disabled people.

As an adult, I keep thinking I have outgrown this discomfort, but in trying to act nonchalant, I generally stick
my foot in my mouth and then fall to pieces inside. Randy
told me a joke several years ago, about a shy boy at a sev-
enth-grade dance who summoned all his courage to ask a
chubby wallflower, whom he liked quite a bit, to dance.
Afterward, when they are standing awkwardly together
and the boy wants to express his affection, he blurts out,
"Gee, you don't sweat much for a fat girl." Randy said that
he could be the boy, and I assured him that he would grow
out of it.

Several months ago at a garden party, I noticed a woman
about my age sitting alone, embroidering. She had long red
braids and almond-shaped brown eyes and kept looking up
expectantly. I went over to talk to her.

"Hello," I said. "What are you making?"

She smiled, held up her embroidery, and said, "A picture,
of the lagoon. I'm doing the egret right now." She sounded
as if she were enunciating carefully through a mouthful of
marbles, and I realized with sudden distress that she did not
have a palate. I was afraid I was going to start laughing out
of nervousness, but didn't, and sat down.

"What's that?" I asked, pointing to a patch of brown
lines.

"Pussywillows," she said. "Pussywillows," as spoken by
a person with no palate, is a difficult word to pronounce.

"It's beautiful," I said. "You're very good."

"It's easy; it's nothing. It's only four stitches; it's pretty
because of the different colors." It was only by staring at
her mouth as she talked that I could understand what she
said. "Really, it's easy."

And I said, loudly and with real admiration, "Well, that's
easy for *you* to say."

After the man on the stretcher was gone, I sat fidgeting,
hesitant to open any more magazines because almost every
one of them had an article on cancer. I have become comfortable when discussing cancer these days, as long as it is

not Wallace's cancer (and I mostly do not think of him as being a person with cancer; I think of him as a person with a mild touch of it that was removed surgically). I feel an impulse to act straightforwardly without invading other people's privacy, and at all costs to avoid patronizing sympathy. When people express sympathy for our family I am never sure if they feel true compassion or relief that it's my family and not theirs, and I keep in mind Alexander Woollcott's line "I am in no need of your goddamn sympathy. I ask only to be entertained by some of your grosser reminiscences."

When Wallace stepped into the waiting room an hour after he left it, I jumped to my feet. "Hi," I said.

"Hi," he said, "ready to go?" He looked perfectly healthy, especially in comparison to the older people in the back room, the ones who *really* had cancer. He opened the door to the clinic and held it while I walked out.

"How was it?" I asked as we walked to the car.

"Fascinating," he said. "I had an examination with the radiology oncologist, and we discussed what two weeks of radiation would be like, and then I waited for my turn with the radiation machine. The technicians drew these little blue marks on my head so they'll know what to aim at with the X rays—see?" He bent down from the waist so I could see the blue dots next to his ears.

"Neat," I said, although I did not like the tattoos at all.

"Then I lay down on the table, and they pointed the machine at my dots—it looks like a dental X-ray machine—and turned it on. There was a faint hum for about three minutes, and then they turned it off. I lay there for a couple of minutes, and then got dressed." We got into the car and I turned on the engine. "And what did *you* do?"

"I read magazines for a while, and daydreamed." I lit a Camel, and eased the car onto the road.

"Let's get a snack," he said. "I'm feeling a bit lightheaded." We were in a mostly residential section with a few office buildings and no place that sold food. "Just head toward the highway; we'll find something."

"What's the doctor like?"

"Young, pleasant, about forty-five, I'd guess. He was wearing Birkenstocks, and his socks didn't match: one was a blue argyle, and one was a green argyle, which reassured me, for some reason. Nice guy. I think I must remind him of his father."

"What was his voice like?"

"Quiet, gentle. He said that I'll definitely lose my hair, and I said we'd have to wait and see, and he said that *no* one believes he'll lose his hair, and all of them do."

"There's a health-food store," I said, pointing. "How about carob almonds?"

"O.K. There's even a space." I pulled over and parked at the curb. "Do you mind going in? I feel a bit tired." He gave me two dollar bills. "Maybe some fruit, too, if there's change."

"O.K.," I said, and went inside.

I found the candy department in the small health-food store and put a few scoops of carob almonds into a plastic bag. I stood staring at the shelves, wondering what else Wallace might like, when I noticed that I was being scrutinized by the man behind the cash register, who turned away when our eyes met; he looked like Jimmy Connors will look in thirty years. I picked up a Hi-Protein carob/peanut-butter bar and made very sure to display it in my left hand; in stores I tend to assume that the manager thinks I'm shoplifting, although I have never stolen anything but penny candy. I go out of my way to make sure my hands and their contents are highly visible, and my eyes always dart furtively around to make sure the manager can see that my intentions are good. I have gone so far as to semifrisk myself as if feeling in my pockets for money or keys. I went to the counter with the candy and gave them to the man, who looked especially suspicious and ill-natured.

He weighed the almonds, rang up a dollar seventeen, picked up the candy, rang up twenty-five cents, and said, "One-forty-two."

There was a basket of beautiful ripe cherries near the cash register, and I said, "I'd also like about sixty cents' worth of cherries." He put two huge handfuls into a plastic bag. "Fifty-eight cents' worth, please," I said. He weighed the bag, removed six or seven cherries, and rang up fifty-eight cents. I handed him the two dollars as he put my purchases into a bag and pushed them toward me. I left the store, with the bag in one hand and the other hand almost above my head, clearly visible.

"Cherries for the mountain," I said to Wallace when I got back in the car. "And a candy bar to fatten you up. And almonds." I handed them all to him, and started the motor.

"Wonderful." He unwrapped the candy bar, and asked if I wanted half as I drove down the road to the highway. I shook my head. He turned on the country-music station, and took a bite of the candy bar. I looked over, and he was chewing slowly, with a puzzled look on his face.

"Curious," he said. "This has the weirdest texture you can imagine, sort of like fried air. Really, you've got to try a bite." He handed it to me, I took a bite, and returned it. The taste was good, but the texture was disconcerting.

"It feels like those peanut-shaped Styrofoam packing things," I said. "But good."

"Moose-turd pie!" he said before taking another bite, "but good!"—which is the punchline to a joke Wallace heard from U. Utah Phillips about fifteen years ago and has been telling ever since.

We drove back to Clement, forty-five minutes on the highway that ran along beautiful lush farmlands with farm animals, and forty-five minutes over the mountain and along the lagoon to town. At the bottom of the mountain Wallace put a tape of Ella's greatest hits on the tape player, and we began eating the cherries. One of the great carefree joys of human life is traveling in a car with a bag of cherries, spitting the pits out the window. We got back to Wallace's house at four.

Randy and Muldoon ran out to greet us when we pulled up, as they would do every day of the radiation. Randy opened Wallace's door and began thumping him on the shoulders. "How'd it go?" he asked.

"Fine. I'll tell you about it inside. Here's what's left of our snacks; finish them off if you'd like." He gave Randy the plastic bag of almonds and cherries, and we both got out of the car.

Randy, my baby brother who is now ten inches taller than I, said, "Oh, boy," and spit a couple of cherry pits at my back as the three of us walked inside.

"I'm gonna kill you," I said.

"Imagine my terror!" he said, patting me on the head.

On the second day of radiation Wallace brought me *The Red and the Black* to read while he was in the back room. "It may explain a few things about the male psyche for you," he said, "and besides, it's an extraordinary book." I read it fifty pages at a time, in the waiting room and in bed, spellbound by Stendhal's descriptions of what could be Clement, one of those American towns where the tyranny of public opinion is as stupid as in the small towns of France. There are innumerable aging Julien Sorels in town, ". . . this young man whose hypocrisy and total lack of sympathy were his usual means of survival. . . ." "I love her beauty but I fear her mind. . . ." "Man was given the power of thought to conceal his thoughts." I have had half a dozen affairs with Julien Sorels over the years, and when I finished the book, I passed it along to several Juliens in the spirit of communication and vindictiveness: none of them finished it.

"It is one of the misfortunes of our age," Stendhal wrote

in 1830, "that even the strangest deviations of conduct do not cure boredom." It became impossible for me to look at many of the adults in Clement without wincing.

Wallace got more and more tired in the afternoons as the second week began, but remained cavalier and uncomplaining. There were afternoons when we would be driving along the farmlands, and I would forget where we were going, and when it came to me that Wallace was getting radiation because he'd had a brain tumor, it was always as a shock. The hypnotism of the long drive added to my feeling of surrealism; it was almost like taking a soporific, without the sleepiness or the dumbness, and it made it possible to discuss our associations of death and dying and aging and even pain—the starkest aspect of all—with a certain detachment, with seriousness and laughter that converged. "This is the shits," he said over and over, "but consider the alternatives." One of the alternatives was the Neanderthal man on the stretcher, but Wallace hadn't seen him.

On the eighth day of radiation, his hair began to fall out, first in individual one-inch strands that gathered on his collar and then in tufts, by the handful. Sarah removed as much as she could with a baby brush, and huge patches of his scalp showed through, surrounded by uneven clumps. It looked like a rodent in a hurry had been nibbling at his head, and he took to wearing a watch cap, although the weather over the hill was consistently reaching ninety.

When we stopped for a frozen yogurt after we left the clinic on the second-to-last day, a small boy at the Frogurt stand stared wide-eyed at Wallace, whose watch cap did not cover all of his skull. His mother hissed at the boy, and he looked away for a second, and then snuck another look. Wallace stared with sudden interest at the list of three flavors.

"I'm starting to scare little children," he said as we walked to our car with the Frogurts. "It is time to do something about it."

"Kids stare at my hair all the time, and big kids used to tease me, but you get used to it. And besides, it'll all be gone soon."

Wallace took his watch cap off in the car; his head looked much more alarming than it had when bald: the scar showed again, and a clump of hair fell onto his Frogurt. "Oh, shit," he said, and looked disgusted. I gave him my frozen yogurt, and said I wasn't hungry. "I want you to cut it all off tonight."

"O.K."

We passed a beauty salon for men and women on our way to the highway, and Wallace smiled broadly. "I got it," he said. "We'll go in, and I'll tell the beautician that my hair feels like it's thinning out a bit on the sides, and could he or she do something with it—maybe even it out a bit and teach me how to back-brush it." We laughed, and when I looked over at him, his head no longer scared me. He was pantomiming a beautician; he squinted doubtfully, looked around from side to side, rolled his eyes, lifted one of the remaining locks gingerly, as if to snip it with the first two fingers of his right hand. The lock pulled free effortlessly, and Wallace threw it out the window.

When we got home that day, I cut all of it off, in the bathroom with a pair of scissors that left only a sixteenth of an inch of stubble when it left any at all. The scar had healed beautifully, thanks in large part to Sarah's insistence that she rub a capsule of vitamin E into it every night, but transforming Wallace back into the Buddhist-monk look-alike made me feel very sad, and old.

On the Saturday after the first week of radiation, I lay on my bed reading when three boys, all twelve years old, showed up at the cabin, with flowers for me from the mother of one of them. "Hello, hello, hello!" they said, bursting into the room.

"Hi, you guys," I said, with affection but not much enthusiasm. "C'mon in."

"So this is where our Slob Monster lives," said the only boy who had never been here before, as the three roamed around the cabin.

"Are you the Slob Monster today, or are you being Mrs. Quiet?" asked the blond.

"Mrs. Quiet."

"You bummed?"

"A little."

"Wanna watch the basketball game? Lakers and Bullets?"

"I'd love to, only I don't have a television."

"You don't have a *television*?"

"Tell us a story, then, O.K.?" The way they act around me is almost the way I act around my uncle Colin: respectful, adoring, and equals. I am always happy to see them.

"O.K.," I told them. "The last time Mrs. Quiet went to a yoga class in town, it was held on the teacher's porch, in the sun. I was told to assume the position called 'Salute to the Sun,' which I did: spine erect, arms stretched outward, palms up, reaching for the sun. I am told to breathe in life, harmony, ecstasy, health, and compassion, which I do, with my eyes closed, and a wasp bites me between my thumb and forefinger, and within minutes my hand looks like the Pillsbury dough boy."

The boys smile and laugh. I laughed, too, becoming the Slob Monster again. I wonder if they will grow up to be adult males who are ruled by their penises and wallets, or if, at thirty, they will visit sad friends.

I had dinner with Wallace and Sarah and Randy every night of the radiation, and then met Kathleen at my cabin for drinks or dope. All five of us felt the surrealism, and did not see very many other people. Our galaxies diminished greatly. I occasionally saw three other friends for beer and drives, but rarely went downtown, and didn't sleep with anyone. I read until I fell asleep every night, sometimes wishing a friend were in bed with me, but mostly not. At the time I did not have a male friend who wanted to sleep with me if I felt like company and hugging instead of sex, and I didn't feel the least bit horny. And there are only a few people outside my family who do not panic or lose interest if I am depressed or quiet, or who do not take it personally when I cease to be entertaining. One friend insisted for so long that she must be a part of my depression that I had to write her off. One friend decided I no longer liked him because I was no longer much fun in his company; he said he had seen me laughing with Kathleen in her car, and that I must not really be as depressed as I claimed—that it must somehow have to do with him, which it didn't. He didn't understand that Kathleen and I laugh together no matter how depressed we are, and when he asked what it is we find to laugh about, and I replied, "Oh, cancer, pimples, aging, being misfits," he said that I should stop seeing her altogether.

On the eighth night of radiation, Kathleen came over to the cabin at nine with a half pint of tequila, depressed.

"What's the matter?" I asked. "What's the thing you're most depressed about?"

"Wallace."

"Oh, that," I said.

I poured us each a shot of tequila, and lay down on the floor.

"Nothing else that I can put my finger on. That's what's so depressing. I have this vague sense of dread right now, you know, that nothing matters, that there's no point, that—like Wallace—you spend fifty years recovering from your childhood, growing up, finally living a free life and— bam!—you get sick. Or that by the time you're grown up enough to know what you really want to do instead of what you're supposed to want to do, you might be too old to do it. I get goosebumps in my stomach, and I can't put my finger on what I'm anxious about. And I can't believe how old I've gotten, in the wink of an eye. This aging business is the pits, slowly deteriorating."

"I think it's *quid pro quo*. Your looks start to go about the time you start growing up, about the time things are starting to gel. . . ."

"*Speaking* of which—speaking of gelling and gelatin—I thought buying some new clothes would lift my spirits. So I went into a clothes store feeling very slinky and thin, and went into the dressing room to try on some pants, and made the mistake of looking in the mirror when I had my pants off. And when I saw my thighs in the three-way mirror, close up, under fluorescent lights, they looked so dimply and purple that I gasped, loudly. Very loudly. So the sales-lady says, 'Everything all right in there?' And I said, 'Oh, uh, yeah, I thought I saw a spider. . . .' " And suddenly, Kathleen was laughing.

On the last day of radiation a corpulent and ravaged woman with the clothes and bearing and voice of a skid-row bum sat on the bench in front of the post office, a tattered paperback copy of *The Thorn Birds* and an open cigar box filled with change and trinkets on her lap. She was drinking from a bottle of vermouth and snarling at nonexistent passersby, loudly, telling the world to go to hell, to go fuck itself.

"Hello," said Wallace as we walked past her.

"Oh go to hell, Gramps," she yelled.

"Jesus," I said when we were inside the post office, "what a mess. There but for fortune. . . ." The woman was a much more disturbing and saddening sight than the younger Burn Outs in town, who by and large seem to enjoy themselves more than the rest of us. When I asked Wallace why he thought the woman affected me in this way, he rubbed his chin.

"I suppose because she doesn't have a chance in hell of starting over, of being less of a mess when she grows up. And besides, she's somebody's *mother*." He opened our post box with his key.

"Not necessarily," I said.

"No, maybe not. But she *is* somebody's daughter." He extracted a postcard and a pamphlet from the box, and said, "I guess this is it. Another communiqué for me from the Gray Panthers, and a postcard for you." He handed it to me. It was a black-and-white photograph of Pope Pius XII with a beam of light emanating from his head.

"Hurray!" Colin's message began. "Your dad's last day of radiation! Drive especially carefully today, dear, you know how your old uncle Colin worries about you. Come see me this weekend; for lunch and maybe a small fight, and remember that God works in strange ways Her tum-tum to perform." I handed the card to Wallace, who laughed at both the picture and the writing, and when we walked back outside, the old woman was gone.

When Wallace disappeared into the back room of the clinic for his last treatment, I sat in the waiting room finishing *The Red and the Black*, across from a woman who looked about my age, pretty and very thin and wearing a blond wig. One of the doctors came into the waiting room, walked over to the young woman, and said, "Your last scan looked a lot better. We'll do another bone scan on Tuesday, O.K.?" The woman nodded amicably. The doctor touched her shoulder and returned to the back room, the young woman smiled at me and left, and chills went up and down my spine.

When Wallace and I returned home that evening, Randy was sitting in the wheelbarrow in the back yard drinking a Mickey's Big Mouth. Wallace was exhausted and, after saying hello to him, went inside.

"You better stay out here," Randy said, handing me his beer. "Sarah has a headache and she's trying to sleep in the window seat. We have to play out here."

"I'm going to get another beer; then I'll come back out."

"Better not," he said. "You'll wake her up."

"Trust me," I said sarcastically. "After all, I *am* an adult."

I went inside, where Wallace was already dozing in the window seat next to Sarah. I tiptoed to the refrigerator, opened it soundlessly, removed a Mickey's, closed the refrigerator silently, tiptoed toward the door, and tripped over Muldoon, who was asleep on the floor. The beer flew out of my hand and hit Muldoon on the head before crashing to the ground. Muldoon yelped and tore into the living room where Wallace and Sarah were now sitting up with groggy impatience on their faces.

"Sorry, sorry," I said sheepishly. "I was just getting a beer." They settled back against the pillows, and I exaggerated tiptoeing toward the door, with my finger to my lips. When I got outside, I opened the beer, having forgotten that I had dropped it, and a geyser of beer shot up into my face. I sputtered, and Randy laughed. I took a foamy sip of beer and sat on the ground next to the wheelbarrow.

"You want me to give you a ride in the wheelbarrow?" he asked. "I don't really fit all that well."

"O.K.," I said, and we traded places. I didn't fit all that well either. Randy lifted the handles of the wheelbarrow and pushed me around the yard for a minute. "Faster, faster," I said.

"Wait here a minute," he said, and tiptoed inside. He emerged with a half-size comforter and Sarah's powder-blue knit cap. He tucked the comforter around me, and handed me the cap.

"What's this for?" I said, putting on the cap.

"I've been watching ladies wheel their babies around all afternoon. I thought it looked like fun." Randy lifted the handles again and wheeled me around the yard, singing Rosalie Sorrels's rendition of "The Hostile Baby Rocking Song," which goes "Oh, this is the day we give babies away, with half a pound of tea." He sang it with Rosalie's menacing Fagin voice. "Oh, *this* is the day we give *babies* away . . ." I laughed, and he started wheeling me toward the gate, still singing. He pushed the wheelbarrow and me out onto the street, and although I felt foolish, there was no one in sight, so I alternately laughed and made baby sounds while Randy continued the lullaby.

One of the town's more prominent drunks drove by, looking like an old pug on morphine, and slowly turned his head around as he passed us. We laughed. Randy pushed me for a few more blocks, and I took long sips of my beer; it was the happiest I could remember being in weeks.

"Oh boy," he said. "Look up ahead." A mother with a real baby in a real baby stroller with a real baby blanket and cap was coming toward us, a couple of blocks away. We were laughing out of control, but quietly, holding it in and almost choking. "Let me do the talking," he said.

He pushed me solemnly down the street toward the woman and her baby. I recognized but did not know the woman, who did not look at all amused when she looked up and saw us approaching. I began to feel even more foolish. When Randy and I were ten feet away from the woman, he said loudly and jovially, "My, what an adorable baby you have." The woman said thank you, looked down, and was about to pass us. She had closely set hostile eyes; the baby looked like J. Edgar Hoover, and was, I think, a girl. "And how old is yours?" he asked pleasantly.

"Ten months," she said, and pushed past us.

"Oh," said Randy, "mine's twenty-three." The woman didn't say another word, and turned down the first cross street. Randy and I became hysterical. He set the wheelbarrow down, clutched his stomach, and roared. I handed him my beer but he shook his head. He picked the handles back up, turned me around toward the house, and pushed me back down the road, the both of us laughing so hard that for the first time in many, many years, I wet my pants.

Back to Work

I awoke on the first of October somehow convinced that it was time for me to get a job, and tried unsuccessfully to sleep the feeling off. I got up to make tea, because coffee had gone up to five dollars a pound, and decided that a job was not such a bad idea. Several years ago when I went into early retirement I promised myself that I would never again wake up to an alarm clock, dress up for work, or work under fluorescent lights, a resolve that I would admire if I did not borrow so much cigarette money from my family and friends. Adults have jobs and make money, I thought, and though I did not particularly want a job, I did want more money, which at this point in my career meant anything upward of twenty dollars a week.

I wrote a classified ad for the local mimeographed newspaper availing my services in yard work, housework, and wine-tasting, at five dollars an hour, and headed out the door toward the newspaper "office," which is four unpaved blocks away. I did not meet anybody on the street whom I knew, because everybody I know has a job. Wallace makes a living as a writer, Randy does yard work, Sarah teaches third-graders, Ben does landscape design, Kathleen does research for a pharmaceutical company, and even Colin gets a monthly check from the state government because he has had so many heart attacks. Before Wallace's surgery I cleaned houses three times a week, but have not worked since except for giving occasional tennis lessons. When people ask me what I "do," I say that I write, although I know that what they really mean is "How do you support yourself?" Last year I cleaned house regularly for a poetry publisher and, while cashing his check at the liquor store, asked loudly, "Can you cash this? It's from a publisher." I think often of a William Hamilton cartoon in *The New Yorker* of two "now society" women sitting at a café table, one woman saying, "Yes, Herb's a writer, but he hasn't gone through the drag of publication yet." Writing is no great shakes in terms of steady income and professional security, but it is much better than working for a living: I know very, very few people who love and are satisfied by their jobs, people for whom work really delivers in the way that love and laughter deliver. Still, I thought as I walked, I might be psychically capable of working two days a week, as long as I could start after eleven.

I reached the newspaper office just in time for the Monday printing, and six hours later the phone began ringing. Adam Arlen was the first to call, and he offered me a housecleaning job for the next day. I said I'd be there at eleven. He said O.K. A few minutes later the phone rang again and a hippie couple I cleaned house for last year offered me another housecleaning job. I said I'd be there Thursday at eleven. The woman said that would be fine. When I hung up, I called Wallace, invited myself for a drink, called Kathleen, invited her along, and left the house before the phone could ring again.

Kathleen and I arrived at the same time and walked into the living room together. Wallace, Sarah, and Randy were sitting at the living-room table watching the World Series out of the corners of their eyes, each with a beer and a project at hand. Wallace was glueing a Japanese teapot back together, Randy was drawing, and Sarah was sorting tiny plastic animals alphabetically into the drawers of a foot-tall chest.

"Hello," said Wallace. "Get yourselves a drink; pull up a chair."

"What is this, crafts time?" Kathleen asked.

"Yeah," said Randy sarcastically, "we're supposed to be making potato prints but we don't have any potatoes."

"What do you want to drink?" I asked Kathleen.

"Whatever you're having." I went into the kitchen to make screwdrivers. "What are you drawing?" she asked.

"Catfish Hunter," who was pitching, said Randy.

"Let me see," she said. "It's excellent."

"No, it isn't," said Randy. "It's stupid."

None of Wallace's children handle compliments with grace. I tend to retaliate with an insult or a joke or a lengthy description of how the opposite of the compliment is true, and I squirm. "Yeah," said Kathleen, "it is pretty stupid, and bad."

I went back into the living room, without drinks, and said to everybody, "Remember that *New Yorker* story about the little boy whose homework was to use 'catfish' in a sentence, so he wrote 'Catfish Hunter wears a red cap'? And his teacher gave it back to him corrected '*A* catfish hunter wears a red cap'?" Everybody laughed, and I sat down at the table.

"Where are the drinks?" asked Kathleen.

"Oh, yeah." I got up and went into the kitchen.

"Jesus, your daughter is beyond hope," she said. "Today she left her racket at the produce stand and her groceries at the tennis court."

"That's nothing," said Randy. "The stories I could tell. . . ."

"Hey, shut up out there," I yelled.

"It's no wonder she can't keep a job," said Randy.

"I got a job today," I said, and walked into the living room with two screwdrivers. I handed one to Kathleen. "I'm going to work tomorrow. So there."

"Doing what?" asked Sarah.

"Housecleaning."

"Heyyy, I'm *impressed*," said Randy.

"Who are you cleaning house for?"

"Adam Arlen."

"The lawyer?" asked Kathleen. "What does he pay?"

"Five an hour. It's what I charge now."

"Good for you," said Wallace.

"Rip-off," said Randy.

"Would you put this guy in the B drawer for 'brontosaurus,' or in the D drawer for 'dinosaur'?" Sarah asked.

"D," said Randy. "It's easier for them to spell."

I absently picked up a small ceramic box, toyed with the complicated latch, and opened it. It contained a small amount of loose marijuana and a crumpled-up ZigZag.

"I *knew* she'd find it," said Sarah.

"It's uncanny," said Wallace.

"You can't hide it from her," said Kathleen. "She can smell it out at fifty feet in the dark."

"Maybe we can get her a job at the airport, sniffing out drugs," said Wallace.

"She can join the trained canine corps," said Randy.

"If you're saving it, I won't . . ."

"No, it's O.K., it's O.K.," said Randy and Sarah.

"Barbara Crandall got her hair done just like yours, except it's gray," said Wallace. "She told me you were her inspiration."

Barbara is one of my favorite people in town, a brilliant, kind, and slightly crazy woman in her fifties. "She did?" I asked.

"She did?" asked Randy, and began to laugh very, very hard.

I ignored him. "I love your hair," said Sarah.

"You do?" I asked. "Can I get you anything? A drink? A pillow? Some money?"

"You don't have any money," said Kathleen.

"I will after tomorrow."

"Then we'll talk."

"I really do love your hair," said Sarah.

"Oh, this old stuff," I said, grabbing a hunk of it. I squirmed. One of the things that makes me uncomfortable about compliments is that they are usually about something that was much too easy to do to deserve attention, or for one of my physical features, which I had nothing to do with, or for things that I did for all the wrong reasons. "Thanks," I said, pleased.

"How's your work going, Wallace?" asked Kathleen.

"Excellently, thanks," said Wallace. The teapot had been reconstructed, and Wallace's hands lay folded on the table. "I've almost finished another story, and I must say I like it much better than the last." He looked as well as he had before the surgery, from the forehead down. Thick white peach fuzz covered his scalp and the scar, his face was well rested and rosy, and the muscles in his face were relaxed. He began to look and feel especially well on the day he went back to writing, which is no small coincidence.

"Good," said Kathleen.

"How much do you make, Kathleen?" asked Randy.

"A thousand something take-home," she said.

"*What?*" he shouted. "A thousand dollars!"

"It's not all that much, really. I mean, I never have any left over. When I made six hundred a month, I spent six hundred a month; when I made eight hundred, I spent eight hundred. I could make three thousand a month and I'd spend it."

"True," said Wallace. "A financial reality."

"Do you order stuffed mushrooms for appetizers when you go out for dinner?" Randy asked.

"Sometimes."

"Do you go to a lot of movies and concerts?"

"Sometimes. In phases."

"I wish *you* were my sister. *My* sister just comes over to steal drugs." He started whispering very loudly. "She can't get a job, because of her hair." Randy's insults and barbs are his compliments. Sometimes we are openly affectionate but more often we insult and tease each other in a friendly fashion. I tell him all the time that he was adopted. It always makes him crack up, no matter how straightfaced I am when speaking.

"I *have* a job," I said. "I have two jobs this week. I don't like to work, and I don't mind not having money as long as I don't have to work very much."

"If I were you, I'd teach five lessons a week," said Randy. "Fifty bucks, easy."

"I get bored with that many; it starts to be work. So I think I'll houseclean twice a week, and do a couple of lessons."

"Yeah, we don't want you to exhaust yourself," said Kathleen.

"I need three days a week to write," I said. "It's what I 'do'; it's what my work is right now. Well, of course I don't make money at it, but I only need fifty dollars a month or so. . . ."

"I wish *I* could live on fifty a month," said Wallace.

"You shouldn't have had children," said Randy. "You should have thought of that twenty-five years ago."

"You know, I go through this grueling experience, I still need a nap or two during the day, I'm back to work on my stories, and there's a thousand dollars in bills on my desk. It's crazy." Wallace shook his head, and smiled. "We're going to have to come up with a scam."

"We can kill Kathleen on payday, steal her check, and pay off your bills," said Randy. "Or another idea I have is this." He pulled the sleeve of his shirt down past his hand, curled his arm up into it, and stuck the fireplace poker up the sleeve. "See, I go into the welfare office and say I lost my arm and can't get a job with only a hook hand. So the welfare people find out eventually that my arm is in my sleeve, and I shriek with happiness to have found it, and then they give me money for being crazy. . . ."

"I feel sorry for you, Wallace," said Kathleen, giving him

a look of condolence. "Really," she said, "all of us who know you and your kids feel sorry for you."

"God knows I tried," Wallace said.

"Not very hard, as I remember," I said. "If you'd been a stricter disciplinarian, we'd all have families and jobs with a good future by now."

"I wonder if you'd be a writer if Wallace weren't," asked Sarah.

I looked at Wallace seriously. He closed one eye. I wouldn't have been the same person if Wallace hadn't been a writer, because Wallace wouldn't have been the same person. If I had not had a father who loved to tell stories, who got to sit in his study all day writing stories and articles— entertaining himself, showing off, recording moments and reflections—while other fathers worked in offices, I might not have wanted to be a writer, but I still would have wanted his favor. The relationship between one's father and one's own sense of ambition is a complicated and usually devious one, and I try not to think about it very much.

Kathleen and I went to the bar after another hour with Wallace, Randy, and Sarah. The skagginess and electricity of the bar are rude awakenings after the comfort and jokes and familiarity of being in a home or car with friends, but the sightseeing is unparalleled. Kathleen went up to the bar and I leaned aloofly against the jukebox. There were a dozen people in the bar, and all but four of their eyes were watching the pool game, even as they had conversations— anything to avoid prolonged eye contact. I waved to several friends and scrutinized the strangers. A man and woman entered the bar and waved nervously to me as they walked to the counter. I stared at their backs and smiled: they are two of my favorite people to watch in town. The hyperpretentious people in Clement entertain me more, with their snobbery and affectations and expensive dogs, than do any group besides my friends. I met Bradley and Renee for the first time at the hot springs retreat where I worked for four months last year. They were there at the beginning of the week when there were few other guests, and Bradley decided to teach their five-year-old son to swim, in the mineral pool. Max did not want to learn how to swim, as he preferred to sit on the pool steps and squirt water through his front teeth. Bradley pried his fingers loose from the side of the pool and carried him out to the deep end. "Wait, wait," said Max. "Kick," said Bradley. Max kicked furiously, and Bradley said, "That's it." "Don't let go," said Max, whining. "*Please.*" "Max, if I let go of you and you kick hard enough and paddle with your arms, you'll float." "Noooo," said Max. Bradley let go and pushed Max away. Max sank. Bradley lifted him, sputtering and crying, into his arms. This went on for an hour, Bradley saying, "Now, *kick*," Max sinking and panic-stricken. On the second day of swimming lessons, Bradley asked Max, who had to be carried to the pool, "Now, Maxie, are you a man like Daddy or aren't you?" Max weighed in the vicinity of thirty-five pounds. By the third lesson Max could tread water, not happily, and Bradley was beaming; I think that when Max grows up, he will know how to swim and he will have massive father problems.

I looked at Renee and Bradley leaning in a casual and stately manner against the bar, Renee a classic blond still-life beauty smoking like Garbo and arranging for her hair to fall forward so that she could seductively stroke it backward. I have always wanted to write a story about a woman like Renee, who speaks with what she thinks of as a child-like voice and a vocabulary of two hundred words, who overdresses, overspends, overflirts, and yet remains somehow likable. I've never written the story, because I cannot figure out how she does it.

I went down to the hotbaths one morning to refill the kerosene lamps, and Renee was the only person in any of the baths. Bradley and Max were outside having a swimming lesson, and Renee was shaving her legs. There was a film of soap and short black hairs and old skin like an oil slick around her.

"That bathrobe is absolutely divine . . ." she said. "Where—"

"Renee, shaving is not allowed in the bath," I said with a clutched stomach and timid voice.

"But why?" she asked. "Doesn't the water drain out?"

"Yes, it does, but slowly."

"Is there a rule?"

"You're our first shaver," I said.

"But I'm almost done. . . ."

"But when I get into the bath tonight, I want to be surrounded by as little of your leg hair and skin flakes as possible." My voice was louder than before, and level. She got out of the bath, stepped into her bathrobe, and walked out of the bathhouse clutching her soap and razor. When she reached the doorway, she turned around and squinted meanly at me. I have always sort of liked her for the mean squint.

Kathleen walked over to the jukebox without drinks. "There's no decent tequila tonight. What do you feel like?"

"I guess I'll have a beer. A porter."

Kathleen went back to the bar, and I went to a table in the corner, where I sat smoking and watching Renee's and Bradley's backs. One morning at the hot springs retreat, Bradley sidled furtively up to me while I was cleaning the kitchen and asked, "Can, uh, women take the waters during, uh, the menses?"

"Yes, of course," I said in a friendly voice, "as long as they're wearing a Tampax."

"Ah," he said, nodding his head with nervous enthusiasm, "I see. And otherwise not?"

I started laughing to myself, as I sat in the bar, with a sudden vision of Renee with her nose in the air and her hair knotted stylishly on top of her head, stepping into the hotbath, wearing a sanitary belt and napkin, razor in one hand and soap in the other.

One of the many things I loved most about the four months at the hot springs was that material walked up to me so many times and introduced itself. A yoga disciple claimed he could make liquids—like a bowl of water—go *up* his penis, but wouldn't show me, because he didn't want to cheapen his ability. A bus-load of young spiritual devotees disembarked one morning when I sat topless on the steps of the aging hotel sewing patches on the playroom pillows. Each devotee wore a gummed label with his name and problem, as in HELLO MY NAME IS SADA AND I NEED TO CAUSE CONFRONTATIONS, and HELLO MY NAME IS FRANK AND I'M PARANOID. A caravan of middle-aged and older nudists arrived one afternoon, took a hotbath, and left when it turned out there were no electrical outlets for their radios. All I could think of was Diane Arbus. I did chores for four hours every morning—milking the goats, cleaning the hotel, tending the garden, taking raisins and oranges to a hostile monk who was living and meditating in the hillsides above the retreat—and wrote every afternoon until dinner. I was introduced to the guests as "Jennifer, our writer." I loved the attention, and I loved getting away with writing all afternoon—I loved pretending that I really was a writer— and I loved the parade of disturbed, eccentric, occasionally peaceful and generally wealthy people who came to take the waters. I quit only when the temperature reached a hundred and seven, and it was the last regular job I've had.

Kathleen returned finally with an Anchor porter for me and a glass of wine for herself.

"What took you so long?" I asked.

"I don't know." She sat down and took a sip of her wine, avoiding my eyes, tapping one foot on the floor, clearing her throat.

"Something wrong?" I asked.

"I want to talk to you about something," she said. "It's

something that makes us both nervous wrecks, and I think it's time to bring it up." She took another sip of wine. "You must have noticed how weird I got—as usual—when you and Wallace were talking about writing." I nodded, with much nervousness in my stomach, and excitement also. "Well, I *always* get weird when your writing comes up. I get real jealous. I go nuts inside. I don't know why I get jealous, since you don't make money or get any attention for it, but I guess it's because I'd rather be doing what you're doing. I mean, I'll have a day in the office where I look at the clock and think, 'Oh good, it's eight-forty-five, only seven and a quarter more hours; oh good, it's nine-thirty, only six and a half hours to go; oh good, it's nine-forty-five, et cetera, and then we'll meet for a drink and you will have been writing all day and you look happy and crazed, like you just had some wonderful sex or drugs. I resent that all of your time is free time, because half of my life is a bore to me, and I feel guilty because I want to write but I don't write. I can't face all that blank paper. But I want to be able to talk to you about your writing without secretly hating you."

"Oh, Kath," I said, feeling very happy and tense, "you'll get around to writing. . . ."

"No, I won't," she said. "You're the writer. And if you sold something, or made good, I think I'd fall apart. I'd simultaneously explode with joy for you—*truly*—and I'd eat my heart out with jealousy." She smiled at me, sadly and shyly. "I'd blow my brains out, I think. Or eat myself to death." She paused. "But I don't want that to affect your work. And now I don't want to talk about it anymore. I just wanted to break the ice."

"Thanks. You did."

"And I love you," she said. "So maybe we'll survive whatever happens. Just as long as you never sell anything.

"Can I buy you another beer?" she asked.

"Heyyy," I said, standing up, "some of us have to *work* tomorrow."

___

At ten-forty-five the next morning I walked above the beach and through the woods up a hillside to the meadow where Adam Arlen lives in a secluded and beautiful wooden house. The massive redwood door was an intricate carving of a lion and an anthropomorphic sun, which I thumped with my fist as I stood furiously wiping my feet on a welcome mat with plastic grass.

"Hello!" Adam boomed as he opened the door. "Come on in! How good to see you!" Adam is the consummate *Esquire* man, except for his hair, which has taken on the crisp, crinkly look of hair that is beginning to vanish. He is about forty, dresses like Prince Charles, and is one of the oiliest, smarmiest people in town.

"Hi," I said, and stepped inside. The house was magnificent, with high ceilings, beautiful wood finishes, lush carpets, huge vases, multitudinous aggressing plants, Rauschenberg-type paintings, no visible dirt, and a four-foot-square fish tank filled with tropical fish, some of them as big as my hand, which all looked like they'd been created by Dr. Seuss.

"So, let me show you around," he said, and we walked from room to room. We stepped into the bathroom, and he said, "This is the bathroom." We stepped into the kitchen, and he said, "This is the kitchen," and so on until we came to the bedroom of his teenage daughter. "This is Andrea's room," he said. It was spotless. There was a framed certificate from the National Honor Society, which Adam pointed to. "Smart as a whip," he said. "Brings home nothing but A's. We've pushed her a bit in this direction, taught her the personal satisfaction in achievement, and it's really paid off. Do you know her?"

"Oh yeah. We used to board horses at the same place."

"That's right. Well then you've noticed she isn't what you might call a beauty, which has been something of a blow to her mother, who was the darling of Cambridge twenty years ago. So both of us feel her grades are going to be more important than if she were a pretty girl. This is the boy's room. He stayed home from school today, but I don't think he'll get in your way. Hello, Trevor," he said, stepping into a bedroom decorated with posters and Trevor's original paintings. A diminutive teenage boy lay on the bed watching *Dialing for Dollars*, red frizzy ringlets against the pillow and his binder on the soles of his feet, which were sticking straight up.

"Hi," he said.

"Hi," I said.

"Jennifer, Trevor; Trevor, Jennifer," he said.

"Hi," he said.

"Hi," I said.

"You the new slavey?" He grinned, bit his lower lip, and looked away. "Just joshing."

"Stay out of her way, *s'il vous plaît*," said Adam, pushing me out the door, and closing it behind him.

"How old is he?"

"He'll be fourteen November eighth. No, the tenth. He looks a lot younger, because he hasn't had his growth yet." We walked back to the kitchen talking, and I noticed for the first time that Adam was only a couple of inches taller than I; so Trevor will probably be a Short Man, and Andrea is not going to be pretty, and I think they are both in for massive parental problems. "He's a fine boy," Adam continued, "quite a character and a joy to those around him, but he's been something of a disappointment to us schoolwise, brings home mostly B's, a couple of C's, always an A in art. . . ."

"His paintings are fantastic. One of them could be a Chagall. . . ."

"Yes, he's good. I was something of an artist myself as a lad, but luckily got good enough grades to really make something of my life. Let's go back to the pantry. And I'm not saying he's a complete letdown just because he doesn't apply himself to his studies. I just hope he works out."

"You can always send him back if he doesn't." We were in the pantry, surrounded by an arsenal of chemical cleaning agents, polishes, brooms, mops, vacuum attachments, and S.O.S. soap pads.

Adam ignored my remark, and handed me a bottle of Mr. Muscle Overnight Oven Cleaner. "I'd like you to spray this in the oven now, and then wipe it up just before you leave. I think four hours is enough. And then you can do the kids' rooms. I'll be in the living room if you need anything."

"O.K." He left, and I sprayed the oven walls with Mr. Muscle, collected the cleaning apparatus I would need, and went down the hall to Trevor's room. He smiled and saluted. He was about the size of an average ten-year-old, and sweet-faced. Shortness can make and break men: some of the most sensitive, ironic, adventurous men I know are shortish, and some of the most boorish despots I know are shortish. "I'll be right back," I said.

I went back to the pantry to get rags. When I walked back through the living room, Adam was measuring white powder into the fish tank, which was a foot shorter than Adam. The two dozen Dr. Seuss fish floated around.

"Feeding time?" I asked cheerfully.

"Oh, no, this is antibiotic powder," he said.

"Do your fish have infections?" I asked jokingly, and laughed a bit. There was a silence. I felt like saying "Just joshing."

"Yes," he said formally. "They do have infections, and I can assure you that there is nothing funny about fish infections."

Everyone has his or her own private hell, I thought, and excused myself after saying that I hoped they all felt better soon.

I began straightening up Trevor's room while he watched *The Donna Reed Show.* "Make yourself at home," he said. I dusted a bookcase and heard a loud musical whispering over the sound of Donna Reed and Carl Betz bickering cutely. I looked up and listened carefully. It was Trevor whispering "Miss You" by the Stones. I went back to cleaning, and it was not at all unpleasant. Trevor's paintings on the wall were accurate and ethereal at the same time. His whispering stopped, and then resumed even more loudly, this time "The Harder They Come." We smiled awkwardly at each other every so often, but mostly I worked in silence. When I began collecting the cleaning components, Trevor said, "There's a beer in the refrigerator if you want it. It's a pretty gross type of beer—Guinness stout. . . ."

"I love Guinness," I said. "It's delicious; it's like dark bread." I thought of James Joyce's line ". . . as we read in the first book of Guinnesses . . ." "It's one of my favorites," I said.

"Oh, you're kidding me," he said, scowling impishly. "I think it's so gross. I think it's like bony syrup."

I laughed, surprised at his accuracy. "I love bony syrup," I said. "I think I *will* have the beer."

"O.K. Well, see you around."

Adam left for his office in the city soon after, and I relaxed a good deal. I cleaned the various rooms for two hours with the radio on loud, absorbed in a curious way with the cleaning, until I got around to the bathrooms and lost all enthusiasm. I greatly resented what I was doing. I opened another beer, and thought about how many B vitamins were in a beer as strong as Guinness. When I finished the living room, I went back to the kitchen and wiped up the Mr. Muscle, which was slimy and green-black and vile and probably deadly to inhale, and I thought that I deserved better than this. I was ten minutes away from exactly four hours, and decided to polish the aquarium glass. I sprayed Windex on it and was standing in front of it with a rag in my hand when Trevor walked into the living room and squinted.

"Polishing the fish?" he asked, and chuckled. "Just joshing."

"Yeah. I'm about done with the house, except for this."

"Once I put red food coloring in the tank and told Dad

I'd dropped a piranha in by accident. Two *months* I got grounded."

I knew a very rich couple in Orinda who grounded their teenage children by restricting their use of the chauffeur: I have strong prejudices against the wealthy.

Trevor had been the high point of the housecleaning, had made it almost worth it. I touched his shoulder when I finished the tank, and said, "Well, I guess I'm done, as soon as I put this stuff away."

Trevor held out his hands. "I don't have any money!"

"I'll get it from your father later. I'll give him a call."

"O.K. Well, thanks."

"Thank *you*," I said, and left soon after.

I called Kathleen at work when I got home, and told her that though I had enjoyed Trevor and the infected fish, I thought I was going to stop housecleaning and go into crime.

"No," she said. "Don't do it. You'd be a dismal flop. I swear, you'd forget where you stashed the goods or what the combination to the safe was; you'd blow your feet off if you had a gun. You'd be an embarrassment to your family and friends when you got arrested trying to remember where your car keys were. We'd pretend we didn't know you."

"I gotta think of a scam," I said. "I'm toying with the idea of ripping off Wallace's stereo and car, maybe Sarah's piano and credit cards. . . ."

"Great, I want a cut. . . ."

"I'll get back to you on it when I've masterminded it."

"I have to hang up now. Actually, I just want to hang up now—but are you free tomorrow night? Shall we go to the bar?"

"Sure. I'll even be able to buy for once."

"I'd say it was about time, but I really don't give a shit. So I've bought you drinks now twenty times in a row. Who's counting?"

I laughed. "Thanks," I said. "I'm going to make this all up

to you when my ship comes in."

"Sure you are, honey," she said.

I walked to my bed, went into the prone, and lay there trying to think of a way around working again. I am not very
interested in the financial rewards of a steady job and I have
put in my time working for other people: I worked a total of
two and a half years after I dropped out of college and before I went into early retirement. I got an apartment in San
Francisco, looked unsuccessfully for work connected to
writing, or reading, and finally registered as a Kelly Girl,
where for three months I did short stints such as taking in-
ventory at Boyle's Payless Drugstore in Daly City, dressing
up as a variety of barnyard animals to pass out brochures
for a foreign-language school, pasting price tags on plastic
Jesuses. I hated it, mostly, made about three hundred a
month, and had to wear nylons roughly twice a week.

One day I walked into the employment office of a huge
engineering and construction firm on Montgomery Street.
The interviewer asked if I could type. I said not very well.
She asked if I had ever done any clerical work. I said no, but
that I had the alphabet down pat. I got hired on the spot as
a clerk-typist in the Nuclear Quality Assurance Plant,
where a bevy of highly paid engineers engineered faulty
nuclear-power-plant sites. My desk was next to the executive secretary's, a hostile fifty-year-old Swiss woman who
could type like the wind and thought I was after her job the
entire six months that I worked there. Her mouth dried out
all the time and she made the smacking noise of disengag-
ing her tongue from her desiccated mouth. Little white
globs of spit formed at the corners of her mouth. I found it
grisly, and started going crazy on the second or third day.

My job, which started at eight and ended at five, consisted largely of separating triplicate forms into three piles:
pink, blue, and green. The executive secretary periodically
complained that I left little flecks of glue at the top of the

triplicate forms. I made friends with four of the engineers, and watched the others as material. One of the latter had been transferred from the Boston office after physically attacking two clients, and his job was to stay sober. He was not allowed to join the others in drinking at lunch, and sat every day like a forlorn walrus, eating his thick ham sandwiches, which looked like pink erasers on white bread. One of the more influential engineers occasionally left Xerox copies of pornographic Peanuts cartoons on my desk—Lucy and Snoopy in compromising positions—and tried to impress everybody by using numerous words that began with the letter Q. It became, after one week, impossible to take proponents of nuclear power seriously, so incompetent and megalomaniacal were the engineers. My four engineer friends joked and very casually flirted with me, took me to lunch occasionally, and just generally made eight hours of clock-watching boredom and frustration bearable. I wrote stories at night to keep from having a nervous bored breakdown, and quit one day when I realized I would rather be outside in a chicken suit passing out brochures.

On my last day, three of the engineers took me to lunch, and gave me a three-record set of Pablo Casals conducting the Brandenburgs. My fourth friend, Ted Aiken, who tried to pretend to be suave but who once got his tie caught under the lid of the Xerox machine and then bumped his head on the lid when he lifted it to free his tie—sort of a young Gerry Ford type—asked if he could buy me a drink after work. I said sure. When I left the office that night, it seemed that everybody except the executive secretary was sad to see me go, and I was shocked but relieved that I, the sorter of the triplicate forms, was dispensable.

After three drinks Ted suggested we go to my apartment and go to bed. I said, "Oh, no thanks."

"Don't you like men?" he asked.

He drove me back to my apartment. As I was saying good-bye, he said, "Now, don't get me wrong, but I've had three stiff ones, no dinner, and I've got to drive all the way to Marin. Would you make me a cup of coffee?"

"No," I said, in a friendly tone. "You'll try something."

"Trust me," he said.

During coffee he complimented me on my clothes, personality, figure, coffee, apartment, tea, and the really special way I had with those triplicate forms. When he finished his coffee, he came over to the chair where I sat and reached for my breasts.

"Let's," he said.

"I don't want to."

"I'll make you happy . . ."

"And then will you leave?" I asked. He nodded romantically.

I showed him to the bedroom, undressed, and lay down on the bed, stiffly. He took off his clothes slowly; the lighting was low but it was not difficult to see that he was built like a hamster. He saw me looking at him, and the first thing he said before he climbed on top of me was, "Soooo, your *tits* are small." It was over in ten minutes, and he left shortly after, well pleased with himself. It was sickening, but not for long.

That was my first steady job. When I think about it, I think about *Something Happened*, the pornographic Peanuts cartoons, Ted Aiken, fluorescent lights, the fermentation in the elevators right after lunch, the asininity of nuclear power, and the little white globs of spit in the corner of the secretary's mouth.

A week after I quit, two months before I turned twenty, I went to talk to the editor of a new magazine in San Francisco, hoping to con her into some free-lance assignments. As soon as I saw the offices, and the dummy issue, and the editor, I decided I *had* to work for her. In her office, I spilled coffee on her desk, developed a tic in my eye, prattled on about my lack of experience and of general worth, tried to make minor accomplishments in college sound professionally auspicious, bit the side of my cheek and made a noise somewhere between a squeal and a moan, and made several nervous jokes. The editor said that there were no jobs but she would keep me in mind. I felt on the verge of tears, and made more small jokes to keep from crying. The editor looked at me for a long time, and then hired me as an assistant editor.

I had my own office, where, amid the most horrifying clutter—mounds of papers, beer cans, books—I was given articles to rewrite, or criticize, or make up headlines for, the letters section to edit and title, freedom to write articles, and interviews to conduct. There were five editors and an art director, all of them brilliant, vastly experienced, sophisticated, and eccentric. All of us drank, especially at staff meetings, some of us smoked dope, all of us worked much too hard, and it was an amazingly happy experience for the first year. I was passionately in love with all six people; they were the big kids and they were letting me play, which is exactly what I felt like I was doing.

Every day at work I marveled at my good fortune and worried that I would be fired. The magazine had a national circulation of one hundred thousand and was filled with black-humor touches. It was even, on occasion, wonderfully gross, and I could see my hand in every issue.

Every day of the next six months was financially precarious, and the business people, who were an anal and generally suspicious bunch, began to pressure us to accept politically offensive advertisements—vaginal sprays, for instance—and paranoia mounted in the office. It was an exhilarating time of editorial solidarity, so clearly us versus them, and we were the ones with the white hats, on the side of truth and creativity. Staff meetings were sometimes still a joy, but more often were infused with sagging morale, jangled nerves, and the resulting mistrust. We were months behind in paying our writers and artists, and one day a woman walked into our offices, held a gun to her head, and demanded to see the accountant, who told her he would put a check in the mail. She said she was going to lose her studio if she didn't have the money: we owed her a hundred dollars, and when she turned the gun on the accountant, he wrote her out a check, which probably bounced.

A few days later the business manager fired the editor-in-chief, the woman who had hired me, and the entire editorial staff quit, one by one. We went out together and got quite drunk, and I was flushed for a long time afterward with having belonged to such a fabulous group, with sadness and relief that we were disbanding, with pride and self-righteousness and especially with the prospect of collecting unemployment, which I managed to do for a year and a half.

I continued the prone until dinner time, when Adam Arlen called to say he would be over with a check in the morning, and that I had done a great little job. I said thanks. When he hung up, I decided to quit housecleaning after I worked for Birth and Arjuna on Thursday and made tortillas and cheese for dinner with a light heart; I knew I would think of something.

Adam dropped off my check Wednesday morning just as I sat down at my typewriter.

"Writing the Great American Novel, hah hah hah?" he asked.

"Nope," I said, standing.

"What are you writing then, a letter?"

"A short story."

"About what?"

"It's about you. It's called 'What Makes Adam Tick?' "

"Ha ha ha," he said. "I gave writing a try once. Everyone told me I ought to be a writer. I'll tell you, there are eight million unfinished novels out there. . . ."

"Thanks."

"I'm not trying to discourage you," he said. "Anyhow, will you clean again Tuesday?"

"No, I've decided to retire again. I'm sorry."

"All right, fine, no problem. Give me a call when you want a job again."

"O.K.," I said, "thanks."

"Trevor said to say hello."

"Thank you; hello to him. And I hope he works out."

I lost some of my enthusiasm for writing after Adam left. If there are eight million unfinished novels out there, there are fifty million abandoned short stories. I looked at the piece of paper in front of me, which was a scrawled, late-night profundity. It said "seeing things, life through prisms of your own judgments, fears, etc." I had leapt out of bed at three A.M., searched desperately for paper and pencil and scribbled it down convinced that I was on to something. I have a collection of these late-night profundities. One says *"Can* have cake and eat it too. *Have* to eat it, or goes stale. And always more cake." One says "blousey women." One says "divine, marvelous, adore, ciao." One says "You can shave my head but leave the bunny alone."

I put a blank piece of paper in the typewriter, and picked up a story I was working on, which was about a bird that crashed into a plate-glass window and came to in the jaws of a cat: there had been a story in the *Chronicle* about a small-plane crash in Africa in which four of eight passengers survived miraculously, set out for help, and were massacred by guerrillas. The gist of my story was that the Lord giveth and the Lord taketh away, and it was called "Hubris." I thought that when the survivors realized that they were alive against incredible odds, they committed hubris by saying "Oh, boy, we're alive; if we survived this we can survive anything; we got away with not dying," and then bam, rebel guns. If the survivors had looked at the carnage and the wreckage and thought about the possibility of being bitten by killer snakes in the jungle and said "Forget it;

what a drag; life sucks wind; let's just sit here and starve to death," they'd be alive today; they would have been rescued by Christians.

I stopped and looked at what I had written, stared into space, and moments later found myself standing at the stove to make tea, and since I didn't feel like having any tea, I sat back down and thought about hubris. A health-food and jogging braggart I knew got creamed by a car while he stood on a curb waiting for the light to change. Two days after my uncle Colin said out loud that he had fooled the gods by surviving another holiday season, he had the heart attack in which he died for several minutes in the ambulance. I forgot or stopped caring about the fifty million abandoned short stories, and my concentration peaked. I wrote about a fraternity party in Pennsylvania at which, after watching several Goucher girls pass out, I said jauntily to the man next to me, "Isn't it wonderful that I can drink so much without getting sloppy?" It was the last thing I said before I fell over, hit my head on the jukebox, and had to be carried to the Goucher bus by friends. When we returned to our dormitory at four A.M., my friends held me up as I stood in front of the check-in window beaming at the woman who held out a clipboard for me to initial. I thought I had her fooled as to my sobriety, smiled at her tenderly, and made huge swirling designs all over the checkout list. When I finished writing about the episode, I realized that it was not so much an example of hubris as of debauchery, but reading through the pages of "Hubris," a short story with no plot, no character development, and no point, I was pleased and excited. I clipped along, absorbed, entertained, filled with glee for several more hours, having forgotten that I was simply pretending to be a writer and about the nonexistent censors reading over my shoulder and about the horrors of failure and humble pie. Instead I wrote, and when I finished, I had the fine sense that I was getting away with something.

Thursday morning I walked to Birth and Arjuna's house, several blocks away from my cabin. They were sitting on the porch of the old wooden house, drinking tea and waiting to go to India, which has been their full-time occupation since I met them two years ago. They have lots of money, and a baby girl who was asleep in a buffalo-skin bassinet on the porch. Birth put her finger to her lips as I walked up, and Arjuna nodded solemnly but did not make eye contact. Birth and I tiptoed inside.

"This is the house," she said, pointing to the inside walls.

"Ah," I said.

"Oh, I forgot that you've worked here before. So you know where everything is. Our room is clean, and Shiva's room is clean, so you only have to do the kitchen, living room, healing room, and hall. Come outside and get me if you need anything."

"O.K."

"But try not to make any sudden noises. We're having Quiet Time. The Stupa is sleeping."

"The what is sleeping?"

"The Stupa. Shiva the Stupa, our child, of course."

"I know what 'Shiva' means, but what is 'the Stupa'?"

"It's Tibetan; it's a symbol of pure awareness. Do you do windows?"

"No."

"Fine," she said. "Fine," and, gathering her white robe around her dramatically, she went back outside.

I cleaned the rooms quickly and without thinking about it, so it was effortless and relaxing. I spent three hours writing a story in my head, about Shiva in twenty years, when she's in jail, having murdered Birth and Arjuna. Shiva goes on trial and on the witness stand says, "O.K., first of all, my name is not really Ethel Porter, it's Shiva the Stupa on my birth certificate. And I did kill my parents. I want to tell you, Your Honor . . . O.K., look, I'm six years old and my grandparents take me to Disneyland, and I'm waiting in line for mouse ears behind kids named Carol and Frank, and the salesman says, 'What name do you want on your mouse ears?' . . . and I had my first little nervous breakdown. I had to sneak off to Girl Scouts, and forge my parents' names on the permission slips. I made s'mores with girls named Cindee and Beth. My mother shows up for my eighth-grade graduation with a huge red blob of paint between her eyes because it's some high Indian holiday, and my father's got a tambourine. Are you getting the picture? When I was a bad girl, my parents used to say, 'Where'd we go off the path with her? We fed her ground-up tofu for her first solid meal; we took her to see Muktananda for her fifth birthday.' . . . So anyway, I go to visit them a couple of months ago, they're sitting on the porch waiting to go to India, my mother's complaining about the weather, and Arjuna's sitting there in one of his 'Nothing negative can disturb my tranquil and beautiful karma' moods, which means he's stewing in his own juices. And something clicks inside of me, and I shot them both through the heart, then poured mu oil all over their bodies—mu was the substance the laboratory couldn't identify. And I'd do it again." The judge dismisses the case.

The only thing left to clean was a tiled mirror wall in the healing room. I immediately cut my forefinger on a jagged corner, stuck the finger in my mouth, looked unsuccessfully for Band-Aids, and, bleeding heartily, went outside.

"I'm bleeding," I whispered, indicating my finger. Birth was nursing the Stupa and Arjuna was reading the *Chronicle Sporting Green*. "I think I need a Band-Aid."

"Do you know what finger that is?" Arjuna asked solemnly.

"It's my forefinger. My right forefinger."

"No, it's your Jupiter finger," he said. "Jupiter was the supreme deity of the Romans." He shook his forefinger at me, and then smiled. "Do you see?" He pointed his forefinger at me and shook it again.

"Oh, I see." I shook my nonbleeding Jupiter finger at him so he would see that I understood. The toilet paper around my right finger was saturated with blood. "Do you think there are any Band-Aids here?"

"No," said Birth self-righteously. "Arjuna and I don't cut ourselves." I went back inside and made a bandage of toilet paper and electrical tape, which worked. I sprayed the tiles again and was all but finished when I cut my left forefinger on another tile corner.

"God fucking dammit," I said, and stuck my left finger in my mouth. I made another electrical tape–toilet paper bandage, and went out with the intention of hiding my second cut Jupiter finger. "I'm done," I said.

Birth gave a sudden joyful shriek when she caught sight of my left hand. "You've cut both of your Jupiter fingers!" she said and shook her finger at me. When Arjuna finished chuckling knowingly into his yogurt, he shook his finger at me also.

"You've learned a big *lesson* today, haven't you?" he asked.

"I certainly have." Both of them looked happy.

"Do you mind a check?" asked Birth.

I walked back to the cabin with a check for twenty dollars in my pocket and electrical tape on the first joint of both forefingers. I saw a casual friend walking toward me, and smiled.

"Hi," I said. I have always liked her; she is about forty, unobtrusively alcoholic, a counterculture clothes horse, and pleasantly off her rocker. When she saw the black tape on my fingers, she said, "Far out." I smiled. Material, I thought, this is material, just like Arjuna and Birth.

"How's your father?" she asked.

"Oh, fine," I said routinely and because it was true. "He's been looking and feeling especially well ever since he went back to work writing a couple of weeks ago."

"I mean, has the pain started yet?" I flinched and looked

back at her levelly, disgusted and fascinated.

"There isn't going to be any pain," I said, "because the surgery and radiation—"

"Oh, that's right," she said, "it's in his brain, isn't it?"

This is material also, this denseness, because there isn't anything else to do with it.

I opened a beer inside the cabin and went into the prone on my bed. I felt tired and relaxed and excited about the abundance of material and the possibilities of revenge therein, yet another reason for writing. There is a fine photograph of Wallace taped to the wall, which I stared at absently. I took the picture at five in the morning on Wallace's last day at the hot springs retreat, with green hills behind him, a stream at his feet, and the early-morning lights the same color as his woolen shirt and his eyes. We had gone bird-watching; I had given him my latest short stories the night before, and he told me that morning to write my stories as I would practice musical scales, and that at some point they would start to gel. He said something also about developing the skill of paying attention, paying attention to every moment, but I was thinking about something else and missed much of what he said.

Monday

On the Monday before Thanksgiving I lay dreaming of a stadium tennis court at which I was watching a match with a boy friend. I noticed out of the corner of my eye a woman who looked very, very much like me except heavier, and in between trying to impress the boy friend, I kept an eye on her; she turned around and smiled at me once, and then moments later was bending forward to grab some papers that had blown from her lap. To my horror and humiliation her tennis dress blew up to her waist and she was not wearing underpants. There was a knocking, and I awoke with shame.

"Hello?" said a male voice from behind the cabin door.

I didn't recognize the voice and immediately disliked whoever it was; the components of my life as I knew it, with Wallace out of trouble and the constant threat of everydayness returning, filtered through my sleepiness, a short current of nervousness went through my stomach, and I turned over to fall back to sleep. I breathed calmly and steadily, with my eyes closed, enjoying the moments of knowing that I was falling asleep again. Sleep, as a friend said, is nectar.

"Hello? Hello?" Knock knock. I didn't move. "You asleep?"

"Yeah," I called, annoyed.

"Sorry. Sorry. I'll come back." I began drifting off, recalling the stadium court and the large bottom of my double fully exposed, shamelessly, with skin as white as my own, thinking it now, tired and warm and vaguely awake, instead of dreaming it.

"What time will you be up?" the voice called.

"God!" I said loudly.

The door opened and a short chubby man with wild black hair and a sweet, serious face bounded in and began tap-dancing next to the refrigerator.

"Happy to see me?" he asked, beaming, tap-dancing away, huge brown eyes flickering, arms outstretched.

"Michael!" I said. "What time is it?"

"Almost eight." He walked over to the bed, removing his down jacket as he walked. "It was wonderful to hear your vicious little voice again after all these years. 'God!' " he whined just as I had, and lay down on top of me. I put my arms around his neck and we kissed, and he bit my nose. He rolled over to one side, and I sat up, rubbed my eyes, cleared my throat, rubbed my nose, blinked several times, yawned and smiled at him. "You're as ravishing as ever, and I have missed you so much. I should have called, hunh?" he said.

I looked at one of my preferred faces in the world, rosy, open, slightly scarred, at the fat belly framed by suspenders, at the slightly receding hairline (he told me years ago that his voluptuousness never bothered him and that the impending hair loss caused him to tear at it in the morning), and shook my head.

"You want a cup of coffee?" I asked.

"Do you want to make love?"

"I want a cup of coffee first. I like to get as nervous as possible before I do anything enjoyable so I can anxiety-attack myself while I'm doing it. And I want to wake up a bit."

"O.K."

I climbed over him and out of the bed wearing a T-shirt

and nothing else, with none of my usual embarrassment whatsoever, went to the stove and lit the burner under the kettle. "Look at those *haunches*," he said, smiling and shaking his head with his eyes closed. "You walking a lot?"

"Oh, yeah, a couple of hours a day."

"Playing tennis?"

"Not much. Teaching mostly."

"Writing?"

"Yeah, a lot."

"Fucking?"

"Sometimes."

"Who?"

"No one special. Horny friends."

"The best kind." He got off the bed and stood looking at the cartoons and photographs on the wall. He took off his suspenders, T-shirt, and blue jeans while I ground coffee beans. When I turned around to ask how he liked his coffee, he had his underpants on his head and snapped the elastic at me as he winked.

"Looks like the electroshock worked," I said.

"Castrating bitches!" he said. "Do you still see the emaciated knuckle-cracker?" Michael took his mug of coffee and snorted derisively. "Poor bastard must be freezing to death these days." The emaciated knuckle-cracker had been six feet, 155 pounds.

"No. Well, every so often. Do you still see the woman you introduced me to last year."

"*See* her? I've been living with her for a year."

"Oh. I didn't know that." Rats, I thought, he *lives* with a woman who is smart and funny and friendly, good teeth, good skin, good income.

"In Pasadena, if you can imagine. We don't really get along all that well. She can't stand me, for instance. So we're off and on—right now we're off and on at the same time. She flirts with *Esquire* hunks periodically so I'll know I'm the luckiest fat show-offy Jew in the world to have this strapping *shiksa*, and then we start picking fights about the drains or money and I get bored and leave for a while, and then she misses me and I miss her and I show up and look more like Marty Allen than the Turk, but I make her laugh a lot and of course I'm the world's most extraordinary lover, hung like a bull moose, and then we get along for a while more. Right now she's sore at me, if you can imagine. I think she's bored. Because, let's face it, I'm a more or less perfect human specimen." He took the underpants from his head and threw them onto the rocking chair as if throwing roses to an audience.

"So what are you doing up here?"

"Seeing you. Getting some work done in San Francisco." He stood up, walked to the bed, and lay down, belly up. "So are you nervous enough or still afraid you're too re- laxed to fully enjoy yourself? Because I'm going to have to go ahead and get started by myself," but he didn't. He looked at me and then at his wrist, as if he were wearing a watch.

"Michael, you come up to see me because your old lady is sore, you wake me up, and then you start saying hup hup hup. . . ."

"I wouldn't do this to anybody else in the world. Think of it as an honor. I wanted to see you. Let me put my heart on my sleeve. I'm crazy about you. I'm crazy about your body, too, and I know you're crazy about me, because I've been totally obnoxious and you haven't thrown me out. I'm one of the few people in the world who think you're per- fect. We're sick in much the same way, and I myself am perfect, so you must be also." Michael and I have known each other for six years, have slept together off and on ev- ery couple of years, have laughed many times until we cried, have talked about all the things I talk about with my closest women friends, have taken LSD together, have sur- vived the vicissitudes and ended up true friends, almost brother and sister. He has acne scars. He will do anything

for a laugh. He is as honest—aggressively honest—a person
as I have ever met; our best laughs have been about our
miserable early teens as semimidgets who were always invited along with the popular kids because we were clowns.
He can be quite annoying on occasion and I trust him in a
way I do not trust men in general. I went over to the bed
and sat down. He held my hand. "To tell you the truth," he
said dolefully, "the last ten or fifteen years have been a real
disappointment."

I laughed, and stretched out beside him, with my hand on
his belly. I thought I would tell him about Wallace's tumor
after we made love, but rehearsed it several times anyway.

"I'm so glad to be here," he said.

"Me too."

"I've felt blue for about a month, until a few days ago. I
just sort of felt like I woke up a few days ago, after thirty-
some years. I'd been preoccupied with punishing Laura for
flirting with this friend of mine, and with punishing my
friend, by being honest with them but also withholding my
love. Then I woke up, decided my life was too short to punish them and that it was infinitely easier to set them up to
punish each other. So I got a ticket for San Francisco, and
here I am. In all of my rotund glory. And on my last day in
Pasadena, I got *really* happy about coming to San Francisco,
escaping, getting to see you, and I went into town and saw
all these people I'd forgotten I like, and the pavement was
slippery from the rain and I was wearing sneakers, and suddenly I become Jacques Tati, Mr. Hulot, with his terrifying
lurches and sidesteps. And what's more, everybody knows
I'm Jacques Tati and I ham it up and my feeling of klutzi-
ness passes and I remember how beautiful it is to clown
around and make people laugh, and how long it's been."

We made friendly, familiar love, in the way that long-
term and nonattached lovers sometimes get to, all the plea-
sures of love and recognition without being stuck with the
person. Michael did not fall asleep when we were done. We

talked about our mothers, lovers, and work. I kept rehearsing how I was going to tell him about Wallace without being melodramatic, but I didn't get around to it for a long time. It was so much easier to lie against him, exchanging notes, details, stories. It was at least as nice as being asleep.

"O.K. I'm thirty-two, right? And I have a brother two years older, like you do, only my brother makes a fortune and has given Mom two perfect grandchildren. So a few weeks ago we're all at a big family dinner, and my mother turns to my cousin's new wife and says, 'Have you met my boys, Jered and Michael? Yes, well, Jered's always been tall and good-looking; even as a baby he was tall, learned to sail a boat by the time he was six; really, a perfect child. And, well, of course Michael isn't quite as tall; in fact, he's a good foot shorter, always the clown; oh, he had us in stiches; it's only too bad he ended up with those damn Shulman thighs. . . .' " I laughed, drowsily. "She'll be telling someone else the same thing in twenty years, I swear to God. . . ." He talked on and on, making jokes, about his family, himself, about his girl friend ("I swear to God, she can't even cook those Chinese soup noodles—you know, you boil the noodles, then add the lizard-flavored stock; well, she drops the packet in with the noodles and boils off the letters . . ."), and about old times with me, all the time stroking or holding my shoulders. "Hey, I've been talking for twenty minutes; let's talk about you for a while."

"Actually, the big news around—"

"Did I mention . . . Oh, go ahead, excuse me."

"In August, it turned out that my dad—"

"Remind me to tell you about being in the sauna with the male midget . . ."

"Beginning of August, my father—"

"Who had *met* Robert Morley . . ."

"Forget it," I said, not particularly mad, and a bit relieved that I had tried to tell him and didn't have to.

"No, go ahead. I won't interrupt. Really. Trust me."

"O.K. The big event was that in August my father had a brain tumor removed . . ." I began, and Michael did not interrupt again except to ask questions. I told him about the symptoms and the surgery and the Black and Decker saw that the surgeon used to connect drill holes in the scalp and the sucking sound that the surgical plunger makes when it lifts up the trapdoor flap of skin and Livingston A and Livingston B and the biopsy and the will and the way Wallace talked after surgery and the Frankenstein scar and the radiation and the girl with bone cancer and the Neanderthal man with the brain tumor, and the positive prognosis and how Wallace liked the feel of the wind against his hairlets and how he looked much older but healthy and how crazy and deranged and strong it had turned out I was and how Wallace and Colin having both been in the Room now saw almost everything but love and work as theater of the absurd, and how my brothers and Sarah had responded—admirably, maybe too admirably, like me—and the Martin Luther King dream, and the tiny blue radiation tattoos on either side of Wallace's ears, and how, even before the first symptoms, Wallace's eighty-five-year-old mother told him of a dream in which he had surgery, and about the cancer dragnet and how well Wallace was feeling these days.

When I couldn't think of any more details or feelings, I shrugged, lying next to Michael, who was looking into my eyes with complete seriousness and perception.

"Some year," he said finally, and slowly. " 'And other than that, Mrs. Lincoln, how was the play?' "

Michael left after breakfast, just before noon. He said he was going into the city and would be back at the cabin at seven-thirty if that was fine with me, which it was.

I called Kathleen at her office and told her of Michael's unexpected arrival, and what a good mood I was in. I told her about his girl friend and how I thought he'd probably be going back soon but that I wasn't sure. I told her about how

much we laughed together and how well we made love together after all these years and how crazy and smart he was,
and that I hoped he didn't stay in Clement too long.

"Yeah, it sounds awful," she said. "No wonder you're
afraid."

"Who says I'm afraid?"

"Aren't you?"

"Yeah, a little bit."

"I would be, too, if someone so neat came along who
loved me and was a great friend and lover. But he lives with
someone, five hundred miles away, so you're safe, don't
you think?"

"Yeah, but if he sticks around for a bit, I would end up
wanting him to stick around longer. I might start waiting
for the phone to ring; that's the worst part."

"That won't happen," she said.

"It might. And there's the part where I might end up liking him more than he likes me, even though I'd *pretend* not
to care. Or else he'll stick around and start to get on my
nerves, when he puts the underpants on his head and snaps
them. . . ."

"Well, first of all, you're mind-fucking like mad; you had
a wonderful morning with an oldtime friend, one of your
best male friends in the world, who thinks the world of
you, and you're already worrying how his mother is going
to react to the divorce. . . ."

"Good point."

"And secondly, let's face it, the worst that could happen
would be that you thought he was going to throw his hat
into the ring with you and you'd get all excited and it
would turn out he goes back to Pasadena, right?"

"Right."

"And maybe he'll hang around for a few days and it'll be
close and fun and then he'll leave and you'll see him again
in a year and it will be three great days again. I'd say—your
father would say—Auden said 'Trust in God and take short

views.' Does that seem like good advice? I really think you have nothing to lose by caring about him, as long as you don't expect anything. You're lucky to have him as a close friend. . . ."

"*That's* what I have to lose. That's the only thing you and I have to lose if we became lovers—each other. That's what always happens to lovers; all that resentment builds up, or almost always anyway. . . . It's so easy to find lovers, and they come and go, but *friends* . . ."

"It's also much easier not to try for anything because you're afraid it'll be a failure or cause pain; it's much easier to keep the walls up even with friends who might be worth lowering the walls for, but you *know* it doesn't work, you *know* it doesn't deliver."

"Well, that's all true," I said, "but—"

"Mind-fuck, mind-fuck," she said. "Whoop whoop whoop."

"I know," I said, and groaned. "I feel so happy—I felt so happy all morning with Michael—and it's a terrible shock to my system to feel this good."

"You definitely sound happy," she said. I know that my voice is a barometer to my moods, as Kathleen's is to hers. It is quite an inconvenience at times, and it is at those times that we say "Oh, fine, fine, everything's *fine*" in tight, whiny voices. "I'm glad for you that Michael's around. I myself think sex is dirty and shameful and disgusting and I'm taking a break from the whole sordid business."

"Do you have time to hear a dream, or should I call you later?"

"Oh, no, I'm free. I'm subconsciously trying to get fired. I'm too good for this job. Life is too short. I came in two hours late; I told an administrator to go suck his nose off; I haven't done a thing all day but look bored. Go ahead."

"Pretty subconscious," I said, "with the subtlety of falling elephants. Only they all probably think you're on the rag. Anyhow." I cleared my throat, and told her every detail of the stadium dream—murky details of the man I was with except that we were definitely lovers and I was trying to impress him, vivid details of my look-alike's naked bottom in the air as she reached for the papers, and a vivid remembrance of the shame I felt.

"Oh, God, it fits right in," she said with just a trace of condescension. I bristled slightly.

"That's too bad, I like it to be a surprise. . . ."

"Oh, don't be like that, Jen; it's a fine dream; you're lucky. So be the look-alike, first person, present tense."

"O.K. I'm sitting at a tennis match and there's a woman behind me who looks just like me, with a man, and I smiled at her but she didn't seem to want to acknowledge me, and then the wind blew some papers I was holding out of my lap so I reach forward, my dress blows up as I'm grabbing the papers—but I *get* them—and the woman behind me is freaking out when I turn around." I suddenly had a vague understanding of the dream.

"Say the last part over again."

"So the wind blows the papers out of my lap and my dress blows up and I'm reaching forward to grab them and my butt shows—"

"There's the important part. That sometimes when you reach for something, your butt shows."

Wallace picked me up for our run to the post office just after noon, another crisp, blue mid-autumn day. His stamina and bloom had returned, and this morning he smiled with a mysterious cheer. He does not make a bigger deal over personal or professional good news than he does over alarming news. His reactions are always clear but restrained.

"You look great," I said, getting in the car.

"That's what Sarah says. It must be true. Last night I got a bit of good news: Carolyn Madison and I got an advance yesterday—a small one, granted—for a book we'd been working on together before I got sick. My agent called last night. That's why I'm looking so well, I think." He drove along the rutted dirt road, just slightly smiling.

"Hey! Great!" I said. "Your worries are over. Now you can take us all out to celebrate—we'll order stuffed mushrooms."

"Exactly what I had in mind. The advance was absolutely perfect timing. I was about to sell Randy to a childless couple in Mexico."

"Let's pick up that hitchhiker; she's a friend." There was a young teenage girl standing by the side of the road in French-cut jeans and a satin boxer's jacket over a cowl. Wallace slowed down and then stopped, and Sandy opened the back door.

" 'Goin' downtown?" she asked. She got in, and I introduced her to Wallace. "Wudder all these books for?" she asked. I turned around and looked at the books on the back seat.

"I'm taking them down to the library," Wallace said.

"Who's Virginia Woof?" She was looking at the second volume of Virginia Woolf's letters.

"Woolf," I said.

"A great English writer, in the first third of the century," said Wallace. "You oughta read her someday."

"Oh yeah? Someone told me she was the lady who climbed to the top of the Statue of Liberty," she said, and all three of us laughed as we drove downhill above the calm, steel-blue ocean. "No kidding," she said cheerfully, "that's what I thought."

"Good thing you ran into us, then," I said.

"Yeah, no kidding. Nineteen eleven to nineteen twenty-two," she read off the cover. "Jeez, she didn't live very long, did she?"

There was a telegram for Wallace from Carolyn Madison in the morning's mail, which read, "All *right*—we got the contract, and you're in good health. I thought you were a goner for sure and that I would be done with this tiresome project." There was a letter addressed to a Ms. Applebottom Larue from Megan, which I tore open—Wallace opens his letters carefully, with his penknife. I destroy most envelopes in the process of opening them. "My darling Ms. Larue," the letter began, "your dearest darling will be in town on Monday, in the afternoon. Having Thanksgiving in town with papa. Will call at my earliest convenience, or call me. It is raining as usual, the horse next door had ponies and I get to have one, see you Monday, I love you, your friend Megan Adler."

"Oh, good, what excellent news—Megan's coming. What day is it?" I asked as we walked back to the car.

"It's Monday. So she's coming today."

"You know who else is in town? Michael. He stopped by the cabin this morning. Two of my favorite people in the world. The gods are smiling on us again."

Wallace started up the car. "Michael, huh? Good man. *And*," he said, in his sarcastic stern voice," I'm glad to see you spend at least a *little* time with men. I mean, all your family hears about is Kathleen and Megan and your favorite ladies in town. Don't you care what the neighbors say? Don't you care about your family?"

"Most of the men I like to be with are taken; somebody's got dibs on them. And the rest live in other places."

"I know," he said. "And I was only kidding anyway."

I called Megan when I got back to the cabin, but no one answered the phone and I sat down at my typewriter to rewrite the story "Hubris." In the interest of not appearing too obvious, I never quite got around to putting down on paper the themes and characters in my mind, but between fantasizing about my first appearance on the Johnny Carson show, the fan letters from Renata Adler, Julia Child, and Mary Tyler Moore, the reviews that would say "Sophomoric, still-water-runs-boring, pedantic, stupid," between worrying that my friends would secretly and guiltily rejoice if I ate literary humble pie or dislike me if my luck was good (because I am prone to these fugitive feelings), between every possible attempt to get in my own way, I wrote somehow triumphantly.

The door to the cabin opened a crack some hours later, and I looked up, knowing that it was Megan and knowing that she would not simply open the door, walk in, and say hello. "Oh Bahhbahhra," she said in her child's Bela Lugosi voice, "they're comming to get you, Bahhbahhra." I started laughing, got up from my desk, and walked stealthily to the door. "Oh Bahhbahhra," she said, repeating the lines from *Night of the Living Dead,* and I threw open the door. Megan gasped, jumped, instantly drew her shoulders up to her ears and then laughed, as I did. We kissed and then hugged briefly, and I did not have to bend down far. She, smiling, reached up, grasped my shoulders, and said, "Let me take a look at you. I'm two inches taller, and my hair is two inches longer. You look great. . . ."

"And you got your ears pierced. But I recognized you the instant I saw you, the very second. . . ."

"I thought you said you got your hair cut like Farrah," she said, walking around the room, picking up books, papers, photographs.

"I was lying." I hung my head. We were both grinning. "It's one of the few lies I've ever told you."

"Ohhhh?" she said, whirling around so that her brown braids swung like ropes, pursing her lips, squinting, "there've been others?"

Her eyes are so pretty, brown and happy, that her mockmad or mock-serious faces look myopic. There is, as with all of my friends, warmth and vitality and a definite aloofness. None of my friends, for instance, is the sort of person who goes around hugging people routinely.

"Yes," I said. "There've been others."

"Like what?" she scowled.

"I told you I was born in San Francisco, Children's Hospital, Caesarean, right?" She nodded solemnly. "I wasn't. I was born on a small star on Berenice's Hair, or Coma Berenices, to poor but proud parents . . . everybody in the constellation had hair like this . . . there was a mix-up at the hospital . . . can you ever forgive me?"

"How's your foster father's hair doing?" she asked, laughing at me. She came over, absently holding a book, and casually leaned against me. "Is he totally fine?"

"Oh, yeah!" I said. "He is, and his hair is growing back. It's fluffier and whiter than before, and he's happy and has a lot of energy—you'll forgive the use of 'energy.' You wanna stop over at his house later?"

"I have to be home pretty early for dinner, but we could maybe stop over for a few minutes. Will Randy be there?" I nodded. "Good. Well, let's have something to eat, and then we can go down to Limpet. How does that sound?"

"Perfect. I haven't eaten for hours." A lack of appetite is one of the phenomena of concentration, and I had thought of my occasional hunger pangs as an inconvenience. I fried two eggs, toasted four pieces of French-bread toast, buttered and put ketchup on them, and presented her with a fried-egg sandwich.

She took a bite, chewed it with a look of quiet ecstasy on her face, and said I made the best goddamn fried-egg sandwiches of anyone she knew except herself.

"Let's take them to the beach," I said, and got out a produce bag. We wrapped them, put them and two oranges in the bag, and went hand in hand down the dirt road above the reef toward the beach. It must have been about four, and the sun was already low on the water, the sky filled with magenta expansions that were reflected, distinctly, on the flat turquoise ocean. We walked along talking about the best books we had read lately, the best movies, the nicest boys we knew, our favorite segments from *Harold and*

Maude, our families, and I filled her in on the new Burn Outs, who were crazier and more hostile than the last batch, some of whom had been assimilated into the street life and some of whom had left and two of whom had died of various overdoses. When we passed a station wagon with a barking, snarling Doberman in it, we both stopped. The dog lunged at us, jaws bared, from behind the back-door window. "Ohhhh," I said to Megan in a syrupy, semi-French accent, "isn't he the sweetest little doggie in the world?" Megan roared, the dog snarled and bared his teeth and barked, and I tilted my head sweetly at him and said once again, "Yes, yes, the sweetest little doggie in the world." We continued walking, Megan still laughing. Megan and I have a rock that we walk to down by the creek above the ridges of Limpet Beach whenever we have a chance, with a glorious view of the sunset above the ocean and whatever animals are on the reef—pelicans, gulls, seals—with no houses anywhere in sight. We sat on the rock with our shoulders touching, and began to eat our sandwiches. The sky was filled with myriad birds migrating, and a line of white pelicans, black primaries outstretched, scooped down with their beaks into the ocean for a moment and then flew upward; there were purples, blues, and pinks everywhere in the water and the sky, the sun brilliant red, just beginning to touch the horizon. Megan's face was light brown, and rosy.

"Jeez, you look so good," I said. "I'm so glad to see you."

"Oh for goodness sakes," she said, and pursed her lips slightly.

"Did I tell you I'm starting a travel agency, called the No-Snakes Travel Bureau, which sends people only to places where there are no deadly snakes?"

"Are you still talking about snakes, for God sakes?" she said.

"I *hardly* ever talk about them anymore, because I hardly think about them anymore. Did I tell you—"

"You've told me every snake story of yours at least once. You've told everyone you know well about your snakes. . . ."

"Did I tell you about the letter Colin wrote about snakes?"

"Jen," she said, looking sincerely worried, "you *sent* it to me, remember? Remember?"

"Oh yeah," I said, nodding.

"Jeez," she said. "I even initialed it under Colin's name." She looked at me, worried.

"Oh, yeah. That was about when I stopped talking about them. *I* can take a hint."

"Some hint," said Megan.

Colin's letter to me at the hot springs read:

> How you *do* go on about snakes! Did you know that medical authorities agree that the biggest danger from a poisonous snakebite—the sort of snake, diamondback rattlers, that you are currently stalking—is from the bacteria lurking in the mouth of the rescuers and on the knives with which the well-meaning panicked rescuers slash the victim before putting on the tourniquet which can lead to loss of limb? And that two or three people in the U.S. die every year from snake bite? Did you know that I hope and pray that this ends all of our communications involving rattlesnakes? Please write to me more frequently—I love you and have your best interests at heart and it makes me sad to hear all of the neighbors talk about how little you love me—BUT NOT ABOUT YOU-KNOW-WHATS.

Under Colin's signature were the initials M. A., Megan Adler, who mailed it back to me, and as I said, I can take a hint.

Wallace had just baked his first batch of cookies in fifty-five years, and was, as Megan and I arrived at his house, removing a tray of black, ashy cookies from the oven.

"Golden brown," he said stentorially. "Megan, how good to see you," he said. He carried the tray of burnt cookies to the sink, laid them next to the piles of dishes, and bent down to kiss Megan.

"Hi, Wallace," said Megan with poise and obvious shyness. "Your hair looks great."

"Thanks. So do you. Have a cookie."

"Ohhh, I think I'll pass. . . ."

"There are unburnt ones on the table," he said. "Would you like to stay for dinner?"

"I'm having dinner over the hill with my grandma and my dad. Is Randy here?"

"He has a job today, clearing brush. You'll have to come for dinner with all of us one night."

"Sure, I will. I want to, with Sarah and Randy and Ben. And I have this book I brought with me you might like, by this guy named Edgar Cayce who talks about God and reincarnation. Well, maybe you would think it was flaky." She went to the table and began eating a cookie. "Good cookie."

"Thanks, and sure, I'll give Edgar Cayce a try." He took a sip of a drink, some dark liquor, neat, and hiccuped. "Excuse me."

Wallace is different these days from how he was before the tumor, somewhat softer, more accessible, and he clowns around more. He hiccuped again with a startled look on his face, and then pantomined great drunkenness, but when he hiccuped again a moment later, a look of distress went across his face. "Dammit, hiccups," he said. "First drink all day, honest." In the next fifteen minutes, when the three of us sat around the dining-room table eating chocolate-chip cookies and listening to the Weavers *Greatest Hits,* the three of us, all show-offs and storytellers, exchanged bits of our lives, all of us laughing, Wallace, Megan, and I, Megan scowling after she said something especially funny, Wallace as always stomping his feet at his punch lines, and hiccuping.

I spent the hour before Michael was to arrive straightening up the cabin, washing dishes, putting my clothes on the floor of the closet, tossing my hair, washing myself quickly, smoking part of a joint, dashing around to swoop up dirty dishes, clothes, and magazines. I went into the bathroom to wipe any old mascara from under my eyes, and stood staring in the mirror as if I were seeing myself for the first time. My hair had reached new levels of disheveledness, and looked like something that ought to be mulched—and also crazed and great and like no one else's hair in the world. My pupils were dilated and my eyes looked sad, even when I practiced smiling. There is a picture of me at three on my wall, white fluff on my head and my mouth hanging partly open and big sad eyes staring sadly at something to the left of the photographer, and it is always startling to see the same face of my older self. My face has changed very little over the years: it's thinner; it has some scars; it's seen more. And Wallace's face, which has aged a great deal in the last three months, is still the face in the pictures on his mother's wall, at two and three years old. I most concretely feel the sense of "I," of being the person In Here, that consciousness at five and eleven and nineteen and twenty-five and sixty-six of "I" when I am slightly stoned and looking into a mirror, looking into my own eyes. "I am here now," I said to myself, and believed it for a few seconds. It has finally occurred to me that it takes years to figure out that this—this here/now business—is not hippie platitude but is, along with loving, the point of all great teachings.

I checked the lighting in the main room, and as I was pulling a cord, the phone rang at the same instant, and I jumped.

I cleared my throat, took a couple of deep breaths, and answered it. "Hello?" I asked, certain that it was Michael canceling, already bracing myself for defense.

"Hello, Jen, Ben." My older brother was speaking in a muffled voice, and my stomach briefly tightened up. "I'm in

Dad's study," he said softly, "and I'm worried about him. He's hiccuping. . . ."

"Still?" I asked with foreboding. He had started hiccuping hours ago. Hiccups are, like everything else, directed from the brain, involuntary reflexes with a nerve center in the brain, in the brain where Wallace had a tumor removed.

"Yeah, and then he groans. You think I oughta call his doctor?"

"Not unless he or Sarah wants to."

"Everybody's getting glum and irritable and sad." There was a silence. "Poor Dad," he said. I had an immediate picture of Dad sitting in the window seat, hiccuping and feeling lousy and probably scared and in total control except of his involuntary muscles, and felt on the verge of tears.

"Well, I guess I'll come on over," I said, and thought of Michael and our date and how bad Wallace's timing was, and what an inconvenience it can be for someone you love enormously to be sick and how sickening it was to be feeling this way and how the last thing I needed on top of the sorrow and frustration was more guilt. My stomach felt very tight, and I felt ever so slightly martyred, and then guilty about it, and then filled with love and solidarity toward my family, and then confused.

I told Ben about my feelings of inconvenience, and he said he understood, and I said I'd be over in half an hour. I hung up and was filled with fury and concern and thwarted expectations of the evening. I tried to breathe evenly into my stomach, and thought rationally that this sort of thinking—about the inconvenience—was just one of the multitudinous distractions I have conjured up, along with doing the dishes and getting a headache, to keep my mind off the sometimes chilling prospects. I thought also that mothers sometimes feel resentful when their children hurt themselves and need a lot of attention because it cuts into the little free time the mother has. I thought about Michael and Wallace and I kicked the refrigerator, grabbed my tennis racket, and began beating the bed, shouting at the top of my lungs. (If I learned one thing living at the hot springs, it was how to shout out some of my anger. I only shout when I'm alone or with Kathleen. It is, only initially, terrifying to hear the sound of one's own voice in fury and frustration, wordless. And it works, for me.) *"Ahhhhhhhhhhhhhhhhhhhh,'* I shouted on one exhalation, mouth wide open, eyes closed.

"Jen?" asked Michael from the doorway. I swung around, mouth partly open. "Am I late or something?" He stuck his head out a bit and tilted it with a look of tentative, curious affection.

"Michael!" I said. I stood with my arms at my sides, shoulders slightly slumped, a bit embarrassed but not surprised.

"What's the matter?" he asked, and came over to me.

I explained about the hiccups, and how pissed off I was that Wallace was having trouble and that I had wanted to spend the evening with him, Michael, and he put his arm around me and sat me down on the bed and said, "Life is the shits; it's disruptive. The outside world is violent and plastic and absurd, and human bodies and relationships can take a terrible beating and still survive it somehow; it's the shits, though; I tell you, *objectively,* I'm nine years older than you and it is the shits; it doesn't make any sense, and it's all we have, which is its validity, and there's the challenge, to have an enormous amount of love and good times . . ." and by the time he finished talking, almost gasping for breath, staring into my eyes, I began to feel almost like a female human being again.

"Thank you," I said.

"You're welcome."

"Will you walk me to Wallace's?"

"Of course," he said. "I'd walk you to the moon."

"Maybe tomorrow," I said, and we started off.

Michael and I walked over to Wallace's under the almost full golden moon above the ridge. I remembered the best description of a full moon I've ever read, Tom Robbins's "a

clownshead dipped in honey." Just before we arrived, holding hands, Michael told me that he had got a ride back to
Pasadena, and thought it was an omen, and thought he'd
probably go back in a couple of days. I wasn't surprised; I
was a bit sad, distantly, and also relieved that I was being
spared the option of having my butt show.

"Oh," I said. I shrugged. "Easy come, easy go."

"I love you," he said. "I wouldn't be leaving, except—"

"Except that you're leaving, right?" We were at my father's gate.

"I hope your dad is all right." I nodded. "And you, too."

"I love you," I said. You have to tell people you love
them whenever you can, or it risks going unsaid, because
they might be dead in the morning. I think I have told every
person I love that I love him or her, and I don't think I've
told anyone I *don't* love that I do.

"Can I spend the night with you tonight?" he asked. "I
could come back to the cabin in a few hours."

We were leaning against each other, something I have
come not to resist so much, arms loosely around each other,
exactly the same height, and I said yes.

Randy was sitting on the porch under the full moon with
his head in his hands and Muldoon at his feet, crying angrily, as if he were working up to a shout but sobbing softly
instead. As I walked up to him, he beat his fist into his palm
several times and then hit a plank of the porch.

"Hey," I said. I sat next to him, our shoulders touching:
Randy and I do not usually like to be hugged when we are
crying; it makes us cry harder.

"Fucking shit," he said through gritted teeth. He
clenched his fist. Our shoulders sagged. If it had been happening to another family, I would have said, blithely yet
concerned, "Hey, look, the hiccups could have any number
of causes, postsurgical, postradiation. Let's see what the
doctor has to say."

"Yeah, you're right," I did say. "Still, let's wait and see...."

"God! I hate it so fucking much; I mean, when is enough enough? I mean this excellent man gets jerked around like this. Why didn't it happen to some asshole or Krishnoid or something? I mean, I can think of thirty people I'd sacrifice easily for Dad if I got the chance. You know? Just go downtown or to a high-school reunion and pick out the real shitheads and douche bags, say, pointing, "O.K., you, out . . . and you with the Dry Look, out . . . and you, sorry, you gotta go, too...." He wasn't crying. The outside lights were not on and the only light was the moon, golden yellow.

Ben was standing over the kitchen sink washing the piles and piles of dirty dishes: when things become frightening in our family, we wash dishes; we actually seek out dishes to wash. The two new kittens, Cattawampas the tortoiseshell and Bunny Wailer the calico, leapt at his legs. Dad hiccuped from the window seat, where he sat reading next to Sarah. "Hello," I said.

Wallace put down his book for a minute, smiled dryly, and hiccuped. He said, "Uhhhh," and shook his head. I went to the window seat, climbed onto my knees between their legs, balanced by holding on to one of Wallace's knobby knees and one of Sarah's knobby knees, shaking *my* head.

Wallace looked tired and irritated. Sarah looked sad and resigned. "Randy's unhappy," he said. "Did he say anything?"

" 'Fucking shit,' " I said, grinning.

"That's about right." He hiccuped, and groaned.

"It hurts?"

"It hurts sometimes. Not much. It hurts for about two seconds. The rest of the time I feel like I've got the flu...."

"All of the kids at school have it," said Sarah.

"Oh, yeah, everyone in town has it, and your white blood cells are a bit low because of the radiation," I said.

"Ohhhhh . . ." said Ben.

"It's not the flu," said Wallace slowly and with a trace of irritation, and I felt fear in my stomach like a siren elicits late at night.

"Make yourself a drink," said Sarah. "Just to take the edge off until the doctor calls." Her eyes were bright and slightly out of focus and she was scratching Wallace's back absent-mindedly while reading a book.

"Have you thought about taking one of the pills you got after surgery? Something to relax you?"

"I'm going to wait until I hear from the doctor."

"O.K." I went into the kitchen, where Ben was still washing dishes, and put my arms around him from the back. He was tapping his foot, and bristled a bit when I first touched him, and then leaned backward against me. I poured myself a shot of Irish whiskey and went back to the living room, picked up a *New Yorker,* and settled into the easy chair, where I sat reading and making occasional cheery black small talk. Randy walked back in as if nothing had happened, and sat with his pen and paper at the living-room table, drawing with obviously great pressure on his pen. "Alexander's Ragtime Band," as performed by Bessie Smith and her band, came on the radio, and I saw Wallace's foot, on the floor in a Bean moccasin, begin to tap. He was hiccuping about every fifteen seconds and groaning afterward, softly. "Jesus Christ," he would say every so often after a hiccup. "Goddammit, why won't they stop?" It was alarming and sad for the first hour, and mostly seemed absurd for the next two. Joe Smith blew his cornet and Wallace tapping his foot, sang along with all the correct words for once, sang with sorrow and discomfort this song which my parents first heard Bessie sing in Harlem. Randy was watching Wallace also and Wallace was oblivious to you, looking down at the pages of his book, singing, hiccuping, tapping out the time. I was filled with loving memories and hope, and the whiskey in my belly made me wiser. The kit-

ten Cattawampas was on his stomach, rising and falling
with Wallace's breaths, bounding back onto the sweater
after a hiccup. Randy occasionally made some general announcement, like "I saw a woman with blue hair yesterday," or "There was a lady in the Guinness book who
hiccuped for eight years or something, whoops, forget it,"
and then went back to drawing.

An hour later the phone rang, and Ben, who had *just*
finished the dishes, rushed to pick it up. He cleared his
throat and said very formally, "Hello?" The four of us sat
up, but Ben's shoulders dropped. "Hi, Megan. Yes, she's
here. Well, we're waiting for a phone call, from the doctor,
so could she call you later, or tomorrow?"

Randy looked as nervous as Ben, and hissed, "Hang up!"

"All right, I'll tell her. O.K. . . . good. See you soon.
'Bye," and he hung up.

"God!" said Randy. "What if the doctor just tried to call
exactly then and now he doesn't call until tomorrow?" He
squinted angrily at me.

"Don't look at me," I said. "Just relax."

"Don't tell me to relax," he said.

"Nyahhh nyahhh," I said. "Relax." I sat reading, defensive, angry that Randy was overreacting, and a bit guilty
that *my* friend had called while we waited for the doctor.
"What was the message?"

"She'll call you in the morning."

Everybody was a bit on edge and trying to contain it;
when there is great tension in a room, while people are
waiting, say, things that get said aren't always meant. We
were saved by the announcement over the radio that a benefit was about to begin, with musicians and comedians
who would play while listeners called in their subscriptions
to the public radio station. One of the radio personalities
Randy and I most like to make fun of, Rose Smythe Bunnington, was going to cohost the show with a mild-man-

nered disc jockey named Jeremy, and Malvina Reynolds, one of my favorite American women, was to begin the show. She sang raspily and beautifully for twenty minutes, and the five of us listened attentively, well satisfied. It was her birthday, as it turned out, and the crowd sang "Happy Birthday" and it was not embarrassing and pitiful as it usually is but a celebration of the ongoing seasons. Malvina Reynolds was seventy years old. The songs she sang were some of the first songs I learned to listen to and sing, and we sang along now when we knew the words, Wallace still hiccuping. My family, with and without our friends, sing and dance—folk singing and reggae dancing—a lot more since the surgery than we have for many, many years.

A local comedian named Buckey Corn followed Malvina, and was pleasant and unaggressive if not funny. He told two jokes and mostly pretended that he was stoned and had forgotten where he was. When he finished, Rose Smythe Bunnington bleated into the microphone, "Oh *Jeremy*, I'm having *such* a marvelous time, really, I'm just laughing myself silly. Why, Jeremy, did you *hear* that joke he told about the midget in the crowded elevator?"

"No," said Randy happily, "Jeremy's been standing there the whole time and he missed it. Why don't you tell it to him?"

Rose proceeded to botch the joke up in every conceivable way, introducing characters who hadn't been in the original, putting the punch line in the early middle, and losing control of herself at one point. "Oh, Jeremy," she gushed, "this is *ever* so much fun, really, and I'm sure our listeners will want to call in a subscription at blah blah blah, won't they, Jeremy?"

"I hope they will," said Jeremy dully.

"Honestly!" she giggled, "that man is *so* funny, ha ha ha ha ha ha ha, and Jeremy, I am not normally a joke person. . . ."

All of us cracked up so loudly that we could only sporadically hear her describing how really marvelous and divine the joke had been. Wallace laughed loudly, and hiccuped.

"Eeeeeeee," Rose squealed before dissolving into laughter. "Will you *look* at what Rachel's doing with the mike onstage now!"

"I wish we could," said Ben. "Jeremy's not speaking to her anymore."

"For God's sake," said Wallace, hiccuping, "call the station. Ask them what she's doing with the microphone!" he shouted, and then half stomped his feet.

"What a disgusting woman," said Randy.

"I bet she's from Minnesota," said Ben. "Real name Sue Ellen Staples."

"I wish the doctor would call," said Sarah, who had not enjoyed the show as much as we had. "It's ten o'clock."

"I hate that fucking doctor," said Randy. "He's probably with his nurse right now on the examination table."

"Relax," said Ben, who was chain-smoking, cracking his knuckles, biting his lower lip, and still somehow looking like the responsible, compassionate eldest son. When the phone rang, his crossed leg twitched outward and kicked the table. He leapt to his feet, composing himself as Randy said, "Heyyy, who's nervous?"

"Hello?" said Ben. Sarah, Wallace, Randy, and I were on the edge of our seats. "Yes, he's here. Just a minute." Ben held the receiver against his chest and looked solemn. "It's your doctor, Dad," he said. "He'll be right with you," said Ben into the receiver. Wallace walked slowly, tiredly, and with anticipation to the phone. There are at least several phone calls in one's life that carry messages after which life is never the same. The doctor was either going to say that Wallace should get to the hospital immediately, that they'd been dreading hiccups, that he was sorry but there was nothing he could do, *or* he was going to say, "Hey, relax, it was to be expected and is no cause for real alarm." I lit up a

Camel. Sarah, Ben, and Randy were all biting or chewing on their bottom lips.

"Hello, Doctor," said Wallace. "Yes, I've been hiccuping for six hours now, no end in sight, and, uh, I was wondering what I ought to do about it." There was a silence. "No, no fever. No real discomfort outside the hiccups. Which hurt a bit afterward ... Uh-huh ... Oh, that's probably true, that the cramping is because I've been hiccuping so long. And, uh, why should I have hiccups?"

There was a long silence of ten seconds that lasted an hour, and then Wallace turned to us with the receiver in the crook of his neck, giving us the thumbs-up sign. "Yes, I see. Well, I'm greatly relieved. . . . Yes, I have a few left. . . . O.K., O.K. . . . Oh, otherwise I've been feeling great. Thanks a million. Good night."

Wallace hung up and we all inhaled expectantly. "A common side affect of radiation on the brain. Absolutely nothing to worry about. I have some pills left over that he says will stop them almost immediately, and they probably won't come back."

"God, all *right*, thank heavens, all *right*," everyone said or shouted, and we all, in our various ways, touched him. Sarah kissed him and went to get the pills. Wallace hiccuped and groaned, and then smiled. "Phew," he said, smiling again with an appreciation the rest of us haven't experienced yet. And once again in the course of a minute, our lives had changed dramatically and not changed, up and down and up and down and up.

Wallace took two Dalmane, and Randy, Ben, Sarah, and I toasted him with hot brandies, and half an hour later the hiccups subsided. As the muscles in our faces relaxed, and the routine bullshitting and insults and understanding and warmth and alcohol caught up with me, I felt confidence in my family and in our gatherings. I thought of friends, of the challenge, of the sword; I thought of vicissitude; I thought of sex and work and I thought that there ought to be a word for "love" that was not so overused; I thought of the trades—what one loses and what one gains in return; I thought that I was on to many things, and when the moon floated past the living-room windows, I thought about the golden yellow moon. "Yes," Wallace said jovially, to a question I had missed from one of the boys, as he rubbed Muldoon's pointy head with the sole of his foot, smiling just a bit groggily. "How did you guess?"

"I just knew you loved killdeer," said Randy, "because they're so pretty and you always point out their zebra stripes and their pretty voice and their bearing. Whadda you like best, Jen? I mean, what is your favorite bird, the bird you're happiest to see?"

"Pelicans, of course."

"Because they're funny-looking?"

"Yeah, and because they're so graceful, too."

"How about you, Ben?"

"Sparrows."

"How about you, Sarah?"

"Owls."

"How about you, Randy. Hawks?" I asked.

"Yeah!" he said, wide-eyed. "How'd you know?"

"Good guess, and you mention them sometimes. . . ."

"Yeah! That's amazing!" said Randy. "I especially like red-tails. And you know what, everybody? I win! I like the right bird; I win the washer-dryer and the seven-inch Sony Trinatron!" Wallace stood up and rubbed the top of Randy's head, tweaked Ben's collarbone and shoulder, put his head down on top of mine for a moment, and held up his hand.

"My roommate and I are going to bed, kids. Thank you all for being around tonight. We'll have to do it again soon." He and Sarah walked out of the living room holding hands. Ben and Randy and I took a loud deep breath concurrently. "Don't forget to lock up," Wallace called from outside, under the moon. "Good night."

An Acknowledgment

I would like to acknowledge the extraordinary debt I owe to the following people:

My aunts Gertrud, Pat, Eleanor and Betty; my uncles Millard, Rex, and Ben; my cousins and my grandmother Nell.

The women without whom I would have been in Napa State Hospital years ago: Mary Lowry, Lynn Atkison, Pam Nyhan, Susan Dun, and Megan Matson.

My closest friends, the clowns and lovers and allies in my galaxy: Betty, Lowell, and George McKegney; Larry and Norma; Lisa DuBois; Ted Hoagland; Pat Gomez; the Kossmans; the Hewletts; the McNaughtons; the Lopez-Salzes; Steve Matson; Becky and Barbara Wilson; Michael Burton; Matty Ehmann; Allan Reeves; Wendy and Bill at Hospice; Danny, Io, and Kora Samara; all of the tennis girls; the eighth-graders; the women at the Roly Poly Bar and Grill; Rosalie Wright; Jon Carroll; B. K. Moran; Mary and Frank Robertson; Baron Corvo; Michael; and Bunny.

My agent, Elizabeth McKee, and my editors at Viking, Maureen Rolla and Cork Smith, all three of whom gave enormously and put up frequently with my paranoid and abusive letters.

And the friends who housed me while I was writing this book; Richard and Kathleen, the Franklins, the splendid Anne and Francis Reeves, and unspeakable gratitude especially to Frances Stewart.

Fairfax, California   ANNIE LAMOTT